PRAISE

ONE MORE SEAT
AT THE ROUND TABLE

"An utterly engrossing, hilarious, and often tender novel of how one hundred-plus creative people made Broadway's legendary, much-loved musical *Camelot* from scraps and sheer determination. Told from the points of view of a clever Gal Friday savoring her first job and a rising baritone hoping for his big break, the plot depicts the 1960 out-of-town tryouts when the show's in trouble. *One More Seat at the Round Table* is an original, charming book. I loved it and was sorry when it ended. All I wanted was to be in the author's chaotic, marvelous world of musical theater."

~ **Stephanie Cowell**, author of *Claude & Camille* and *The Boy in the Rain*

"In *One More Seat at the Round Table,* Dormady Eisenberg spins a delicious, surprising concoction of a story, giving a true insider glimpse of one of the most iconic Broadway musicals. Replete with dramatic ups and downs, off-stage romances and rivalries, and sparkling with wit, this book should be required reading for every theater geek or lover of musicals."

~ **Susanne Dunlap**, author of The *Portraitist* and *The Courtesan's Daughter*

"Masterfully researched and artfully written, *One More Seat at the Round Table* is historical fiction at its best, offering production intrigue, vocal rivalry, death, hospitalizations, and romances within Lerner and Loewe's 1960 hit *Camelot*. Prepare to lose your entire day as Susan Dormady Eisenberg's Gal Friday guides us in a riveting story of love, courage, and sacrifice. The book is peppered with utterly captivating insights into Broadway show-doctoring and the elements needed to transform a production from disaster to shining splendor."

~ **Henry A. Young, Jr.**, former executive director, the New York City Center Joffrey Ballet

"A delightful discovery awaits all who are smart enough to purchase this novel, *One More Seat at the Round Table,* and succumb to its inherent pleasures. It's a love story for all who are curious about the theater and the American musical form as it delves accurately into the intricate evolution from the rehearsal process to a series of opening nights ultimately landing on Broadway. The two main characters who romantically find their paths through their respective places within the art form and into each other's lives accurately reflect the obstacles to having a career in the professional musical theater. Ms. Dormady Eisenberg is a vivid storyteller and her incorporation of the historic personages who populate the original *Camelot* production provides a colorful adventure as the novel embraces theatrical history.

~ **Joseph V. Melillo**, executive producer emeritus,
Brooklyn Academy of Music (BAM)

"A wonderful, suspenseful, and engaging novel about the making of the musical *Camelot,* replete with famous historical figures such as Richard Burton and Julie Andrews. We see the real streets of New York City, both the glitz and the seamy side, then go backstage with the actors and witness the grit it takes to create a show that mesmerizes audiences and lasts through the ages. The real story, though, is the evolution of the two main characters, Jane and Bryce; how Jane fights for autonomy and must prove herself to be seen and heard in a man's world; and how even with obstacles and road-blocks, both art and love triumph."

~ **Louise Nayer**, author of *Burned*: A Memoir
and *Narrow Escapes*: A Memoir

ONE MORE
SEAT
AT THE
ROUND
TABLE

A NOVEL OF BROADWAY'S *CAMELOT*

SUSAN DORMADY EISENBERG

atmosphere press

Published by Atmosphere Press

Cover design by Matthew Fielder

Author's Note: A synopsis of the musical *Camelot* as staged on Broadway after March 19, 1961, may be found on page 338-340.

atmospherepress.com

For my sister Nancy Peck,
with love and gratitude

"Like it or not, the credulous eye and the quixotic heart are part and parcel of the theater. The theater is not so much a profession as a disease, and my first look at Broadway was the beginning of a life-long infection ..."

- Moss Hart, *Act One* (1959)

"In the end I have come to realize that I wrote not because it is what I do, but because it is what I am; not because it is how I make my living, but how I make my life ... I feel the same sense of coming home every time I begin to write. Now, if I can only remember everything Moss told me ..."

- Alan Jay Lerner, *The Street Where I Live* (1978)

PROLOGUE

Brock Remsen's Journal

August 29, 1958

No doubt about it, success has been an answered prayer that's causing tears for my friends Alan Lerner and Fritz Loewe. Despite the popularity of their *My Fair Lady,* still selling out in New York and London, Lerner fights with his wife and says he doesn't know what to write next. And Loewe's still recovering from a near-fatal coronary last spring.

Sure, *My Fair Lady* gleams with Shaw's dialogue from *Pygmalion,* and it's a tough act to follow. But I've solved their problem. Last Sunday, *The New York Times* ran a review of T.H. White's novel, *The Once and Future King.* It's a faithful version of the Arthurian legend in which "might for right" supplants violence and love won't conquer all. And it's right up Lerner's alley, so this past Monday, I bought the hardback and tossed it on his desk, saying, "Here's your next musical."

Alan looked leery. He'd seen the review but wasn't convinced. Then half an hour later, our *Fair Lady* director phoned to say he'd read the same review. "You should adapt it, Alan," Moss Hart suggested. Great minds!

It's only Friday, but Hart's set to direct, Loewe's on board, and the lawyers are chasing the rights. "Here's my chance to write a show with a big idea," Lerner said today. "Peace and justice as my central theme. What do you think, Remsen?"

I think Alan's on fire again! His working title is *Jenny Kiss'd Me,* and now it's full speed ahead to Arthur's court in Camelot. And maybe I'm speaking too soon, but this one should be another slam dunk for Broadway's most famous creative team.

Who needs George Bernard Shaw?

PART ONE

NEW YORK REHEARSALS
SEPTEMBER 1960

"Life beats down and crushes our souls and theater reminds
us that we have one."
-    American acting teacher Sanford Meisner

"Life is like a beautiful melody, only the lyrics are messed up."
-    Hans Christian Andersen

1.
TWO BIG
BREAKS

Jane

I don't have psychic powers, but at various times in my life, I've felt a prickle along my neck when something big was about to happen. Although such moments have been rare, I had one that late-August day in 1958 as I whirled through the revolving door of the Hotel Piccadilly coffee shop on West 45th Street.

Bathed in sweat after a long trek from Murray Hill, I claimed a wobbly table and grabbed a few napkins from the dispenser to wipe my face. Then I removed my straw hat and white gloves, which proper ladies wore back then, and glanced at the menu I knew by heart. I'd come here once a week since July, and the joint was filling up with tourists and regulars, most of them chatting in pairs. But everything seemed normal, and I had to wonder if my neck barb had come not from a moment of prescience but from the baking heat of summer in New York.

The Piccadilly was in the heart of the bustling theater district, and its coffee shop was the one place I felt at ease in my adopted city. I'd read somewhere that most Broadway producers lunched elsewhere—Sardi's or Café Edison—but on different days, I'd spotted David Merrick, with his shaving-brush mustache, and skinny Hal Prince on the red-topped stools at the counter. And since those two guys had hits on Broadway, I longed to hand them my resume, which I carried in a black Coach shoulder bag, a graduation gift from my parents. Having landed here in June with a newly minted drama degree, I hoped to snag a theater job, but so far had only found the nerve to send out letters. (Would producers get irked if I interrupted their meal, or would they praise my chutzpah, a Yiddish word I'd recently learned? I didn't know, but neither Merrick nor Prince had looked approachable, so my courage took a powder.)

When a scowling waitress with iodine-tinted hair lumbered over, I ordered ham on rye and a Coke, no ice. Feeling famished—I always skipped breakfast—I craved a side of fries, but it was hard to make it on a junior secretary's pay, so thrift was essential. Yet, while this shop cost more than the coffee shop at the Barbizon, the women's hotel I'd chosen to please my folks, I never tired of its crowded, noisy atmosphere. Then, after lunch each week, I strolled the narrow streets of the 40s, browsing theater marquees and display cases as another girl, one who liked clothes and jewelry, might window-shop on Fifth Avenue. But my passion was Broadway, and it still amazed me that I lived in a town where plays and musicals were performed *every night*.

The waitress brought my Coke in a tall glass brimming with ice, and it was clear she hadn't heard my request over the din—the shop was getting full. And for some reason, I missed my college roommate, Sarah Wilkins, an aspiring singer-actress who should've been auditioning for the fall season. Sadly, Sarah's parents had whisked her home to Albany after graduation and made her take a job in a bakery. "It smells so sweet in there, I get headaches," she'd groused in a recent letter. "But I'm squirreling away every dollar and will join you at the Barbizon soon."

Reading my friend's wistful words, I felt glad I'd banked my birthday checks from relatives for the last decade. I'd used my savings to relocate from Maryland and pay my bills while searching for work. Of course, Sarah's inability to plan was part of her charm, and I missed her spontaneity. Who could forget the time we—

The waitress slapped my sandwich on the scarred wooden tabletop along with the check, wrenching me back to the present. I took a demure bite of ham while watching a tall thirty-ish man slide onto a stool at the counter. He was pressed and starched with dark wavy hair and might've been an ad exec or stockbroker—too well built for a model. But he carried a light-green canvas messenger bag instead of a briefcase, and from his straight posture and melodic voice—I strained to hear him order—I guessed he was an actor and maybe a singer.

My waitress with the orange hair promptly brought the guy's burger and fries, grinning at him with dingy dentures, and I chuckled at the woman's lame attempt to flirt. While the actor drenched his food in Red Wing ketchup, the off-brand the Piccadilly served, I decided he was a looker, at least from this angle. After wolfing down my sandwich and tossing coins on the table, I grabbed my hat and gloves and walked to the door, where a playful impulse stopped me. Instead of leaving, I turned and zinged the guy with my best smile (and unlike the waitress, I had nice teeth).

By dumb luck, he was looking my way, and as our eyes met, he returned my smile, flashing nicer teeth than mine. In that instant, I knew why he drew me like a magnet. Everything about him told me he *belonged* here. He wasn't a newcomer like me or a visitor from the hinterlands. Theater was in his marrow, and I yearned to ask him how that felt.

But I lost my chutzpah, just like with the producers, and raced out the door, my floral dress swirling around my now-squishy knees: his smile had unstitched me. I fled down 45th, passing the Plymouth and Golden Theatres, swerving left at Eighth Avenue, then skirting the Manhattan Hotel and turning up 44th. As I hurried along this fabled block, passing the Majestic Theatre, then Sardi's Restaurant, I realized I'd never flirted with a stranger before. And I had to wonder if my telltale prickle had been about him. *Lordy, Jane, get a grip.*

By the time I reached Broadway with its camera-toting tourists and yellow cabs careening in and out of lanes, I'd put the actor—if he was an actor—out of my mind. As the traffic light changed, I ignored the pulsing neon signs above Times Square and dashed through the crosswalk with the other pedestrians. Then I raced up 44th like the Road Runner in those movie-house cartoons. If I made a beeline to my office, I might reach my desk before my boss, a fiend for punctuality, left her tidy inner sanctum and noticed I was late getting back from lunch.

The steamy dog days gave way to a cool fall and damp gray winter, and although I returned to the Piccadilly each week, I didn't see the Red Wing-loving guy again.

On a February morning in 1959, I was waiting on the Lexington Avenue subway platform, skimming *The New York Times*, when I read that Lerner and Loewe, creators of *My Fair Lady*, were writing a new musical about King Arthur and his faithless Guenevere. The librettist and composer, along with their director, Moss Hart, planned to produce the show, which would open in the fall of 1960.

Startled when my train squealed to a halt, I felt a fresh surge of moxie. I'd begun to salivate at the show's title, *Jenny Kiss'd Me*, and while elbowing my way into a car reeking of onion bagels and dirty wool, I vowed to insert myself into the rarefied realm of Lerner, Loewe, and Hart, whose earlier show remained a standing-room-only hit.

But as I reached my stop in Murray Hill, a neat residential neighborhood, I woefully told myself I hadn't impressed anyone so far. I was a show-biz virgin camping out in a secular convent. Nights in my airless room, I penned overheated letters to producers whose names I found in playbills, mentioning my love of theater and my eagerness to do any job to break in. But I hadn't received a single reply, and this seemed unfair since I was seeking backstage work. Why didn't my pragmatism set me apart from all those stagestruck actors and actresses who pined to see their names in lights?

Even as a teenager, a flighty phase for most, I'd never wanted to perform. After stage-managing two musicals with help from my high school drama teacher, I enrolled in the Drama Department at Catholic University, where I impressed the program head, Gilbert Hartke, known in D.C. as "the theater priest." In my freshman year, he'd said, "Janice, we need girls like you."

Girls like "Janice" Conroy? Hartke bragged about knowing the legends of stage and screen, but couldn't recall his students' names. But I supposed he'd meant "we need girls in tech," and with Father's blessing, I tried set design, crew, carpentry, prop management, and yes, stage management. Dirt under my nails became a badge of honor, and after four years, I thought I'd gained the chops to apprentice behind the scenes on Broadway.

Yet, since I'd made no progress with theater, I felt lucky to work for the literary agent, Emily Burgoyne, whose office occupied the ground floor of a brownstone on East 38th. "Em" dressed in wrinkled linen and wore heirloom jewelry like a tony graduate of Miss Porter's and Smith. From what I could tell, she lived on the royalties of dead authors, though she still accepted submissions from the living. But since the phone seldom rang and few visitors stopped by, I finished my duties quickly and spent my remaining hours reading *Variety*.

Then one rainy day, my boss asked me to comb through the "slush pile," the expanding cache of unsolicited manuscripts gathering dust on an extra desk. "You've got a quick mind, Jane," she said. "Read them all, reject what you don't like, and pass on what's promising. See if you can find us the next Truman Capote."

"I'll try," I assured the generous woman in her forties who'd inherited the business from her father. And I came to like my expanded duties since, other than a noon deli run for Em's tuna sandwich, I could read all day without guilt. Maybe I'd discover authors we could nurture together. Maybe the "publishing game" (my boss's slang) was my soon-to-be-discovered vocation, though I hated to renounce the stage this soon. Yet how on earth could I break in?

I chose to view my literary tasks as a detour and settled into a pleasant workday routine. On weekends I scoured the museums, walked through Central Park, and had coffee with school friends who were also seeking their fortunes in the city. Sometimes I caught act two of Broadway plays and musicals, sneaking in at intermission and taking an empty seat while grandmotherly ushers with varicose veins turned a blind eye. It was a way to stay informed about theater without shelling out three bucks for a balcony ticket.

Since my parents doubted my ability to support myself, I paid my bills without asking for their help. My Barbizon cell cost six dollars a week, and I ate for spare change at the automat or Malachy's at 63rd and Third. (At the latter, the chatty Irish proprietor allowed unescorted ladies to sit at his bar, a privilege that women on their own were denied elsewhere.)

———◆———

Discouraged about my prospects in the spring of 1959, I asked Miss Burgoyne if I could take off Good Friday and the following

Monday. That Holy Thursday night, I boarded the train to my family's colonial home in Bethesda, where I slept in my old room, plastered with Broadway posters, and savored my mother's clove-and-pineapple ham on Easter Sunday—she was a terrific cook who'd tried in vain to teach me her skills. With my brother fishing in Aruba and my sister visiting her husband's folks in Florida, I had my parents' full attention, which was nice, and that Monday I was delighted when my favorite uncle, Max Conroy, came to call.

Max was my dad's younger brother, an imposing Navy man who'd married and divorced in his thirties and now worked at the Pentagon. His hands were scarred with mismatched pigment—from exposed raw skin to fiery red patches—because of burns he'd suffered in World War II, and though I'd always wanted to know what happened to him, he never discussed the details. But he was one adult who always listened to me with interest, so I kissed his smooth cheek smelling of Old Spice when he entered my parents' parlor. I admired his pressed pinstripe suit and charcoal tie and was glad we could chat alone when my mother ran out to the kitchen.

"Owen tells me you're trying to break into theater," Max said while I poured his tea. (He meant my father, a cardiologist who'd been summoned to D.C.'s Sibley Hospital, where he sent patients in need of urgent care.) "How's your search going?" my uncle asked, settling his lanky body on the Chippendale sofa.

"It stalled out," I said, pouring my own Darjeeling. After sliding into a Queen Anne wing chair, I met his piercing gaze. "I'd like to work on Lerner and Loewe's new musical, but after sending letters to everyone on their staff, they don't know I'm alive."

"Why didn't you ask my help?" he asked, raising his bushy gray brows. "Or maybe you're not aware I went to Annapolis with Lerner's production man, Brock Remsen. We also served together in the Pacific, and we're still close. I speak to him once a month."

"Brock?" I asked, smiling. "Great name."

"His name is Edmund," Max said. "Lerner dubbed him 'Brock' because he's a cross between a brick and a rock—steady, in other words. And, look, I'll be glad to recommend you. I'm sure he'll have some job you can do." He wiped his mouth with a linen napkin. "I hate to ask, but do you type?"

"Sixty words a minute," I told him, grateful for his surprising offer.

———◆———

It turned out Brock Remsen already had a crack assistant. But Max continued to sing my praises throughout the next year, which was why, on a sunny Monday in July of 1960, I found myself in a rehearsal hall foyer in the West 40s surrounded by singers and dancers. Their sweat smelled like fear, but unlike those chorus hopefuls, known to theater folk as gypsies, I was waiting to see the assistant to the producers.

I'd told Emily what I was up to—she seemed disappointed—and asked for the day off. Before leaving the Barbizon, I'd pulled my reddish-brown hair into a chignon and donned a houndstooth Chanel jacket from a vintage clothing shop, a white blouse whose Peter Pan collar I'd managed to scorch, and a gray flared skirt with black pumps. I'd added black frames over my blue eyes, and when I checked myself in the mirror—I was a slim five-foot-six—I felt satisfied.

"You're Max's niece," Brock Remsen said as he ushered me into the rectangular studio with metal tables and chairs along the wall. Several men were already seated, but not wishing to appear nosy, I stared at the floor. When Mr. Remsen pointed to an empty table, I slid onto a folding chair, and he sat across from me. "Your uncle's always been proud of you."

"Thanks for telling me," I said, flustered by his praise. "I gather you and he went to school together." Getting a closer look, I definitely would've taken Mr. Remsen for ex-military. He was tall and trim with a silver crewcut and had to be in his forties like Max. The one theatrical touch was a silver goatee that my uncle would've thought too flamboyant.

"We played football together in college," Mr. Remsen went on. "I quit the service after the war, but your uncle stayed on. He's done rather well for himself."

I smiled. My uncle had "done rather well," all right: he was the Under Secretary of the Navy. "Max may lose his post if Nixon loses the election," I muttered.

"Well, Lerner tells me his Harvard classmate, the junior Senator from Massachusetts, will be our next president. I'm a political dunce and have no idea where he gets his info." With a shrug, he added, "My assistant left me high and dry, and since Max sent me your resume last year, I phoned Gilbert Hartke." He leaned back as someone played a lilting tune on the piano.

Was that from the score? I nearly swooned at the idea of hearing new music by Loewe.

"Hartke thinks you're aces at detail work," Mr. Remsen continued, "which is what I need. Someone who'll help me keep track of script revisions. Changes come like lightning once we're out of town. I need a person who's compulsive."

"I love detail work. The more changes, the better."

"During rehearsals, you'll mainly run errands, but there will be other tasks, too." Brock Remsen looked me in the eye. "You're not applying for this job to meet famous actors, are you?"

"That idea hadn't occurred to me."

"Good," he said with a chuckle. "My assistant has to stay as neutral as Switzerland. Before you can say 'Merlyn,' we'll be putting out fires in the dressing rooms."

"I once put out a dorm room fire. Nothing to it."

"Splendid! You're my new Gal Friday. You'll start here a week from Monday at 10 a.m. sharp. For now, go to Jenny Productions at 120 East 56th and see our administrator. She'll talk to you about salary, employment policies, and all that good stuff."

"Don't you want to know about my typing?" I asked when my future boss stood.

"Kiddo, if you can type slow with two fingers, that's all I need," he said, extending his hand. "Welcome to *Camelot*. That's the name of our show."

"Isn't it *Jenny Kiss'd Me*?"

"Alas, that name was already used by Jean Kerr. Care to read Lerner's book?"

"Are you joking?" I asked. "I'd love to."

"Here," he said, handing me a script bound in soft leather. On the cover, stamped in gold, was the name *Camelot*. "Guard it with your life." He paused. "Listen, Jane, Lerner wears black specs like yours, and it might be better if you don't copy him. Do you own another pair?"

I whipped off my frames. "My vision's fine. I was trying to look brainy."

"A schemer, huh?" he asked with a snort. "You'll fit in well around here."

"Thanks so much, Mr. Remsen."

"You may not thank me when you hear your meager salary. And please call me Brock." He shrugged. "The theater's casual, Jane. We mostly use first names."

A short, sallow, middle-aged man bellowed, "Edmund, dear boy, will you join us?" The guy wore a paisley ascot and spoke with a slight German accent.

"Right away, Fritz," Brock replied, confirming that the speaker was the composer Frederick Loewe. My new boss grinned and waved me toward the door.

I threaded my way through the gypsies, wondering which of them would make the cut. After leaving the building, I floated to the corner of Eighth Avenue. Cabs honked, and pedestrians circled around me, and when I smelled pretzels warming on a cart, my stomach growled. But I headed uptown, eager to hear my employment details. Later on, I'd call my uncle and report my news.

Maybe I'd also send him a bottle of 86-proof Old Forester, his favorite bourbon. Without Max's help, Brock never would've seen me. (I knew because I'd sent Remsen three chirpy letters that he'd ignored.) But against all odds, I'd landed a real backstage job, which might disturb my parents since they felt it was offbeat to work in the theater. And perhaps their opinion made sense in a family that regarded the Honorable Maxwell Conroy as its black sheep. (Instead of becoming a doctor like my grandfather and father, he'd made the Navy his career, which didn't seem unconventional to me.)

As I strolled north, sharing the sidewalk with workers in search of lunch, I thought about my family. I was a middle child who'd grown up with two "pleaser" siblings—an older sister, Alice, a housewife and rabid Junior Leaguer, and a younger brother, Brendan, a medical student at Georgetown. Sadly, I had never found common ground with either of them. Yet I'd somehow inherited my uncle's fierce streak of independence.

As I passed a market with street-front shelves of lush fruits and vegetables, I decided I'd ripened as a person during my "salad days" in New York. Smiling at my reflection in a deli window, I felt ready for the challenges of *Camelot*, believing my Gal Friday job, lowly as Brock Remsen had made it sound, would eventually lead to the career I wanted.

Bryce

It was the idea of working with Richard Burton that daunted him, making him think he should skip his *Camelot* audition tomorrow. He'd seen Burton in *Time Remembered*, the actor's second Broadway show, and thought the man was nice-looking, brooding, and utterly brilliant.

Also, kind of short. Wouldn't Bryce (at six-foot-three) tower over Burton, who was, at most, five-ten? Would that be a problem, or would all the knights be tall?

It might not matter. His agent told him Alan Lerner had written speeches for King Arthur that would leave the other actors in the shade. Bryce was nonetheless dying to observe how the Welshman worked. And he was especially pleased that his agent was sending him for a featured role as a knight that would pay a higher salary than chorus work.

Bryce switched off his bedside lamp and tried to count sheep, but his mind wouldn't shut down. He was scheduled to perform for Lerner, Loewe, Moss Hart, and Franz Allers, the musical director, at the 46th Street Theatre. If things went as planned, the stage manager would feed him some lines, but the producers mainly wanted to hear his voice, since they hadn't found an understudy for Lancelot. Could this show be his "break"? Could he quit his day job waiting tables at Sardi's at long last?

Would his surname be an issue? It was Christmas.

As he breathed deeply to calm his thoughts, he pledged to give the audition his best shot. He'd pursued a useless bachelor's degree in accounting—his father's idea—and sometimes felt insecure among conservatory-trained singers. On the other hand, he'd been working since college at the Lambertville Music Circus, a summer tent theater, steadily moving up to featured roles, and he'd recently played Tom Baxter in

Redhead, this season's opener at the Paper Mill Playhouse. He'd been well cast as the romantic lead and was praised for his acting and singing at that New Jersey venue where many famous actors had cut their teeth. His new agent, Andy, a go-getter at Ashley Steiner, signed him after *Redhead* and felt he'd be ideal for *Camelot*.

The next day at 10 a.m. sharp, Bryce opened the stage door on 46th and nearly hit Dan Elsdon, who was pausing inside before entering the wings. Bryce guessed that Dan was his main competition. The guy was six-two with angular cheek-bones and a plush baritone that sometimes veered flat when he got nervous—they'd worked together at the Cape Playhouse in Massachusetts. Now they smiled at each other, but before they could say hello, a girl with cornflower blue eyes and a reddish-brown ponytail greeted them, introducing herself as Jane Conroy, assistant to Brock Remsen.

Miss Conroy stared at Bryce for a long moment, blushing the pink hue of cotton candy. "The producers are, uh, waiting," she said, "and since we're using alphabetical order, you, uh, Mr. Christmas, will read first, followed by you, Mr. Elsdon. Then we'll repeat this order for the singing. And you'll meet Robert Goulet, who's playing Lancelot, though I don't know why he's here." She sighed. "Good grief, I should keep such thoughts to myself."

"You don't like Goulet?" Elsdon asked with a crooked grin.

"He's fine," Jane replied. "But I'm a worker bee. My opinion means nothing."

"It sure does," Dan remarked, squeezing the girl's bare arm.

Bryce gritted his teeth. Wasn't Elsdon engaged to a New York socialite, one of the Biddles? He'd noticed that actors who were attached often made passes at lovely girls. "I've heard of Goulet," Bryce said, lying with gusto. "He's got a terrific voice, right?"

Jane nodded. "Mr. Allers says Goulet has the best voice he's heard in a decade."

Bryce saw Elsdon's high-wattage smile fade and hoped he'd gained the upper hand. Unlike his rival, he sang well under most conditions without the benefit of Elsdon's Juilliard pedigree. As they walked through the dark wings to the stage, Bryce repressed a grin, believing his bright timbre would impress Franz Allers, a conductor known for being precise.

A man with dirty-blond hair waited center stage, and Jane introduced Bryce and Dan to Nate Wicker. Bryce recalled seeing the actor off-Broadway in *Much Ado About Nothing* with Eric Christmas—no relation. He was thirtyish. Nice features, but average height.

"Nate will read with you," Jane said. "He's Sir Dinadan and will understudy Arthur."

"I'll be ready for flu season," Wicker drawled in a faint Texas accent.

"Hiya, Christmas," said Bernie Hart, a gray-haired man with black glasses who sauntered over from the wings. He was Moss Hart's younger brother, and since he was a Sardi's regular, Bryce knew him well. They'd even shared a drink at the restaurant's "little bar" once or twice. "Mr. Elsdon, I'm the stage manager," Bernie added, "and there's a chair at stage left for you."

Dan Elsdon nodded and ambled away.

"The big dogs are out there," Nate told Bryce, nodding toward the house. "They need to hire someone today. Why not you?"

"Thanks," Bryce said, eyeing Jane Conroy as she walked away, admiring her curves.

Bernie placed a script in Bryce's hands. "I told Mossie you're good, Christmas. Don't make a liar out of me."

"I won't," Bryce said. "I'm in your debt, Bern."

"You and Nate will do the scene when Lancelot meets

Arthur for the first time. Lancelot whacks Arthur in the chest, bragging that he's the right arm of His Majesty without knowing he's whacked the king himself."

"Funny," Bryce said.

Bernie Hart smirked. "I've marked your lines in yellow. Give 'em hell, boyo."

When he finished reading, Bryce knew he'd nailed the scene. He walked off stage, and as Elsdon took his place, Bryce slid onto the folding chair and sighed. Why hadn't he brought a thermos of tea? Dust motes filled the air, and his mouth felt parched. Not great for singing.

He focused on his breathing, trying not to hear Elsdon's line readings. When Dan returned to the wings, he smiled as though he, too, had aced his acting. Bryce stood and strode across the stage to a console piano. The accompanist asked if he'd brought music, and he removed folded pages from his green canvas bag. He'd chosen an Irish folk tune, the kind of ballad a knight might croon to his ladylove.

The pianist played the opening bars, and Bryce sang Yeats to a tune by Britten:

Down by the salley gardens, my love and I did meet,
She passed the salley gardens with little snow-white feet.
She bid me take love easy, as the leaves grow on the tree,
But I, being young and foolish, with her did not agree.

He couldn't sense a reaction from the "big dogs" in the dark, though few actors chose art songs for auditions. A baritone might typically select "They Call the Wind Maria" from Lerner and Loewe's *Paint Your Wagon* to flatter its creators. But after a few lines, Bryce realized he was in excellent voice and strove to embody the hopes of a shy suitor.

As the second verse began, he sang louder, infusing his tone with energy.

In a field by the river, my love and I did stand,
And on my leaning shoulder, she laid her snow-white hand.

He'd studied with one teacher since high school, a retired Eastman professor, and his technique, though not showy, was consistent. He didn't make faces or use extraneous gestures; he had the ability to be still and let emotion shine through the music and text.

She bid me take life easy, as the grass grows on the weirs;
But I was young and foolish, and now am full of tears.

Silence greeted him as he finished. Then a man in the house wearing black glasses stood and called, "Please wait, Mr. Christmas," before slumping back into his aisle seat.

Bryce passed Elsdon, who was heading for the stage. He slipped into the hall and went upstairs to a dressing room where he couldn't hear Dan's polished baritone. He'd had that pleasure at other auditions, and Elsdon's talent had unsettled him.

After exactly four minutes, he was climbing downstairs when Miss Conroy appeared, asking him to hurry. Heading through the wings, he stopped at center stage and stood near Elsdon. Bernie quickly introduced Bryce to Alan Lerner, the man with black glasses, as well as Frederick Loewe, Moss Hart, Franz Allers, Lerner's assistant Brock Remsen, and Robert Goulet, who was tall and handsome with sapphire eyes.

"Welcome aboard, Mr. Christmas!" said Lerner, whose brown hair was styled into a well-oiled pompadour. "Mr. Elsdon will play Sir Sagramore, and we'd like you to play Sir Lionel and understudy Mr. Goulet as Lancelot."

"I'd be honored," Bryce said.

"We'll have fun," Goulet said, blue eyes shining. "Call me Bobby." He extended his hand, and Bryce shook it, noticing a lit cigarette in the other. How could anyone who was serious about his voice *smoke*? Some actors insisted nicotine made them calm, but good singers weren't that reckless. Smoking weakened the cords and reduced lung power. Why didn't "Bobby," who was likely in his late twenties, know this?

"Am I excused?" Nate asked, and Brock Remsen nodded. After Wicker left, Bryce wanted to tell the team he'd loved *My Fair Lady*, but these were princes of the theater who didn't have time for brown-nosing. And to underscore his hunch, they all stalked off.

Elsdon abruptly said, "See you at rehearsals, Christmas." Then he trailed after Wicker, perhaps peeved that Bryce was chosen to understudy Lancelot.

Jane Conroy joined him. "You were upstairs when they told Mr. Elsdon there's a full cast read-through on Saturday, September 3rd. It's at 1 p.m. at the 54th Street Theatre."

"Thanks," Bryce said. "Have we met, Miss Conroy? You look awfully familiar."

"Our paths crossed, uh, once before. At the Piccadilly coffee shop."

"I have lunch there sometimes," he admitted. "I'm a captain at Sardi's, and Mr. Sardi hates it if we come to work hungry."

"Mr. Sardi's going to miss having such a conscientious worker," Jane said with a bright smile. "Congrats on landing a featured role. I'll see you next week, Mr. Christmas."

"Bryce," he corrected before the girl vanished into the wings.

As he exited the stage door, he wanted to shout his good news to the heavens. He decided to stop at Dinty Moore's, a joint up the street known for succulent burgers with onions.

Since it wasn't a Broadway matinee day, the lunch crush hadn't begun. He sat alone at the long wooden bar, catching glints of brass accents throughout the large front room, and though it was barely 11 a.m., he ordered a Heineken and toasted himself. He knew he'd forever view his *Camelot* audition as a high point in his career, having been hired instantly on his merits. It was a relief not having to wait on tenterhooks for a callback, and he'd hit paydirt with a new show by Lerner, Loewe, and Hart. He was Broadway-bound at last, and having just turned thirty, he'd met one of his life goals.

Since he wasn't due at Sardi's until 4 p.m., he drank a second beer with his burger, missing the Piccadilly's Red Wing ketchup. *Oh, jeez,* he thought with a start, Jane Conroy was *that girl.* His mind flashed back to the day she'd turned and smiled at him before rushing out the coffee shop door. He'd had to stop himself from chasing after her because her looks and manner had attracted him. He'd thought about her for several days afterward, wondering who she was.

But that was two summers ago. In the meantime, he'd kept company with a book editor, Rina Markoff, a relationship he'd ended in June. Taking another slug of beer, he warned himself that rebound affairs rarely lasted, and since he'd waited years to make his Broadway debut, the last thing he needed was the distraction of a new romance with its endless wild cards and upheavals.

"Another beer, sir?" the bartender asked him.

"Just the check," he said, thinking he had time to run home and take a nap before his shift. His boss, Vincent Sardi, Jr., would be pleased by his news, since Mr. Sardi was supportive when his actor-servers snagged a theater job. And because Bryce's chance to originate a role in a show like *Camelot* was truly special, he knew he'd be the talk of the kitchen that night.

2.
MOSS MAKES
A TOAST

Jane

Before I left my room for *Camelot's* first read-through that
Saturday, I marveled that I'd run into the gorgeous guy from
the Piccadilly at auditions. What were the odds? And since I'd
see him again today, I took extra care with my hair, letting it
fall to my shoulders, and my clothes, pressing a white blouse
until it was crisp and donning a black pencil skirt that showed
off my svelte figure.

Then I frowned at myself in the mirror since I'd been honest during my interview. Snagging my post was a stepping
stone to my future, not a ploy to meet actors.

I grabbed my white straw hat and white gloves, thinking
it was the last time I'd wear white accessories: Labor Day
weekend was here. Locking my door in the hall that reeked of
pine carpet cleaner, I reminded myself that backstage flings
were another name for office affairs. Hadn't I read an article
in *Glamour*, the magazine *for the girls with a job,* warning
women to keep their work lives separate from dating? Heading for the center stairs, I had no idea why my neck hair rose
to attention before I'd seen Bryce Christmas two years ago.
And after I noticed his wide-set eyes, blue as a gas flame, and
his alluring smile, I'd wanted more than his French fries that

day. But we were colleagues now. I needed to make the most of *Camelot* and let this gifted actor do the same. (Lordy, the fellow could sing.)

I walked through the Barbizon's opulent lobby featuring palm trees and an Oriental carpet. Outside, I surveyed the hotel's exotic entrance with its pink-coral bricks and beige sandstone. Its facade had sure impressed my father on the day he drove me here, insisting that if the place had been good enough for the former Grace Kelly, now Her Serene Highness of Monaco, it was good enough for Jane Conroy.

So far, I'd met Ford Agency models and ballet students, two kinds of girls whose heads looked larger than their tubercular bodies; high school grads learning to type at Katharine Gibbs; college grads answering phones in ad agencies while hoping to write copy; and *Mademoiselle* college-competition winners called "Millies" whose prize was to edit an issue of the magazine. And I'd met young actresses, often at the indoor swimming pool, where they moaned about their demeaning group auditions known as "cattle calls." I hadn't gotten close to any of those boarders, though I sometimes shared meals with Edie Edmunds, a scrappy cub reporter at the *New York Herald Tribune*.

Having left the Barbizon early, I strolled up the block to number 158 and eyed the red door of a modest townhouse. It was the former home of playwright George S. Kaufman, a place described by his writing partner, Moss Hart, in his memoir, *Act One*. Brock had introduced me to Moss, but I hadn't mentioned I was living a stone's throw from where Kaufman had asked him to collaborate. Why would he care?

I retraced my steps, irked by the reek of dog poop as I walked to Lexington Avenue. (Some pampered East Side pooches didn't make it to the curb.) But it was a perfect Labor Day weekend, warm and sunny, though the city seemed abnormally quiet. Many folks had likely decamped to Coney

Island or the beaches of Long Island to savor one last gasp of summer. But how could riding a roller-coaster or catching some rays compare with watching (and hearing) a new musical by Lerner and Loewe? I almost pinched myself since this was the moment I'd longed for.

Picking up my pace, I passed coffee shops, drug stores, markets, laundries, and the back door of Bloomingdale's before descending into the subway at 59th. Perspiring a little, I welcomed the coolness of the underground platform, and ten minutes later, I was strolling down Seventh Avenue toward 54th.

Hard to believe I was seconds away from meeting Julie Andrews. In college, I'd seen her brilliant performance in *My Fair Lady*, and we were about the same age; Julie would soon turn twenty-five, a birthday I'd marked in June. Not long ago, I'd read she'd married her childhood sweetheart, a set designer named Tony Walton, and since designers traveled for their work, I assumed Mr. Walton would be gone a lot, giving me a chance to become Julie's chum.

(Chum was a word the actress used in a newspaper profile while she was doing *The Boy Friend*, her 1954 New York debut. In that same article, she mentioned she'd lived at the Hotel Piccadilly, planting the seeds of my fascination with the place.)

Beyond La Scala, a small Italian restaurant, I saw the blank marquee for the 54th Street Theatre, which, Brock had explained, used to be called the Adelphi. In the mid-1950s, the place was used to film *The Honeymooners*, Jackie Gleason's TV show that was performed for a live audience. Lately, it had been refurbished and renamed, and after *Camelot* left for Toronto in three weeks, *Bye Bye Birdie* would move here from the Martin Beck. "Alan, Fritz, and Moss were lucky to find an empty theater for rehearsals," Brock said when he'd given me a tour.

I felt my heart pounding as I cleared the outside door and

headed for the stage, removing my hat and gloves. As expected, the crew had set up rows of folding chairs facing the house—these were for the cast. The guys had also placed *Camelot's* costume sketches by Abelard and set designs by Oliver Smith on large easels at either side of the rows, and a few techies were now standing around talking, swigging Coke out of green glass bottles.

The stage and house lights were on since Moss Hart told the company they could invite their families and friends to this first reading. Yet, while guests would hear the actors, the long production table facing the cast would surely block the view from the orchestra section. (Maybe some clever spectators would sit in the mezzanine above the action.)

Creeping downstage, I saw a young woman sitting alone in the first row of chairs and couldn't believe my eyes: it was Julie Andrews. Observing her from a distance, I thought she was beautiful with a peaches-and-cream complexion. Her short brown hair was teased and sprayed, and she looked slim and stylish in a white blouse with cuffs and a floral skirt.

Mustering my nerve, I walked up behind her and chirped, "Hello, Miss Andrews."

She jumped as though I'd pinched her and stood up, letting her script fall to her feet. "Good heavens," she said, turning around, "you gave me a fright."

"Sorry," I murmured before retrieving her script. "I'm Brock Remsen's assistant, Jane Conroy. I wanted to introduce myself in case, uh...in case you need anything."

"How'd you do?" Julie said in her British accent, accepting the leather-bound book from my shaking hands. "May I ask a favor, Jane? Could you try not to sneak up on me?"

"Of course," I said, wanting to fall through the floor.

Without another word, Julie Andrews sat down and opened her script, dismissing me.

"Miss Conroy," called Nate Wicker, wearing glasses with black frames and a sports jacket with a tie. He didn't greet the leading lady but chose a seat two rows back.

"Let's whisper," I said, drawing near, "so we don't disturb anyone."

"It doesn't hurt to tread lightly the first day, darlin'," Nate advised. "Actors are always competing with their last success, even stars."

"I see." But it hadn't occurred to me that Miss Andrews, who'd been the toast of Broadway as Eliza Doolittle, might be worried about her new show's table read.

"The principals will return here tomorrow," Nate said, "but the ensemble will rehearse at the New Amsterdam. Correct?"

"Correct. Did you invite anyone today?"

"My wife, Shari, is here." He paused. "Ah, the king enters, and if you want my advice about him, speak when spoken to."

Richard Burton ambled toward the first row. He was a striking man with short brown hair and acne scars on his cheeks. He wore a jacket and tie and looked slimmer and less muscular than I remembered from seeing him in movies. After nodding to Nate and me, Burton slid onto the seat next to Julie, and the two leads struck up a conversation. I turned toward Nate, but he was reading his script, so I didn't disturb him.

When Brock Remsen entered with Alan Lerner, Fritz Loewe, and Moss Hart, I ran to Brock's side. Among my duties was to bring the producers coffee, water, and sundry items they requested. Today, however, urns of coffee, hot water for tea, and platters of cookies and pastries filled a long table at stage right, which meant I might be spared the gofer routine.

The noise level picked up as Lerner, Loewe, and Hart strolled downstage to greet Miss Andrews and Mr. Burton. Bobby Goulet joined them, followed by David Hurst (Merlyn) and Robert Coote (King Pellinore), the veteran British actor who'd played Colonel Pickering in *My Fair Lady.* Jumping up, Julie Andrews yelled, "Cooter!" and the pair hugged like survivors of the Blitz—or maybe survivors of the well-publicized tantrums of their former leading man Rex Harrison. Eighteen singers and twenty-one dancers gradually arrived, whispering hellos while moving to the back. Dan Elsdon (Sir Sagramore) and Bryce Christmas (Sir Lionel) sat next to Nate (Sir Dinadan); they were featured actors who also sang in the ensemble.

Bryce and Dan waved to me while the last principals trickled in: Marjorie Smith (Nimue), Nell Dean (Morgan Le Fey), and Roddy McDowall, the film and stage star who'd begged to play Arthur's son Mordred even though his character didn't enter until act two. (Brock had told me about McDowall's many calls to Alan and Moss. "His presence in *Camelot*," my boss explained, "is what's known as 'luxury casting.'")

When the company was seated—I'd moved to the rear—Moss Hart stood before us with his back to the audience. He was a dapper man in his mid-fifties with a receding hairline and was rumored to be so anxious he saw his psychiatrist daily. But he carried himself with panache, and even before he asked for quiet, the chatter ceased.

Moss Hart commanded respect just by showing up.

"On behalf of Alan, Fritz, and myself, I want to welcome you to *Camelot*," Moss called in a light tenor voice. "It's thrilling to launch a new musical, but as some of you know, it's harrowing, too. The hardest work is done out of town while we're sleeping on saggy beds and drinking cold coffee from cardboard cups, and missing our families. But look around, ladies and gents. All of us excel at what we do. We'll weather the rough spots and return to New York with a marvelous show. So, before we start this grand journey, I want to make a toast." He looked around. "And here's the Veuve Clicquot."

While crew members passed out plastic coupes of champagne,

Moss beamed like a master of ceremonies, accepting his drink from Robert Downing, the production stage manager. When everyone had a coupe, the director said, "All right, friends, raise your glasses to *Camelot!* God bless us, everyone, and screw Tiny Tim."

Some cast members yelled, "Hear, hear!" while others chugged their "Veuve Click," as my dad called this vintage. Then the actors passed their empty glasses to crew guys at the end of each row. After Moss asked the cast to find page one in their scripts, he turned to his brother Bernie, one of our three stage managers, and asked him to announce the stage directions.

The read-through commenced as Sir Dinadan, Sir Lionel, and Merlyn discussed the imminent arrival of Guenevere, a bride the king had never met. Arthur was hiding in a tree but climbed down to sing "I Wonder What the King is Doing Tonight." Fritz played the piano while Alan performed this first number in a nasal tenor that sometimes strayed off pitch. But Alan's ability to convey the humor and conviction of his words made up for his vocal flaws; everyone applauded at the end.

I was swept away, and for the next two hours, I blinked back tears, grateful that I was part of this astounding show. *God bless Uncle Max and Father Hartke*, I thought. Their influence had placed me in a world of enchantment.

Act one ended, and Bernie Hart called for a break. Most company members rose, heading to the restrooms or visiting the snack table. Moss, Alan, and Fritz formed a huddle, and since Brock didn't need me, I sped through the wings and dashed up some concrete stairs. The doors to the dressing rooms were unlocked, so I entered one—dusty, reeking of old smoke—and let myself cry. Though the leads hadn't sung a note, I'd fallen in love with Loewe's rapturous melodies and Lerner's clever lyrics and book. Some of the acting was already polished to a sheen, and after Richard Burton intoned Arthur's closing act-one monologue, the "proposition" speech, in which he acknowledged Guenevere and Lancelot's passion, then forgave his wife and best friend, the cast and the audience had clapped and cheered.

Had Moss been too negative, predicting "harrowing" times and "rough spots" out of town? Because *Camelot* seemed perfect, even without the voices of Julie and Bobby. Yes, the show was long, even at the act-one mark, but it would be pruned and shaped by its veteran creators. (Maybe Moss Hart did need a shrink. His worries seemed premature and overblown.)

I wiped my eyes and fluffed my hair and went downstairs. I was moving steadily through the backstage throng when I smacked into a short man with slicked-back dark hair and a thin black mustache, wearing a suit that fit like a second skin. He reared up like a spooked pony, and I apologized, having no idea who he was. The man regained his balance, smiled, and murmured, "Pardon me," and as I watched him cross the floor and kiss a lady in a white knit suit, I knew I'd nearly toppled Abelard, the acclaimed Hollywood costume designer who'd dressed Grace Kelly and Ingrid Bergman. (The woman he'd greeted was his wife, Lolo Weston, a movie actress with a platinum pageboy.)

Alan ran over to greet Miss Weston and pump the designer's hand, and Moss joined them. I stared at the quartet, guessing I'd meet many celebrities through *Camelot*. But at least I hadn't brought shame on myself for simply brushing against Abelard's bespoke lapels.

"Hey, Jane," Brock called as I was about to sit. "Fritz just reminded Alan they're going to a black-tie shindig tonight." He paused. "I'm sorry, but you'll have to run to the tailor and pick up Alan's new tux. He wants you to leave it with his housekeeper." He handed me a scrap from a yellow legal pad.

"Here's the info."

I numbly retrieved my belongings and followed Brock through the wings, aware that he was limping, an impairment I hadn't noticed before. We wound up near the stage door, and he glanced over his shoulder, perhaps to ensure we were alone. "Look, this is strictly confidential. Is that clear?" I nodded, and he sighed, adding, "In July, Alan's wife took their toddler son to Europe, and when she landed, she called and told him she wasn't coming back. Can you imagine being that cruel? Alan adores his little boy."

"It's awful," I mumbled.

"Well, for a while, Alan couldn't function, and he had trouble completing act two. Now he's muddling through, but barely. His wife always kept track of their calendar, which is why you're retrieving his tux. Anyhow, be here tomorrow at two for the first rehearsal of the leads." He gave me a ten-dollar bill. "I know you'd rather stay, kiddo, but you'll see the show ad nauseam from now on. Take cabs and keep the change."

Though I was sorry for Alan's distress, I felt like a lowly Army recruit who had to obey distasteful orders. After clearing the stage door, I decided my day had plunged from the sublime to the ridiculous in two hours. Exhaling a sigh, I glanced at the yellow scrap before hailing a cab.

Since it was a holiday weekend, the taxi sped to the tailor in the East 60s, waited, then drove me to Alan's address at 42 East 71st, a more elegant townhouse than George S. Kaufman's old home. A middle-aged maid in a gray uniform answered the bell and accepted Alan's tux in a garment bag. After I jumped back in the cab, the driver sped down Fifth Avenue, giving me a sun-dappled view of Central Park. It was among my favorite New York places, though everyone told me it was dangerous to walk alone in its forested glens.

Unable to shake my misery—after all, I'd been banished—I

went back to my room at the Barbizon and fell asleep for two hours. Feeling no better when I awoke, I went to Malachy's, a hole-in-the-wall on Third Avenue whose front window was strung with Christmas lights all year long. It smelled of spilled ale and mildew. Though the place featured a dozen wood tables, some unoccupied, I sat at the bar and ordered a Guinness from the part-time bartender who'd once introduced himself as Dickie Harris. He was a nice-looking man with brown hair, fiery blue eyes, and a nose he'd broken once or twice. The first time we met, he claimed he'd known "the poor wee McCourts" back in his native Limerick.

"Tough day, darlin'?" he asked in a mellow voice. "You look knackered."

"Yup, knackered," I said, repeating a word Dickie used often.

He had his own Guinness at hand, and after serving me an enormous glass with a layer of foam that might've been cream, he raised his mug, saying, "Slainte (*Slan-sha*)."

"Slainte," I said before we both chugged some of our ale. Then I ordered a hamburger on Alan's dime while the Saturday band—musicians who played the tin whistle, concertina, guitar, and fiddle—launched a round of Celtic tunes. Some of the patrons clapped along or drummed the tabletops, and I perked up. My dad's grandparents hailed from County Mayo, so I had Irish roots.

"Aren't these fellas grand?" Dickie Harris called over the music. The Guinness had given me a buzz, and I wondered if anyone would dance. Well, I wouldn't ask Dickie. He was attentive to every girl who came in and was, in his own words, "a bit of a lad." It was a quaint expression, but I got his general drift.

Bryce

You're not in Lambertville anymore, he thought, walking home after the *Camelot* read-through. He'd admired the acting of Burton, Andrews, and McDowall, and though his character Lionel had few lines, he'd sing in all the choral numbers plus understudy Goulet, which meant working with Nate Wicker. Since Nate seemed like a stand-up guy, Bryce looked forward to knowing him better, whereas Elsdon was more competitor than comrade. Bryce was still surprised they hadn't picked him to cover Lancelot since, on a good day, Dan could out-sing anyone and was handsome as sin. You had to wonder why he wasn't a star at City Opera.

With taxi horns crooning the rush hour, Bryce waited at the corner of Ninth, musing that it might grow tiring to shuttle back and forth between the New Amsterdam on 42nd and the 54th Street house. But shows came together in rehearsal halls or empty theaters with their stale smells and greasy dust motes, and he couldn't wait to help *Camelot* evolve into a polished production.

After stopping to buy his supper at the corner deli, he sprinted to his brownstone on West 56th. He climbed steep stairs to the landing, opened the massive wood door, and checked his mailbox—just bills—before running up three flights. He was in great shape from weekly sessions at the gym and was breathing normally as he entered his long narrow railroad flat. But when he switched on the light and cockroaches scuttled across his counter, he vowed to call the super. Yet, no matter how often that hard-working man sprayed his kitchen, the blasted bugs wouldn't die.

Bryce put a Coke in his ancient fridge that sputtered when he opened the door, as though it hated being disturbed. Needing a beer, he withdrew a Heineken before placing his meal on his dining table at the front of his living room. His apartment faced the street, and afternoon light poured in through two windows facing a metal fire escape. New York brownstones were in various states of renovation, and some still had communal toilets in the hall. His apartment had a water closet and a shower since the building owner had removed the bathtub from the kitchen, a quirk still found in former tenements.

Removing his suit jacket and tossing it aside, he decided the stars of *Camelot* were probably renting luxury apartments, and as he ate chicken soup with a plastic spoon—he loathed washing dishes—he wondered when he'd be flush enough to move somewhere nice.

His father had expressed the same sentiment when Bryce called to announce he'd snagged his first job on Broadway. His dad, a good-natured though humorless soul, was a tenured Econ professor at Rutgers who'd insisted Bryce study accounting. That field, his dad used to say, would provide a secure living, the proverbial "something to fall back on" if his theater ambitions tanked. But dealing with numbers made Bryce's head spin, and he'd much preferred waiting tables until his stage career blossomed.

At Sardi's, from which he'd taken several leaves of absence, he could eavesdrop on the meetings of producers and directors and glean useful nuggets about the business. Since he was tall, his customers could spot him, and he took pains to recall the minutia of their orders, such as someone's wish to substitute fries for mashed potatoes or green beans for peas. He made sure water glasses were refilled and bread was replenished, which earned him hefty tips. He was so efficient he'd been promoted to captain, sporting a maroon blazer instead of the cherry-red waiter's jacket. The best parts were that the hours flew, and he earned enough to get by.

Well, his Sardi days were over for now; maybe forever if *Camelot* led to other roles. Still, his parents had been grudging about his news. "Don't count your chickens," his mother said. "Don't burn your bridges with Vincent Sardi," his father advised. No wonder he felt unsettled whenever his horizons expanded. He'd grown up under an effing wet blanket. It astonished him that he could still summon the will to audition despite the constant rejections that came with the territory. There had been nights when he'd come home and bawled into his beer, wondering if he should stop struggling to perform.

Maybe his days of doubt were over, too, he mused, eyeing his prized possession, a 1956 "mahogany satin" Steinway console he'd bought from a voice teacher who was moving up to a baby grand. He'd studied piano for years and played well enough to accompany himself when he vocalized, believing the Steinway's exceptional sound made him work harder.

After finishing his supper, Bryce cleared the table and settled his long body on the sofa, a hand-me-down chintz settee from his folks. He switched on a lamp and began reading *The Once and Future King*, the quirky latest version of Arthur's legend that Lerner adapted for *Camelot*.

He was engrossed in *The Sword in the Stone*, the novel's first part, when his bell rang. He placed the hardback on an antique trunk that doubled as a coffee table and headed to the intercom in his foyer, thinking one of his female neighbors had forgotten her key. It happened so often that he figured the girls used this excuse to chat with him. This time, though, a husky female voice called, "Sorry to drop in, darling, but I wanted to see you." He pressed the buzzer, waiting for his old flame Rina Markoff to climb the stairs, knowing she wouldn't break a sweat.

"Rina," he said, feigning pleasure as he opened his door. "What a nice surprise."

"Is it?" she asked, barging into his apartment as if she were expected.

"I'll take that." He pointed to a bottle in her arms, and she gave him the syrupy Mateus that made his stomach churn. "Let me take your coat," he added, but she was already handing him her calf-length fur. During their time together, he'd felt sorry for the poor raccoons someone killed to make this monstrosity that smelled of Chanel Number Five. Truth was, he hated to put it in his closet where his coats and jackets might pick up its scent. Since Rina was watching, however, he placed the fur on a hanger, leaving the closet door ajar for ventilation.

"I read in the *Times* that you got a featured role in *Camelot*," she said. "I wanted to mark the occasion. But is that Tim White's pitiful novel over there?"

"Why pitiful?" He uncorked the Mateus on his kitchen counter and grabbed two wine goblets from a cabinet before joining Rina in his living room.

"He distorts the characters," she said, sitting on the couch. "He presents Lancelot as an ugly Frenchman who'd give Quasimodo a run for his money. And Arthur comes off like an idiot. Our house published it, but I hope Alan Lerner doesn't perpetuate Tim's vision."

"The script is quintessential Lerner," Bryce said, pouring wine for both of them, then sitting next to her. "He must know a thing or two about desire. I read he's on his fourth wife, and he's only forty-two." He took one sip of the Mateus and placed his glass on the trunk. "The novel's first chapter is charming."

"That's the only part with charm," she insisted. "You know I'm an astute judge of fiction. I wouldn't bother with the rest if I were you." Rina was an editor at Putnam with a master's in lit from Yale. She knew her stuff, but if she didn't like a particular book, she refused to let anyone else form an opinion.

While she sipped her wine, Bryce gave his old flame a discreet once-over. She was still lovely with blonde hair, hazel eyes, and asymmetrical features, though she kept herself too thin for his taste. This was astonishing since she lived on borscht, blinis, caviar, and sour cream sent to her weekly from the Russian Tea Room, compliments of her wealthy father.

"Well, Sir Lionel," she said, "are you interested?" When he didn't answer, she crossed her legs, showing shapely thighs. "We should celebrate. You met your goal. Broadway by 30."

"Yes," he said. "But you need to know we're going out of town in three weeks."

"Then there's no time to waste," she murmured, standing.

Bryce got up and kissed her wide mouth. She tasted like the wine she'd brought.

Telling him she needed to use "the loo," she kicked off her heels and ran down the hall.

He followed her, heading to his room, stripping off his white oxford shirt and tie on the way. He felt tense about starting rehearsals tomorrow, so for his money, Rina had resurfaced at a good moment. Perching on his mattress to remove his shoes and socks, he recalled that despite the lady's tendency to boss him around, she always let him lead in the sack. He hoped they'd quickly reignite their sexual chemistry since, otherwise, they had little in common. But since he'd been honest about his imminent departure, he felt no guilt about wanting a romp with her.

Yet, as he took off his slacks and tossed them in a heap, he pictured Jane Conroy's lovely face and wavy auburn hair. He'd never forgotten her smile on that hot August day in 1958, and now he imagined her pert breasts under the blouse she'd worn today.

When Rina slipped in, her naked body glowing from inner heat, she noticed the bulge in Bryce's briefs. "You couldn't wait?" she asked, sounding confused.

"Nope," Bryce said before hastily leading Miss Markoff to his bed.

3.
PREMATURE EXIT

Jane

As Brock predicted at the first reading, I got to attend endless *Camelot* rehearsals. It surprised me that all the men wore ties and most women chose dresses (except Julie and me, who favored slacks). And at one point, Alan apologized for the tux incident, claiming he had no wish to turn me into his valet (pronounced "val-it"). His kindness eased my fears that the producers viewed me as a mindless, low-level drudge.

Because of Moss's directing process, however, I hadn't seen most of act two during the first ten days. And after spending my time running between rehearsal spaces, I still came home to a claustrophobic room and group bathroom down the hall, a situation that was wearing thin. The poor old Barbizon was like living in a down-at-the-heels convent—I'd seen my share since I'd been taught by nuns through twelfth grade. But as my friend Sarah Wilkins observed over penne at Sardi's, the noisy bistro with red banquettes, known for star caricatures on every wall, there was little point renting an apartment when I'd be leaving town with the show for six weeks.

"You're right," I told her. "But, Sare, you still haven't mentioned how you got here."

"I developed migraines from working in that awful bakery,"

Sarah said, adding that her grandmother had shown some pity and offered to fund "one frugal year in the city." Two days earlier, she'd checked into the Barbizon and planned to start a round of musical auditions. I'd already asked Brock to make a call since Rodgers and Hammerstein were replacing chorus members in *The Sound of Music*. They needed sopranos to play nuns, and blonde, zaftig Sarah screamed "wholesome" from every pore.

"I can't thank you enough for asking your boss to help me," she said after the pasta plates were removed and a waiter in a red blazer and black slacks brought our Baked Alaska.

"My pleasure," I murmured as blue flames jumped from our dessert, then died out while we hoisted our forks. Diving into the charred meringue, I mused that, until recently, Bryce Christmas had worked here and must've looked smashing in his uniform. "Listen, Sare, I also have surprising news. One of our singers learned she's expecting and gave notice last night."

"You're kidding," Sarah said. "*Camelot*'s hiring?"

I nodded. "Show up at the New Amsterdam roof tomorrow at one and our musical director, Mr. Allers, will listen to you. Sing an aria. He likes a classically trained sound."

"You and I might go on the road," Sarah said happily.

I grinned because my friend was a messy traveler. But it would be great fun if we could tour together, and the *Camelot* ensemble would be stronger with her agile coloratura. I also hoped to earn points with Franz Allers, an Eastern European perfectionist, for finding a soprano who could sight-read. He loudly harped on the failings of the chorus, though he often praised the "musicianship" of Bryce Christmas and Dan Elsdon.

Not wishing to make Sarah nervous, I skipped her audition, but when my boss later showed up at 54th Street, he announced that the maestro had hired Miss Wilkins on the spot. She'd sung Adele's "Laughing Song" from *Die Fledermaus* and "knocked it out of the park," which pleased Brock. "You know your sopranos," he said, patting my hand in the avuncular manner he'd used since I joined the staff. (Unlike the other straight men in the company, Brock didn't flirt with me or anyone else. As a result, I trusted him completely.)

As my boss took off, I felt two large hands grab my shoulders.

"Afternoon, love," said Richard Burton in his resonant voice that brought to mind a cello, lyrical and sometimes mournful. When I spun around, he flashed a wolfish grin, sharing none of Brock's scruples. With a second's encouragement, he'd pull me into a stage-level dressing room and make advances. "What are we doing?" he asked. "I left my script at home with my notes."

Richard was dressed in a red sweater and tan slacks. (Someone told me he often wore red to honor his Welsh roots.) "Moss is blocking part of act one, scene five," I said. "From the moment Arthur introduces Lance to Jenny."

"Isn't it peculiar?" Richard asked. "Guenevere's nickname should be Gwen or Gwenny."

"T.H. White calls her Gwen *and* Jenny. But why don't I find you a script?"

"No need, love," he said. "I know my lines. But you might fetch me a cup of Earl Grey."

"Right away, Mr. Burton."

"It's Richard or Rich, and you're a dear." He paused. "I suppose you hope to act?"

"No—uh, Richard," I said. "I want to do production."

"How marvelous," he said, chuckling. "That's a first in my experience. Any girl I've met backstage has longed to be on stage."

"I never acted even at school. Working tech has always

been my dream."

"Ah, well, it's a wise woman who knows herself."

His attention delighted me, but I sensed danger. "I should get your tea."

"The steamier, the better," he said with a wink.

Since his last comment wasn't about Earl Grey, I was glad to head out. But since visiting the neighborhood deli was an eight-minute round trip, I returned promptly, and as Richard accepted his tea, he slipped me a dollar, giving me a large tip. By now, Julie Andrews, wearing a beige blouse and matching trousers, and Bobby Goulet, in a blue cardigan and dark slacks, were chatting on stage. Since Brock was off meeting with Alan, I waited on the proscenium, hoping to watch the principals rehearse.

Today's scene should've started with "The Lusty Month of May" for Julie and the ensemble, but we were skipping the music. A stagehand lurched forward to remove the ghost lamp, a naked bulb atop a long pole, and another techie lowered the house lights. The setting was supposed to be a garden near the castle with trees, a fountain, and a gold bench for the queen, but a second crew member merely brought a canvas folding chair.

Moss Hart appeared at the rear of the house and strolled down the aisle. He looked suave in a gray pullover and gabardine trousers and, today, wore soft suede shoes like moccasins. He stopped at the edge of the orchestra pit, calling, "Good afternoon, everyone. As you know, the next scene is pivotal since it's when Guenevere begins to loathe Lancelot."

"But he works a miracle later on," Richard said. "What's not to love?"

Burton's quip broke the tension, and the leads laughed. But this was the scene that also planted seeds of conflict between Arthur and Guenevere, as well as Guenevere and Lance, so the dramatic stakes were rising.

"I believe Jenny's animosity stuns Arthur," Moss said. "He admired Lance's strength in the last scene and felt his remorse when Lance realized he'd bashed the king. So, I want to see disharmony start to build." He paused. "Jane, you're welcome to come down here with me."

Surprised that Moss had called me by name, I dashed toward the wings and found the pass door to the house. Moss held an unlit pipe between his teeth and was now sitting on the aisle in row L, so I claimed the seat one row ahead of him.

As the leads took their places, I thought about the various scenes they'd rehearsed over ten days. The opening was a beguiling play within a play, with Merlyn scolding Arthur for hiding in a tree until his princess-bride arrived from a neighboring kingdom. Arthur jumped down and told Guenevere his name was "Wart," extolling the charms of Camelot in the title song. When courtiers appeared, calling him "Your Majesty," Arthur sheepishly dismissed them and slowly explained how he pulled a sword from a stone and became king. Though Guenevere had just told him she planned to run away, she was moved when Arthur said he aspired to be worthy of her, and they gleefully ran off to get married.

When the next scene began five years later, Arthur and Guenevere (a.k.a. Jenny) were hatching the idea of the Round Table where "might for right" would establish a new moral order. The following scene brought the young Frenchman Lancelot du Lac to Camelot as he sang "C'est Moi," a paean to his perfection. Then he bested Arthur in a mild skirmish before swearing fealty to the Round Table.

Each scene was witty and eased the plot toward the moment, unfolding now, when Arthur introduced his queen to the priggish, pious Lancelot. And now, eyeing the actors, I recalled that Moss let the leads position themselves wherever they felt comfortable. (Brock told me that Moss believed a director was the custodian of the show, whose foremost goal was to honor the text.)

"Please begin," Bernie Hart called from the seat at the far end of Moss's row.

King Arthur entered the garden, followed by Lancelot. He introduced the young knight to Guenevere, who wanted to discuss the previous comic moment when King Pellinore and his sheepdog had stumbled into the garden. (In the actual show, singers and dancers would be milling about in the background, laughing after Pellinore's exit.) What followed now was a short, increasingly tense exchange as pompous Lancelot made a disastrous impression on the fun-loving queen.

"Hold on," Moss called, rising.

I guessed why he was stopping: Bobby's line readings had been stiff. Of course, Lancelot himself was stiff, and maybe this was Goulet's interpretation.

Moss dashed up the aisle as far as the pit while Richard, Julie, and Bobby rambled downstage to chat with him. I longed to hear the director's comments, but stayed put. After Moss returned to his seat, the actors began again. This time, Arthur appeared bemused—even worried—about Guenevere's chilly response to Lancelot. His interactions with the queen were livelier, and it was clear that a few words from Moss had energized their exchange. But Lancelot's line readings remained lifeless, and I heard Moss whisper, "What in hell was that?"

He jumped up, calling, "Stop." He again ran toward the stage and motioned to Bobby, who strolled down to the footlights for a private chat. After Moss reclaimed his seat and the trio began anew, Arthur and Jenny were animated, but Lancelot was blah.

Moss leaned toward me, whispering, "I'd like to smack him upside the head." Then he squeezed my shoulder and took off down the aisle again, briefly vanishing before appearing center stage. Whatever he said to Bobby made the actor's ruddy complexion lose its color.

I felt bad for Goulet. According to the bio he'd submitted for the Toronto playbill, he'd done a few leading roles with the Kenley Players, a summer stock company in Ohio. *Camelot* would be his Broadway debut, but while he'd had vocal training, he hadn't gone to acting school. Maybe he felt petrified sharing the stage with Burton, one of the finest actors working in theater and film, and Andrews, who'd been acclaimed for *My Fair Lady*. Yet why hadn't the guy hired a drama coach before rehearsals began? Had he thought his good looks and splendid baritone would be enough?

"Jane," Julie called from the proscenium. Rehearsal was apparently over, and Moss was heading into the wings with Richard and Bobby. "Will you wait for me?"

My heart wobbled in my chest. Julie hadn't spoken to me since September 3rd, but now she was smiling as she entered the house. "I need to visit Helene Pons, then get to a chorus rehearsal," she said. "I thought you'd like to see Helene in action, since she's a legend." Reaching my seat, she added, "You and I got off on the wrong foot. Please chalk it up to first-day jitters."

"I shouldn't creep up on people," I said, standing. "But I'd love to tag along."

I'd watched with interest in recent days as female cast members were dispatched by the stage managers to the Pons Studio, one block west on 54th, where Broadway's renowned dressmaker was refining their costumes. I knew the men were sent to Ray Diffen Stage Clothes near the Plaza and had lately noticed that Bryce Christmas, Dan Elsdon, and other knights were sprouting facial hair, maybe at Diffen's request. (I thought Bryce, with his dark mustache and goatee, looked sexier than before, which was saying something.)

Now Julie and I walked through the lobby, exiting beneath the marquee, which now advertised Dick Van Dyke, Chita Rivera, and Kay Medford in *Bye Bye Birdie*. It was another warm day, and we hiked west, passing a row of brownstones. Julie had long legs and didn't dawdle, and we met few pedestrians. "So, how does the show look so far?" she asked as we dodged cars while jaywalking across Seventh Avenue.

"It's—great," I stammered.

"Is it, Jane?" Julie asked.

"You and Richard are amazing," I said. "Bobby—"

"Could be stronger," she said. "Richard, Roddy, and I see that, but we don't want to criticize him to Moss." She sighed. "I trust you'll keep my confidence."

"I will, and please keep mine," I said. "Bobby was on a different wavelength today."

"I had the same problem at the start of *My Fair Lady*," Julie confessed. "I wasn't cutting it in rehearsals, and the producers thought they should replace me. I'm sure Rex Harrison was leading that particular charge. Then one weekend Moss closed down rehearsals to work one-on-one with me. He bullied and cajoled and gave me the line readings until I couldn't see straight, but by Monday, I *was* Eliza Doolittle. There's absolutely no doubt that he saved my job."

"What a clever way to help you," I said, touched by her humility.

"I wish he'd do the same for Bobby, but he's got a lot to juggle with the show running so long. Maybe in Canada." Julie shrugged. "Let's talk about your friend, Miss Wilkins. I think she may become my second understudy."

"That would be great for her," I said, though Sarah hadn't known about this possibility. And neither had I.

"I'll hear her today," Julie said. "Then I'll rehearse 'The Lusty Month of May' with the chorus, which should be great fun. I'll get to sing, dance, and lark about. In fact, it's the 'May' costume we'll see in a moment."

As we pressed on, Julie mentioned she'd married Tony Walton, her childhood sweetheart, the previous year and wished he could stay with her in Toronto and Boston. "His career's thriving," she said, "and I couldn't be happier. But the road can get bleak when you're alone, and I assume he'll be flying in and out."

I felt flattered to be Julie's confidante, and when she asked if I had "a beau," I said I'd had a steady guy in college but was now unattached.

"Don't be alone with Richard," Julie advised. "He's married to a lovely woman named Sybil, and they have a little girl who's three. But he'd like to seduce every lady he meets."

"I've heard that," I said.

"Bobby's mind is on his work so far, which is refreshing."

"Roddy McDowall isn't married, is he?"

"Roddy's a confirmed bachelor, and I adore him."

"Confirmed bachelor" was the code term for homosexual, and Mr. McDowall wasn't alone; many men in the chorus were gay, some more open about it than others.

"Can I tell you," I continued, "that Sarah and I saw you in *My Fair Lady*? You became her role model, and I felt honored to breathe the same air for one afternoon."

"You're sweet," Julie said. "I just remember working like a horse and feeling tired all the time and never being able to go anywhere because I had to save my voice. It was worth the price, but non-actors think it's all champagne and roses and parties with Noel Coward. Instead, it's trips to the ENT and having Rex Harrison and Cecil Beaton call you filthy names." She gave a bawdy laugh. "Not to my face, of course, but it hurt when people told me."

"I'm sure it did," I said, startled to learn she had an earthy streak.

When we reached a skyscraper on the next block, we took the elevator to the 13th floor. A receptionist with white hair said, "Hello, Miss Andrews. They're expecting you." Julie led me down a narrow hall past several workrooms where men and women were bent over cutting tables or seated at whirring sewing machines. We entered a messy room with costumes on racks, floor-to-ceiling mirrors, and bolts of colorful fabric propped against the walls.

"Ah, you're here, darling," said a petite sixtyish woman in a black knit dress with scissors dangling from her belt. Julie introduced me to Mrs. Pons, whose dark hair was arranged in a bun, and the woman riffled through some gowns on hangers before giving one to the star. As Julie slipped behind a screen, two assistants stood by: a blonde woman in an orange shirtwaist and a brown-haired man in a blue shirt and gray slacks with a tape measure around his neck.

Mrs. Pons peered at me. "Are you Julie's assistant?" she asked in a French accent.

"For now," I said. "Is there anything I can do?"

"Yes, dear. You can stop slouching. You're too pretty to have bad posture."

I giggled because Helene Pons was spot on: I did slouch when I got nervous. As the leading lady came back, skirt rustling, I murmured, "How lovely!" She wore a light-blue taffeta gown with a V-neck and long taffeta royal-blue sleeves.

The man sank to his knees, holding a pin cushion. "Are these the right shoes?" he asked.

"Yes," Julie said. "I'm wearing flats for the entire show."

"Unlike Miss Doolittle's toe-pinching Edwardian boots," Mrs. Pons said, tugging the gown downward, checking the fit at Julie's waist while the man measured for length.

"The dress should come up two inches," the man said, starting to pin the hem.

Mrs. Pons moved in front of Julie to assess her helper's opinion. "I agree," she said.

"My waist needs more give," Julie said. "I'll be dancing and twirling things on poles, and I need the freedom to move." She studied herself in a mirror. "Also, I don't love the neckline."

Mrs. Pons nodded. "I'll call Abelard. I think a round neck will show more bosom, which never hurts." She turned toward a table and picked up a pale-blue piece of organza. "Feel this, Julie," she said, offering the fabric. "It's for the overskirt."

Having seen Abelard's original sketches, I remembered the May dress would be appliqued with daisies. The pale-blue taffeta sleeves would extend halfway down Guenevere's arm, but for now, only the royal-blue undersleeves were attached to the dress. When finished, the top sleeves would have flowing organza tails to create a medieval flair.

"Your costumes will be ready in a week," Mrs. Pons told Julie. "Come back then, darling."

Ten minutes later, Julie and I were elbow-to-elbow with other diners, sharing a mammoth corned beef sandwich at the Carnegie Deli, where the walls displayed photos of famous actors. Two matrons across the noisy room recognized my companion, pointing and staring, though they didn't interrupt us. I had to speak loudly to be heard, and I thanked Julie for inviting me to her fitting. "You told them exactly what you wanted," I said. "Mrs. Pons admires your candor."

"Helene clucks over me like a mother hen," Julie said, raising her voice above the racket. "But every woman she dresses looks tall and elegant on stage."

After a quick lunch, we retraced our steps on Seventh Avenue, passing 54th Street as we hurried downtown. When Seventh merged with Broadway, we dashed beyond peep shows and strip parlors and souvenir shops with obscene playing cards in the window, a tawdry stretch.

"I love the old Ziegfeld theater on the New Amsterdam roof," Julie said when we reached 42nd, an unsavory street at any hour. "That's where we rehearsed *My Fair Lady*. It's grimy, dusty, and dark. I always feel I need a bath when I leave."

"It feels otherworldly," I said. "The ghosts of the showgirls probably like our rehearsals." I paused. "May I ask you something, Julie? I hope you won't take offense, but sometimes I have trouble hearing you sing in rehearsal."

"No offense taken," Julie said. "I've been marking to conserve my voice. You see, my cords were in shreds after *My Fair Lady*, so I'm building my stamina slowly. The baritones in our show are big guys who sing at full-throttle, but I can't afford to push out sound like they do." She sighed. "Even Moss asked why I'm quiet, but by the end of rehearsals, I'll be singing out."

We walked another block past nudie shows and theaters advertising triple X-rated films to the Amsterdam, an old Broadway house that now played first-run movies. I trailed Julie inside to a pair of elevators that whisked us to the top floor. Stepping into a hallway, we found a large open space where Hanya Holm, the choreographer, was demonstrating steps to twelve knights. Hanya was a short lady in her sixties who wore her brown hair in a bun. She addressed the male dancers with a German accent, calling, "Feel the sensation of air. It's all around you."

"Hanya's a gem," Julie whispered. "But when she gets cross, she wants the moon."

We entered an adjoining room that contained a full proscenium stage. Some rows of seats remained in the back, but most had been removed; in their place were metal tables and folding chairs arranged in a line. Brock sat at one with Alan. Robert Downing, the production stage manager, and his three stage managers—Bernie Hart, Edward Preston, and Jonathan Anderson, who doubled as the choral assistant to Mr. Allers—were at the other. The featured knights, Nate Wicker, Bryce Christmas, and Dan Elsdon, lounged in the first row of regular seats; all seemed to be reading.

Sarah sat three rows behind the actors, and when I saw her terrified expression, I swallowed hard. But when Brock spotted Julie and me, he summoned Sarah to the front of the room and introduced her to the leading lady. Sarah whispered, "It's an honor to meet you."

"Sarah's going to sing 'Goodnight My Someone' from *The Music Man*," Brock told Julie. "You should decide if she should be your understudy."

"Shouldn't Fritz and Franz Allers make that decision?" Julie asked.

"They'll weigh in. But for now, take a seat, Jules. And Sarah, please get to center stage."

My friend looked as though she was being sent to the stake like Guenevere at *Camelot's* finale. But while Brock, Julie, and I joined Alan, Sarah climbed the side steps and moved into position. The pianist played the intro bars of Meredith Willson's haunting ballad, then Sarah began softly. As her volume picked up, her silvery tone had a bit more heft than Julie's light crystalline sound. When she finished, everyone clapped, even the guys rehearsing with Hanya Holm. Sarah blushed before she climbed down the stairs and shyly approached the team.

"You're my ideal understudy," Julie said, standing. "Welcome."

"Thank you," Sarah said, looking dazed, as though Julie's praise was hard to take in.

"I'll speak to Fritz," Alan told Julie. "Now Hanya wants to watch a run-through of 'Then You May Take Me to the Fair' before we rehearse 'The Lusty Month of May.'"

Alan nodded at Bernie, who called, "Messrs. Wicker, Christmas, and Elsdon to the stage."

Before those guys could rise, however, Fritz Loewe darted toward us from the rear of the room, heading for Alan. Brock had told me the composer wore lifts in his shoes, and he teetered as he stopped short. His cheeks were flushed, and he was panting.

"What's wrong?" Alan asked, rising.

"Dear boy, something's more than wrong," Fritz said. "Abelard is dead."

"Dead?" Alan asked. "How?"

"He had a heart attack today in Hollywood," Fritz said. "I just heard it on the news."

"Abelard's wife is here in town rehearsing a play," Alan muttered. "I had dinner with her the other night."

"I think we should discuss what we're going to do," Brock said. "The act-one costumes are ready, but Abelard was still tinkering with the rest."

"That's unlucky," Fritz said, shaking his large head.

"Brock, you take rehearsal, and I'll call Lolo," Alan said. "Jane, you run uptown and alert Moss. Tell him we'll put our heads together tonight." He twirled a lit cigarette in his fingers. "And Jane, also tell Hanya we're ready for her, but don't breathe a word about Abelard."

I took off toward the choreographer, who always wore the same black blouse and skirt, sans stockings or tights, and soft black dance shoes. When Hanya stopped drumming, I repeated Alan's words before darting toward the elevator.

In a mental fog, I ran toward the subway on 42nd, dodging greasy-haired men in tight pants who were passing out flyers for strip shows. Alan had entrusted me with a vital message for Moss, which was akin to addressing the real king of *Camelot*. And while waiting on the crowded subway platform, I distracted myself, wondering why the director hadn't coached Bobby privately as he'd done for Julie in *My Fair Lady*. He'd seemed quite unhappy with Goulet's acting.

Maybe it was a matter of priorities. Moss Hart was married to the actress Kitty Carlisle, and they had two school-age kids. I'd spotted the three of them waiting for Moss one night under the 54th Street marquee, Mrs. Hart swathed in mink despite the mugginess of fall. Maybe the director wanted to spend time with his family before leaving town, knowing he'd have endless opportunities to help Bobby on the road.

Well, the day's one nice surprise was that Julie had opened

up. I longed to take her out for drinks and hear her many yarns about *My Fair Lady* and *The Boy Friend*, and maybe I'd approach her on the road when her husband was elsewhere.

As I exited the subway at Carnegie Hall, I knew I'd crossed an invisible line from green college grad temping at the Burgoyne Agency to young working woman paying her dues in her dream field. I woke each morning eager to discover what the day would bring, and it was seldom what I anticipated. Now, for instance, I felt sad about Abelard, having seen the stunning taffeta gown he'd created for "The Lusty Month of May." The designer hadn't been around since the read-through, but he'd kindly apologized when I'd nearly knocked him down. Now, as I recalled the lines on his face and his sagging jowls that first day, nausea rose in my throat. Abelard had probably been about fifty. My dad's age.

Approaching the stage door, I sighed. I'd only known three people who died—a classmate in a freak accident during high school, a college friend's mother from cancer, and my ninety-year-old Irish great-grandma from a stroke. Even my four grandparents were alive and well, but a key member of the *Camelot* team wouldn't see his elegant designs come to fruition.

Slipping into the backstage corridor, I planned to find Moss, then run to St. Patrick's and light a candle to honor Abelard's memory. Maybe I'd also light a candle for Alan, since the poor guy looked thinner and paler every day. (Marital woes? Missing his son? Writing problems?)

I spied Moss seated in a canvas chair, watching Bobby perform his first solo, "C'est Moi." Franz Allers, balding and short, was conducting a pianist in the pit, and Moss grinned as Bobby sang about Lancelot's purity and strength. Creeping down stage right, I was startled anew by the richness of Bobby's baritone. This was the first time I'd heard him sing except in "The Quests," where chorus members joined in, and his voice reminded me of burnished silver.

"Wait, Robert," Mr. Allers called as the piano ceased. "You must stop using rubato."

"Was I using rubato?" Bobby asked, sounding coy.

"You know you were," the conductor said brusquely. "You can be a jazz singer on your own time. In this show, you must adhere to Mr. Loewe's time signature. Once more, please."

Bobby grinned, then sang the song again. When he finished, Mr. Allers called, "Better."

Moss rose and walked toward the pit for a word with the maestro. Then he faced Goulet, saying, "You're free to go, Bobby. Have a good evening."

"Moss," I said, inching close to the director. "I'm here with an urgent private message."

He looked worried, but neither of us spoke until Bobby vanished.

"It's terrible news," I murmured. "Our designer Abelard has died."

"How tragic," Moss said with a grimace. "He was younger than I am. Heart?"

"Apparently," I replied. "Alan said he'll call you later."

"Thanks, Jane," Moss said. "I'm afraid I'm late for an appointment. Please excuse me."

"Of course," I said before returning to the stage door, eager to gulp some fresh air. But as I reached the sidewalk, I thought of Bryce Christmas, wishing I could speak with him about the ups and downs of rehearsals. So far, it had been easy to avoid him, but whenever our eyes accidentally met, I detected a flicker of interest before one of us looked away.

The afternoon sun warmed my bare arms, and I keenly recalled the finesse Bryce had brought to the folk tune he'd sung at his audition. His approach to singing seemed naturally rhythmic, while Bobby sometimes placed the vocal emphasis on the wrong notes. (Mr. Allers had objected to Goulet's "rubato," which meant the speeding up or slowing down of a tempo. Sarah and I had discussed this musical term when she began voice lessons at Catholic U.)

Crossing Fifth Avenue, I glanced up the block, thronged with people toting shopping bags, and saw the stone façade of St. Patrick's with its neo-Gothic steeples looming over midtown. The cathedral had opened in 1879, a fact I learned at age twelve when my Girl Scout troop toured the city. Though I no longer went to Mass each Sunday, I still believed in my faith and was glad New York had erected this historic Catholic church.

I climbed the front steps and withdrew a white lace square from my bag to cover my head—I always carried one. Creeping through a massive bronze door, then a second set of wooden doors, I smelled incense and vividly recalled the high Masses in my childhood when the pungent lingering fragrance had made me sneeze. Stopping short, I marveled at the beauty of the white marble arches and stained-glass windows in the nave.

Remembering poor Abelard, also Alan, I walked to the brass candlestand near the wall and lit votive candles for each. Then I dropped coins in the donation box and walked up the aisle, finally sliding into a chocolate-brown pew. When I knelt and began to whisper the "Our Father," comfort coursed through me, and I stayed at St. Patrick's for half an hour, praying that nothing else would go wrong for *Camelot* itself or for any of my cherished new acquaintances.

4.
KERFUFFLE
WITH THE KING

Bryce

He'd noticed Abelard (and his natty silk suit) that first day and knew the designer had come out of retirement to create the *Camelot* costumes. And, sure, it was sad that the man died young, but the producers were acting frazzled, and everyone knew the show needed their undivided attention.

Two days after the company's loss, Moss addressed the ensemble on the New Amsterdam roof, reporting that Abelard's colleague, Tony Duquette, would finish the costumes. Tony, a balding man in his forties with huge eyes and protruding teeth, had agreed to deliver everything before they left for Toronto, so Moss assured the cast that preparations would proceed "without another hiccup."

Despite the director's show of confidence, Bryce didn't sleep well that night. The next afternoon, when he arrived at 54th Street to rehearse the scene in which Lancelot returns from his quests and is knighted, he felt out of sorts. But since he'd never formally met Burton and both of them were early, he approached the star and offered his hand. Burton shook grudgingly, then returned to his paperback edition of *Great Expectations*.

Feeling like a dolt, Bryce took a seat down front. What the

hell had possessed him? He was reticent with strangers, and Burton, though friendly with Wicker and Goulet, had never looked at him cross-eyed. Maybe it was because, as Bryce feared early on, he was five inches taller; or maybe the leading man limited his circle to a few trusted acolytes.

He left the star with his Dickens, wondering who'd willingly reread that grim novel. Sitting back and closing his eyes, he thought about Rina, who pleased him in bed. He hadn't realized how lonely he'd been, and it was fun to hear her stories about fractious authors since he'd grown weary of focusing solely on himself, an actor's occupational hazard.

Even so, Rina was deeply unhappy in spite of her publishing career, and her chronic negativity depressed him. Lately, his eye often lit upon Jane Conroy, whose optimism was a shot of adrenaline when the rest of them felt low. She was blessed with classic good looks but seemed unaware of her beauty, and she was unfazed when straight guys in the chorus (and a few lesbians) made blatant passes. He liked her spirit and lack of guile, but he watched her discreetly since he and Rina were a couple—for now, anyway.

Moss Hart strolled past Bryce, trailed by Lerner and Loewe. All three stage managers trickled in, followed by tiny Hanya Holm; the super-tall set designer, Oliver Smith; and the lighting designer, Abe Feder, a ringer for Jack Benny. Brock Remsen and Jane joined the production team at their table as singers and dancers flopped into orchestra seats. But why was Bobby Goulet lurking in the aisle? Did he look hollow-eyed and pale from carousing with Burton? (Rumor had it that nobody could match the leading man for the volume of booze he consumed, apparently without getting drunk or suffering hangovers the next day.)

"Hey, Christmas," Nate Wicker called from the row behind. "Are you ready to wait a while? They're actin' like long-tailed cats in a room full of rockers."

Bryce spun around, thinking Nate's Texas slang undercut his sarcasm. "Everyone's here today. Even Smith and Feder."

"Hope y'all brought something to read," Nate added, holding up a copy of *From Russia, with Love.*

Bryce showed Nate his fat hardback of *The Once and Future King,* which, despite Rina's poor opinion, he liked enormously. But realizing he couldn't concentrate, he was stashing the book in his canvas bag when Bernie Hart called, "Company on stage for the knighting scene."

Everyone took off toward the pass door leading into the wings, then to the stage where Burton and Andrews were posing on the steps in front of twin thrones. Robert Coote stood on Burton's right, and Nate slowly ascended a set of stairs to stand on Julie's left.

Moss Hart, who'd also entered from the house, strolled over to Bryce. "Bobby's green around the gills," he said, "so you'll play Lancelot. Go put yourself near Mr. Coote. When Lancelot's name is called, walk over and kneel while Richard taps your shoulder with his sword, Excalibur. Then get up and turn. Walk straight ahead. Exit stage left."

"Will do," Bryce said, feeling self-conscious since he hadn't yet learned Lancelot's stage business. But he instantly stalked over to wait with Robert Coote, another actor who'd barely acknowledged his existence.

As Sir Lionel, Bryce had once rehearsed this interlude leading to the act-one finale. The scene took place in *Camelot's* Great Hall amid the pageantry of the court. When it was finished, the set would be multi-leveled with rows of knights and ladies on the diagonal on both sides of the king and queen; more lords and ladies would be on risers at the end of those lines with standard bearers on both sides of twin balconies featuring intricate latticework. All the surfaces would shimmer with gold leaf. The effect would be stunning.

"Places," Bernie Hart yelled from the production table.

The rehearsal pianist soon played the solemn background music as Sir Dinadan called for the knights to be invested. Lancelot held his breath while Sirs Colgrevance, Bliant, Guilliam, and Castor approached King Arthur, knelt, and received shoulder taps from Excalibur.

When Lancelot was called, he walked forward and knelt, bowed his head to receive his tap, and peeked at Guenevere, whose blue eyes were boring into him. Then he stood, walked downstage, and strode stage left. The music faded, and one by one, the ensemble processed off stage, leaving Arthur alone for his last act-one monologue, known as his "proposition" speech.

Crowding into the wings, the cast fell silent as though holding a communal breath. Arthur spoke in a torrent of words, revealing his shock at the love he'd seen on Jenny's face three scenes ago when she bowed to the love-struck Lancelot after the jousts. The king's words built to an emotional crescendo that was both heartbreaking and inspiring as he told himself his wife and best friend had not chosen their passion and remained devoted to him and his Round Table.

As Richard finished, wild applause, cheers, whistles, and bravos echoed from the wings as well as the house. When Richard walked downstage with his sword, Moss and Alan ran down the aisle and stood before the pit—a de facto moat—to congratulate him. The ensemble trickled on stage, talking softly among themselves.

Bryce thought he should say something since he was playing Lancelot. He walked over and waited while Julie complimented Richard. Then he stepped forward and extended his hand for the second time that day, saying, "Mr. Burton, you were so—uh, short."

"What was that?" Burton growled, his gray eyes flashing daggers.

Reeling from his gaffe since he'd planned to praise the star, Bryce stammered, "I meant you were so *brilliant*."

After a beat, Burton asked, "You're Christmas, aren't you? Do us a favor, sport."

"Of course," Bryce said, relieved at the actor's casual tone.

"Stay the frigging hell away from me," Burton barked.

"Forgive me; I misspoke. I was deeply moved by your speech."

"Ladies and gentlemen," Bernie Hart called, "Moss wants to start again from the top of the knighting scene. Places, please."

"Remember, *Yuletide,*" Burton said. "Keep your bloody distance, and I mean *meters.*"

"What's eating him?" Nate Wicker asked Bryce from behind.

"He thinks I insulted him. He's livid."

"Aw, he'll cool off," Nate said with a chuckle. "He's got a big heart."

Bryce didn't answer, wondering if Burton would ever lift his edict. He wasn't sure how long a meter was, but staying a foot away would be hard backstage where space was tight. And what was with that "Yuletide" crap? Christmas wasn't a stage name, whereas it was commonly known that Burton had been Richard Jenkins at birth and later took the surname of his foster father, a Welsh acting teacher.

<hr>

After repeating the finale, Richard departed and the chorus ran through "The Lusty Month of May" with Julie and Robert Coote and a skittish, sometimes incontinent sheepdog. This was the number that came before the tense first meeting of Lancelot and Guenevere, which led directly into "Then You May Take Me to the Fair." So, Julie, Bryce, Dan, and Nate now rehearsed that song in which the queen naughtily asked Sirs Lionel, Sagramore, and Dinadan to challenge Lancelot to a joust on the same day. When they finished, the four of them grinned at one another.

A supper break followed, then Julie and the ensemble returned so Moss, Fritz, and Hanya could watch "Guenevere," the show's penultimate number, which narrated the fate of Jenny and Lance, who'd been caught by Mordred in the queen's bedroom and accused of treason. The singers gathered on the 54th Street stage for the first time, having formerly rehearsed this number at the New Amsterdam.

"As you know," Moss called from the house, "we haven't yet named the two singers who will perform the solos in 'Guenevere.' After consulting with the maestro, Alan, Fritz, and I have chosen Bryce Christmas and Dan Elsdon. You'll each sing a few verses."

Everyone applauded, and Bryce smiled proudly. He'd hoped for this plum.

"Kudos," Dan said.

"To you, also," Bryce replied, glad to be paired with a baritone he respected.

Bernie Hart approached, handing them copies of the music and lyrics with their names printed above their vocal parts. Before moving away, he told Bryce, "Nice going, boyo."

Franz Allers raised his baton and the next two hours were among the most gratifying of Bryce's career to date as he sang his solos several times. He made gestures that Hanya refined, and he felt the gravity of the awful moment when Dinadan led Guenevere from the wings at stage left to the wings at stage right, where the stake was supposedly waiting. Offstage, Lancelot was riding in to rescue Jenny from a cruel death by fire, but since Bryce and the ensemble served as a Greek Chorus, these events were sung oratorio-style instead of shown. Facing the audience, Bryce used his voice to create tension, and he heard Dan do the same.

"We obviously chose the right singers," Fritz remarked as

the rehearsal ended, and Moss echoed the composer's praise. But then he called to Bryce, asking him to stay.

His stomach took a dive, as though he'd been summoned to the principal's office. But Bryce collected his things and made his way to the production table where Moss was seated. The company had cleared out, so other than a techie setting up the ghost lamp on stage, he was alone with the eminent director, who signaled for him to sit.

"I gather you had a dust-up with Richard today," Moss said.

"He thinks I insulted him," Bryce said. "I was nervous and babbled the wrong word."

"I see," Moss said silkily. "Well, I'm afraid I have bad news."

"I'm out as Bobby's understudy?"

"Not *that* bad," Moss said. "But we've asked Dan to cover Lancelot, too. And if Bobby's out again during rehearsals, Dan will work with Richard. For the show, we'll flip a coin. Remember, Julie also has two covers."

"I'm sorry for causing a flap."

"Look, you did a smashing job in 'Guenevere' just now and your other solo in the 'Fair' number. You're a convincing actor, too. I predict you'll go far."

"Sir, I don't know what to say," Bryce replied. "Your good opinion means the world."

"My brother told me you were gifted, and you are. Since your singing voice carries well, my one note is to rein in your volume when you speak. Let your intonation show your emotion. Otherwise, you come across bluff."

"I'll do that," Bryce murmured. "Thank you again, sir."

"No more 'sir.' Moss is fine. And, look, Bryce, I should be thanking you. You come prepared, and you're willing to try whatever we ask. So, you had a kerfuffle with the star. It happens." The director smiled before grabbing his Burberry raincoat and strolling up the aisle.

Before Bryce could gather his jacket and bag, Jane Conroy appeared at his elbow. "I thought everyone had gone," he said, delighted to see her.

"I waited," she said. "It's been a great night for you. Want to have a beer at Charlie's?"

"I'm afraid I have plans," he said, wishing Rina wasn't waiting at his flat.

"Maybe another time," she said, sounding disappointed.

"Oh, what the hell," Bryce said. "They have a pay phone. I'll tell my friend I'll be late."

"Great," Jane said. "This will be my treat to celebrate your new solos. You know, I've never heard a voice like yours. It sounds like gold satin."

"Well, shucks, ma'am. I'll blush if you keep on like that."

They set off in the evening shadows, chatting about the choral rehearsal. Walking down Eighth, they passed scummy strip joints, and when a toothless man accosted Jane, Bryce took her arm. She didn't pull away until they reached the popular theater hangout. Bryce opened the door under a green canopy, allowing Jane to precede him inside, where the smoke was thick. They entered the dark, cave-like bar and sat on backless wooden stools.

"I'll have a bottle of Michelob," Jane told a bartender with an onyx mustache.

"Make that two," Bryce said, thinking the barkeep was an actor. "I think I need to get off the damn clock," he muttered.

"The clock?" Jane asked.

"No matter who I see in this part of town, I assume they're in the business."

"Because they all are," she replied with a laugh. "Hey, don't you need to make a call?"

"Thanks for reminding me," he said, touched by her thoughtfulness. "Be right back."

He dashed to the pay phone housed in a booth, and when Rina picked up, Bryce told her a "techie" had taken him out to celebrate his new solos. "I'll be an hour at most," he promised.

"That's fine," she said, yawning audibly. "But come home soon so *we* can celebrate."

When he found Jane again, she was pensively sipping her Michelob from the bottle. Bryce poured his beer into a chilled glass, saying, "To *Camelot*," and they clinked.

"I went to the dressmaker with Julie," Jane said, "and it was fascinating to watch Helene Pons at work. But I didn't realize how often the cast would be going to Pons or Diffen."

"Working with Diffen has been a rite of passage," Bryce replied. "Ray is meticulous. But I've never worn hose before, and they're not only snug, they're warm. I hope I don't sweat too much under the lights." He paused. "So, Jane, how did you get a job with this show?"

"I'd love to say it was persistence, but my uncle went to school with Brock Remsen and sent him my resume. When Brock's other assistant quit, he tracked me down, which means I'm the luckiest theater grad alive."

"You have a theater degree?" Bryce asked.

"I fell in love with theater when my mother took me to a touring production of *Oklahoma!* It played the National Theatre in D.C. when I was seventeen—we live in the suburbs. I sat in my seat sniffling, and my mom thought I hated it." She snorted. "I was mesmerized. I knew from the very first song that I had to be part of this magic world. You see, it was my first professional musical, and I became an instant convert."

"What did your parents say when you told them?"

"Oh, I didn't tell them. They would've squashed my hopes like a bug. But I'd already stage-managed two shows in high school, and I confessed my new goal to my guidance counselor, a savvy nun. Since I'd already gained admission to Catholic University, she suggested I major in theater instead of English, and she pulled strings to make it happen."

"Did you like Catholic's program?"

"It was humbling. Everyone I met was super talented, even the other tech majors. But I dug in my heels, and things began to click, and from everything I've seen so far, production is the right place for me. I just need to find the exact niche." She paused. "Your story's different from mine. You must've always known you had gold in your throat."

He grinned, savoring their conversation. "I found out in high school when I got the lead in *Pirates of Penzance*. My folks let me start voice lessons, and my teacher decided I had the goods. He gave me a solid technique, and I still work with him." He took a sip of beer. "I grew up in Jersey," he added, "and had the advantage of seeing a slew of Broadway shows that inspired me. But since my college degree's in business, I had to play catch-up when it came to training. When I moved to New York, I worked nights and took acting classes with Stella Adler most days."

"Stella Adler?" Jane asked. "I'm impressed. What's she like?"

"She's a genius, but she's tough. She thinks research is vital to creating strong characters, along with a good imagination. Her method is different from Strasberg's, but I'd still need to conjure the death of my old pet dog to cry on cue." He laughed. "Miss Adler would definitely frown on that."

"I figured you'd studied acting from your ease on stage." She paused. "I'm glad to know you, Bryce. Since we're heading out of town, I might need a guy friend. Is that too forward?"

"Not at all," he said. "I should mention I'm seeing someone, but she's not in the show."

"It's good you're involved," Jane said quickly. "I shouldn't complicate my job with—"

"Nobody else feels that way. By Toronto, it'll be like Noah's Ark. Everyone in pairs."

"Then let's make a pact that you and I will stay lone wolves on the ark."

"I'm a lone wolf by nature," he said.

"Me, too," Jane said, raising her bottle. "To restraint on the road."

"To restraint," Bryce said, clinking again. "From now on, I should call you Cookie, short for 'smart cookie.'"

"Better than plain Jane," she said.

"There's nothing plain about you, Miss Conroy," he said, drinking her in. "Listen, I had a run-in with Richard today. Did you hear any talk about it?"

"No," she replied. "But Richard can be testy."

"By the way, I saw that '53 production of *Oklahoma!* in D.C. It impressed me, too."

"You were in the District then?" Jane asked.

"I was drafted for Korea out of college in '52 and did basic at Fort Meade near D.C. Then I moved to Fort Bragg in North Carolina, then back to Meade." He shrugged. "I felt bad about not seeing action, but I was POG material with my accounting degree."

"My dad was in the service. Isn't POG a person who's not a grunt? It's not a nice term."

He laughed. "There are worse terms."

"You carry an Army messenger bag, don't you?"

"It's an Army-issue camera bag, and I treasure it." He removed the weathered green satchel from the back of his chair and showed her the nametape—*B.A. Christmas*—on the outside flap. Then: "Thanks for the beer, Jane. But now I should go."

Jane paid the bartender, and when they were standing outside under the green canopy, she told him she needed a taxi. Bryce stepped into the street, raised his arm, and a yellow cab screeched to a stop. "I want 63rd and Lex," Jane told the driver as she jumped in back.

"This should cover it," Bryce told the cabbie through the open window, handing him a few bills. He waved to Jane as she rode away, then strolled up Eighth Avenue humming "Guenevere." Along with telling Rina about Hart's decision to appoint a second understudy for Lancelot, he'd share the director's positive remarks. But he wouldn't mention his spat with Burton. Rina didn't suffer fools gladly, so why draw attention to his clumsy slip of the tongue?

It was a humid night, and the hookers were sitting in second-floor windows on side streets, showing bare flesh. He absently wondered what Toronto would be like. Then he reflected on Jane's wish to have a male friend on the road. It cheered him to know she wasn't a vapid suburban girl slumming in the city before she married a dull fellow from home. Hell, she might love theater as much as he did. She was certainly right about that *Oklahoma!* tour.

He walked faster, trying to avoid the crush of people on the sidewalk. Rina, he glumly mused, was not a kindred spirit. During their previous eighteen months together, he'd bought costly Broadway seats for Williams's *Sweet Bird of Youth* with Paul Newman and Geraldine Page and Hellman's *Toys in the Attic* with Maureen Stapleton and Irene Worth. Rina had slept through those plays and spoken disdainfully about Bernstein's *West Side Story.* Over steaks at Downey's after the latter, she'd argued that musicals were an inferior art form, which stunned him since he favored musicals over dramas. (In fact, he'd never witnessed a tour de force like Burton's in any show.)

Lord knew what Rina would make of *Camelot.* But since he'd be away for six weeks, he assumed her attempt to resume their relationship would end as abruptly as it began. This meant she wouldn't have a chance to nitpick the show in his presence, a happy thought.

Reaching his building, he felt a jolt of optimism. The rebound problem he'd worried about at Dinty Moore's was moot since he no longer felt emotionally attached to Rina, and aside from his run-in with the leading man, his prospects hadn't seemed this bright in years. And while he'd respect Miss Conroy's adorable call for restraint, was there any reason he couldn't get better acquainted with this fascinating girl?

Toronto, Bryce decided while climbing his front steps, couldn't come fast enough.

5.
JANE TO
THE RESCUE

Jane

The last days of New York rehearsals felt like limbo. Time dragged, the jokes in the book fell flat, and the saloons within spitting distance of rehearsal were filled with cast members after 11 p.m. The only one who didn't go was Julie, who wanted to protect her cords, whereas Bobby smoked and drank as though his voice was immune to abuse.

"I'm bored with the taverns near Times Square," Richard told me on September 20th as the full company assembled. "Do you know any East Side pubs? Irish perhaps."

"Malachy's at Third and 63rd," I said. "You can't get more Irish than the owner, Mr. McCourt. And you might meet Dickie Harris, a cheeky barkeep from Limerick."

"Dickie Harris from Limerick?" Richard asked. "You mean Richard Harris? The actor?"

"He's an actor?" I asked.

"Up and coming," Richard said with a grin. "I met him in the West End in the Fifties, but he's doing movies now." He pecked my cheek. "Thanks, love. I'll try Malachy's tonight."

Nell Dean sashayed up to us, batting her thick false eyelashes at her leading man while snubbing me. She was a nicely stacked redhead, and I watched Richard put his arm around

Nell's waist before they moved toward his dressing room.

After I joined my boss at the production table out front, Brock said, "Don't try to match the cast drink for drink when you're out with them." We were waiting to watch a complete show run-through, one of several Moss had scheduled, and I couldn't wait to see all of act two. "I also heard some dish about you, kiddo. Someone saw you and Christmas going into Charlie's. Are you an item like Nell and Richard?"

"Of course not," I told him with a shrug. "We're pals."

"Pals, eh? Well, make sure to protect your heart. Bryce seems like a straight arrow, but he's an actor. Believe me, no matter how nice they appear, they're all on the make."

"I appreciate your advice," I said, annoyed. "Is everyone happy with the show?"

"They're not saying much yet," Brock said. "And here they come."

The production team walked down the aisle like members of a wedding party: Moss, Alan (in white gloves), Fritz, Hanya Holm, Oliver Smith, Abe Feder, Tony Duquette, Robert Downing, Ed Preston, and Trude Rittman, a German lady with short hair and glasses who arranged the dance and choral music. They noisily claimed chairs at the three tables as Mr. Allers mounted the podium from where he'd conduct the piano.

"Hey, Brock," I whispered. "What's up with Alan's gloves?"

"He wants to remind himself not to bite his nails," Brock whispered. "He's bitten them down to the quick, and lately, he's drawing blood."

I assumed Moss would give a speech, but over the loudspeaker, Bernie Hart called, "Places for act one," then two commands for the house lights, then "Music." After Mr. Allers had the pianist play the end of the overture, Sir Dinadan and Sir Lionel walked on stage, and act one commenced.

"Well, Fritz," Alan said, turning to his partner nearly four hours later after the cast was dismissed for dinner, "we have work to do."

"Work, dear boy?" said Fritz. "You mean major surgery."

"I agree," Moss said. "Even if we speed up the pace, some musical numbers should go."

"Which ones?" Fritz asked, sounding alarmed.

"Let's head to Patsy's and confer," Moss said.

I jumped up, thinking I wouldn't be asked to join them at that intimate Italian restaurant with linen tablecloths and leather banquettes and the best ravioli I'd ever tasted—Brock had taken me there. The waiters, portly middle-aged men, were brusque, but the owners knew Brock and sent us complimentary cannoli and espresso.

"You'll take notes, Jane," Alan said, removing his blood-stained gloves.

Flattered, I followed Brock, Alan, Fritz, and Moss up the aisle. Hanya Holm and Trude Rittman flounced off with Tony Duquette, but they didn't join us. It was another mild September evening, and I softly asked Brock why Mr. Allers had drifted away alone. He replied that even the conductor didn't attend brainstorming sessions with the producers.

This made sense when the discussion would focus on cuts. Nobody wanted to see his or her work discarded, but the show was running two hours too long, which meant that half of *Camelot* might be tossed out like yesterday's newspaper.

"Don't look worried," Brock told me. "We're exactly where we should be at this point."

"You should know," I replied, but I doubted his rosy assessment.

⎯⎯◆⎯⎯

Alan, Fritz, and Moss were methodical. Instead of making hasty decisions at Patsy's (where Frank Sinatra was dining with Joey Bishop), the producers ate Fettuccine Alfredo and crusty Italian bread paired with good Chianti. When the entrees were cleared away, they ordered coffee, and each gave his impressions of the show. Alan asked me to jot down the songs that might be extraneous, and Moss suggested "Then You May Take Me to the Fair," the quartet in which Guenevere asked the top knights to joust with Lance. "We could cover the meat of that song in dialogue after 'The Lusty Month of May,'" he said.

Frowning, Alan said they could also drop "The Quests," a fifteen-minute depiction of Lancelot's achievements. "Why does he need any quests when he's already brought Lionel back from the dead?" he asked. "He's already proven himself."

"But that song is logical," Fritz said. "Lancelot wants to leave the court to cool his ardor for the queen." Then Fritz claimed he could live without "Fie on Goodness!" a choral number in which the knights longed for their old brutal ways, now forbidden by Arthur's civil court.

"And Hanya's ballet for animals in Morgan Le Fey's forest scene doesn't advance the plot," Moss said. "It does the opposite, in fact." Both Alan and Fritz muttered their agreement.

Brock did a quick calculation on a cocktail napkin. "Those cuts would shave off twenty-five minutes of performing time," he said. "Two songs in act one, and two more in act two."

But when the company assembled after the dinner break, the producers ran through the full act one again. I sensed they were scrutinizing the "disposable" numbers they'd discussed, and when rehearsal ended, I felt glum. Maybe it was the sad foreshadowing of Richard's "proposition" speech or knowing some actors' solos would be slashed.

After Moss gave notes, Sarah and I walked home along 57th Street, passing Carnegie Hall, the Russian Tea Room with its snazzy red canopy, and Bendel's, a trendy boutique. Neither of us said much, and the street itself lacked its usual after-hours hum.

"I'm in over my head," Sarah confessed after we crossed Fifth, moving past Tiffany's.

"You mean, having to learn the part of Guenevere?"

"With that and—don't pass out, Jane, but I slept with Sir Sagramore."

"What?" I almost tripped on a crack in the sidewalk. The devout Catholic girl I'd known in college had planned to stay a virgin until her wedding night.

"Don't judge me," Sarah moaned. "Dan asked me to his house to run lines. He's Lancelot's understudy now, and we did the scene in Jenny's bedroom. Only this time, Mordred didn't burst in, and we wound up doing the deed." She laughed ruefully. "Was he ever shocked when I bled all over his white sheets."

"Did he use a rubber?" I asked.

"I don't think so," Sarah said, starting to sniffle. "What if I get pregnant, Jane?"

"I'll have one of the knights cut his head off," I said as we crossed Madison with its many galleries, all closed at this hour. "Listen, Sare, I thought I was pregnant once. I slept with Billy Cosgrove in our last year of college, and my period was late. But it was a false alarm."

"I can't believe you didn't tell me about Billy," Sarah said.

"I felt ashamed."

"You and I are running with a fast crowd, Jane. We better take charge, especially since you're clearly interested in Bryce. But we've all heard he's back with his old flame."

"Bryce told me he was involved," I muttered. This was a sore subject.

"That must've been a letdown."

"It was, but what were the odds a man that attractive would be unattached? And since Dan's gorgeous, too, are you sure he's available?"

"As far as I know," Sarah said. "So, I plan to buy condoms

and put them in my purse."

We walked for a long while in silence, but if Sarah had asked for advice, I would've told her to swear off sex and focus on her professional debut. And I would've felt like a hypocrite because I'd seen a doctor and gotten a diaphragm after moving to New York. Having had sweaty sex with Billy in a D.C. firetrap, I knew it was easy to succumb, so I planned to be careful next time. "Sarah," I said as we approached the Barbizon, "I know your dad worked for Red Wing when your family lived in Fredonia. Where can you get their ketchup?"

Sarah replied that her father bought Red Wing ketchup directly from the factory and kept a supply on hand. "I'm sure he'd send you some. But what's this all about?"

"I like Red Wing, too," I fibbed. "Could you ask your dad to send me one bottle, special delivery, care of the Royal York Hotel in Toronto? I'll reimburse him, of course."

"There's more to this than you're telling me," Sarah said, "but I'll call him tonight."

<hr>

The next few days, the producers held full-show rehearsals, and it was hard not to worry that *Camelot* still ran three hours and forty minutes. It was clear to me that Hanya's animal ballet would be the first number to go, but Brock thought the producers would keep it in until after the Toronto opening. "Hanya's worked hard. They'll give her a chance to see it."

"That's considerate," I said as Brock and I watched from the last row of the house.

Throughout this performance, I focused on Roddy McDowall, who slithered in at the top of act two. He was magnificent. If Richard wasn't playing Arthur, Roddy might have stolen the show with his portrayal of the king's illegitimate son who planned to destroy the Round Table. You could tell Roddy savored Mordred's nastiness, especially when he burst in on Lance and Jenny in the queen's bedroom, catching them in a clinch.

Brock whispered, "Roddy's so great, I hear they might write him his own song. Can you believe it, Jane? Another song!"

That day when act two ended, Julie wheeled out a cart from the wings. She'd served daily afternoon tea to the principals and now offered the same hospitality to the ensemble. The company crowded around, accepting Styrofoam cups from her graceful hands.

Standing off to the side, I felt privileged to be part of this generous company. Yet I wondered how running errands and taking notes would help me in a future job. I wasn't learning to call the show, as stage managers did, because Brock was a general assistant. So even though I was soaking up the Broadway ambience, I was treading water.

How could I broach my concerns to Brock without insulting him?

Nate sidled up to me, saying, "What a wild group. You know the song, 'I Wonder What the King is Doing Tonight?' Well, the girls in the chorus like to sing, 'I Wonder Who the King is Screwing Tonight?' And we haven't even left New York."

We shared a laugh, and I confessed I'd heard that when Nell wasn't looking, Richard was squiring other ladies to his dressing room. (I hoped this gossip was false since I'd met and liked his wife, Sybil. And how many women could a man seduce while putting away numerous vodka shots each day and starring in a musical?)

"Burton's stamina is prodigious," Nate said before strolling away.

I sighed since Nate was among the actors who'd formed a Burton clique, spending hours with the star. (I'd once observed that when Richard was nervous, he twisted the gold ring on his pinkie, and I'd recently seen Nate do the same thing—*except Nate had no ring.*)

"Jane Conroy," a high-pitched voice called, and I turned to greet Francine Tristan, the show's press agent, who was the living embodiment of Auntie Mame. She was five feet tall and wore low-cut dresses with spiky heels. "Darling, I need help setting up interviews with Alan and Fritz in Toronto." (She pronounced the city's name "Torono," which I later learned was the Canadian way.) "Could you ask Brock to give me a jingle at my office tomorrow?"

"Of course," I said, whipping out a notebook and pen from my pocket.

"Good girl," Francine said as though she were addressing a two-year-old. "And how are the cuts coming along? Rumor has it this one's a bladder-buster."

"They're making progress," I said, wondering why Francine hadn't peeked in herself.

"The dear shits will have a field day."

"Who are the dear shits?"

"They're gadflies who attend all the out-of-town shows. When they come back to New York, they spread vicious gossip. And they're flying up to Toronto in droves."

"That's unfortunate," I said. "So, how are the photos coming?" I'd watched Richard, Julie, and Bobby leave a few rehearsals to visit the studio of Friedman-Abeles, the team that photographed most Broadway shows. The partners worked on West 54th, close to Ninth, but I'd never been invited to go.

"Fine," Francine said. "Joe Abeles has taken great portraits of the leads in street clothes and one or two costume shots. But I'm not scheduling the production photo call yet. Leo Friedman will do that after our first New York preview." She smiled. "Why do you ask?"

"Brock asked me to be your point person for the photo call."

"Goody," the press agent said with a cackle. "It helps to have a pretty girl on hand when I'm asking the actors to pose. They sure as hell don't like taking orders from me."

————◆————

I was surprised to receive a message at the Barbizon that my mother was coming to New York on Thursday and hoped to meet for dinner. This was tricky to arrange, but I got Brock's permission to leave the afternoon rehearsal for a 5 p.m. reservation at the 21 Club, my parents' favorite New York haunt. And since the evening run-through was at 7:30 p.m., I knew I'd have ample time with my mom. I brought a beige cloche hat, navy shift, short tan gloves, nylon hose, and navy pumps, changing in the ladies' lounge. Then I slipped out through the lobby at 4:45 p.m. and hailed a cab to 52nd Street.

Since I was early, I stood in front of 21 studying its thirty or so cast-iron jockeys, some meant to be Black, some white, all about three feet tall. Lining the balcony above the club's wrought-iron fence, the jockeys tickled me with their brightly painted silks. They were quintessential New York, like the celebrity portraits at Sardi's, and I was still admiring them when my mom slid out of a cab. Tish—I thought of her by her nickname—wore a yellow chiffon cocktail dress and crème cashmere stole, and with her blonde updo and unlined face, she looked forty instead of fifty.

As usual, I felt eclipsed by my mother's glamor, but we cheerfully descended the steps to the door. Tish checked in with the maître d', who ushered us across the red carpet to the Bar Room with its red-leather banquettes, red-and-white checkered tablecloths, low lighting, and toys whimsically hung from the back ceiling. We snagged a prime table in front of a picture window, and while the Bar Room was more casual than the upstairs dining rooms, the patrons around us wore dressy clothes like ours.

Tish ordered a martini from a server in a white jacket and charcoal slacks, but I wanted to stay sharp and requested soda water. When the drinks arrived, I shyly asked my mother why she'd come to town.

"I'm here with my bridge club," she said. "We're staying at the Waldorf and touring the Cloisters tomorrow. On Saturday, we have tickets for something called *Once Upon a Mattress*."

"I caught that show," I said. "It stars this young comedienne named Carol Burnett and has music by Richard Rodgers' daughter. It's terrific." I was in awe of Mary Rodgers because she was one of the few women who'd composed a Broadway musical. (When I told Julie I'd seen the show, she confided she'd loved it and thought Miss Burnett would be a big star.)

After a second waiter brought a basket of bread, I took a slice and slathered it with salty butter. "You mean you didn't come here to see me?"

"Well, I timed it so I could see you," Tish admitted. "You're about to leave for Toronto, and your uncle Max told us it's a milestone to go out of town with a show."

"He's right. It feels like an honor." I explained I'd have rooms at the same luxury hotels as Lerner and Loewe and my boss, who knew Max.

"That should be safe," Tish said after sipping her martini. "You know how we worry."

Since our time was limited, we ordered as soon as possible. When the server left us, I said, "I guess a backstage job isn't what you had in mind for me, but I love it. I'm surrounded by amazing artists, and the music makes my heart sing. I tried a literary agency, and it was pleasant, but theater feels like home."

"Then it's not a passing fancy?" Tish asked. "Dad and I were hoping you'd get it out of your system, move back to D.C., and teach drama at a private girls' school."

"Not a chance," I told her. "I see my work for *Camelot* as the start of a career."

Tish silently sipped her drink.

"You must have an opinion," I insisted as the waiter delivered my green salad.

After another server brought Tish's shrimp cocktail, she said, "My opinion is: I wish I'd never taken you to *Oklahoma!* I think that show fueled your present ambitions."

"Oh, Mom," I said. "Ali's given you two grandchildren, and Brendan will be a doctor like Dad. You were bound to have one kid who didn't toe the line."

Tish speared a shrimp and popped it in her mouth. "I read a statistic the other day, Jane. Only one in three women work outside the home. Now that number should increase since there's no reason educated girls can't earn their own living. But a Broadway job is so unconventional, it's radical. We didn't think you'd get anywhere, or we might've objected."

"Sorry to upset you," I replied, feeling irked.

"I'm not upset. I'm—wary. But one thing I've discovered about parenthood is that your offspring will surprise you." She put down her tiny fork and patted my hand. "You do seem fulfilled. I hope you enjoy your time in Toronto and Boston. And by the way, Dad and I know you'll be busy. We won't expect to hear from you much."

"It'll be hectic for sure."

"How do you like working with Julie Andrews? Is she friendly?"

"She is. In fact, she's an ally." I chuckled. "I mentioned I was coming here for dinner, and she said her agent gave her a twenty-first birthday party at 21 when she was starring in *My Fair Lady*. It was in a private room, and they had a band for dancing. Fabulous, huh?"

"Tell me something you've learned," Tish said with a conspiratorial smile. "Something you never would've guessed about Broadway if you weren't on the inside."

After swallowing a bite of salad, I said, "I'm still pretty new. Can I think about that?"

"Please do," Tish said. "But I'm interested. I love the theater, and I used to sing well. But I never would've had your pluck."

Over "chicken hash," a modest name for 21's chicken, sherry, and cream concoction served on spinach and white toast, Tish offered news of the family and I shared stories about *Camelot*, glossing over Richard's wandering eye. Later, as we drank coffee, Tish mentioned she'd volunteered to work for John F. Kennedy's presidential campaign. "Some of the girls wear these cunning red-and-white striped dresses with blue belts that say *Kennedy*. But at my age, I'll probably be hidden in a back room."

"I doubt that, Mom."

When the check came, Tish gave her Diner's Club card to the waiter, who returned to say the card had been declined. "I'll need cash or an American Express card," he added.

Blushing, Tish asked if she could have a moment. The waiter made a face but took off. I riffled through my purse, saying. "I have two dollars."

"I'm short on cash, too," my mother said while checking her wallet. "What'll we do?"

"I'll go get some money," I said, rising, purse in hand. "You should order dessert and coffee. I'll be back in a trice." I strolled past the long wooden bar as if I didn't have a care in the world, then dashed through the foyer, relieved the maître d' had left his podium. I escaped outside, and though a cab was dropping two well-heeled couples at the curb, I knew the pre-theater traffic would be clogging midtown streets.

Having no choice but to walk, I hurried over 52nd to Fifth and barely felt my feet touching the sidewalk as I passed a historic Episcopal church, St. Thomas, before crossing the avenue.

Sprinting up 54th, I dreaded having to ask one of the stage managers for petty cash, but Brock wouldn't return from dinner for a good half hour. Just as I reached a small deli across Sixth, five members of the *Camelot* cast came out the door: two female dancers, Dan Elsdon, a dark-haired actor with a round face named Jack Dabdoub, and Bryce Christmas. All of them waved and hightailed it up the block except Bryce, who stopped to flash an approving grin. "You look stunning, Jane. Hot date?"

"I had a date with my mother at 21."

"Fancy," he said. "But why do you look forlorn?"

"The restaurant rejected my mom's Diner's Card, and we didn't have enough money to pay. I'm hoping to find Bernie Hart so I can borrow some cash. Believe me, the waiter's not happy with us. I'm afraid he'll call the police."

"How much do you need?" Bryce asked, reaching into his back pocket.

"Twenty," I mumbled, my cheeks feeling hot.

He removed a crisp bill from his wallet. "Here you go," he said. Then he gave me another ten. "And a little more, just in case."

Floored by his kindness, I almost cried. "I'll get it back to you tomorrow."

"No rush, and don't worry about the waiter. This happens nightly at Sardi's. The guy may be concerned about his tip, but he won't call the cops."

"You're a lifesaver, Bryce," I said, choking back emotion. "I should return."

By the time I reentered 21, I was sweating like a stevedore, and when I found Tish, she was staring into a full cup of coffee. "Success," I said, sliding into my chair. "No dessert, Mom?" I asked, swabbing my brow with my napkin.

"I lost my appetite," Tish murmured. "I told the waiter I sent you to my hotel to get the money." She bit her lip. "I feel terrible about this, but you're resourceful."

When the waiter began to hover, I gave him Bryce's twenty plus two bucks from my purse, enough for a tip. He bowed before leaving us one last time.

"I have funds in the Waldorf safe," Tish said. "Why don't we have breakfast tomorrow and I'll repay you." But after we cleared the front door and were standing on the sidewalk, my mother whispered, "I hate telling Dad."

"Why tell him? Call Diner's Club and straighten it out. Then enjoy your weekend. Someday you and I will laugh about this caper."

"Oh, sweetie," Tish said, hugging me, "you've definitely grown up since you moved here. I'm grateful for your quick thinking. Let's find a cab, and I'll drop you at rehearsal."

Later on, while I watched the evening run-through, my mind wandered back to dinner. I'd never interacted with Tish as an equal before, and I hoped she'd support my theater ambitions going forward. Hadn't I proven I was mature enough to call my own shots by rescuing her from humiliation?

———◆———

At the end of our final week in New York, the company gathered for a Saturday afternoon run-through before we left for Canada, some flying, some driving, and some traveling by train. We'd have half a week of stage rehearsals at the O'Keefe Centre before opening night, but everyone's nerves were in overdrive.

Moss had invited wives and families to attend this last rehearsal, and before curtain, I ran into a buxom raven-haired woman at the rear of the house. From her photos in the *Times*, I recognized her as Shari Hempel, the New York City Opera mezzo who was Nate Wicker's wife.

"You're Miss Conroy, aren't you?" Shari asked. "Nate

speaks warmly of you."

"He's terrific," I replied.

"Usually," Shari said. "But he's gotten erratic since hanging around Mr. Burton. I'd love to join you in Canada, but I'll be here singing one of the three little maids in *The Mikado*."

"Nate usually rises above the chaos."

"Let's hope that continues," Shari said before gliding away.

I thought Nate's wife had aptly sized up Richard. The crazier things got, the more he drank, and his resilience probably made life harder for his acolytes. (Richard had taken me aside and thanked me for recommending Malachy's, confirming that "Dickie" was indeed his old pal Richard Harris. "Keep your eyes peeled, love. You'll see him in movies. And he sings, too.")

As the pianist played the last bars of the overture, I plopped down next to Brock at the production table. Studying the opening scene, I watched two enormous "horses," devised by Tony Duquette, which trotted on stage and bowed to Guenevere. They were outfitted in full court regalia and were as tall as elephants. (I pitied the chorus members inside those bulky costumes.)

As the first scene continued, I gleaned the answer to my mom's "insider" question. In my naivete, I'd once believed that performing was about getting something from the audience, such as applause or approval. But now I realized our *Camelot* actors, singers, and dancers got their reward from sharing their talents, and it didn't matter who was sitting beyond the footlights. They would've given their utmost if I had been out there alone.

I'd explain this insight to Tish on the phone one day soon. But now I thought about the "fulfillment" side of my job that she'd also mentioned. I loved working on this show, as I'd claimed. But I'd committed the sin of omission because my duties were so easy that a ninth-grader could've done them. What was the challenge in toting messages between rehearsal halls? The big difference between my current chores and fetching Em Burgoyne's deli lunch was that my main task at the agency—reading submissions—required brains. Had I been so blinded by my love of theater that I'd taken the wrong path in life? (In fairness to Brock, he'd repeatedly assured me that my role would expand out of town.)

It soon dawned that while my mind was elsewhere, Richard and Julie had been doing the scene in which Arthur woos and wins Guenevere, the first of two transcendent moments in *Camelot*. I sighed as the pair ran offstage, seemingly destined for "happily ever after."

"If only the rest could be like that," Alan said to Brock.

"It will be," Brock told his friend.

And that was my boss's role in a nutshell: he had to whisper words of support when he should've told Alan that his two acts didn't jell.

Three-plus hours later, the finale was just ahead. I knew it would be magnificent, an impression I always felt in my bones.

Dejected and defeated, the king waited for daylight to attack Lancelot's army. Making noise, a lad of fourteen named Tom showed himself and said he hoped to join the Round Table and fight for right. As Arthur learned that reports of his new moral order had spread throughout England, he grasped that his struggles had not been in vain.

In a voice mixed with sorrow and triumph, the king began a reprise of the title song, this time with elegiac lyrics. Halfway through, the king dubbed the boy "Sir Tom of Warwick" and sent him home to live and grow old and extol the glory that was Camelot.

This was the show's finest moment and perhaps Lerner

and Loewe's greatest achievement. Even the finales of *Briga-doon* and *My Fair Lady* couldn't touch it for sheer dramatic impact, since Richard Burton's acting and singing were heroic and heart-rending.

As the last New York rehearsal ended, my eyes filled with tears, and I asked myself again: was Brock's job what I wanted? To be cheerleader-in-chief to a Broadway titan?

Absolutely not. Which meant I had some thinking to do.

Wiping my face, I stayed put as the house lights came up, and Moss ran down the aisle toward the orchestra pit. Brock stretched, and Alan turned sideways to speak with Oliver Smith.

As the actors moved downstage to hear Moss's notes, Bryce Christmas, standing in front, made eye contact with me, and I sat up straight and boldly returned his gaze. It occurred to me that even if the actor was destined to be my friend (and nothing more), he was someone I could trust at this topsy-turvy crossroads.

"Ready to hit the road for Toronto, kiddo?" Brock suddenly asked.

"You bet," I told him, staring into Bryce's shining blue eyes.

PART TWO

TROUBLE IN TORONTO
OCTOBER 1960

"What I had not yet learned, and would have to learn the hard way, was that once in rehearsal a play—and everyone and everything connected with it—is sent spinning down a toboggan slide on which there is no stopping or turning back. Whirling down the slope one can only take the twists and turns as they come and hope to have sufficient luck to land safely. It is a marvel to me that so many do, for there are no exceptions made—the same rule applies to everyone—and the toboggan slide is especially iced for each new play."

- Moss Hart, *Act One* (1959)

6.
O'KEEFE
OPENS

Bryce

Since he liked the slow pace of railroad trips, he'd traveled overnight from New York on the same train as Richard Burton and Robert Coote and managed to stay out of their way. He was the first to get off that last Monday in September, and a woman with a rubbery face and light curly hair hurried up to him, saying, "You must be Mr. Christmas—they said you're tall. I'm Mary Jolliffe, the O'Keefe Centre publicist." She explained she was waiting to escort "the stars" to the King Edward Hotel where Burton, Coote, and other leads were lodging.

As his colleagues stumbled onto the platform, still drunk from whatever they'd consumed over many hours, Miss Jolliffe raised her eyebrows and Bryce made a mad dash into the historic Union Station, the plushest train depot he'd ever seen. He exited onto Front Street, a wide boulevard similar to Fifth Avenue. Miss Jolliffe might need help corralling her sozzled charges, but he was the wrong man for the job. It was a mistake to alienate any press agent, however, and he'd apologize when he saw her again.

The late afternoon sun was shining and his hotel, the Royal York, was across the street. It was an elegant, high-rise building that looked like The Plaza. After checking into his room, he stretched out on one of his twin beds and wondered if Jane Conroy would join him for supper. But his eyes closed, and when he awakened, it was too late to call Jane or anyone else. He'd heard "the big dogs" and the production folks were also at the Royal York, and he wondered how he and Dan landed in such a tony hotel. It was supposed to be a ten-minute walk from the O'Keefe, also on Front Street, where *Camelot* (and the theater itself) would open on Saturday night.

Feeling rested after his nap, Bryce explored his room and found a note on his dresser:

Greetings, Bryce!

Bobby has the flu, so you'll play Lancelot in rehearsal until he's well.

Yours, Bernie

PS - Moss also has flu. Steer clear of infected folks for the sake of your priceless pipes.

He was confused since Moss told him Elsdon would play Lancelot if Goulet had to miss rehearsals. Was Dan ill, too? Viruses careened through casts like wildfires in dry brush. But he had to smile at Bernie's "pipes" remark. As he knew from Sardi's, where Bernie was famous for his puns, the younger Hart brother had inherited his family's humor gene.

When he ambled toward a dining table for two, he found a bottle of Red Wing ketchup tied with a red ribbon. A note on hotel stationery said:

Dear Bryce,

Welcome to "Torono." I got you this gift so you'll feel at home when you're eating burgers and fries in here.

See you soon—

Your Friend,
Cookie

He laughed before ordering Jane's suggested meal from room service. Then he left a message with the front desk clerk, thanking his "friend" for her thoughtful surprise. As the evening dragged on, he was disappointed not to get a return call, but after his supper—he'd enjoyed the Red Wing—he sat in an overstuffed chair and immersed himself in Harper Lee's *To Kill a Mockingbird*, a novel Rina had given him as a farewell present.

Rina told him one of the characters, an oddball kid named Dill, was based on Truman Capote, who'd been Miss Lee's neighbor when they were kids in Alabama. Hearing insider trivia was one benefit of dating an editor, but he was hard-pressed to think of others. In the days before he hit the road, he'd felt increasingly impatient with Rina's pessimism. Even their parting conversation last night at Grand Central had ended poorly.

"You realize that if Kennedy wins, Khrushchev will think he's an easy mark and declare war on us," she remarked as they waited for his train. "My parents came here from Russia. They say he'll blow us off the earth."

"How could that happen?" Bryce asked. "Our military's more powerful."

"No, it's not," Rina scoffed, her voice rising. "So don't you dare vote for Kennedy."

Bryce frowned, unwilling to debate politics since he hadn't yet studied the candidates. As soon as he was able to board, he pecked Rina's cheek and fled, hoping she'd take a hint, but she stayed on the platform in her perfumed fur. He waved with forced cheer as the train passed her, but her bereft expression made him wish he'd told her it was over. Instead, he'd taken the easy way out to avoid an unpleasant farewell. And for his entire ride to Toronto, he felt ashamed of his cowardice and dreaded giving Rina the news by phone.

Bryce awakened early the next morning, rested and eager to explore. Since rehearsals wouldn't resume until Wednesday, he had a precious day to himself. A welcome packet on his bureau invited company members to visit the O'Keefe Centre as long as they didn't interfere with the installation of sets and sound equipment, so he'd head there first.

He ate breakfast in his room, happily dousing his eggs with Red Wing, which reminded him of his Piccadilly lunches when he sat at the counter with famous producers—David Merrick, Hal Prince—and feared he'd never get to Broadway. But here he was, staying in a luxe hotel, preparing for his out-of-town debut in Lerner and Loewe's seventh musical. And bless Jane's kindness, but where did she get a bottle of Red Wing? He'd never seen it at the market.

Bryce set off along Front Street around 11 a.m. The weather was cooler and less humid than in New York, and he wore a leather bomber jacket and wool scarf to protect his "pipes."

He passed the beige Union Station with its Roman colonnades, then the beige Dominion Public Building with more colonnades, both reminding him of limestone Beaux Arts buildings in Washington, D.C., say the Russell Office Building or the Herbert Hoover Department of Commerce. (He'd boned up on architecture while he was stationed near the capital.)

He soon passed the Bank of Montreal, another Roman-style behemoth that was kitty-corner from his destination. As he got close to the O'Keefe Centre, he assessed its design as ultra-modern. The exterior was an immense stone rectangle with a slanting stone canopy that jutted beyond the front facade like a ramp. Bryce had read that a train station once occupied the site and kept strolling for two more blocks until he glimpsed a skein of railroad tracks in the distance. He returned to the O'Keefe with its eight glass doors and entered the lobby, where he muttered, "Holy crap," and then felt lucky he was alone.

There were white marble walls and bronze-and-granite staircases at both ends. Straight ahead was a red-crème-and-black mural by a famous Toronto artist. (A newspaper article he'd read over coffee mentioned the hundred-foot-wide, fifteen-foot-high painting that was called *The Seven Lively Arts*.) When he cleared some mirrored doors, he found himself in a huge auditorium—3,000 seats, he'd heard—with cherry-wood seats upholstered in red plush. The carpet was gold, and cherry panels adorned both sides of the stage, an odd decorative touch.

The curtain was up, and the lighting designer, Abe Feder, stood on the proscenium calling to crew guys on ladders. Bryce also spotted Oliver Smith and one of his trim male assistants at a production table in row L or M. Tall Oliver yelled a few commands to three crew members loafing on stage. No part of his set was visible, but various scenes boasted upstage turrets, multi-colored flags, and high platforms resembling chalices. (Shades of the Holy Grail?) All the backdrops were painted in vivid colors, and some had elaborate drapes. The production was sumptuous and occasionally quaint, such as when Pellinore entered with his enormous white-and-brown English sheepdog.

Bryce retraced his steps, moving through the lobby and taking another peek at the mural before returning to Front Street and rambling to the corner of Yonge (called "Young"). He walked one long block and found the glass stage door. Inside the lobby, a beefy security guard sat on a stool at a high counter, and after asking Bryce's name, he handed him a lanyard with a badge and a key marked 2-4.

"Welcome to the O'Keefe," the guard said. "Always wear

your badge and sign in when you arrive or leave. To find your dressing room, take the lift one floor up, and you'll see a hallway straight ahead. But during the show, you might prefer the stairs—they're faster, and you won't get stuck." He laughed. "Not that anyone's had a problem yet. *Camelot*'s our maiden voyage."

Bryce thanked the guy, and when he was inside the "lift," he realized he'd never worked anywhere with a backstage elevator. He exited into a spacious foyer adjoining a hallway of principal dressing rooms. Finding number 4, he saw his name on an index card along with Wicker and Elsdon, and when he unlocked the door, he found a fruit basket with a note from Hugh Walker, the O'Keefe's general manager. This was a gracious welcome, and he was amazed by the room's long vanity—three mirrors—and padded chairs, its daybed with a pillow and fluffy quilt, two sinks, and a separate bathroom with a toilet, shower, and third sink. Compared to the dressing rooms he'd visited in turn-of-the-century New York theaters, this was a palace.

Bryce chose the vanity closest to the door and removed his makeup and personal items from his canvas bag. He was arranging them before the mirror when Wicker breezed in. He, too, seemed surprised to encounter such luxury and claimed the vanity in the middle. They compared notes about their hotels ("elegant") and the sawdust and paint smells of the new auditorium, which Wicker had just toured.

"The sound technician's raising Cain," Nate said. "I was there when Lerner arrived, and the sound guy told Alan the new house is deader than dead."

Bryce chuckled. "Are the star dressing rooms at stage level?"

"Stage right. Space for Richard, Julie, Bobby, and Robert Coote."

"Not Roddy?" Bryce asked.

"Roddy's a mensch. Given his billing, he should have one, but he gave his to Coote because the guy's older than most of us. So, Roddy's up here."

"Have you seen Dan?" Bryce asked.

"Dan's making hay with the lovely Miss Wilkins. I saw them yesterday, cooing like newlyweds." He shrugged. "That girl sings almost as well as Julie. How's that possible?"

"It's a matter of which vocal timbre you like," Bryce said. "I prefer Julie's for theater, but Sarah sounds lovely, too. She could have a big career."

"You too, Christmas." Nate paused. "You sound better than Dan or Bobby."

"But they're stellar," Bryce mumbled.

"Your singing has more soul, and you're a better actor."

"Back at you, Nate. You're one of the best actors we've got. I want to see your Arthur."

"Thanks," he said. "I'm learning from Burton. It's like attending a daily masterclass."

"Speaking of Burton, do you have any advice about how I can handle him?"

"Find your light, say your lines, and behave like he's the one with the problem. He'll respect you, whereas if you try to appease him, he'll act mean, just to be contrary." Nate laughed. "Hey, would you care to have lunch, then find the bars? We'll need liquid courage once things get going. This show isn't ready to open in four days. How will they trim a full hour?"

"Hell, don't you think Moss can prune this monster and turn it into a hit?"

"From your mouth to God's ears," Nate said. "Let's roll."

The first establishment on a list Nate had gotten from his hotel's front desk was the Savarin, a brief stroll to Adelaide and Bay Streets. Bryce and Nate had a beer in the Men's Beverage Room, a dark-paneled lounge, before climbing upstairs to the Windsor Room with its dark-wood tables and chairs. "The buffet looks good," Bryce said, and after Nate nodded, they filled their plates.

Since it was a clear afternoon with abundant sun, they walked to Wellington Street and grabbed a second beer at the Cork Room. By the time they found the Brass Rail on Yonge, an all-day strip club, Nate was keen to ogle the "nearly nude girls" promoted by a neon sign, but Bryce begged off. They moved on to the Colonial Tavern, then learned it had been gutted by fire. "This was supposed to be a terrific jazz club," Nate said as they eyed its sooty remains.

Their last stop was the King Edward Hotel, where Bryce noticed a bar across the street with a vertical sign saying *Letros*. "Wonder what that is," he muttered.

"The hotel clerk told me it's an upscale gay bar," Nate said. "The boys in the chorus will love it." He paused. "Hey, Bryce, we covered so much ground I think I need a nap."

"Likewise," Bryce said, "but this was fun. I'll see you at rehearsal." Nate saluted and disappeared into his hotel, which looked even nicer than the York. Bryce took off again, using a pocket map to locate Yonge, then Front, getting his bearings. He'd enjoyed his time with Wicker and was glad they'd kept the conversation light. Nate spoke proudly of his daughters, Elizabeth and Erika, pulling out his wallet to share their photos. Yet his colleague's interest in seeing nude girls made Bryce wonder if Wicker lived by the actor's code of the road, meaning faithful to one's partner at home but free to stray on tour.

Back at the Royal York, Bryce phoned Jane but again got no response. Weary from wandering, he took another long rest, then ordered room service. After supper, he called Rina, planning to end their affair, but he lost his nerve. Was there ever a "right" time to give your lover the old heave-ho? Probably not, but that didn't excuse his delay.

Jane

On Friday, the day before opening, I stood at the rear of the O'Keefe Centre watching the stage, my stomach hurting. The show was in shambles, and even Brock, known for his even disposition, was snappish. Alan Lerner's estranged wife had flown into town with their toddler son, and Alan couldn't cope. Though Brock asked me to run interference with the woman he sarcastically called "Madame," a Shalimar-scented blonde in her thirties, I failed him. She told me she had no use for "functionaries," and if she couldn't see Alan, she wanted to speak with Brock *tout de suite.*

"She grew up in France," Brock explained during the break between acts. "She became a lawyer, or maybe it was a doctor. Now she's retired and utterly bored. Watch your back."

"Why did she come to Toronto?" I asked.

"To reconcile. I gather Alan's open to the idea and completely thrilled to see his child, but he's popping tranquilizers like jelly beans." Brock smirked. "I'm going to ask Kitty Hart to step in when she arrives. Nobody messes with Kitty, not even Madame Lerner."

As the tech rehearsal lumbered toward the act-two finale, I decided Oliver Smith's magnificent sets looked puny on the O'Keefe's immense stage. And the sound was god-awful. Panels on either side of the proscenium were supposed to control the clarity and volume, but the sound technicians hadn't mastered them. Though Franz Allers was conducting in Toronto, the orchestra seemed to be playing in Montreal, three hundred miles away.

Bobby Goulet, now saying Lance's farewell to Arthur, had done his best that afternoon, but his voice was hoarse from coughing. (Bryce had played Lancelot at two previous rehearsals, dazzling me with his complex portrayal, and the show seemed flat without him.)

"Alan told me Bobby has a whopping crush on Julie," Brock whispered, "and maybe Goulet feels shy around her. Maybe it affects his ability to emote. But Julie's a faithful wife, so Bobby will strike out." He didn't speak again until the curtain closed and the house lights came up. "Three hours and forty minutes," Brock moaned as Alan and Moss, standing three feet away from us, now raced down the aisle. "When we add applause, the show might run three hours and fifty minutes. Why did they wait until *after* we open to cut Hanya's animal ballet?"

"You said it was because—"

"That was rhetorical." He grinned. "And this new house may be stunning, but we should've premiered at the good old Shubert in New Haven. The O'Keefe gave us this barn for free, but we had no idea they'd make such a fuss. They're flying in stars from across the globe."

The dear shits, I thought. "Maybe they'll love *Camelot*," I ventured.

He rubbed his temples as though he had a headache. "Do you have a gown for the opening night party at our hotel?"

"I didn't know I'd be invited," I said, having assumed that just the producers, the stars, and the designers would attend the black-tie soiree. Since I hadn't worn a gown since my high school prom, I hadn't brought any semi-formal dresses with me when I moved to Manhattan.

"You're not Cinderella, Jane. Of course, you're invited. Why don't I slip some petty cash under your door? Head to that big department store Simpson's, and buy a cocktail dress."

"Oh, Brock," I murmured. "You don't have to—"

"Oh, but I do. My wife Lisa's a Barnard math professor who can't get up here, and I need a date nobody will talk about. Also, tomorrow's Julie's birthday. I know you're tight with her."

"Thanks for the heads-up," I said. "Should I check on Mrs. Lerner?"

"Don't waste your time," he said. "Why don't you relax after Moss gives notes? Things may get rough starting Sunday. We won't be sleeping much." He sighed. "If you see any cast members later, spread some cheer, will you? Tell 'em the show looks great."

I saluted before trailing my boss to the production table in the orchestra section. Moss, Alan, Fritz, Abe Feder, Tony Duquette, and Oliver Smith were conferring loudly. Glancing around, I also saw the tall, snow-haired orchestrator Robert Russell Bennett, the dance arranger Trude Rittman, and Hanya Holm rambling toward the producers. When the curtain opened again, I glanced up as the cast loudly assembled downstage to wait for notes.

"It was a noble effort," Moss told Alan and Fritz, "but it's nowhere near ready."

"Let's hope the critics are kind," Alan said. "Maybe they'll extol its potential."

"Words to live by," Moss said, then he strolled toward the pit, mopping his forehead with his handkerchief. His cheeks were moist, and I knew he was still battling the flu.

Having heard the director's opinion, which echoed my own, I dashed out through the lobby, passing the red-creme-and-black mural, and made my getaway. The afternoon light was growing dusky, and I hiked toward my hotel, admiring the Dominion Public Building and the train station, which spanned the blocks between the O'Keefe and the Royal York. As for seeking out cast members to "spread cheer," I wasn't in the mood. It would've been fun to have a pajama party with Sarah, but she was glued to Dan Elsdon, an attachment that worried me.

On Saturday morning, I felt dizzy trying to navigate Simpson's, a crowded department store similar to Garfinkel's in D.C., where I'd often shopped with Tish. After wandering past Jewelry and Cosmetics, I bought some long white gloves that I'd need to accessorize a formal outfit. Then a clerk directed me to the third floor, where I found a knee-length sleeveless emerald-green crepe dress with a tasteful v-neckline and crisscrossing bodice above a swingy flare skirt. It looked as though it had been designed for me, and my saleslady in cat's-eye glasses called my choice "chic."

(Before leaving for Toronto, I'd packed my black patent-leather pumps, a black satin evening bag, and my fat Mikimoto pearls, thinking I'd wear them for opening night with the plain navy shift I'd picked for my dinner at 21. But now my outfit would turn heads—and I had my boss to thank.)

Toting my Simpson's dress in a plastic garment bag, I rode the elevator to Fine China and bought a blue Wedgwood heart-shaped trinket dish with the image of a woman in a billowy gown—Guenevere? Since the gift wrap desk was nearby, I had Julie's Wedgwood swathed in paper with golden squares that resembled the floor of *Camelot's* Grand Hall. (Since Brock had given me a whopping hundred and fifty dollars, I had enough to cover my purchases. I planned to repay him, though he'd insisted it wasn't necessary.)

I cabbed it back to the hotel, planning to nap, then shower and arrange my hair in an updo before eating a grilled cheese sandwich from room service. I knew I'd feel comfortable with Brock tonight since he'd treat me as his niece, but as I kicked off my shoes and fell on my bed, I felt pangs of disappointment. After Bryce received a belated invitation to the party, he'd called to ask if I'd be his date. When I confessed I had to go with Brock, he said, "Maybe he'll get busy schmoozing. Then you and I can catch up."

His remark tickled me, though I'd hardly seen Bryce since

we'd come to Toronto. He'd been swamped playing Lancelot each day, and I'd had to attend production meetings at night. Despite agreeing to my absurd restraint pledge at Charlie's—I felt embarrassed in hindsight—Bryce might be sleeping with some lissome beauty in the chorus, which would serve me right; I adored the guy and hadn't let him know. But the idea of being his casual bedmate made my stomach roil, and since he'd told me he had a girlfriend in New York, I was acting aloof.

The opening night curtain for *Camelot* at the O'Keefe was supposed to be at 8:15 p.m., and I figured the cast would arrive earlier than usual. I whizzed through the stage door at six to be safe, and my first stop was stage right to deliver Julie's Wedgwood dish. It was my first view of the star dressing rooms, and I was impressed by the amenities—a large vanity with lights and a plush chair, a velvet sofa, a console piano, fabric chairs for visitors, and a large private bathroom with a shower. Each surface in Julie's room held a bouquet from well-wishers, making the place smell like a florist shop.

I put my package near a pile of telegrams and left without studying the family photos on her mirror. I hurried through the wings to the backstage foyer and took the elevator two floors up to the ladies' chorus room, which held twenty girls whose names were posted over different parts of the vanity. I left a gift for Sarah, a star paperweight engraved with *Camelot, 10-1-1960*, and a "break a leg" message on hotel stationery. Tonight was truly special since Sarah was making her debut as a card-carrying member of Actors' Equity.

With wings on my heels, to quote Mr. Hammerstein, I ran downstairs to the spacious room shared by Bryce, Dan, and Nate, which smelled of male cologne and more flowers— Dan had received an enormous mixed bouquet. I left a small wrapped box for each of them—a monogrammed shot glass from Bloomingdale's—and a tiny gift card.

In my crepe frock and long gloves, I did feel like Cinderella heading to a ball, and when I studied my reflection in Bryce's mirror, I thought my outfit, updo, and makeup made me look sophisticated. Then I felt self-conscious, hoping to avoid Bryce until later. But my wish went awry when he burst in, wearing a leather jacket over a white dress shirt and dress slacks, part of the tux he'd put on for the party. He stared at me before hanging a garment bag on his rack.

"You caught me," I mumbled. "I brought you a gift."

"You take my breath away," he said, his blue eyes darkening.

But I was the one who couldn't breathe, much less answer. I'd never been alone in a closed space with Bryce, and I could smell his aftershave, a spicy popular scent called Canoe.

"Dan's on his way up," he continued. "But listen, Cookie, I have something important to tell you. Maybe we can leave the party early."

"I'd—like that," I told him, flashing my warmest smile. "Have a good show, Bryce."

"Thanks," he said, opening the door for me. "Nothing can save us except Burton. We can't hear the orchestra, and Feder placed glaring spotlights above the stage, so we're virtually blind out there." He snorted. "We'll probably open and close tonight."

"Possible," I said, crossing into the hall, then twirling around to face him. "But you know what Tallulah Bankhead said, don't you?"

"No," he replied, crossing his arms. "Enlighten me."

"She said, 'It's one of the tragic ironies of the theater that only one man involved in it can count on steady work: the night watchman.'"

Bryce boomed out a laugh and shut his door. Now I chuckled,

too, wondering how I'd pulled that maxim from memory. But I hadn't wanted to spout a hollow platitude since we all knew the show was a mess. Even so, I had unwavering faith in Alan, Fritz, and Moss, who possessed the experience they'd need to fix *Camelot*. As for Richard, Julie, and Roddy, they were sensational; even Bobby, though a bloodless actor, was heroic when he sang.

Waiting for the elevator, I longed to know what Bryce wanted to confide. And since I'd heard tonight's host, E.P. Taylor, the O'Keefe Brewery owner, expected four hundred people at his shindig, my boss probably wouldn't object if I left his side to chat with others.

———— ♦ ————

At stage level again, I watched the crew arrange the sylvan setting for Guenevere's arrival. I especially loved the giant birch tree Arthur sat in while he sang his first song, "I Wonder What the King is Doing Tonight."

Crossing the wings, I glimpsed a small girl with brown braids lurking outside Richard's dressing room. "Hi, there," I called, and the child ran to me and hugged my knees. Soon the girl's blonde, doe-eyed mother, Sybil Burton, appeared in the doorframe.

"Come in, won't you?" Sybil said, so I shyly entered Richard's lair and perched on his couch with his wife and daughter. Sybil and the little girl wore party clothes, and Richard was clad in a striped robe that displayed a mat of brown chest hair. "You look smashing," he told me.

"Thanks," I murmured. "Have a good first show, Richard."

"Daddy says it will stink tonight," the child said sadly.

"Not quite, love," Richard drawled. "Daddy said he'd do his best to make it stink *less*."

Sybil and I smiled, then I excused myself and chuckled

aloud at Richard's gallows humor. He didn't seem worried, and that buoyed my mood as I entered the Green Room, a small lounge that was the appointed meeting place for Brock and me, Moss and Kitty, Alan and Madame, and Fritz and Tamara, the composer's much-younger girlfriend. But I was the first to arrive, and since a man in an apron stood behind a makeshift bar, I asked for soda water, hoping it wouldn't spoil my lipstick.

As soon as Brock strolled in wearing black tie, he beamed at me, saying, "Why, Miss Conroy, it's a new you!" He declined to order a drink, adding, "I was out front, and it's like the Oscars with TV crews, klieg lights, and celebs galore. Would you like to see? There's no point staying here since Alan's in the wings rowing with the missus."

"Let's go," I said, eager to avoid the unhappy Lerners.

It wasn't until the curtain fell that I had a moment to absorb *Camelot's* glamorous but unwieldy opening performance. Why had Moss walked on stage beforehand and told the audience, "*Camelot* is lovely, but you're going to be a lot older when you leave here tonight"? His prediction had been accurate: the show began at 8:50 p.m. after speeches and the playing of the Canadian national anthem and ended at 12:40 a.m.

When Brock and I reached backstage, company members were hugging each other, though Bryce and Sarah weren't among them. "Brilliant, Richard!" Roddy McDowall called to the leading man, kudos echoed by Julie, Robert Coote, and Bobby before that trio headed to their stage-right dressing rooms.

A while later, during our shared trip by limo to the Royal York, Julie thanked me for my "precious" gift and said she'd keep it in her dressing room as a good luck charm. Brock amused Julie and her dapper husband, Tony Walton, with his report of a small blaze in a lobby elevator halfway through act one. "The publicist called the fire brigade and cleverly averted a crisis."

(The other thing that "burned" tonight, I decided, was the scenery as Richard's incandescence pushed the show past its slow spots. Julie had been a spritely, vocally superb Guenevere, and Bobby stopped the show with his solo that opened act two, "If Ever I Would Leave You.")

When our group entered the hotel ballroom on an upper floor, we were greeted by our host, Edward Plunket Taylor, a balding man with horn-rimmed classes clad in white tie. Mr. Taylor absently shook hands with Brock and me before moving on to Julie and Tony, whom he engaged in conversation. (Brock and I were clearly chopped liver.)

The hall was filling up with VIPs and members of the *Camelot* company. Flowers adorned pedestals, and buffet tables offered all manner of food. Bars were crammed into all four corners, and linen-swathed tables with candles formed an inviting circle in the ballroom's center. A string quartet played waltzes, though it was hard to hear the music above the chatter.

I was tongue-tied observing tall Carol Channing in a platinum wig; petite Agnes DeMille, who'd choreographed *Brigadoon*; dancer Marge Champion with her director husband Gower Champion; Broadway baritone Alfred Drake; publisher Bennett Cerf who appeared on TV's *What's My Line*; and Alexander Cohen, the dour producer who'd booked *Camelot* into the O'Keefe.

"Quite an affair," called Francine Tristan, gliding up to me after Brock left to fetch our drinks. I complimented the press agent on her mauve satin gown and sable stole, and she grinned, saying, "I just heard Herbert Whittaker, one of the top critics, telling someone it's a nice production that needs work. Guess we'll hear more from Herb on Monday. And don't look now, but that sexy Bryce Christmas is heading our way with Vincent Sardi."

As Bryce and a balding, kind-faced man approached, both in black tie, Francine said, "Vincent, how kind of you to come." Turning to Bryce, she purred, "Your voice is divine."

Bryce thanked Francine, then turned toward me. "Miss Conroy, I'd like to introduce my longtime boss, Mr. Sardi. They call him 'the Mayor of Broadway.'"

"Lovely to meet you," Vincent Sardi muttered. "As for you, Christmas, we've surely seen the last of you in a maroon blazer. We'll soon be commissioning your portrait for our walls."

"That would be amazing, sir," Bryce said. "What would you like from the bar?"

Mr. Sardi requested champagne, and when Bryce polled Francine, she asked for the same. I explained that Mr. Remsen was getting my drink, and he soon returned with my tonic water. My boss greeted everyone, but when Bryce disappeared into the throng, I felt homesick.

I slipped a few paces behind my party, though I waved to Sarah on Dan Elsdon's arm. From a distance, I watched Moss and Kitty Hart, the latter in a blue silk gown and sapphire necklace, chatting with Mr. Taylor and a short lady who resembled Mary Martin, though Brock had already told me she was Mrs. Taylor.

My eyes filled with tears that were sure to wreck my mascara. I might never attend such a swanky event again, but what I cared about was the *show,* not all these strangers who'd come to celebrate the opening of Mr. Taylor's auditorium. Mercifully, I didn't sense that the theater folk who'd come from New York were the gossipmongers Francine had warned me about, but I nonetheless felt like the mother of a sickly child who couldn't withstand the taunts of bullies. I'd much preferred having *Camelot* all to myself.

Was I going nuts from the stress? The whole point of

everyone's work was to share the production with the public. *Jane, get a grip*, I thought, and then I recalled having that same thought after I'd seen Bryce for the first time.

I wiped my eyes with my gloved left hand, leaving a dark smudge on one finger, and took a sip of tonic. The string quartet now played "Happy Birthday" as four waiters wheeled a multi-tiered cake with tall shimmering candles to Julie and Tony's table. Julie smiled, ever gracious, but I wondered if she'd fancied her intimate twenty-first party at 21 more than this noisy spectacle. Well, I couldn't guess Julie's reaction, but I had to get the hell out of there. Brock was yakking with Alan in his new tux and his ornery wife, clad in a black gown and diamond choker. Since Bryce was busy with Mr. Sardi, who would miss me?

My head ached as I fled, waving to Nate, who sat with Nell Dean. Bobby and Richard stood together, drinks in hand, though the Burton girls had left. When I was alone in the elevator, I had to stop myself from wailing. It was after 2 a.m., and I was whipped, but after the chaos I'd seen on stage, I decided to request a wake-up call. The cast would perform tomorrow, their one Sunday show, and the producers would surely meet by 11 a.m. for a grim post-mortem.

I was unlocking the door when a smooth male voice called, "Hey, Cookie." Turning, I saw Bryce Christmas, his bow tie unfurled. "I came so we can continue our talk from earlier," he said. "I'd invite you downstairs for a drink, but the bar's swarming with people."

"Come in," I told him, shedding my heels and gloves as Bryce walked past my twin beds to a round table. He pulled out a chair and held it for me.

"Question," he said. "Did the sound system act up as we began 'Guenevere' tonight?"

"I'm afraid so. I couldn't hear your first two verses because of static."

"I've never been out of town with a show," he said, sitting opposite me, "but Jack Dabdoub told me it's usually like this." He grinned. "A taste of hell."

When his expression turned somber, I assumed he'd come to announce he was serious about the lady in New York. Tapping my foot, I wished he'd say his piece and vamoose.

"We all loved the shot glasses," he said. "We plan to buy a bottle of vodka."

"Why should Richard have all the fun?" I said, stifling a yawn.

"Look, Jane, Monday's our night off, and I'd like to take you to dinner. Mr. Sardi told me about a charming French place." He paused. "You could wear that fantastic dress."

"Is that a good idea?" I asked sharply. "You said you were involved."

"Remember before when I mentioned I had something to share? It's that I'll be calling my lady friend in New York and ending our relationship. To be clear, I would've done that even if I wasn't dying to know you better. We're just not compatible."

Thrilled but trying to act nonchalant, I said, "Then I'd like to have dinner on Monday."

"Wonderful," he said, his blue eyes glittering. "I'll pick you up here at 7."

"Hey Bryce, I'm sorry I proposed that dumb restraint pact. Do you mind if we forget it?"

"That was my next subject," he said. "But I'd still like to call you Cookie."

"I wish you would," I replied. "You know, I couldn't help wondering something as I watched you with your old boss. Is it fun to work at Sardi's?"

"Fun? Not exactly. Vincent Sardi's cordial but demanding. And you also have to please the chef and the maître d'. It's sort of like trying to please Lerner, Loewe, and Hart. And God help you if you let one of the stars steal their portrait."

"They steal them?"

"All the time," he said. "The frames aren't nailed to the wall, so it's easy."

"But why would they do that?"

"Mostly because they hate their likeness. But Mr. Sardi respects the artist, a guy named Don Bevan, and goes along with whatever Don does." Now Bryce stifled a yawn. "I'll be happy to tell you my Sardi tales sometime, but it's getting late." He rose, and I trailed him to the door. When Bryce was in the hall, he grabbed my hand and smooched the soft spot above my knuckle. "Sweet dreams, milady."

"Same to you, Mr. Christmas," I said, aware of the wet spot his lips had left on my skin.

After closing my door, I did a mad dance around the room. I'd been drawn to this man since our paths had crossed again at auditions and was crestfallen when he'd told me he was seeing someone. Was it possible that, going forward, he might beam his attention on me alone?

I stopped twirling and caught my breath. It was too late to call Sarah, who was likely sleeping with Elsdon two floors below, and I could hardly phone Brock.

Removing my sensuous crepe dress, I gleefully recalled Bryce's comment that he wanted to know me better. Still, given the zaniness of life on the road, was this a good time to start a relationship? I answered not only to Brock, but to Alan, Fritz, and Moss, three theater titans I now addressed by their first names. What would my life be like if I added a boyfriend to this mix?

Oh, who was I kidding? I had to take my shot with Bryce Christmas. And as I pondered my growing attraction to him while removing my makeup, I knew I'd have trouble taming my excitement enough to sleep. Though it had been a mixed evening for *Camelot,* it was a triumphant night for Jane "Cookie" Conroy.

7.
ALAN'S
ACHING GUT

Jane

I'd showered and dressed and was sipping a second cup of coffee when my phone rang on Sunday. It was Brock, asking me to attend a meeting in Alan's suite at 11 a.m. "We won't see reviews until tomorrow," he said, "but the producers heard enough carping at the party to know we're in deep guano."

"Over the running time?" I asked.

"For starters," Brock said. "Please be your usual upbeat self. They need shoring up." He paused. "Where did you go last night, kiddo? I couldn't find you."

"Sorry, Brock. I had a headache."

"A headache named Christmas?"

I laughed nervously. "Bryce tracked me down, as a matter of fact."

"I hope he behaved himself, or I'll be taking heat from Max." He clicked off, and I thought he'd sounded peeved. It hadn't occurred to me until this moment that Brock might feel responsible for me when the company was out of town.

I got to Lerner's suite with ten minutes to spare. His wife and child weren't there, but Alan was pacing the parlor as he'd paced the rear of the O'Keefe during the premiere. I sat primly on his couch, wondering how I could act "upbeat"? What was the point of pretending *Camelot's* opening had gone well?

"Hanya's going to hate us," Alan moaned, plopping down on a second couch across from me. "Her ballet has to go, but the bigger cut we have to make is 'The Quests' number. With those two gone, we'll shave off fifteen to eighteen minutes."

I chewed my lip. "I know it's not my place to offer an opinion."

"Opine away," Alan said. "I could use a fresh perspective."

"The animal ballet slows the plot at the moment when Arthur's stuck in the forest just before Lance sneaks into Jenny's room. And after Lancelot brings Lionel back to life, his Quest number seems repetitious. The show might be stronger if you cut them, and these thoughts aren't original. Moss said the same thing at Patsy's, remember?"

"I do now," he said before lighting a new cigarette. "Thanks, Jane."

When Alan abruptly resumed pacing, I thought I'd upset him. But as soon as Moss, Fritz, and Brock stumbled in, all bleary-eyed from Taylor's party, Alan suggested those very cuts, and his partners agreed. Since Alan had to write transitional dialogue, Moss and Fritz gave him ideas for lines before Kitty Hart showed up with sandwiches and beer. Clad in a boxy red Chanel suit with red pumps, her brown hair teased and sprayed, she had to be the classiest waitress on the planet. I jumped up to help, earning a rare nod of approval from Moss's wife.

Before breaking for lunch, Fritz said, "I hear the sound people have learned how to adjust the acoustical panels, which means we might hear the orchestra tonight."

"I'll have the new dialogue for rehearsal tomorrow," Alan said. "We can put in our initial changes for Tuesday."

"Excellent," Moss said. "I'll ask Bernie to post a rehearsal notice."

I woke up on Monday, October 3rd, blissfully anticipating my date with Bryce. We'd waved to one another after the Sunday show, and I couldn't wait to get through today so I could put on the green crepe dress he'd admired on opening night. I was in a great mood until I saw Brock's stony mien when we met for lunch at the Royal York's coffee shop.

"The verdict's in," Brock said. "One wag wrote that *Camelot* is '*Gotterdammerung* without laughs,' and that'll be quoted far and wide. A few others are benign. But as Lerner says, the critics get their fun dancing on a playwright's grave, and Nathan Cohen did a jig in the *Daily Star*. He called the show bulky and cluttered, claiming act one's too long and act two's too short. He said Burton's working on a higher level than his colleagues, which makes the show unbalanced, and Bobby's stiff. But wait till you hear his main idea."

I sighed, believing some of what the critic had written was on point.

"Cohen suggests we cut the only part of the show everyone likes, the opening scene when Arthur meets Guenevere. He thinks we should start with the 'The Lusty Month of May.'"

"That would mean cutting almost half of act one," I said. "Well, at least we don't perform tonight. And from what I hear, the actors don't read reviews."

'That's what they tell people to save face, Jane. They read 'em and weep. And from what I just saw in the *Globe and Mail*, Herbert Whittaker's almost as harsh. He finds Julie passionless and hates the scene when Arthur says farewell to Lance and Jenny near the end. He calls it 'disastrous.' But I don't get that comment at all."

I bit into my turkey sandwich, dreading the rehearsal ahead. The cast was weary, and the ensemble would be sorry to lose two numbers that showcased their talents.

"We have another problem," Brock said, spearing a French fry. "The final scene of *Camelot* depends on King Arthur's chemistry with Tom of Warwick."

"Richard is so stirring I hadn't noticed."

"The boy we have now is fine," Brock said. "But he's leaving for reasons his mother didn't explain. Maybe she wants him to focus on school." He shrugged. "Bottom line, Moss and Alan are sending me to London to find a replacement."

"London?" I asked, my heart sinking. "For how long?"

"A week, ten days. Whatever it takes. I leave Thursday, and you'll be the producers' assistant in my absence." He smiled. "You look stricken, Jane. But I have complete faith in you."

"Thanks," I said. But how could I function with Edmund Remsen in a different hemisphere? It was obvious why Alan created a nickname that combined "brick" and "rock." He was both along with my north star, and I vowed to be worthy of his trust.

I spent the afternoon watching the rehearsal from the rear of the O'Keefe, and this time I realized Tom of Warwick was very good. No wonder they were concerned about replacing him.

I took some notes, but mainly wondered how I'd hold my own with the Broadway heavyweights at the two production tables. Oliver Smith, Abe Feder, Hanya Holm, and Tony Duquette didn't know my name or what I did, and I wished I was already at dinner with Bryce. From reading his bio, I knew he had a lot of experience; he could give me sound counsel.

When the cast was dismissed, I took a cab to the hotel, showered, styled my hair, and put on makeup. Believing I looked hot, I donned my least ratty underwear and slipped into the swirly crepe dress, hoping to dazzle my beau. When the phone rang, I attacked the receiver, thinking it was him,

but it was Brock telling me to get to Alan's suite *pronto.*
Put off by his brusque tone, I said, "I can't, Brock. I have a date."

"Cancel it," he snapped before hanging up.

Not knowing how long I'd be busy, I wrote a note with Alan's suite number and taped it to my door, though I guessed Brock wouldn't be pleased if my date showed up. But if he was sending me to Alan, maybe my boss wouldn't be around.

It seemed surreal when I slipped into the Lerners' suite and saw Alan lying on the floor, eyes closed, clutching his stomach. Madame, clad in a leopard coat, blonde hair uncombed, was kneeling over him as their toddler son cried "Mama, Mama" while pulling on her furry sleeve. Looking around, I noticed Moss speaking softly on the phone.

"You certainly took your time," Madame growled at me. "We call our little boy Chouchou." (She pronounced it "Shoeshoe.") "Take him into the bedroom and order dinner. He likes macaroni and cheese and apple juice. Go!"

Risking the woman's displeasure, I rushed to Moss's side as he hung up. "What's the problem?" I whispered.

"No idea, but an ambulance is on the way," he said. "Brock's meeting us at Wellesley Hospital. You're to stay with the little boy."

"I'm expecting—Bryce Christmas," I stammered. "We had a date I'll need to cancel."

"Sorry," Moss said. "Thanks for coming on short notice."

I warily approached Chouchou, who was a small blond cherub. Trying not to scare him, I crouched down and asked if he'd like to play.

"No!" he screamed. "I want Mama!"

"I'll read you a story," I said. "We'll eat mac and cheese."

"Mama!" he shrieked.

"You can't negotiate with a two-year-old," Madame barked. "Take him away."

I grabbed the kid's sticky hand, but he was stronger than he looked and held his ground. Thinking I'd have to pick him up (and fretting he'd soil my expensive frock), I got a reprieve when Bryce appeared in the doorframe, dressed in a tailored navy-blue suit and toting a dozen white roses tied with a blue ribbon. I pointed at Chouchou, then the bedroom, and he grasped my meaning. After handing me the flowers, he swooped the wriggling boy into his arms and followed me into the master. I sniffed the roses, my favorite flower, and set them on a side table before closing the door.

When Bryce put Chouchou down, the kid cried, "More."

"You want another ride, little man?" Bryce asked.

Chouchou put his arms up, so Bryce gave him a piggyback spin around the room. Then he dropped the boy gently on the bed and sat near him.

"Alan is going to the h-o-s-p-i-t-a-l," I told Bryce. "I've been pressed into service as a sitter." I shook my head in frustration. "Mrs. Lerner told me to order dinner, so I'll be having mine here. It could be hours before they return. I'm so sorry."

"There's a phone over there," Bryce said, pointing to the night table. "I'll call the French restaurant and cancel, and we'll order room service. My treat."

"You'll keep me company?" I asked.

"Yeah, and I'll even change the kid's diaper. It's ripe."

"That would help," I said.

"I used to watch my young cousins in high school. Guess it's your lucky night."

"It might be your lucky night," I teased. "Let me find what you'll need." I walked into a den off the bedroom and found a table holding diapers and rash cream. "In here," I called.

Bryce carried Chouchou like a sack of potatoes, and the kid squealed with delight. Bryce set Alan's son on the table, and I ran out, closing the door. Becoming a mother wasn't my goal. Was it too much to hope I could get through life without ever changing diapers?

When noise leaked in from the parlor, I opened the French doors and peered out. Three medical technicians in blue were transferring Alan to a stretcher as Madame stood by, looking scared out of her wits. Moss patted her hand, and Kitty flew in wearing a mink stole, not a hair out of place. (Apparently, the Hart children had not traveled with their folks to Toronto.)

The med techs hoisted Alan on the stretcher and carried him into the hall, followed by Mrs. Lerner and the Harts. I felt awkward in the bedroom among the Lerners' personal belongings (such as the mauve silk peignoir that lay on the rug), so I opened the doors.

"All set," Bryce said as Chouchou ran ahead of him into the parlor. "We boys are hungry, so let's order."

After a tasty macaroni and cheese supper, Bryce, Chouchou, and I had a pleasant evening, mainly because Bryce kept the kid busy. He was reading the story of the *Three Little Pigs*, huffing and puffing with enthusiasm, when we heard a tap from the hall. I answered, finding Moss on the threshold.

"We need to speak in private," he said, so I showed him into the bedroom. "Good news. Alan will recover fully. Alas, he has bleeding ulcers and may be in the hospital for a while."

"That's a shame," I said, knowing Alan's crisis would be a setback for *Camelot*.

"It is," Moss said. "And since Alan's wife drives him batty, you'll be running to his bedside with messages. With Brock in London, I'll be relying on you, and everything I say must be kept confidential. Don't tell anyone about Alan's illness, even your boyfriend out there." He laughed. "Good choice, by the way."

"He saved us all tonight by taking charge of Chouchou. I'm not great with kids."

Moss smiled warmly. "Maybe not, but you're great backstage. You're dedicated and resourceful, and we all know it.

Before we return to New York, let's have a serious chat about your aspirations. I'm sure you don't want to stay a Gal Friday, and if I can help you move forward in your career, I shall."

I was bowled over by his kindness. "Thank you, Moss."

"One last thing. Mrs. Lerner won't be back until they find a room for Alan. She said her boy probably won't settle down without her, so don't worry about putting him to bed."

He offered a courtly bow. Then he called goodnight to Bryce and Chouchou as we strolled through the parlor. After Moss left us, I felt amazed that he'd said such encouraging things to me. If I'd been alone, I might've done another mad dance across the carpet.

"Your eyes are closing, little man," Bryce told the boy. "How about we get you into your PJs, and I'll sing you a funny song?"

"Okey-dokey," Chouchou said. "Later, gator," he told me.

"Night night," I said, thinking the kid was tired and might fall asleep.

"He's out," Bryce said ten minutes later, joining me on the sofa. "What did Moss say?"

"They have no idea what's up." I shrugged. "So, where does that leave us?"

"Well, despite the unconventional way we spent the evening, I'd like to skip dating and go steady." He grinned. "Your turn, Cookie."

"This might sound strange," I said, "but the first time I saw you at the Piccadilly, I got the idea you were someone I could care about." I smiled. "I'd like to go steady."

Bryce moved closer and took my face in his hands and kissed me, gently at first, then urgently. I kissed him back, inhaling his male essence and the scent of his aftershave, losing my bearings. But when I realized where I was, I pulled back, saying, "Mrs. Lerner could return any time, so we can't—"

"You're right," he said wistfully. "I should go back to my

room. Call me later?"

"I will. Hey, you were the Pied Piper with Chouchou to-night."

"I love kids," he said, rising, then helping me to my feet.

"Thanks for my flowers," I told him at the door. "I'll put them in water. I adore roses."

"I'm glad," he said, squeezing my arm. "See you later, ga-tor."

"In a while, crocodile," I replied.

But despite our light-hearted farewell, I dearly missed him as the hours ticked by, and I hoped to visit his room when Alan's wife returned. I'd slept with my college boyfriend out of curiosity, but I desired Bryce Christmas, body and soul. When we landed in bed, I hoped to see mouth-watering lust in his baby blues, and maybe gratitude since I'd be wearing a dia-phragm. (No sensation-blocking condoms for *my* man.)

At midnight, I glanced around the parlor and noticed a photo of Alan and his wife, perhaps from happier days. They posed before a blazing hearth in ski clothes, Alan's arm tightly circling her waist, their eyes bright with hope. Was the picture snapped in Europe during their courtship? Was Mrs. Lerner sorry she'd given up her profession to become a full-time wife/mother/socialite?

I sat back on the couch, pondering the mysteries of cou-plehood. Nobody could peer inside a marriage the way you could look inside an engine to learn what made it go. But if Madame had excelled at her career, she might resent being an appendage to Alan instead of a person admired for her intel-lect.

I checked on Chouchou, who was snoring in his crib, and when I returned to the couch, my mind floated back to Bryce's kiss, the first time we'd had intimate contact. Could souls travel through lips? Because I'd felt a soul connection as our mouths came together. It hadn't surprised me that Bryce knew what to do or that he'd made me feel wanted. But he'd gathered me close without touching anything but my face and claimed me in a way that seemed almost holy. I'd kissed boys before, but they'd been just that: boys. They'd been careless with my body and my feelings, seizing me like hunters attacking prey. But Bryce was a man—a gentleman—and as I thought about his confidence and grace, my eyes filled with tears of joy.

That was the moment Mrs. Lerner chose to return, tossing her leopard coat on a chair. Startled, I jumped to my feet, and when she noticed my moist eyes, she said, "My son couldn't have been that bad. But what have you done with him?"

"He's asleep," I said. "He was an angel tonight, and for that, you might thank Mr. Christmas. He kept Chouchou entertained." I grinned, all innocence, and for the first time in our brief acquaintanceship, Madame didn't scowl or make a snippy retort. Instead, she pursed her lips and padded toward the bedroom, presumably to check on her sleeping child.

Bryce

Jane failed to appear like a nymph in the night, nor did she call. He undressed and went to bed around 2 a.m., guessing Mrs. Lerner had been delayed at the hospital.

While eating eggs in his room on Tuesday morning, Bryce was beset with longing he'd never felt before. He'd gone out with girls in high school and lost his virginity in his freshman year at Rutgers. He'd formed a casual attachment to a civilian clerk during his Army years, which had heightened his loneliness instead of easing it. And somehow, he'd convinced himself he cared for a Yale-trained actress he met at Lambertville, then Rina, who'd requested his table at Sardi's one night and baldly propositioned him.

Jane Conroy was different. He'd spent enough time with her to know he yearned to make love to her until she hummed with pleasure and begged for more; he yearned to protect her from pain; he yearned to spend his free hours making her laugh, a tinkly sound he found infectious. He yearned to serenade her with the romantic songs of Loewe, Rodgers, Gershwin, and Porter.

Passion was fueled by chemistry, as Sky Masterson told Sarah Brown in *Guys and Dolls*—he'd played Sky in summer stock. And he'd felt an electrical charge when he kissed Jane, a spark that could, with little tending, become an inferno.

He recalled a chat with Dan, who'd learned from Sarah that Jane was a doctor's daughter from Bethesda, raised Catholic though she wasn't devout. Sarah also mentioned that Jane disliked kids, which Bryce gleaned from seeing her with Chouchou. But she was clever, confident, and mature beyond her years, with a quick sense of humor that endeared her to pals.

He already knew he wanted their relationship to grow and, yes, last.

He was tempted to call her, but since he'd see her at the theater, he showered and dressed and grabbed coffee downstairs. He met Nate Wicker at the corner of Front and Younge, and they walked together toward the stage door. "Richard called me late last night," Nate said. "Something's up, and Moss is going to explain. Richard also told me Moss's father just died. He sent his brother Bernie to Florida to arrange the funeral. Stoic, huh?"

Bryce hadn't heard about the director's loss, and he didn't let on that he knew what Moss might reveal about Alan. Gossip would spread if he admitted he'd spent the evening in Lerner's suite with Jane, and he wanted to shield their attachment the way you'd protect a fragile bud trying to bloom.

Edward Preston, one of the stage managers, was waiting near the security desk, and he told Nate and Bryce to take seats in the auditorium. Since it was easier to get there from the street, they returned to the O'Keefe's front doors and hurried through the lobby, eventually falling into fifth-row seats. Moss was on stage with Fritz, and Jane stood off to the side, looking distracted. She didn't wave to Bryce, though their eyes locked several times.

When the cast was in the house, Moss and Fritz walked downstage.

"Ladies and gentlemen," Moss said, "Alan was taken to Wellesley Hospital last night. He has a gastrointestinal ailment, but he's resting comfortably and should be released in a few days. Please don't try to visit or call, but I'm certain he'd appreciate cards or notes." He sighed. "We'll have to do without Brock Remsen, who's gone to London to find a new Tom of Warwick. A young man named Eddie Reynard will step in tonight, so make him feel welcome. And for the present, Jane Conroy will function as my assistant. If you have concerns you'd normally share with Brock or Alan, speak to Jane."

Moss turned to Fritz, who said, "Tonight, we'll see how it goes without the animal ballet and 'The Quests.' Moss and I have agreed not to make further changes until Alan returns, and I speak for all of us when I say thank you for your forbearance."

Fritz stepped back, and Moss said, "In five minutes, let's start with act one, scene eight. We'll continue through the Grand Hall knighting scene. Then we'll do act two, scenes three and four, with Morgan Le Fey. Anyone who's not in the forest may leave after the Grand Hall."

After Bryce and Nate returned to the stage door, Nate entered the wings, and Bryce took the elevator to his dressing room. When someone knocked, he was thrilled it was Jane, and though he wanted to sweep her into his arms, he suggested they sit on the daybed.

"I got hung up with Mrs. Lerner," she said. "She was so upset she made me sleep there."

"I thought as much," Bryce said. "How about tonight?"

"I have an after-show meeting with Moss," Jane said. "With Brock gone, I think the soonest we can meet is Sunday, our next night off."

Dan Elsdon burst through the door. "Am I interrupting?"

"No, I'm just leaving," Jane said, standing. "Have a good rehearsal."

"Are you two a couple?" Dan asked Bryce when they were alone.

"Yeah, we are," Bryce said, sitting before their vanity. "How's it going with Sarah?"

"She's a darling," Dan said. "But I haven't told her about my fiancée, Dominique."

Bryce frowned. His roommate was proving to be a ruthless Don Juan. But Elsdon was similar to many actors he'd met, and his lack of ethics was not Bryce's business. He abruptly excused himself and loped downstairs, thinking he should call Rina that night before curtain. He didn't want to emulate Dan's selfish behavior, and it wasn't fair to pursue Jane in Toronto while his old flame pined for him at home.

In the wings at stage left, he was nearly mowed down by Moss, who said, "You're good with kids, Bryce, so I'm making you the chaperone for our new Tom. Be at the stage door at half-hour to meet Eddie Reynard. I'm assigning him to your dressing room and moving Nate to Robert Coote's room for now."

"Glad to be of service," Bryce told the director. But he wasn't happy about having to supervise a kid while preparing to perform. What next? Would they ask him to watch Pellinore's incontinent canine, who looked like the "shaggy dog" in that Disney movie?

Jane

I was back to carrying messages, this time from Moss to Alan, cabbing it a mile or so to Wellesley Hospital. And maybe because my dad was a doctor and I'd spent hours with him at Sibley Hospital near the U.S. Capitol, I *loathed* hospitals. (Later on, I realized my dad had taken me on his rounds hoping I'd feel inspired and become a nurse, but I had a weak stomach. Case in point, I'd once stepped in vomit in his cardiac unit and gagged so much I had to leave the floor. And still, my father kept dragging me to Sibley.)

I'd visited Alan in his sunny private room twice that week, and when I got there on Saturday at noon, he was scrunching up his face while eating lime Jello-O. "Pull up a chair," he called, "and tell me the dish."

Since I'd brought good news, I cheerfully obeyed, removing a tabloid from my bag. "We got a great review in *Variety*," I said, handing him the folded paper.

"Well, well," he said. "That means the dear shits didn't infect all the press with their opinions. Honestly, not since Rodgers and Hammerstein's first flop had I seen so many fake smiles at an opening night party." But he set *Variety* on his bed. "Summarize it, will you?"

"It's by someone named McStay," I said. "He says the show needs trimming, but the production is so colorful and so grand he hates to see anything cut. He likes the cast, the costumes, and the choreography."

Alan was quiet for a minute. Then: "Has Moss pruned the book?"

"No, he's waiting for your return."

"Kitty called and told me Moss can't shake the flu."

"But he's working. He and Fritz cut the two numbers you'd discussed and put in your new dialogue. It now runs three hours and thirty minutes."

"Still too long. Any word from Brock?"

"He wired us. He's returning this week with two British boys—one who'll play Tom and an understudy. In the meantime, the local kid's doing well."

After a beat, he said, "I don't see much of my wife."

"Your doctor told her to stay away."

"Smart man," he said with a smirk. "Please tell Moss I might be here another week."

"Is there anything I can get you, Alan?"

"How about a new act two?" He furrowed his brow. "As you must know, Fritz and I had major Broadway hits with *Brigadoon* and *My Fair Lady,* and we won an Oscar for *Gigi.* I thought I was finally ready to write a musical with themes that reached beyond whether a man and woman can make their love endure, which was the subject of those other three."

"*Camelot* is that show," I said, astonished that Alan was being so frank.

"But *Camelot's* not working," Alan said. "It has the right elements and the best cast we could hire on either side of the Atlantic. And I don't think Fritz has written a more lyrical score. But something's missing on my end, and when I start obsessing over it, my gut aches and I'm afraid I'll make my ulcers bleed again. Thus, when new ideas come to me, I shut them down and do another damned crossword puzzle. I've never felt so useless."

Who but Alan Jay Lerner would use the word "thus" in conversation? Repressing a smile, I asked, "What did you like about T.H. White's book?"

"Ah, that's easy. I liked the author's wit and his contemporary slant on the Arthurian legend. His Arthur is a man of timeless ideas, which is why he's the once and future king." He paused. "I think it was Shakespeare who said, 'Some men are born great, some achieve greatness, and others have greatness thrust upon them.' Well, my Arthur combines all three forms, which I hope comes across. I view him as a great statesman like the U.N.'s Dag Hammarskjold. But maybe my Arthur's also a fool for letting Lancelot destroy what he built."

"Lance doesn't destroy anything," I blurted out. "He doesn't even touch Guenevere in your version. Mordred's the one who wrecks the Round Table."

"You're right, of course." Alan's face brightened. "The first thing I'll do when I get back is beef up Mordred's lack of morals. He's pure evil."

"Mordred was a bad seed, whereas Arthur was a light in the Dark Ages."

"Yes, and it's clever the way Tim White used the legend to craft an anti-war novel in response to Hitler. I think he succeeded, and I've also introduced the anti-war angle, but I don't want to be heavy-handed. Yet it's possible I haven't gone far enough."

I swallowed, feeling out of my depth. I hadn't read White's book and couldn't comment.

"That's enough shop talk," Alan said wearily. "Before I forget, I hope Chouchou didn't give you trouble the other night. Since I heard you got him to sleep, you must have a way with children."

"I can't take any credit," I said, standing. "Bryce Christmas was with me. He kept Chouchou so busy, your little boy conked out."

"Bryce has hidden talents," Alan said. "Please thank him for me."

"I'll do that. And since the matinee's underway, I should head back." I walked to the door, then stopped and turned. "Alan, *Camelot* shows the relevance of 'might for right,' and I think it contains a strong anti-war message for this era."

"Thank you, Jane. You've cheered me enormously. Come back any time."

I took my leave, amazed that Lerner had shared his aims for the show. And as I strode down the hall, breathing through my mouth so as not to smell the antiseptic reek, I also wondered why Moss Hart wasn't using Alan's absence as an excuse to fix the flaws everyone could identify.

Waiting for a taxi at the corner of Wellesley and Homewood, an area of coffee shops and small stores, I recalled a college course I'd taken on the plays Moss had coauthored with George S. Kaufman. Why was a playwright who'd won the Pulitzer Prize not filling the obvious void? (Brock once let it slip that Alan had initially asked Moss to coauthor *Camelot's* book and later changed his mind.) But while jumping into a cab, I answered my own question. Hadn't Brock told me Moss felt his main job was to honor the text? In this case, it was Alan's text. So, revising *Camelot's* book was Alan's exclusive bailiwick, which had to be a source of frustration for a writer as versatile as Moss.

The taxi pulled up in front of the O'Keefe, whose tilted overhang gleamed with scores of tiny lights. After paying the driver, I ran into the lobby patrolled by a security guard and two ushers. The guard checked my security pass and opened the door to the house, where I stood in the back watching Roddy McDowall. He was cheerfully fouling the air as Mordred, the illegitimate son of Arthur and his half-sister Morgause, though she didn't appear in Alan's script.

Now Julie and Richard began to whistle, sing, and dance in "What Do the Simple Folk Do?" Though it began as a witty number, it revealed the seeds of marital angst and ended on a bitter note, and I always enjoyed watching it. As the audience gave the stars an ovation, I slipped out through the lobby and reentered the building through the stage door, showing my security pass to another guard.

Soon Julie and Bobby would be in Guenevere's chamber, preparing to part forever. Then "Guenevere" would start, and since Bryce sang the opening two verses, I slipped into the cavernous wings at stage left and stood near Eddie, our new Tom of Warwick. I might not have noticed the blonde woman in front of Ed, except the lady had drowned herself in perfume and wore a ratty raccoon coat. I wished one of the stage managers would banish her, since cast members might sneeze or cough from her excessive use of Chanel Number Five.

Dressed in a dark cloak and hood, Bryce sang with his usual power and finesse, supported by the chorus, and after Lancelot rescued Guenevere off stage, the lights went out and the ensemble trickled into the wings. As Sarah passed by, she mumbled, "We need to talk. Wait for me at the stage door after the show." Then Bryce appeared, waving to the lady in fur. But when he finally saw me, his face turned scarlet under his makeup. Tapping my shoulder, he whispered, "I have a problem. Call you later."

The blonde woman seemed riveted by the emotional farewell of Arthur and Lancelot, then Arthur and Guenevere, and by process of elimination, I guessed she was Bryce's old flame. Yet her arrival had to be a surprise because before I'd seen Alan, Bryce kissed me in his dressing room, and we'd considered having "a quickie" on his daybed. Then, thinking better of the idea, we'd vowed to wait until after our date on Sunday. To ensure that nothing came between us this time, I told Moss I had an unbreakable engagement, and he'd given me permission to skip a night meeting with the production team. Since Brock wasn't due back until Wednesday, the coast had been clear until now. (Surely Bryce would send the lady packing by tomorrow, wouldn't he?)

When Sarah and I were seated in the Savarin dining room after the matinee, Sarah ordered two club sodas. "We have to stay clear-headed," she primly explained.

"Is it Dan?" I asked, observing the crowd of diners at dark wooden tables. Many had come here from the matinee. This was clear because their tables displayed the O'Keefe's red-orange playbill with a knight in burnished armor below a huge white *Camelot* logo.

"Who else but Dan?" Sarah asked. "Turns out he's engaged to a socialite. That's all he said when I told him my news." She paused. "Jane, I missed my period."

Tempted to speak, I held my tongue. (Otherwise, I'd start ranting about Dan.)

"His fiancé Dominique Biddle is a friend of Mrs. Lerner's. Yet Dan claims he'd never met Alan before and got his *Camelot* role without anyone's help."

"Who cares how he got his damn job?" I snapped. "What will you do?"

"Have the baby and keep it. Sarah Bernhardt did that, and it didn't hurt her acting career."

From the Bernhardt biography I'd read at school, I knew my Sarah was nothing like the steely, unconventional Divine Sarah. "Will your parents support your decision?"

"No, they'll want me to have the baby and give it up for adoption."

"Well, I can't see you doing that. You'd worry about your kid for the rest of your life."

"I'm going to raise it on my own," she declared. "I was thinking you and I could rent an apartment together." Our sodas came, and we both ordered baked ham with au gratin potatoes.

"We'll look for a place," I said calmly. "As soon as we get back."

"Please don't tell anyone." Sarah sighed. "I don't think Dan will breathe a word. Since I was a virgin when this began, he knows the baby's his, and he's promised child support. But he doesn't plan to dump Dominique, who's had two rich husbands and is older than Danny."

"He's got the morals of an alley cat," I bristled.

"And I'm the biggest idiot in the world because I still love him. Isn't that pathetic?"

"He's a bigger idiot," I said. "You're having his kid, and he's going to lose you both."

We dished about the company until our meal came. I ate my cheesy potatoes and little else, wondering what I'd say the next time I saw "Danny." But Sarah had a healthy appetite for a woman in turmoil, so maybe she really was eating for two.

I stood on stage behind the closed curtain as Moss gave notes following the second Saturday show, and afterward, it pained me to watch Sarah cross the wings with Dan. Then I saw Bryce pulling the new Tom by the arm. It seemed likely his old flame would be waiting outside his dressing room, so I planned to stay away.

Nate Wicker wandered over, saying, "Hey, stranger. I've hardly seen you since we came to 'Torono.' Want to go out with us tonight?"

"Who and where?" I asked.

"Richard, Nell, Bobby, Joan from the chorus, and me. We're off to Le Coq d'Or, which is a club with a rockabilly band called 'Rompin' Ronnie Hawkins and the Hawks.' Richard read that Ronnie is entertaining and wants to hear him. The rest of us are going along for the ride."

"Count me in," I said, figuring Bryce wouldn't take Rina to such an offbeat place. "I've never gone drinking with Richard. Might be an experience."

Nate chuckled. "Right this way, love. You can wait for us in the Green Room."

I fell into step near Nate and asked if he'd learned anything new about Burton lately.

"Matter of fact, yes," he said. "He has this odd pre-show ritual. Just before he's due on stage, he goes to the side of the curtain and stares at the audience. Then he lets loose a stream of curse words, berating the folks out front for coming to judge him. It's kind of frightening, but when he's finished, he's completely calm and ready to give them his all."

"I'd love a peek at that," I said.

Nate left me at the Green Room door, then took off toward his dressing room. I slipped into the lounge where dark-haired Tony Walton was sitting on a bench. He politely stood, and then we both sat, ignoring the drinks and snacks on a nearby table.

"It's a wonder Moss can do anything, sick as he is," Tony said. "Julie's afraid she'll be next." He offered me his winsome gap-toothed smile. "Are you going somewhere tonight?"

"Yes, out to hear music with Richard and his cronies. Rockabilly or some such thing."

"We've heard the Toronto clubs get wild after midnight," Tony said. "I'm taking Julie straight back to the hotel for a warm bath and hot tea." He laughed. "Sounds sedate, I suppose."

"Sounds smart," I murmured, thinking I should go to my own hotel.

Julie stalked in, her face scrubbed, a scarf covering her hair. She kissed Tony's cheek, then turned to me. "I hear you're going out with Richard's gang," she said. "Careful, darling."

"Yes, careful, darling," Richard quipped, entering the Green Room with Nate.

Both wore jackets and ties, and I was glad I'd dressed nicely in a green crew-neck sweater, white long-sleeved blouse, and red tartan-plaid wool skirt. (I'd chosen my clothes that morning and looked a bit school-girlish for club-hopping, but there was no time to change.)

"You're wearing Welsh colors, love," Richard added.

"You've had an influence on us all, Richard."

Nate offered his arm, and as we crossed the wings, Nate and Richard joshed each other, and I knew I should beg off. I was afraid I'd given Nate the wrong idea by agreeing to go drinking as his date. But Bobby, Nell Dean, and petite Joan Augur were standing at the security desk, and my common sense deserted me.

"Nice of you to join us, Jane," Bobby said, and I was nearly knocked off my pins. Since the start of rehearsals, Goulet had looked straight through me, as though I was beneath his notice.

As we exited the stage door, we met a throng of rabid fans wielding pens, and Richard, Bobby, Nate, Nell, and Joan stopped to sign autographs. A limo was idling at the curb, and I took shelter in its long back seat. Ten minutes later, the actors joined me, and the driver sped north to "the strip" of clubs and bars on Younge. When we reached Le Coq d'Or, the maître d' escorted our party past the Saddle Bar with its red-leather stools to a table for six in the main room, a sea of white leather chairs and brown tabletops with paper placemats.

It was after midnight, and "Rompin' Ronnie" was singing on a low platform, backed up by "The Hawks." He wore a suit and tie and loudly belted "Mary Lou," which brought to mind the vocal style of Elvis Presley. Ronnie had a curly dark pompadour and wide pleasant face, and when he launched into "Dizzy Miss Lizzy," a song from the radio, his energy picked up. He danced, hopped, jumped into the air, and whooped. As I glanced around the table, Richard, Bobby, and Nate seemed amused, and when the band took a break, Richard ordered bottles of Bollinger and told us to check our menus. "Eat hearty, friends," he said. "Tonight's on me."

After we'd ordered, "Rompin' Ronnie" touched Richard's

arm, introduced himself, and drawled, "I've heard y'all are magnificent in *Camelot*."

"Thank you, sir," Richard said, grinning. "We're enjoying you and your merry band."

Ronnie smiled. "I was wonderin' if you'd mind if we introduced you fellas from the stage. We want our audience to give y'all a round of applause."

"How very kind," Richard said, standing to face Ronnie. "But I'll give you and your men free tickets to *Camelot* if you don't. Please come as my guests, then visit me backstage."

"All of us?" Ronnie said. "Why, thanks, Mr. Burton. We'd love to."

"Call Mary Jolliffe in the press office at the O'Keefe. I'll ask her to arrange it."

Ronnie thanked Richard once more, then stomped off toward the cowboy bar.

"Nice chap," Richard said. "But I fear he would've had all of us singing next." Everyone laughed, and I tried to ignore Nate's arm, which he'd draped around my shoulder. As Richard reclaimed his seat, he began necking with Nell, whereas Bobby was talking with Joan, who seemed to be a platonic colleague. Was it possible Nate's intentions were just as benign?

"Don't look now," Nate whispered, "but Bryce just walked in with his lady from New York. I think he'll pretend not to see us so he doesn't have to spar with Richard."

Instead, Bryce and his Chanel-scented flame walked over and said hello. "Too close, Yuletide," Richard barked, although Joan and Nell warmly greeted Bryce and "Rina Markoff." The woman smiled and burbled compliments, saying she'd watched the afternoon and evening shows and loved them both.

Bryce discreetly rubbed my neck, so I turned to Nate and kissed his cheek, a dumb move considering I was sending the exact wrong signal. But I was miffed at Bryce for not ending his affair with "Miss Markoff" before she flew into town. I hoped to make him jealous, and when the host showed Bryce and Rina to a table at the other end of the room, I felt saved by the noise and bustle of the waiters who brought our food. But, as I'd feared, Nate had read my kiss as an invitation, and now he swiveled around and stuck his tongue down my throat. His breath was sour, and I pulled away. Wanting to taste something good, I downed a full coupe of Richard's delicious champagne. Then another.

"Rompin' Ronnie and the Hawks" returned to their platform and began a song called "Forty Days" as Ronnie strutted and jumped. I grabbed my purse, telling Nate I had to powder my nose. "Be quick," he said. "I'll miss you, darlin'."

I dashed past the Saddle Bar into the ladies' room and wiped my face with a wet paper towel. The mirror was filmy, and I couldn't see well enough to touch up my lipstick. Had I been wrong about Bryce, I asked myself, viewing him through the "filmy" lens of romantic illusion?

When my head began to spin from the champagne, I grabbed the sink to steady myself as Rina Markoff barged in.

"You're the little tart Bryce is chasing," Rina spat out. "Well, I'll be here for a week, Toots, and by next Saturday, you'll be a distant memory."

It was tempting to insult the woman in kind, but I returned my lipstick to my purse and marched out of the room. I wanted to visit Bryce's table and shriek at him, but I couldn't take a chance of falling on my face, so I bolted out the club's front door. The bouncer hailed a cab, and while riding past the neon lights on "the strip," I told myself that Nate, who lodged at the King Edward, wouldn't track me to the York after I'd run out on him.

I was in bed an hour later, tossing and turning, imagining Bryce having sex with Rina down below. I sat up and began to gag, but presently took a few deep breaths. Feeling calmer, I decided I hadn't misread Bryce's character. He hadn't known

Rina would come to Toronto, and if I wanted the guy, I had to give him time to sort things out. Even if he fell into bed with his old flame, sex wasn't much without passion—I'd learned this from screwing my college boyfriend. For all I knew, Bryce might want me more after a night with Rina, who'd looked haggard in the dim restroom light.

Settling myself under my blanket, I now thought sadly about Sarah. She'd put me on the spot at supper, asking me to share an apartment, but did I want to become a second mom to her infant? No, I craved peace and quiet, not a baby squalling all night. And as I considered my dilemma, I concluded Dan Elsdon had to ditch his fiancée and marry my friend whom he'd knocked up the first time she'd tried sex. But was there anyone in my orbit who could possibly persuade Dan to do the right thing?

8.
HART'S
QUIXOTIC HEART

Bryce

He vowed he wouldn't sleep with Rina, but after running into Jane at that crummy club, he downed three gin gimlets. Later, when his old flame made advances, he succumbed, though afterward, he left her bed and slept in the other twin. He woke with a start at 7 a.m., and as Rina sawed wood, dribbling saliva from her open mouth, he felt guilty even though he and Jane weren't yet lovers. Unable to calm himself, he rolled out of his sheets, donned a flannel shirt and jeans, and took the elevator to the floor above.

He assumed Jane would be furious, but she answered her door with a smile and invited him in. She was dressed in a lavender blouse and tweed slacks, her brown hair in a ponytail, and Bryce learned she was an early riser, the same as he.

"I met your friend in the restroom last night," Jane said. "She said she was staying for a week, and you'd be over me by then."

"I owe you an explanation," he said, thinking his head might explode from morning-after regret. "She showed up out of the blue before the matinee yesterday. I should've called her long before now and explained about us, but I told her yesterday between shows. She was hurt, and we decided to talk later on. Then we had the bad luck of running into you."

"Want some coffee?" Jane asked. "Room service brought a pot and two cups as though they knew I'd have a guest."

"Thanks," he said, following her to the small round table where she was already pouring coffee from a carafe. "I like it black. And I'd be grateful for two aspirin, if you have some."

Jane retrieved the white tablets and a glass of water from the bathroom and put them on the table before him. "Bryce, I've got my hands full," she said before sipping the hotel's weak brew. "Alan won't be back for a while, which I'm telling you in confidence, and Sarah, one of the most trusting girls I know, thinks she's newly pregnant by Dan Elsdon."

"I feel bad for both," Bryce said before swallowing the aspirin with water.

"What I'm saying is, you can take your time with Rina. Then we'll see what's what."

"It might help if she goes when she's ready." He gulped some coffee. "She stayed in my room last night, but this morning I'll ask my understudy Jack Dabdoub if I can bunk with him."

"I guess our first date has to wait again," Jane said. "And listen, Sarah doesn't want anyone to know her situation. But if you have any ideas for persuading Dan to marry her—"

"Elsdon and I aren't exactly friends," he said, rising. "But I'll see if I can get through to him." He walked around the table to peck Jane's cheek. "Thanks for the coffee, aspirin, and compassion." Heading for the door, he heard Jane behind him and longed to kiss her for real, but he merely turned, saying, "A week from now, everything will be peachy. That's a promise."

Alone in the corridor, he decided he'd been too drunk to reject Rina's overtures the night before, a mistake he could rationalize as break-up sex. But it would be unfair to give his old flame the wrong message twice, so while she was in town, he'd keep her at arm's length and sleep elsewhere even if he had to rent another room. He just hoped it wouldn't be for long.

Rina brought a manuscript to edit, so that Sunday afternoon, Bryce read the last third of *To Kill a Mockingbird* while she sat at his dining table, pencil in hand, crossing out lines and making comments in the margins. He went to rehearsal on Monday, and since his old flame wanted to see *Camelot* a third time, they had an early supper in the hotel's Princess Lounge before setting out for the theater. It was a brisk October night, and they walked in silence until Rina asked about Burton's "Yuletide" remark on Saturday night. "Was he insulting you?"

"He's annoyed with me, but I don't know why." It was a white lie he didn't mind telling.

"Does Miss Conroy know?" she asked.

"Rina, let's not argue before I have to perform."

"That girl lacks something," Rina remarked. "I suppose she's pretty in an Irish milkmaid way. When I told an agent friend that I was seeing *Camelot,* she told me her secretary left her to work for this show's production chief." After a pause, she added, "Jane Conroy looks harmless, but she must've slept with someone to get her job."

"That's enough," Bryce snapped, and Rina shrugged as if to say, "Believe what you want." He assumed it was hard to get a position with a producer even if a relative had contacts. But when he and Rina reached the O'Keefe's front entrance, he suspected she was trying to plant suspicions about Jane, which was ironic since he was the one who'd strayed.

"Rina, it just occurred to me that you hate musicals," Bryce said, holding the door for her. "Yet you wanted to see *Camelot* three times. How come?"

"Partly because I love your voice," she said. "But Lerner's script is deep. It's not there yet, but with proper editing, it should work."

"I'm happy you think so," Bryce said, feeling encouraged since she was tough to impress.

As arranged, they met Mary Jolliffe in the empty theater lobby. She gave a comp orchestra ticket to Rina, and Bryce left the ladies chatting like lifelong cronies—and why not? They were successful women in their thirties and he'd sensed they'd get along.

He retraced his steps and walked around the corner to the stage door where Eddie Reynard, age fourteen, was waiting inside. The kid was lanky with ginger hair and green eyes, and Bryce believed he'd be a heartbreaker in a year or two. "How's it going?" Bryce asked when he and Eddie were rambling to the elevator.

"I don't think Mr. Burton likes me," Eddie groused, a lock of hair falling in his eyes.

"Join the club," Bryce said. "But what do you mean?"

"He never talks to me when we're waiting to go on."

"He's concentrating," Bryce said. "His last scene with you has to pack a wallop."

"Roddy McDowall talks a little," Eddie said. "I asked him about *Lassie Come Home,* and he said Lassie's real name was Pal. Do you think he was pulling my leg?"

"Probably not," Bryce said. "I read somewhere that Lassie was played by a male dog."

After they were seated in their dressing room, Eddie reading a *Superman* comic book and Bryce putting on makeup, Dan opened the door. But he lingered in the hall to give Sarah Wilkins a sloppy French kiss before entering and slapping his gear on the makeup table.

"Hey, Elsdon," Bryce said. "Watch those public displays, will you?"

"Why?" Dan asked. "I bet Eddie's seen his mom and dad do that."

"Nah," Eddie said. "My mom hates all that kissy-face stuff."

After doing a stretch, Dan sat before his mirror. "I heard Wicker and your girl Jane went drinking with Richard and Nell. Where the hell were you?"

"I was there," Bryce replied, refusing to take the bait. "Hey, Ed, could you run to the Green Room and get us some Cokes?"

"I'm not allowed to drink Coke," Eddie said.

"Live a little," Bryce replied. "It'll be our secret."

"Thanks, Bryce," Eddie said before dashing out and slamming the door.

"I gather Sarah told you her news," Bryce remarked.

Dan kicked off his shoes, then stood to remove his corduroy slacks, which he hung on the rack along the wall. "There's nothing like getting a girl preggers to make a man feel virile."

Bryce frowned. "Unless you want to get a reputation as a total louse, Elsdon, I think you need to propose before her daddy buys a shotgun."

"*You're* not her daddy, Christmas, so butt out. Look, I've told Sarah I'm engaged, but I'm not going to leave one of the most prominent women in New York. And since Dominique's a woman of great sophistication, she doesn't care what I do on the road."

When Eddie returned with three cans of Coke, he said, "Mr. Burton was nicer to me in the Green Room. He asked me to tell Yuletide to steer clear." The boy chortled, opening his Coke can with a snap. "I just have to find out who this Yuletide character is."

Elsdon smirked at Bryce, saying nothing.

Ignoring his colleague, Bryce began patting his foundation into place. He decided Dan was the biggest asshole he'd met in show business, and that was saying something.

———◆———

Keeping their word, Moss and Fritz made no other changes that week. Each night the show trudged on for three-and-a-half hours, or sometimes longer, depending on the amount of applause. The cast rehearsed daily, and Fritz became a martinet with the chorus, egged on by Maestro Allers. But Moss seemed depleted, which Bryce and his friends whispered about. It was hard not to notice that their director delivered his notes with less humor and encouragement than before Alan took ill.

Bryce also felt uneasy backstage since Elsdon and Wicker had stopped speaking to him. He'd offended Dan by confronting him about Sarah, and Nate probably blamed him for Jane's flight from Le Coq d'Or. Then again, Nate might be mimicking Burton's distaste for him. Nights after the show, he was stuck with Rina, who believed she could cure his infatuation with Jane. Strangely, she accepted that sex was off the table—Jack Dabdoub was letting Bryce use his extra bed—but she planned to stay all weekend, wrecking his hope of seeing Jane on Sunday night.

Brock Remsen had just returned with a kid named Garry Whitson, who'd start playing Tom at the Saturday matinee, so Eddie Reynard was leaving. Before they changed into their costumes on Eddie's last night, Bryce gave him a blue-and-white Toronto Maple Leaf cap since Ed had told him that hockey, not acting, was his main interest.

"You're cool, Bryce," Eddie said, donning the cap and admiring his reflection in the mirror. "Thanks."

"My pleasure," Bryce said, relieved he wouldn't have to supervise Garry Whitson, who'd share a dressing room with Rufus Devane, a second teenager from England who'd serve as Garry's understudy.

When Jane slipped into the room, she grinned at Eddie in his cap. "May I have a word, Mr. Christmas?" she asked.

"I'll rustle up some Cokes," Eddie offered, then took off.

"He's a cutie," Jane said.

"So are you," Bryce said, rising. "I'm happy to see you alone."

"Would you like to go on an outing tomorrow?" she asked. "Brock asked me to bring Alan home from the hospital. I thought we could have breakfast before we pick him up. You'd be back in plenty of time for the matinee. Apparently, Alan plans to come straight here for a meeting with Moss and Fritz." She laughed. "Fritz plans to introduce a new overture next week. Does that sound like he's rearranging the deck chairs on the Titanic?"

"Actually, I think a new overture might help. As for tomorrow, I usually have breakfast with Rina, but I'll tell her I've been called in early to work with Moss." He sighed. "By the way, our director doesn't seem pleased with anything Goulet does."

"Brock thinks Moss needs to guide Bobby more." Jane paused. "There's a little place on Wellesley near the hospital. It's called Café Colette. Should we meet there at nine?"

"A rendezvous? That'll be fun." Bryce moved next to Jane, pulling her close. "You smell wonderful." He pressed his lips to hers, and she returned his kiss, and before they came up for air, he'd pushed her toward the daybed, where they fell into a heap.

"The door isn't locked," she murmured.

"I know." But he began to nuzzle her neck.

When someone spoke in the hall, Bryce jumped up and pulled Jane to her feet, noticing her cheeks were pink. "About tomorrow," he murmured. "After we drop Alan, let's come back here. Nobody'll be around that early." He stroked her face. "Cookie, I can't wait any longer."

"Neither can I," she murmured, and when they kissed again, Bryce felt her heart pounding against his chest.

Jane

After the finale that Friday, the company assembled on stage for notes, and I waved to Brock before he introduced Garry, the new Tom of Warwick, a gangly fourteen-year-old with dark hair styled into a bowl cut. Poor Brock looked exhausted from his London jaunt, and so did Bernie Hart, who'd returned to the stage manager's console from his dad's funeral.

Moss also appeared pale as he introduced Francine Tristan, who'd flown in from New York and was standing with a skinny blonde lady. "*Camelot* has scored a coup," Moss announced, "and our valiant press agent has come here to tell you about it."

Francine swayed on her heels as though she'd drunk too much on the plane. "I'm happy to announce," she said, "that *Time* Magazine will feature Alan and Fritz on its November fourteenth cover to celebrate their partnership."

"Bravo!" Richard called, sparking a round of clapping and cheers.

"*Time* has sent us an intrepid researcher in the person of Joyce Haber," Francine added. "Joyce will nab you in hallways or call your rooms, and we hope you'll give her your full cooperation as she gathers background details." She turned. "Care to say a few words, Joyce?"

The blonde lady stepped forward like a Miss America contestant. "Hello, *Camelot* company," she said, her tone dripping with practiced warmth. "I look forward to chatting with many of you soon. Thanks in advance for your help."

As Miss Haber stepped back, Francine nodded to the director.

"I'm delighted to report that Alan will return tomorrow," Moss said, and the company clapped again. "Fritz and I are proud of what you've done this week, but we've decided to slow the changes. There will be choral rehearsals each afternoon to keep us musically sharp, but the principals are excused. For now, I'll give you my notes, then please go home and rest." He laughed. "Or hit the bars. Whatever floats your boat."

I peeked at Bryce, who was gazing at me with such longing I felt giddy. But then I looked past him and saw Rina staring my way with venom, and I knew the woman wouldn't go quietly. Now my gaze shifted sideways where Sarah was hanging onto Dan like a life raft, and I wished I hadn't gotten Sarah into *Camelot*. She would've been better off as a nun in *The Sound of Music*. Yet never in a million years had I dreamed she'd fall into bed with the first attractive actor who put the moves on her.

On Saturday morning, I was dressed and ready to leave for breakfast with Bryce when the phone rang. It was Brock, sounding harried. "Change of plans, kiddo," he said. "You get up to Moss's suite as soon as you can, and I'll fetch Alan at the hospital."

"What happened?"

"Another crisis. But I think I'm the right one to deal with Alan."

After Brock rang off, I called Jack Dabdoub's room but got no answer. In a panic, I grabbed my things and dashed out to the elevator. When it stopped, I came face to face with Bryce, which solved the problem of how to reach him. Explaining Brock's instructions, we hurried to the Harts' suite, where Moss was lying on his couch, looking flushed and sweaty. A bald, portly man leaned over him, listening to Moss's heart with a stethoscope.

"We're from the *Camelot* team," I said. "What's going on?"

The man stood up as Bryce and I moved closer. "I'm Dr.

Francisco," he said. "Mr. Hart's having angina and shortness of breath. It might be a coronary. I've called for an ambulance."

"We'll ride with him," I said.

"Only one person can go," the doctor said.

"Then I'll get out of your hair," Bryce told me. "Will I see you before the matinee?"

"Let's try to meet in your dressing room," I said, wistfully watching Bryce take his leave.

Three burly men pushed their way inside, wearing blue hats with visors, white shirts, dark ties, and navy trousers. One of them called, "We're the St. John Ambulance Brigade," and I realized they were the same team who'd come for Alan.

"I'm the hotel physician," Dr. Francisco said. "Our patient is having a cardiac event. I gave him nitroglycerin, and he needs oxygen *stat*. This lady's his advocate."

I held Moss's clammy hand as the ambulance techs shoved a glass coffee table away from the couch. "Kitty's—coming—today," he whispered. "Tell her."

"I will," I said before the brigade slid Moss onto a stretcher.

"He's fortunate they got here so fast," the doctor said. "I think he's in some danger."

I thanked the physician, then ran after the medical technicians who were transporting Moss, my hands growing cold from Moss's poor prognosis. I watched the techs enter the elevator before moving inside. We passed a crowd in the lobby—though nobody from the *Camelot* cast—and moved toward a sedan-style ambulance parked outside. The techs slid Moss into the rear and eased him onto a gurney before helping me board.

The driver switched on the siren and whizzed through the busy streets of Toronto. One tech placed an oxygen mask over Moss's face while another found a vein and began an IV.

A short while later, the ambulance parked at Wellesley

Hospital's Emergency entrance, and I jumped onto the driveway. Two guys removed Moss's gurney, then placed it on the pavement and held it taut until they set up its legs. I followed as one brawny tech pushed Moss through a pair of doors, down a long hallway, and into a treatment room. When a plump nurse in a white dress and cap slipped in, the tech removed a health form from his pocket and took off. After scanning the report, the nurse pulled a curtain around us before taking Moss's vitals. Since his eyes were tightly closed, I began to shake, fearing he might die.

Brock came through the curtain, breathing hard. "How's he doing?"

"Not sure," I said as a tall young man joined us. His name tag said "Dr. Levine."

"Please wait outside," said the nurse. "Dr. Levine's our top cardiac man. Lucky for your friend, he's here this morning."

"I represent Mr. Hart's family in New York," Brock announced. "I'll stay."

Grateful to be excused, I meandered out to the waiting room and sat on a none-too-clean fabric chair, wishing I'd brought Bryce. Why had we allowed ourselves to be cowed by that unctuous doctor?

It felt like an eternity before my boss came to find me, saying, "I haven't yet told Alan." He claimed the adjacent chair, adding, "His discharge is running late, so I left word for Kitty at the hotel. It's good timing that she was returning here today."

"She'll be shocked," I said.

"Maybe not," Brock said. "Moss had his first heart attack before he turned fifty, and they're working hard to make sure this one isn't fatal." He rubbed his chin. "Someone at the hotel saw him being wheeled out and called a local radio station, so they've likely reported his collapse. Guess I should shake a leg before Alan hears the news from someone else. You come, too,

Jane. You can't do anything for Moss."

I saw sorrow on Brock's face, and while we took the elevator upstairs, I realized how starry-eyed I'd been about working on Broadway. As Julie had told me on the day we visited Mrs. Pons, the theater was hard work, but I'd never imagined I'd be visiting hospitals this often.

When we reached Alan, he was sitting in a wheelchair waiting to leave, and he stood and twirled around, eager to demonstrate his return to health. "Why do you two look bereft?" he asked, sitting again. "I'm my old self. I can't wait to confer with Moss."

"Yes, well, about that," Brock began, but he clammed up when a nurse's aide dashed in to change the bed and tidy the room. I tried to distract Alan, telling him about Joyce Haber, whom he'd agreed to meet the following morning.

As soon as Alan's nurse and a young Asian orderly arrived, the nurse gave Alan some discharge instructions and two prescriptions before the orderly wheeled him through the open door. Brock and I were preparing to follow when a tall Black orderly pushed a gurney into the room Alan had just left. I recognized Moss's receding hairline, though his face was covered by an oxygen mask, and Brock must've noticed, too, because he turned as white as the sheet covering Moss's lower half.

At the hospital's main entrance, Alan eased into the back of a waiting Cadillac. We joined him, and as the car zipped off, Brock said, "Alan, I'm the bearer of bad tidings. Moss had a heart attack this morning. He's just been admitted, and the doctor told me he might be here for weeks or even months."

"Months?" Alan asked. "You mean we've lost our director?"

"Sorry to be blunt," Brock said, "but you'll be dealing with that researcher from *Time,* and you need to know the facts. As of now, nobody can predict when Moss will recover."

When the car made a U-turn, I saw Kitty Hart in a Burberry

raincoat emerging from an orange-navy blue cab. Her eyes were red, no doubt from crying.

"I need to see Fritz right now," Alan said, sounding defeated.

"He's waiting for you in the Green Room," Brock said.

"As a courtesy, we should alert Richard and Julie," Alan said. "But we shouldn't reveal the gravity of Moss's condition to anyone."

All of us were mute until the Cadillac parked in front of the O'Keefe.

"I haven't seen the show for ten days," Alan said as the driver jumped out to open his door. "Can it survive this new crisis?"

"I think so," Brock said. He exited on the far side and circled around to Alan while I trailed behind. "But, remember, you're our leader. Fritz writes glorious music, but he comes across disengaged in a crunch."

"Cold as the Alps," Alan said. "But it's a defense mechanism. Fritz is a big softie." He sighed. "Look, musicals open and close with the weather. The main thing is for Moss to recover, however long it takes."

I was touched by his altruism, and that's when I knew he revered Moss Hart.

When Alan showed up at the Green Room, Fritz greeted him with a brisk hug.

Giving the partners their space, Brock and I escaped into the hall. "Fritz is a very private man," Brock said, "whereas Alan will tell you his deepest secrets even if you'd rather not know." We strolled across the wings, exiting in the foyer near the stage door. "I don't need you this afternoon," he told me. "But I'm walking back to the hotel. Coming, kiddo?"

I told him I had stuff to do and waved him on his way.

When Brock was out of sight, I asked the guard if any actors had signed in.

"One," he said, checking the sheet. "Mr. Christmas."

And he's my gift, I thought.

On the second floor, I found a public restroom where I inserted my diaphragm, then rinsed my mouth with water. Checking my reflection in the mirror, I added fresh lip gloss and shook my hair loose from its ponytail. Feeling shaky with anticipation, I walked up the hall and knocked on Bryce's door.

He answered wearing nothing but a bath towel tied around his waist, and he gently pulled me inside. Locking the door, he said, "I knew you'd get here, Cookie. How's Moss?"

"I'm not supposed to talk about it," I said, trying not to gawk at the silky hair on his arms and legs. I couldn't remember seeing my old boyfriend's body in the light.

"I got calls from cast members who heard about Moss on the radio. Just tell me if he's holding his own."

I nodded, and Bryce took me into his arms and kissed me until warmth flooded every cell of my being. Then he pulled me to the daybed and sat nearby. "I have great news. Rina and I are officially kaput. She's gone to the airport."

"How did that happen?" I asked, shyly touching his chest hair, which felt as soft as down.

Bryce took my palm in one of his beautiful hands. "I told her the truth. She has too much pride to stay."

"The truth?" I met his expectant gaze.

"You and I haven't known each other long, Jane, but I've never wanted anyone this much. And there's a reason for that. You see, I love you."

"You do?" I asked in amazement. "I love you, too. At least, I think I do."

"You *think* you do?" he teased, ripping off his towel and moving close. "Well, I plan to turn that wan comment into an unconditional 'Hell, yes!'" He brought my hand back to his chest.

Laughing nervously, I stroked him again, letting my eyes stray downward. His body, every part of it, was beautiful, and while this impression was sinking in, he smoothly removed my blouse and bra and helped me lie down. When he grabbed a condom he'd hidden under the pillow, I said, "No need. I'm wearing a diaphragm."

"I think I've died and gone to heaven," he said dreamily.

Afterward, when we were lying on the narrow mattress, both of us sweating, I knew I'd follow him anywhere to feel his hands on my skin again. "I do love you, Bryce," I whispered. "You're really good at—this."

"Takes two," he said, raising himself on one arm. "I'm so content I could stay here all day, but Dan comes early, and Nate's with us again. How about if we have supper after the show tonight? I hear they have dancing at the Walker House. We can have our belated first date."

"Let's hope I'm not on call for another emergency," I said, sitting up. "By the way, I know how to dance."

"You know how to do everything," he said with a wicked grin.

I grinned back, astonished that this stunning man was mine alone.

I put on my green crepe dress and black heels and took pains with my hair and makeup, and when I waltzed into the Green Room at 7:50 p.m., Brock and Alan whistled. Fritz squeezed my arm paternally, though his absent girlfriend was around my age.

I had no idea why Brock wanted me at this meeting, but I sat on a straight chair and waited as Richard, in a navy velvet tunic and blue hose, and Julie, in a pale-blue satin gown and long blue gloves, claimed the bench near the wall.

Alan and Fritz stood in front of their stars. "From Fritz's

message to the cast after the matinee," Alan said, "you're aware that Moss went to the hospital. Kitty has assured us he's stable and his doctors think he'll recover. Please don't tell anyone else, but there's no way of knowing when he'll return."

"Poor Moss," Julie said.

"Yes," Richard said. "The poor chap's had flu for two solid weeks."

"We're not sure who we can find to take the reins," Fritz said.

"But that's our first priority," Alan said. "Try not to worry."

"Why not direct it yourself, Alan?" Richard asked. "Anyone else is liable to muck it up."

"Alan will have his hands full fixing the book," Fritz said.

"I appreciate your confidence in me," Alan said. "But be careful what you tell Miss Haber from *Time*. She'll know Moss went to the hospital, but we're not sharing any details."

Richard snorted. "She already told me that in light of Abelard's death and Alan's illness, *Camelot* should be called 'a medical,' not a musical."

"She's a wordsmith," Alan said ruefully. "We'll see that in *Time* before they're finished."

Through the backstage loudspeaker, Bernie Hart called, "Fifteen minutes, ladies and gentlemen. Fifteen minutes till places."

"Well, it's 8 p.m.," Fritz said. "All I can say now is 'Good show!'"

"Yes, indeed," Alan said. "Please, my friends, *don't* break a leg."

Richard and Julie laughed without mirth, then sprinted off to finish dressing.

"I didn't want to mention it," Alan said, "but I'll tell you three, and it's not to leave this room. Kitty called me to her suite at the hotel and told me Moss doesn't want to be replaced."

"How odd," Fritz said. "He's well aware that a ship needs a captain."

"Moss no doubt feels he'll be back with us soon," Alan replied.

"Look at how long it took me to recover from a heart attack," Fritz said. "Let's talk after the show and make a short list of directors."

"Fine, I'll see you on stage," Alan said. "I'll give the cast their notes tonight. But now I better take a seat and watch what's been happening in my absence."

"I'll be at the rear of the house, as usual," Fritz said before tottering off in his lifts.

"He's been ornery in the past," Alan said, "but Moss's crisis and my ulcers are making him impossible. *Camelot* may be our swan song."

"I don't think so, Alan," Brock said. "You know how Fritz gets when he's out of town."

"He's never been this bad," Alan said. "And I know what you're thinking. It's never *been* this bad." He looked at Brock and me. "You two are excused for the evening." And he fled the Green Room as Bernie Hart called, "Ten minutes, ladies and gents. Ten minutes till places."

"You're looking lovely," Brock told me. "You must have a date with Christmas."

"Yes, we're moving past the buddy stage."

He frowned. "Out-of-town flings seldom flourish when the show returns to New York."

"He loves me," I said.

"Like Elsdon loves Wilkins?" he asked. "The man's engaged to a rich society dame, but Sarah nips at his heels like a puppy." He paused. "I should watch tonight, so excuse me."

When my boss stomped away, I felt hurt that Brock was taking out his worries on me. But the overture would start in five minutes, and since I'd received permission from Bernie to view the show from stage left, I entered the wings and saw Richard peeking through the curtain, uttering curses at the audience, just as Nate had described.

I suppressed a giggle because Richard's language was vile, but then he climbed into the huge tree where, as Arthur, he'd spy on Guenevere.

Since Richard hadn't noticed me, I simply stepped into the shadows as the actors took their places. I heard applause out front and assumed Mr. Allers was mounting his podium; and my heart rose like a kite on a breeze as the orchestra began to play. The new music Fritz recently added gave the show a more dynamic start than his original overture.

I heard a spritely drumbeat as Sir Dinadan and Sir Lionel—Nate and my darling Bryce—marched on stage, followed by Merlyn, played by a German actor who wore a fake beard and flowing robe. As the knights left to search for the missing king, Merlyn yelled for Arthur to leave his hiding place, sparking applause when Richard jumped down. After Merlyn berated him for acting childish, he exited, and Arthur sang "I Wonder What the King is Doing Tonight," a witty number that should've evoked laughs from the audience but rarely did.

Before the crowd could applaud at the song's end, Guenevere raced on stage like a gale of wind and sang her wistful first solo, "The Simple Joys of Maidenhood." The audience clapped at Julie's entrance, and by the time Arthur bewitched his future queen with the "Camelot" number, he was barreling toward his "sword in the stone" speech. It ended with his declaration of love before he and Guenevere ran off together.

I sighed with pleasure, having adored this idyllic scene since early rehearsals. The "play within a play" should've been a preview of the alchemy to come, but the show slid downhill from here except for Richard's genius, some funny dialogue, and the singing of Julie, Bobby, Bryce, and Dan. Yet Richard always moved me when he crooned "How to Handle a Woman," and Julie once confided she felt the same way.

During the act-one finale, after Richard gave his "proposition" speech, everyone was rapt, both in the house and the wings where the cast jammed together to listen. As the curtain fell and applause erupted in the theater, I was always surprised to hear the company clapping too.

Richard bowed to his colleagues and loped toward his dressing room, trailed by Julie and Mr. Coote. The ensemble dispersed, most heading stage left where they could take the stairs to the upper floors. But since I'd told Bryce where I'd be standing, he came to find me. "You sounded amazing tonight in the 'Fair' number," I told him.

"Cookie," he said gravely, "you'd better come upstairs."

"What's wrong?" I asked as he pulled me through the wings.

"It's Sarah. She missed the Great Hall scene, and when Dan went to check on her, she was locked in our bathroom, crying and calling for you."

"Sarah wouldn't miss a scene on purpose. She must be in a bad way."

Inside the dressing room, Nate was seated at their vanity, and Dan was kneeling on the floor outside the bathroom. Nate didn't speak, but as Bryce sat with his back to the mirror, Dan stood up and moved, letting me approach the bathroom door. "Sarah's bleeding," he whispered. "That can't be good, right?"

Shrugging at Dan's question, I called, "Sarah, let me in," and the door instantly opened. I found Sarah curled up on the floor, holding her belly.

"I'm having a miscarriage," she wailed. "I felt the urge to pee, and blood came out."

While leaning down to feel her cool brow, she told me she hadn't flushed, so I made myself look in the toilet. Small red clots floated in the water like blobs of paint. "You should lie on the floor and raise your legs up to the toilet seat," I told her.

"I'm going out to call my dad. But try to stay calm. My sister had spotting in early pregnancy, and it was nothing."

"I'm freezing," she said, lifting her legs to the commode. "Can you get a blanket?"

Back in the dressing room, Bernie Hart was calling, "Ten minutes, ladies and gents. Ten minutes till places for act two" over the intercom. I asked Dan to take the spread off the daybed and cover Sarah.

"Did she—lose the baby?" he asked while grabbing the coverlet.

"I don't think so," I said. "But she should stay off her feet. Look, when you three go down for act two, could someone tell Bernie that Sarah's ill and has to leave? My dad's a doctor, so I'll try to reach him. If he says it's all right, I'll take her to my hotel room."

Bryce had already changed into his long tunic for act two. "I'll tell Bernie about Sarah and cancel our reservation for dinner."

"We'll never have a date," I moaned before running to the pay phone near the elevator. Since cast members were lurking in the hall, however, I dashed downstairs to the security desk, asking to make an emergency phone call. While my father was giving me his opinion, the actors were called to the stage for act two. When I returned to Sarah's side, she muttered, "What did Dr. Conroy say?"

"He said many women have breakthrough bleeding in the first trimester. But he's going to make some calls in the morning and try to make an appointment for you with an OB, even though tomorrow's Sunday." I gave her my hand. "Let's get you up."

Sarah eased her legs off the toilet seat and stood, shivering. "Bernie Hart talked about me over the intercom," she said. "He announced I was sick and had to leave."

The lively opening notes of the Entr'acte spilled through

the loudspeaker. "Why don't I go to the chorus room and get your stuff," I said. "I'll come right back, and we'll take a cab to my hotel. You should stay with me tonight."

"Thanks, Jane. I'm so—" She choked up, and her words trailed off.

"Tell me something, Sarah. Did anything happen before you began to bleed?"

"Dan and I had words. He won't end his engagement, so I'll have no choice but to go home to my parents. My plan to live with you was selfish. You have a life of your own. You shouldn't be saddled with my mistake."

"Periods get delayed," I said. "Maybe you're not even pregnant."

By the time *Camelot's* curtain came down, Sarah was dozing in one of my twin beds, wearing a borrowed nightgown. When someone knocked, I found Elsdon on my doorstep. "Forgive me for intruding," he said. "I had to check on her."

I stepped aside and watched the actor bend over Sarah and tenderly stroke her cheek.

"You know something, Dan," I said. "You're a bit of a lad, but for what it's worth, my dad thinks Sarah and the baby will be fine. *If* there's a baby."

"Thanks, Jane. Look, I'll be in my room if you need anything. Don't hesitate to ask. And by the way, Bryce is concerned. But he's not going to call so he doesn't disturb Sarah."

I passed a restless night and was up, dressed, and drinking coffee by 7 a.m. The phone presently rang, and my father said he'd arranged for Sarah to see a Toronto OB at noon. This was a monumental favor, so I said, "I owe you, Dad."

"Let me know the outcome," he said. "With these new HCG tests, the doctor can give Sarah an answer today." He laughed drily. "Don't let this happen to you, Jane dear."

I felt relieved when I hung up, knowing our suspense would end soon. Thankfully, there was no show today, and I hoped Sarah would feel well enough to rehearse Monday afternoon and perform at night.

Since my friend was asleep, I took the elevator down to Bryce's room, where he greeted me dressed and smelling of Canoe. "How's our girl?" he asked, stepping back so I could enter.

"I'm taking her to the doctor later," I said, seeing his room for the first time. It was neater than mine, as though he'd just checked in.

"Well, you're here now," he said, "and we have unfinished business from last night."

"We do," I said before Bryce gave me a long, lingering kiss. He tasted of toothpaste and coffee, and, without warning, he swooped me into his arms and carried me to his bed, tossing me onto his barely rumpled sheets.

<hr />

My hope of having a Sunday date with Bryce was scuttled when Brock ordered me to attend a meeting with Alan, Fritz, and "a mystery guest." The team asked me to take notes, and it seemed ironic when the four of us departed for La Chaumière, the French restaurant where Bryce and I were heading the night Alan's ulcers sent him to the ER.

We took a cab across town, stopping before a white brick house with casement windows. The place held a labyrinth of dining rooms, and the *Camelot* party was ushered to a table for six near a fire in a marble hearth. I spied white linen cloths, hurricane lamps with white tapers, white roses, and white-and-gold china flecked with pink roses and green leaves, the Limoges pattern my grandmother owned. Wall sconces threw off ocher light, and I dearly wished I was there with Bryce, his warm hand cradling mine.

"Are you still with us, Jane?" Brock asked, and I noticed the men were waiting for me to sit before they took their chairs.

"How is Miss Wilkins?" Fritz asked after we ordered drinks. "She's one of our best sopranos, and she missed act two last night."

"Just a stomach bug," I replied.

(The obstetrician had examined Sarah and believed she was newly pregnant. After he took urine and blood, he ran a test and called two hours later to confirm his diagnosis. He assured Sarah that first-trimester bleeding was nothing to worry about, advising her to rest with her feet up whenever possible. Otherwise, she was free to continue her activities.)

"I've heard Moss is holding his own," Alan said, "but I've had no luck finding a replacement yet."

"Keep looking," Fritz said.

We were presently joined by a balding man, probably in his late fifties, who wore thick black glasses like Alan's. My bosses stood, and the men shook hands; then Brock gestured toward me, saying, "Philip Burton, I'd like to introduce my assistant, Jane Conroy."

"The Other Burton," as I dubbed him, leaned down and extended a moist paw, then took a seat. A waiter removed the sixth place setting, so everyone could spread out, and took Burton's drink order. "Philip is Richard's father," Alan told me. "Also a fine director in his own right."

"Why, thank you," the Other Burton said, blinking twice.

"I heard you gave Richard notes on Friday," Alan affably continued. "He was inspired at the Saturday matinee and evening shows."

"I thought so, too," the Other Burton mumbled. "I saw both."

"I'm sure you have thoughts on the book," Fritz said.

"Perhaps the music also."

"Music isn't my purview," the Other Burton said. "I did take the liberty of making some comments on a spare script Richard gave me. I hope you don't think that's presumptuous, Alan."

"Not at all," Fritz assured him.

But when Alan smiled, he set his jaw, and I knew he was offended. The waiter broke the tension by delivering the drinks, and Brock gave a toast to *Camelot*.

Wrinkling his brow while accepting Burton's annotated script, Alan said, "Ah, here are the hors d'oeuvres."

Appetizers of all kinds arrived on a silver cart, everything from escargot, stuffed mushrooms, and stuffed olives to pureed cottage cheese with scallions and cognac, marinated anchovies, and quenelles of shrimp. But my stomach ached, so I stuck with the mushrooms.

"The reason I wanted to chat with you isn't about the show per se," the Other Burton said. "In point of fact, I'm worried about Richard's emotional health. He's vastly upset about Moss Hart's illness, and he's worried about his singing. He needs more support, you might say."

"But he's doing well," Alan said. "He didn't seem upset when we told him about Moss."

Burton blinked again, reminding me of an owl. "He's the star of your show. He wants to be a tower of strength for his colleagues, but deep down, he has misgivings."

"Thanks for passing on your impressions," Fritz said. "We'll—make sure he's happy."

"I suppose you think the show is overly long," Alan said.

"I'm afraid I do," the Other Burton replied before swallowing some anchovies.

"Don't be afraid," Alan said, putting his fork down and lighting a cigarette. "It *is* long."

Brock stopped eating. "Yes, but having a chance to work

out the kinks is why we go out of town."

"Maybe Nathan Cohen was right," Alan said. "Maybe I sent the show on a fool's errand from the first scene." He muttered, "Excuse me," rose from his seat, and zipped away.

"I apologize if I distressed Mr. Lerner," the Other Burton mumbled.

"You didn't, dear boy," Fritz said. "His ulcers must be paining him."

Brock and I exchanged glances, then resumed eating. It was a long time before Alan returned, and the rest of the meal went smoothly. Philip regaled them with tales of Richard's youthful triumphs on the British stage, but I left La Chaumière feeling that while the Other Burton had helped us by mentioning Richard's "misgivings," he'd also inflamed Alan's worries.

--------♦--------

For the next two days, I spent a kind of honeymoon with Bryce, sharing ecstatic moments between 11:30 p.m. and 8 a.m. Castmates invited us to go drinking, but we kept to ourselves, ordering late-night meals from room service and scorching our sheets with passion.

Though not a virgin, I was a novice, which became clear after Bryce and I had sex the first time. My college boyfriend had deflowered me but hadn't worried about my satisfaction. Intercourse had been such a letdown back then, I'd begun to believe that female pleasure was a myth, and I gave up screwing Billy out of boredom and disappointment.

I didn't reverse my opinion until I heard myself shrieking in Bryce's dressing room that first time. I'd never had an orgasm before, and I feared my initial one was a fluke, like the eruption of an inert volcano. But it happened again and again, whenever we got naked, though never in the same way. Bryce was skillful and ardent, and seemed wild about the way I looked, smelled, and warmed to his touch. And since I longed to please him, I asked what he liked, and he happily confessed his wants.

Maybe the biggest surprise was that by the time Bryce stripped off his clothes—and mine—I was primed for the sacred moment when he'd push inside. I felt closest to him then, so close that when we were apart, I missed him with a physical ache, as though part of me had been torn away. I now got butterflies watching him on stage, knowing he'd be mine again when the curtain came down, and I also viscerally felt Guenevere's misery. The queen had never had the thrill of being possessed by Lancelot, and yet she was punished for cheating on Arthur. Strangely, I wished they'd forget the script at least once and have one another before Mordred burst in, a notion that was so crazy I realized I was living in a desire-sodden haze.

It was becoming harder to withhold what I knew about the producers' plans. I wasn't supposed to share this stuff with anyone, and I worried I'd accidentally tell Bryce in bed when my guard was down.

More than once, Brock remarked that I looked "radiant," and I feared that anyone else observing me would figure out why. I also had trouble concentrating, which was the result of being besotted. I was tempted to ask Sarah if she felt the same about Dan, but I cherished the intensity of my new feelings and wanted to keep them private. (I knew this phase wouldn't last. How could it?)

⬤◆⬤

On Thursday afternoon, the company was called in to rehearse some changes for the end of act two. Alan had cut a riveting scene in the king's study in which Arthur and Mordred argued about Guenevere's fate and Mordred threatened to destroy everything his father held dear. Alan left in bits of dialogue, adding these to the "Guenevere" number, and he also rewrote verses of that song which Bryce, Dan, and the chorus had to learn.

That afternoon Alan also told the cast he was freezing the show until Boston. "We're still running too long, but we're not changing anything for the public."

On Friday around 3 p.m., as I watched the retooled "Guenevere," Brock called me to the lobby and gave me an envelope. "We need you to bring this to Moss," he said. "He can't have visitors except Kitty, but Alan got special permission. We're asking you to go, Jane, because he's less likely to grill you. If you discuss the show, keep it light. We don't want to upset him. And if he asks if we're replacing him, tell him you don't know." He sighed. "Not that we've had much luck with the directors Alan's pursued so far."

"Right," I said, glad I'd brought my coat and purse to the lobby. "I'm on my way."

Wellesley Hospital was a nine-minute cab ride from the O'Keefe, but who would've dreamed its proximity would be a boon to *Camelot*? I had this mournful thought while ambling down a long hall on the fourth floor. After passing the nurses' station, I found Moss's private room, which was speckled with sunlight. He was sitting up in bed wearing his reading glasses, with a book on his lap. The nurses had removed his oxygen tent, which Brock had mentioned to me, but he was still hooked up to several IVs. He looked wan but alert.

"How lovely to see you, Jane," he said, as though I'd entered his hotel suite for a cocktail party. "Alan said you'd be dropping by."

Feeling shy, I walked over and gave him the envelope.

"Thank you, dear girl," he said, setting his delivery on his swing table where the nurses had placed a water pitcher and cups. "Sit down and talk. I'm lonely."

"How are you feeling?" I asked, fighting panic as I dragged a metal chair close to his bed. *Don't say the wrong thing.*

"Not too bad." He shrugged. "How does the show look? Any shorter?"

"Much. They've cut twenty-five minutes, including your cuts. It's tighter."

"I feel like a wretch for leaving all of you in the lurch."

"We miss you," I assured him. "But everyone's trying to cope."

"How's Bobby?" he asked.

"The same. But when he sings, does anybody notice?"

Moss chuckled softly. "I got so frustrated with Goulet, I didn't do him any favors, and believe me, I regret not taking him in hand in New York. But maybe it's for the best that I'm off his back. I might've destroyed his confidence, and who knows? He might shine when he gets his sea legs." After a pause, he said, "We never had that chat about you, did we, Jane?"

"Oh, Moss, I'd feel wrong doing that now."

"You're very capable. Do you still want a theater career after *Camelot*?"

"More than ever," I said. "It's a nuttier world than I imagined when I was in college. But the ups and downs make it thrilling. It's like that toboggan ride you mentioned in *Act One*."

(I'd read his memoir on September nights when rehearsals had left me too tense to sleep.)

"I almost forgot that metaphor," he murmured. "I still think it's apt."

"After watching you in action, I think I'd like to direct. I stage-managed in college and directed two short plays, and although it's a long shot for women, I'm intrigued by the idea."

Oh God, I wanted to flee. I hadn't known I felt this way until the words spilled out, and it seemed likely that Moss

Hart, playwright and director extraordinaire, would tell me I was presumptuous. But I had to sit there waiting for his response.

"I can name several ambitious women who've directed on Broadway and elsewhere," he said. "There will be more, and since I've asked Alan not to replace me, you should seize any opportunities you can. In Boston, for instance, you might ask to work with the new Tom of Warwick or volunteer to take understudy rehearsals. Brock Remsen respects you, and if you make yourself indispensable to him, you'll reduce his stress and build your resume."

"Oh, Moss," I said. "I've never told another person this idea."

"My advice is *don't* tell people. You'll hear all the reasons you should become a wife instead. My one caveat is to make sure you and your romantic partners are on the same page. Men can marry and have children and leave town with impunity. Women have it much harder. They're judged by a double standard."

Stunned by his open-mindedness, I stood. "I should let you rest, but thank you so much for your encouragement. I hope you'll be back with us soon."

"Have no fear," he said drowsily. "You haven't seen the last of me."

He began to breathe heavily as he slept, and I felt sad knowing Moss Hart would likely disappear from my life. But I felt grateful for his wisdom and support. And since the company's travel day was Sunday and I'd fly to Boston with Brock while my boyfriend took the train, I'd have time to plan how to make myself "indispensable," as Moss suggested.

At the hospital's main entrance, I came upon Kitty Hart as she walked through the automatic doors. "Jane, dear," Kitty called.

"Alan told me you were coming. How's Moss?"

"I left him dozing," I said, admiring Kitty's thick brown hair, coiffed in a short, teased style with "wings" at both sides. She wore a belted tweed suit, gloves, and brown pumps and carried a Chanel bag with the intertwined Cs. "Mrs. Hart, I planned to call you." I continued. "I—well, I need your help. And since Moss is sleeping, could you have coffee with me? There's a place across the street."

"Let's," Kitty said. "Moss likes you, and I've hardly shared two words with you in New York or Toronto. I fear we're not going to Boston." Her eyes filled with tears, and I took her arm. We walked to Café Colette, where I'd planned to meet Bryce on the morning of Alan's discharge. After ordering at the counter, I bought two coffees to the small table where Kitty was glancing mournfully out the window. "This must be so hard for you and your children," I said, placing the steaming mugs on the wooden tabletop.

"You know what the hardest thing is?" Kitty asked, using a paper napkin to dab her moist brown eyes. "Getting answers I can understand from the doctors here. Trust me, Jane, it's a nightmare. Either I miss the physician on call, or he dashes in, barks a few words I can't decipher, and leaves. And I wind up not knowing my husband's condition."

"I might have a solution," I said, sitting across from her. "If you authorize my father to call Moss's doctor here, he can get the straight scoop and you can talk to him."

"Your father?" Kitty asked, raising thickly penciled eyebrows.

"My dad's a D.C. cardiologist. He understands what it's like for the spouses of heart patients, and he's used to explaining complex medical facts."

"And he wouldn't mind?" Kitty asked, sounding dubious. "Isn't this a lot to ask?"

"Well, a simpler way would be to persuade Moss's nurse

to write out what's on his chart. Then make a list of questions for my dad. I'll come to your suite and call him and put you on. Then I'll make myself scarce, and you can ask him anything you want."

"Oh, Jane," Kitty said, her face lighting up. "If you're sure your father would be willing, how about tonight? I'll go upstairs and get the details now. Could you be at my suite at seven?"

"That should work," I said. "My dad comes home early on Fridays."

Kitty took a sip of coffee before pushing her cup away. "You said you need my help?"

"Yours or Mrs. Lerner's. I gather you both operate in the same circle."

Kitty laughed drily. "Yes, but I'd avoid Alan's wife if I were you. She somehow got the impression you and Alan had a fling when she was in Europe."

"Alan's never looked at me cross-eyed or any other woman except Mrs. Lerner."

"That's what Moss and I told her," Kitty replied. "Now, what can I do for you?"

Reeling from Kitty's absurd comment about Alan and me, I said, "My friend Sarah Wilkins is in the chorus. She got in trouble with Dan Elsdon, and since she was a virgin, there's no doubt the baby's his. But he's engaged to a friend of Mrs. Lerner's, Dominique Biddle."

"I know Dominique well," Kitty said. "She's my neighbor. She's immensely wealthy and awfully pretty. And I'm sure she'll be horrified to hear this news. You see, Dan will be her third husband, and she's unable to bear children, which is her biggest sorrow. That said, I think she knows he's unfaithful out of town."

"It didn't happen out of town. Dan seduced Sarah in New York during rehearsals."

"I see. Well, in Dominique's moral universe, that might be a hanging offense." Kitty laughed. "Why, Miss Conroy, you naughty girl. You want me to spill the beans so Mrs. Biddle will end her engagement, clearing the way for your *enceinte* chum."

"Exactly, because Dan cares for Sarah." I suddenly recalled the tender way he'd stroked her face while she slept in my room. "But he needs a nudge to break up with his fiancée."

"I'll talk to her," Kitty said. "Dominique should know she's marrying a cad." Kitty tapped my hand like a schoolmarm. "But, darling, your plan could backfire."

"I know. And Sarah deserves better than Dan. But a baby needs two parents."

"I couldn't agree more." Kitty grabbed her gloves and Chanel purse. "I'd better see Moss's nurse so I'll be prepared to speak with Dr. Conroy."

"He's Owen. And I'll see you at seven, Mrs. Hart."

"Kitty," she said, rising. "And thank you, Jane. I'll feel better if I know what to expect."

I watched Kitty Hart cross the street, hoping I'd done the right thing by asking her to intervene in Sarah's crisis. Brock had called me a "schemer" at my interview, and maybe I was. But what was the harm in using my small bit of influence to help my friend and her baby?

Drinking my coffee, I recalled my Irish great-grandma's favorite saying: "If wishes were horses, beggars would ride." Yet Sarah was no beggar, and despite her error in judgment, she might ride into the sunset with Dan if this Biddle woman decided an out-of-wedlock Elsdon baby would be inconvenient.

I felt optimistic after my chats with Moss and Kitty, and since it was a lovely fall day with azure skies and cream-puff clouds, I decided to walk back to my hotel. Passing shops and restaurants, I mused that my time in Toronto had fundamentally changed my life. I'd formed my first serious relationship and was hatching a daring plan for my career. It might be nice to stay in town longer and savor my growth on both fronts.

Well, we were off to Boston, and whatever happened there, I was sure Bryce and I would fall more deeply in love. As for *Camelot*, the show's future depended on Alan, and I couldn't guess how he'd juggle the loss of Moss's steady hand and the pressure of fixing his long, unfocused book. The company grapevine reported that veteran members of the ensemble feared our show might close before it reached New York. But I hoped they were wrong.

I prayed I'd still have a job a month from now.

PART THREE

During *Camelot's* four weeks in Boston, Julie Andrews thought Alan and Fritz were "the loneliest men in town."

- From the *TIME* cover story on Lerner and Loewe, November 14, 1960

9.
THE OTHER BURTON TURNS UP

Bryce

Two things were clear to Bryce on Monday, October 24th, as he checked into his room at the Parker House, the old Boston hotel where the Parker House roll was invented. First, he was madly in love with Jane after their last week in Toronto. Other than choral rehearsals and evening shows, they'd spent every moment together, and he believed that when they got back to New York, they'd start shopping for an engagement ring. It was happening fast, but he was certain. While the sexual side was spectacular, their bond felt deeper and richer than just physical fulfillment. Jane was "the one." In the words of Oscar Hammerstein, a diehard romantic, "Once you have found her, never let her go," and Bryce planned to heed this advice.

Second, he had to accept the glaring signs that *Camelot* seemed as doomed as Arthur's Round Table. He believed this because, after the final bows in Toronto, he and Jane had gone to a cast party at the Franz Josef restaurant. In a private corner as they ate Viennese pastry, Jane said, "Please don't tell anyone, but Alan's torn between the wishes of Moss, who doesn't want to be replaced, and Fritz, who wants a new director. Brock says Alan is paralyzed, and he's back to popping pills, which is how his ulcers began. Well, pills and his troubled marriage."

That evening Bryce said he thought married life would be hard with the imperious Mrs. Lerner, who'd recently asked him to watch Chouchou again so she could run around Toronto with the *Time* researcher. (He'd complied but declined payment, hoping to earn Alan's goodwill for being a sport.) In the meantime, he'd heard Joyce Haber would join them in Boston, which had to be a bad wrinkle. The woman seemed ruthless, and he worried her article would wind up being another nail in the coffin of their show.

He sat on his saggy double bed, thinking the Lerners' marital angst might determine whether *Camelot* closed in Boston. Alan might also flounder without Moss Hart. Should Bryce call Mr. Sardi and ask if he could wait tables again for the Christmas season? Jane wouldn't care; she'd begun to grasp the truth of Tallulah Bankhead's quip about theater jobs. But would her father, a D.C. doctor, welcome a waiter into his family? A featured actor in a Broadway musical might impress Dr. Conroy, but even that was a stretch since professionals often cast a jaundiced eye on performers.

Bryce felt his old insecurity gnawing at his self-esteem. He could hear his own father's reedy voice, exhorting him to choose a reliable career over "the vagaries of show business." He rubbed his mustache, then picked up the phone on his night table and placed a station-to-station call to the Ashley-Steiner Agency. When Andy Carver's secretary patched him through, Bryce asked his agent to be on the lookout for new opportunities.

"Are you serious?" Andy asked. "You're in the hottest show of the season." But after Bryce outlined *Camelot's* woes, Andy replied, "Bryce, I wasn't going to tell you yet, but you're up for the romantic lead in another new musical. The producers saw you in Toronto and think you're ideal. This one opens in April, and Cyril Ritchard is directing. Interested?"

"Definitely," Bryce said, feeling calmer after he hung up.

Yet he wasn't pleased with his cramped room overlooking School Street. The wallpaper was peeling, and the place stank of cigarettes. According to a pamphlet he'd found on his bureau, the Parker House was built in the 1920s on the site of an 1855 hotel, and he hoped to spend little time here. But one of the city's main streets, Tremont, was around the corner, and if he walked south along Boston Common, he would quickly reach *Camelot's* next venue, the historic Shubert Theatre.

It seemed inconvenient that Jane was lodging clear across town at the Ritz-Carlton, where Lerner and Loewe had suites along with Richard, Julie, Roddy, Bobby, and Robert Coote. Most of the ensemble was farmed out to modest hotels, but he and Dan were neighbors, which Bryce learned after bumping into Elsdon down the hall. Dan stopped him to confide that Sarah had quit the show after another bleeding mishap.

"Jane told me she flew from Toronto to her parents' home in Albany," Bryce said. "I gather she's confined to bed." He felt increasingly disgusted with Elsdon, who once confessed he hadn't used condoms and feared he'd wrecked Sarah's promising career. This was sad since on the day the girl auditioned at the New Amsterdam, Bryce thought her sparkling coloratura resembled the voice of Beverly Sills, an impression he'd later passed along. Sarah had laughed and murmured, "Not a chance," a refreshingly humble response. But the poor thing lacked the sense to pour piss out of a boot. Who slept around without using birth control?

"I'm fond of Sarah," Dan told Bryce. "But I may not see her again unless—"

"You call off your engagement?" Bryce asked.

"Let's just say I'm reviewing my options."

"You have one option, Elsdon," Bryce said. "Look, I'm not trying to bust your balls, but if you shirk your responsibility toward a girl you got in trouble, you're not worth spit."

"This may come as a surprise, Yuletide," Dan said, "but I

agree with you." Then he slipped into his room and slammed the door, leaving Bryce to wonder how things would turn out.

Jane called at 5 p.m. to announce she had to attend a dinner meeting in Alan's suite with Brock and Fritz. "I'm in room 1125. How about if you come over at ten? I can't wait."

"Neither can I," Bryce said. "Is there rehearsal tomorrow?"

"There's a tech run-through Wednesday at ten," she said. "The crew's having fits with the set. The O'Keefe was too big, but the Shubert's too small." She sighed. "And now I have to run."

After Jane hung up, Bryce heard his stomach growl, but he waited until 6 p.m. before heading to Dini's Seafood Grill, dubbed "a Boston classic" by his hotel desk clerk. The November night was cold, and he could see his breath, but this block of Tremont was part of the Freedom Trail, and he enjoyed passing the Gothic church called King's Chapel and its old graveyard. He'd never been to Boston before, and he liked the feel of it right off.

He soon reached Dini's, which had a large, unfussy dining room with maple chairs and white Formica table tops. He was seated at a deuce along a maple partition and was sipping a Heineken when Roddy McDowall came in. Looking dapper in a blue blazer, silk paisley ascot, and tan slacks, the star was alone, so Bryce stood and waved. He hadn't shared more than a word with McDowall in New York or Toronto, but Roddy cheerfully joined him, saying, "Did you hear the latest? They might fire Bobby."

A wiry waiter dashed over to take Roddy's drink order, then raced away. Startled by his colleague's bombshell, Bryce asked, "Why would they do that?"

"Whenever a show doesn't work out of town, they look for

ways to make improvements, and they think his acting is weak." He shrugged. "Well, you won't have an issue. You're great as Lionel *and* Lancelot. Maybe they'll ask you to replace Goulet."

"I wouldn't feel good profiting from Bobby's troubles," Bryce said. "But I'm a big fan of yours. You're downright scary as Mordred, and I admired you on Broadway in *Look After Lulu.*"

"You're one of the few who saw *Lulu,*" Roddy said. "It closed in a month. But playing Mordred is a hoot. And contrary to the naysayers, we'll make it to Broadway."

"Who's gunning for Bobby, anyway?" Bryce asked as Roddy's martini arrived.

"I heard Alan spoke with Moss by phone, and they concurred. But it's absurd. I think Alan should own up to the real problem: his book." Roddy glanced at the menu. "I have no idea what scrod is, but Boston's known for it, so I'll give it a try. When in Rome, eh?"

"I'll try it, too," Bryce said, surprised to be dining with one of his boyhood idols. He liked Roddy's perspective, but felt concerned for Bobby and hoped the crisis would blow over.

As the waiter brought bread and butter, Roddy yakked about his Hollywood friends, namely Elizabeth Taylor and Gregory Peck. Though he was neither arrogant nor boastful, he entertained Bryce with tales as smooth as sea glass, no doubt refined by repetition. Bryce wasn't eager to admit he'd spent years waiting tables between summer stock and regional roles, so after they ordered a second drink, he asked Roddy about *Lulu's* director, the same star his agent mentioned. "Is Cyril Ritchard nice to work with?"

"He's a delight," Roddy said. "A prince of the theater like Moss Hart. He's also a devout Catholic who goes to daily Mass, much the way Moss sees his psychiatrist."

"Whatever gets them through the insanity of the business," Bryce said.

After they finished their entrees and ordered brandies, Roddy asked Bryce about his background. They split the check and left Dini's at 9:45 p.m., and Bryce assumed Roddy would accompany him to the Ritz. But the star explained he had an engagement, and as Roddy walked south, Bryce guessed he was meeting some gay castmates in the Combat Zone, the red-light district whose clubs reputedly catered to all tastes. Feeling a buzz from two Heinekens and a Hennessy, Bryce hailed a taxi since he wasn't sure Boston Common was safe at night.

The cab cruised past small stores and coffee shops along Tremont, passing the corner of Boylston where the Colonial Theater marquee advertised *All the Way Home,* another show on its way to Broadway. The driver soon turned right, then took a sharp right onto Charles, passing Boylston again, then speeding between the Common and the Public Garden. It wasn't long before the cab stopped on Arlington Street in front of the renowned Ritz-Carlton.

A doorman in a navy uniform opened Bryce's door, and he glanced at the Garden with its wrought-iron fencing and quaint Victorian street lamps. He cleared the Ritz's gold revolving doors and ran up marble stairs, passing a dark-paneled bar and the Firestone and Parsons jewelry store. In the carpeted hallway, he stopped in front of a grand staircase on one side and a set of elevators on the other. Ahead was the lobby and the reception desk, where the staff wore black-cutaway jackets. Bryce was glad he'd donned a tie, dress shirt, and khaki slacks with his leather jacket; otherwise, they might've kicked him out.

Hopping on the elevator, he hoped Jane would be waiting. When he found her room on the 11th floor, however, the door was locked, and he felt conspicuous loafing in the hall. He retraced his steps and cooled his heels on a bench in the foyer. Jane presently showed up, looking pale. "Tough day, Cookie?" he asked, standing up.

She dove into his arms and began to sniffle. Pulling away, she took Bryce's hand and led him down the hall. They entered a suite high above the Garden's treetops, with a shimmery skyline straight ahead featuring the neon sign for the Parker House. (Had Brock arranged these plush accommodations? A Gal Friday would normally lodge with a minion on the production team, and Bryce recalled Rina's catty speculation about how Jane got her job.)

"I have no idea how I got a suite," she said, reading his mind. "It's one of the few without a working fireplace, but we'll enjoy it, yes?"

He nodded since everything from the light fixtures to the drapes looked expensive and new. He peeled off his jacket, thinking Jane must be the producers' pet.

She curled up on a sofa in the parlor, and Bryce inquired if he could bring her anything. She asked for club soda, pointing to a bottle on her dresser, and he poured the warm fizzy water into a glass before joining her. She took a sip, saying, "Sorry for the tears before. Changes are coming so fast, I can't keep up."

"Roddy McDowall told me they might fire Goulet," Bryce said.

"That's on the table, apparently. And Alan spent part of yesterday and all of today calling every director he knows. He thinks the word's out in New York and Hollywood that *Camelot's* a dud. Who'd want to take over and risk hurting their reputation?"

"Not many," Bryce said.

"He'll continue searching to please Fritz, but Brock will direct for the short run. Alan hopes to write all day tomorrow, so we may have new scenes to rehearse after the tech on Wednesday." Jane smiled. "I asked to work with the two new kids playing Tom of Warwick and Alan gave me permission. Isn't that neat? I'll get directing experience."

"You want to direct?" Bryce asked. "Since when?"

"I was inspired watching Moss. Hey, I know it's a long shot, but what do you think?"

"Well, I haven't heard of many women directors. That doesn't mean—"

"I spoke with Moss at the hospital, and he encouraged me. But he warned me that my partners would need to be on board, or it wouldn't work."

"It's your call, Cookie, but maybe we should get through Boston before worrying about what's next." He leaned over and placed his mouth against hers. "Lordy, I needed that," he said, pulling away.

"Me, too," she said. "Our meeting tonight was grim. Nobody raised his voice, but Fritz thinks Alan is being loyal to Moss at the show's expense, and Alan feels defensive. Brock's afraid for Alan's health, so we got nowhere."

"Can you believe I had dinner with Roddy?" Bryce said. "He's the real thing."

"That's what everyone says," Jane said with a yawn. "Do you mind if we go to bed without—the usual? I'm wiped out."

"I'm beat myself," Bryce said, though he wanted to make love to Jane until she forgot everything but him. But he excused himself and took shelter in the bathroom where he mused that directors traveled from theater to theater, often outside New York. Like stage management and company management, directing was not especially conducive to family life.

Then again, neither was acting.

He unwrapped a fresh toothbrush he removed from his pants pocket. While scrubbing his teeth, he decided he'd underestimated Jane. Theater was a passion they shared, but he'd assumed she'd quit working when they tied the knot. He was mistaken, and he wondered if he should spell out his worries and discourage all talk of directing. Was he tolerant enough to marry someone whose career might compete with his? He'd hoped to take Jane on the road, assuming he toured again, until they had a child or two. But now he recalled how she'd treated Alan's son when they babysat, ignoring the boy and letting Bryce do everything.

Okay, this is what he got for falling head over heels without discussing the essentials beforehand. (If she didn't want kids, he wasn't sure their relationship could survive.)

Feeling tense, he emerged from the bathroom and was surprised to find his ladylove lying naked on an enormous bed, propped on one arm like a temptress. "I got my second wind," she said. "Are you up for some fun?"

Smiling, Bryce began peeling off his clothes. He decided to worry about potential conflicts later. For all he knew, her interest in directing would evaporate as reality set in.

When he was naked, he gazed at her body, his mouth nearly watering. He'd been with women who satisfied him, but they'd acted relieved when intercourse was over, as though they'd bravely endured a root canal. Few girls had been as responsive to his roving hands or as relaxed when he thrust inside. Sex with Jane was nothing short of a revelation.

Later, when both of them were lying together, limbs entwined, she said, "I thought I'd be embarrassed if someone did that to me, but it felt natural." She grimaced. "Is it all right—uh, down there?"

"Beautiful," he said, leaning over to kiss her. She looked so delectably unkempt, hair flying everywhere, lips swollen. Sexy as all get out.

"Too bad Lancelot and Guenevere couldn't have this," she said.

"Lance goes to her chamber with mischief on his mind. Then Guenevere mentions Arthur and kills the mood." Bryce chortled. "Hell, Cookie, who are we kidding? Lerner doesn't let them do the deed because Julie Andrews isn't that kind of gal."

"That's the reason?" Jane asked, grinning.

"It has to be. T.H. White makes it clear that Lance and Guenevere sleep together."

Jane yawned. "I feel naive compared to you."

Bryce laughed again, turning out the light. As Jane crawled into his arms, he felt utterly content. When she dozed off, making funny little sleep sounds, he warned himself to stay neutral about her directing ambitions. A conventional wife and mother might be dull, whereas Jane Conroy was unpredictable. Marriage to her would always be an adventure.

Jane

I left Bryce in my bed, concluding it was sometimes better to give than receive. Before he was fully awake, I'd burrowed under the covers and made him moan with pleasure. Then I'd brushed my teeth, showered, and dressed before calling room service. The nice part of having a suite was that the waiters didn't see my guest, though I ordered coffee and muffins for two. After a quick breakfast, I grabbed my belongings and hung the Do Not Disturb sign on my door.

On the sidewalk outside the Ritz, I surveyed the Public Garden, which had a sheen from the morning sun, and promised myself to explore the grounds. This was my first trip to Boston, and I hoped to see more of the city than my route to and from the Shubert. After the doorman hailed a taxi, I enjoyed a glimpse of Boston's theater district, which featured the Colonial on Boylston and the Majestic and the Wilbur on Tremont, as well as the historic house down the block where we'd spend the next month.

The cab dropped me outside the Shubert with its marble and glass canopy and high arch above "Palladian windows" on the second floor—I'd read about its design. Unlike the immense modern O'Keefe, the Shubert, dating to 1910, appeared small and narrow. Next door was a restaurant, the Paddock Café, with picture windows, and just beyond was a liquor store, a corner deli, and the alley leading to the stage door.

I slipped through one of six doors into the foyer with its box office behind grilles and entered the lobby with Victorian murals, crystal chandeliers, marble walls, red carpeting, and a built-in refreshment counter. The sound of hammering leaked through the theater's open doors, and once inside, I beheld a gem of a playhouse with 1,500 red-velvet seats in the orchestra, mezzanine, and balcony. It boasted marble boxes at the mezz level and more chandeliers, but the place was intimate compared to the O'Keefe, which could hold twice as many patrons.

I watched techies with beer bellies huddling downstage while listening to the commands of Oliver Smith. Abe Feder stood upstage, calling to men on ladders who were setting lights. Feeling cheerful, I returned to the lobby and ran down the steep stairs to the ladies' lounge.

Brock was waiting in a small powder room with Garry Whitson, who'd play Tom of Warwick, and Rufus Devane, his understudy. Both boys, skinny and baby-faced, were about fourteen, and they stared at the carpet as Brock said, "Miss Jane's going to coach you today. And when she thinks you've done enough, she'll take you to the deli for ice cream." Then he addressed me. "Afterward, walk them to the Parker House. Their moms will be waiting."

"Sure thing," I said before he asked for a private word.

"I'll be in the lobby with Julie and Richard," he said when we'd moved across the room. "We're doing act one, scene three, while Alan writes lyrics for Roddy. Don't forget you have a lunch meeting with Lerner and Loewe."

After Brock sprinted upstairs, I asked the boys to sit on a loveseat while I opened the script. "I'll be playing the king today," I said. "I know I'm a poor stand-in for Mr. Burton."

"We're not important enough to rehearse with him," Garry said.

"You're important," I said. "You'll rehearse with him another day."

"My mum says he drinks like a fish," Garry said.

"My mum says he chases skirts," Rufus said. "Whatever that means."

"Hold on," I said. "Mr. Burton is the star of our show, and you're *never* to comment on his personal life. Now let's start with you, Garry. Go over near the stairs. Pretend you're in the wings, and when I say your cue, enter. In a few moments, Rufus, you'll do the same."

The character of Tom had sixteen lines in the last scene of *Camelot*. He proudly told the king he'd stowed away on a boat as Arthur and his knights were leaving to fight Lancelot's army. Tom bragged that he wanted to kill a lot of men to defend the Round Table. The king was stunned to learn this heroic boy had never met a knight but had only heard of their bravery and their motto, "might for right." Arthur requested Tom's name and hometown, knighting him on the spot. Then he ordered "Sir Tom of Warwick" to run behind the lines—and live—and tell everyone he met about Camelot. As the war began, Arthur told Pellinore he'd won his battle, believing history would remember his achievements.

The scene's power got to me whenever I watched Richard, but as I worked with Garry and Rufus, I realized that neither boy brought conviction to his lines. After Rufus made his mock exit, I asked whether they had read T.H. White's novel.

"My mum says that book is for adults," Garry said.

"My mum says that, also," Rufus added.

"Let's sit again for a moment," I suggested.

"Are we done?" Garry asked as the pair returned to the loveseat.

"Not yet," I said, claiming an adjacent chair. "Have you both seen *Peter Pan*? The Disney version that played in the movies."

"I saw that," Garry said. "In the *cinema*."

"Me, too," Rufus mumbled.

"Good," I said. "Remember the moment near the end when Peter Pan flies off to rescue Wendy and the Lost Boys from Captain Hook? He gets there just in time to save the boys from walking the plank."

"Yeah," Garry said. "So what?"

"Well," I said, "when Tom stows away on the boat, he plans to help the knights preserve the honor of the Round Table. He's on fire with the idea, and when he meets King Arthur, it's like the moment when Peter Pan saves the Lost Boys. It's *that* great."

"Honest?" Garry asked.

"Yes," I replied. "But you both sound like you've crossed the street to buy a candy bar. Like it's no big deal. You need to know that your character, Tom of Warwick, becomes the hero of the finale. Like Peter Pan when he defeats Hook."

"Nobody told us that," Rufus groused. "Mr. Remsen didn't explain it that way."

"Mr. Remsen has a lot on his mind," I said. "But remember, King Arthur might die like the Lost Boys at the plank. Then you show up and give him a reason to fight on."

"I'm gobsmacked!" Garry said. "Can we try the scene again, Miss Jane?"

"Just call me Jane," I said. "And this time, I want to feel your courage. *Be a hero.*"

"You go first, Garry," Rufus said, and Garry ran sideways as I moved to the center of the room. I took a breath, then fed the kid his cue.

With a sense of daring, Garry made his entrance and spoke his lines with palpable emotion. When he finished, Rufus clapped.

"Much better," I said. "Now you go, Rufus."

With a grin, Rufus cheerfully took his cue. He was a bit more subtle but no less convincing than Garry, and when the scene ended, Garry clapped and I beamed at the two of them. "We'll go for ice cream now," I said. "But we'll return here tomorrow at 9 a.m. and practice again before the tech rehearsal."

"Will Mr. Burton be happy with us, Jane?" Garry asked.

"You'll blow his socks off," I said. "But keep practicing with your mums."

When I got back to the Ritz, huffing from a hike through the Public Garden, Bryce was gone. He'd left a note thanking me for breakfast, and since he had a free day, I regretted we couldn't spend it together. But I was obliged to attend a script conference.

I showed up at 1 p.m. sharp at Alan's sunny suite, number 1004, which had a fireplace and the same view of the skyline I saw from my rooms. Alan was on the phone, still wearing his pajamas. (Fritz liked to joke that Alan picked up the receiver first thing each morning without knowing who he was going to call.) Alan nodded to me, then ended his chat before heading for his bedroom, so I helped myself to a sandwich from a platter on a side table.

I was still eating when Fritz dashed in, hair askew, looking as though he'd slept in his clothes. He was followed by Joyce Haber from *Time*, clad in a tailored boucle suit with a velvet collar, her blonde hair teased at the crown. I realized Brock had forgotten to tell me Haber would be there, which was odd since Fritz normally barred outsiders from his work sessions with Alan.

"Joyce, dear," Fritz said, "make yourself at home. Do you care for luncheon?"

I almost laughed since it was like Fritz Loewe, ever formal, to call sandwiches on Wonder Bread "luncheon." But Haber declined his offer and claimed the parlor's second sofa, setting her file folders and a notebook on the mahogany coffee table. "I prefer not to have an audience when I do interviews," she said, glowering at me, but when Alan returned sporting a mint-green blazer, tan slacks, and loafers, the *Time* lady smiled without repeating her complaint. (Did Alan know his cuticles were bleeding?)

"Joyce will ask us questions," Fritz said, "and then she'll go interview Roddy."

"Excellent," Alan said, pouring coffee from a silver pot. (He discreetly wiped his nails with a paper napkin—he'd obviously seen the blood—before joining Fritz on the sofa.)

"Are you two rewriting the entire show here in Boston?" Haber asked.

"Richard Rodgers once said he'd never open a can of sardines without going to Boston first," Alan replied.

Haber tittered, and Fritz, who was fingering a piece of jade he'd withdrawn from his pocket, admitted that he and Alan planned to slash their three-hour-and-thirty-minute show down to two and a half hours.

"We're also adding a song for Roddy and a new one for Julie, but these will replace two we're cutting," Alan said. "And yes, I'm revising the entire book in Boston."

"I assume," Haber said, "that you'll be getting help from Mr. Hart when he returns."

"We assume so, too," Alan said. "For now, we're letting Moss recover in Canada."

"I spoke with Miss Andrews," Haber said. "She called you 'the loneliest men in town.' Do you know why she'd describe you that way?"

"From her time with us in *My Fair Lady*," Alan said, "Julie knows the welfare of a large company rests on us." He grinned. "I call Fritz 'Sir Aggravate' because I test his patience."

"But I love Alan," Fritz said. "We're not alike, yet we blend like coffee and cream."

"Whereas Gilbert and Sullivan detested one another," Alan said. "Affection is really not required for a successful collaboration."

"Yet we clicked that first day back in '42 when we met at the Lambs Club," Fritz said. "I lost my way to the men's room and ran into Alan. You know the rest."

Haber asked Lerner and Loewe to elaborate on how they chose Broadway musicals as their "métier" and how their backgrounds and education influenced their partnership. I listened intently, making an occasional note so I could tell Brock. After forty minutes of grilling, the *Time* researcher thanked the partners, grabbed her papers, and showed herself out.

"Well, that was tiresome," Alan said. "I hope the publicity's worth our time."

"You're the cover story," I blurted out. "It'll be published before *Camelot* opens."

Alan sighed and lit a cigarette, and Fritz put the jade back in his pocket. "Did you track down Joe Ferrer?" Fritz asked.

"I talked to him earlier, yes," Alan replied. "He's directing a movie and can't step in. But look, Fritz, I can handle the writing and directing, as long as Brock takes some rehearsals." He smiled. "Jane here just had a session with our new Toms. How did that go?"

"The boys were unsure about the value of Tom's role," I said. "I think I convinced them."

"Let's work on Roddy's song," Fritz said. He crossed the room and sat at the white baby grand. Addressing me, he added, "This will replace Roddy's reprise of 'Fie on Goodness!'"

Alan pulled a straight-backed chair toward the piano and whipped a notebook out of his pocket before sitting down. "We need to make Mordred more evil. I jotted down the seven deadly sins that he calls virtues and did a riff on those. Here's what I wrote so far." He began reciting lyrics that poked fun at Courage, Purity, Charity, and Humility.

"Hmm," Fritz said. "I see it as a patter song. Something like this?" He played an allegro melody, and Alan improvised the lyrics as he sang along.

I thought they aced it. They'd worked together for almost twenty years, writing three so-so musicals until they had a 1947 hit with *Brigadoon*—Alan had just described their history to Haber. Yet the ease with which Loewe set Lerner's words impressed me; they moved seamlessly from verse to verse, dashing off the song in thirty minutes. Then Lerner sang it through, a fast, funny, cynical solo that would establish Mordred's appalling lack of morals.

"We'll give it to Roddy now, but he can't introduce it for a couple of weeks," Alan said. "First, I have to shorten act two."

"*Bonjour,*" Madame Lerner said, using her key to enter the suite.

"Hello, darling," Alan said, rising, then turning to Fritz. "My wife has a few ideas, and since we're having a story conference, I told her she could sit in. You don't mind, do you?"

Fritz shook his large head, but his nostrils flared as though he smelled something foul. "May I use the phone in your bedroom?" he asked Alan.

Alan nodded, and Fritz tottered across the room and disappeared.

Madame took Joyce Haber's spot on the couch. She wore a patterned dress and heels, and her hair was styled into a bob and teased at the crown like Haber's. "Chouchou's in the bedroom with Nurse," she told Alan. "They're listening to Debussy."

"Good." Then Alan glanced at me, saying, "I want my son to hear classical music instead of show tunes. It's better for his brain development."

Fritz returned, and five minutes later, he answered a rap on the door. His girlfriend Tamara loped in, wearing a wrinkled white blouse and skin-tight black leggings, her bone-straight black hair falling to her slim waist. She sat near Madame, who moved away as though Tamara harbored a dread disease.

Fritz told Alan, "Since your wife's here, I felt Tamara also should give her opinion. She's seen the show many times, and five heads are better than two." He sat near his girlfriend as Alan handed out five scripts. Then he pulled his chair close to his partner.

"When I spoke with Oliver Smith earlier," Alan said, "he suggested we eliminate our present act two. Since act one is happy and romantic, he thinks we should make it longer and merely hint at Arthur's future troubles. Oliver says there's no way to make a downhill saga go uphill."

"That's daft," Fritz said. "I don't think it would be dramatic enough, and we'd have to cut Morgan Le Fey and Mordred altogether."

"Exactly," Alan said. "Look, I've given this a lot of thought, and we should definitely cut or compress some moments in act one. But the big changes should come in act two. The only part I won't meddle with is the final scene with Tom because the plot should build inexorably to the moment when Arthur realizes Camelot won't be forgotten. We just need to get there sooner."

"I'm sorry you cut the quest song," Madame said.

"Me, too," Tamara declared. "And the animal ballet. That was so cute."

"We can't make decisions based on 'cute,'" Alan said. "We'd never get anywhere."

Fritz grinned like the cat who ate the canary. "Should we perhaps take a break, Alan, and reconvene later? Alone?"

Alan jumped to his feet. "Good idea. I think speaking with Joyce Haber wore us out. And since this is my suite, will all of you please leave? I have a headache."

"Let's go, Tamiboy," Fritz said.

"Right away, Babybear," Tamara replied, rising, and I had to pinch the inside of my wrist so I wouldn't giggle. Why did Fritz and Tamara use those cloying pet names in public?

After the others left, Madame stood, air-kissed Alan's cheek, and departed. "Well, that was a waste of time," Alan said, sounding irked.

"I like the new song for Mordred."

"I do, too," Alan said. "But you should go do something fun, Jane. Take a break."

Smiling, I saluted and headed for the hall, eager to escape Alan's doldrums. Waiting for the elevator, I decided Oliver Smith's suggestion was off the wall. But Nathan Cohen, the Toronto critic, had offered a similar suggestion: cut the first five scenes.

Well, the troubles of the partners had given me time for myself, a rare boon. Even if Lerner and Loewe patched up their differences later, Brock would join them, and I'd have a night off. So, I entered my suite and raced to the phone. When Bryce didn't answer, I left a message at the Parker House and decided to nap.

For a while, I was too keyed up to sleep. I wished I'd used the afternoon to tour the Isabella Stewart Gardner Museum, which was built in the style of a fifteenth-century Venetian palazzo. My parents had discovered the Gardner when my dad was in medical school at Tufts, and Tish had encouraged me to visit. "They're not working you to death, I hope," she remarked in a recent call, to which I replied, "Not at all. Frankly, my job got more interesting on the road."

This was accurate. Today, I'd felt proud of my work with the young Toms of Warwick, believing I'd improved their acting. Didn't that mean I might have enough talent to direct?

I was dreaming of my family's home in Maryland when the phone rang. It was Bryce, and while checking my watch, I realized I'd slept all afternoon. He told me he'd walked some of the Freedom Trail with Nate, then he asked me to dinner.

"You mean an actual date?" I asked. "Where?"

"Café Danube, which is supposed to be romantic—also dressy. I'll be at your door at six. I thought we'd go early since we have a long day tomorrow."

I threw off the covers and padded to the shower. As the warm water caressed my back and neck, I was glad Bryce had picked a restaurant where we might not run into anyone from the cast. We hadn't tried to hide our affair, but tonight I wanted Bryce to myself. He'd never fully opened up about himself, and I hoped a "romantic" cafe would offer the right backdrop to help draw him out.

⚬ ◆ ⚬

Café Danube was on Newbury just past Clarendon, half a mile from the Ritz. On our walk, Bryce and I held hands in the chilly dusk, passing stores, galleries, tea shops, brownstones, and a Gothic church visible in the haze of street lamps. Our destination was the second floor of a rectangular brick building near a salmon-colored mansion with cone-shaped towers. "That place could be in downtown Camelot," Bryce joked, pointing across the street. But I'd learned it was common to come across old buildings in Boston juxtaposed with modern ones, and I'd begun to love this city where the seeds of revolution had taken root.

After climbing upstairs from the street, we entered a dimly lit room with sconces and heard Slavic strains from a violinist.

We were shown to a spacious table for four, swathed in white linen with candles and gardenias. As Bryce removed my wool coat, which Tish had sent to the Ritz, he noticed my new black frock with its plunging neck. "Where did you get this slinky number?" he asked.

"My mother sent it as a gift," I said, handing my coat to the maître d'.

The ambience was intimate, and when we were seated and I glanced at Bryce across the table, my heart fluttered. He wore his navy suit, and his blue eyes darkened in the candlelight. "I ordered wine before we got here," he said.

A sommelier in white tie arrived with a silver bucket holding a bottle of Meursault. The man opened the vintage, handed Bryce the cork, and gave him a taste. With Bryce's approval, he poured the golden-green French wine into crystal goblets.

"What are we celebrating?" I asked, picking up my glass.

"Us," he replied, raising his glass. "And *Camelot*, which brought us together."

"And the Piccadilly," I said before we clinked. "So, who told you about this place?"

"Nate," Bryce said. "He and his wife spent their honeymoon in Boston."

A waiter offered us menus, and I was miffed that mine didn't list the prices, as though ladies didn't need to consider the cost. But I didn't want to spoil the mood, so I scanned the entrees: chicken goulash with mushrooms; fermented sauerkraut with pork chops; potatoes paprikash; cabbage rolls with veal; goose liver with truffles. Heavier cuisine than I usually ate.

"Looks authentic," Bryce said. "My *nagymama*, which means grandmother, and my *anya*—meaning mother—are Hungarian."

"Hungarian sounds musical," I said, thinking I'd try the iced cherry soup and chicken goulash. I finished my wine, and a new server dashed over to refill my glass. Bryce asked what

I'd like and when the main waiter came back, he ordered our meals. This annoyed me further. (Why hadn't he let me speak? My father never ordered for my mom in restaurants.) A bread basket came along with complimentary savory crepes filled with onions, spices, and ground beef, topped with sour cream. "These are tasty," I said, telling myself to let my irritation go.

"They're called *hortobagyi palacsinta*," Bryce said. "I grew up with this food."

"Know what, Bryce? I want to learn everything about you. In some ways, we put the cart before the horse."

"We couldn't stop ourselves, but you're right. I don't even know who you voted for."

I thought he was kidding. "Kennedy, of course. Who else?"

"I chose Nixon," Bryce said.

I nearly fell off my upholstered silk chair. "But Nixon's a creep."

"Well, I don't trust Kennedy not to obey the Pope."

"I'm a Catholic like Kennedy. *I* don't obey the Pope. Not always."

"Don't get steamed, Cookie. We don't have to share the same politics or religion." He laughed. "I knew you'd be the kind of person who'd use an absentee ballot. I had a neighbor forward mine."

"I never changed my residence, so my mother sent my ballot to the Ritz." Willing myself to calm down, I recalled that we'd never talked politics, so why should it be a wedge? "By the way, what is your religion?"

"I was raised Episcopalian," he said. "But I don't practice a particular faith."

"You're an agnostic?" I asked, feeling my chest tighten.

"I believe in the Golden Rule," he said. "But not in organized religion."

When the wine steward refilled our goblets, I gulped my second glass of Meursault in three swallows. After another waiter brought my appetizer, served in a cup floating in ice, I waited for Bryce to try his veal rollups before tasting my cherry soup. It was so tart I screwed up my face, causing Bryce to grin. Oddly, I wished I could run back to my suite. His admissions made me feel I was out to sea in a leaky kayak. Or had I sloshed down too much wine on an empty stomach?

"I went to Catholic school with nuns for twelve years and then Catholic University," I murmured. "I've never met anyone who doesn't believe in God."

"I believe in a higher power," he said softly. "I just don't know how it all works. My mother was born Jewish, but she converted to please my father. I think she paid a big emotional price, and I got a bad feeling about religion from watching her struggle. My family went to church, but unless I'm misjudging my parents, those visits were part of their social life." He shrugged. "I think my father's god is John Maynard Keynes, so Dad probably voted for JFK. Didn't I read that Kennedy's good pal Galbraith is a Keynesian?"

"I read that, too," I said before eating more soup, growing used to its taste. Bryce dove into his rollups, which resembled Chinese egg rolls, and after our appetizer plates were removed, I studied his handsome face in the candlelight, grateful for his honesty. He'd known I was an Irish Catholic and could've hedged about voting for Nixon.

The violinist in a black vest and dark slacks approached, saying, "I'll now play '*Csárdás*' by Vittorio Monti." He began the familiar song with slow, almost plaintive passages that grew into a frantic solo. As his bow flew across his instrument, we stopped eating and gave him our full attention. When he finished, Bryce tipped him and said, "*Koszonom szepen.*"

"You thanked him in Hungarian," I said as the musician strolled to another table.

"My n*agymama* taught me some words," he said. "I'd like

to visit Koka, her hometown, but after the upheaval four years ago, our State Department has made it hard to travel there."

"Did your mother's family come here long ago?"

"My mother was born in Budapest, and her parents emigrated in 1910, the same year the Boston Shubert opened. I'm an only child, and nobody in my family thought I should be an actor except my grandmother. She loved my voice and went to bat for me." He sipped his wine. "How about your background? Irish, I imagine."

"Yes, my dad's grandparents fled the Irish famine in the 1840s and settled in Vermont. But my mom's grandparents came from London. My folks met as kids and married out of college; in fact, they moved here for my dad's med school years. Then they settled near D.C. after his Georgetown residency." I shrugged. "I have a sister and brother who are model offspring, but I'm not close to either. I'm sure they're all waiting for me to quit the theater."

"That might be a long wait," Bryce said.

"I'm just glad I found a backstage job, so maybe I'll have a shot at directing. If I apply to Yale School of Drama, Moss might even recommend me."

"You've made up your mind?" he asked.

"Not yet," I said. "Getting into Yale would be hard, and even if I got accepted, I might decide it's not for me. But one good thing is that New Haven's close to New York, so we could see each other." I felt myself blush. "Unless you're planning to dump me when we get back."

"New York to New Haven should be an easy commute," he said.

As our main course arrived, Bryce leaned back to give the waiters some room, and I felt surer of him after sharing our religious views and family details. My parents might not rejoice if I brought home an Episcopalian Republican, but my Irish Catholic father was an anomaly among the many WASP physicians who practiced at his hospital. Many doctors were Republicans, so perhaps my folks would tolerate Bryce's politics. (I'd relished learning that he was half-Jewish.)

"This looks awfully good," I said, eyeing our food. "Thanks for bringing me here. It must cost a fortune, though my menu didn't have prices."

He laughed. "I knew you'd notice that. It's old-world gallantry."

"Well, you're my newfangled knight. And I'm curious about something. The initials on your Army bag are B.A. What's the A for?"

"On-drish," he said. "Spelled A-n-d-r-i-s."

"Elegant," Jane said. "My middle name's Patricia."

"That suits a posh girl like you," he said, beaming. "Hey, it's funny we've never talked about this, but what's your favorite music? I mean, beyond show tunes?"

"I love the kind of song you sang at your *Camelot* audition."

"*The Salley Gardens*?" he asked, sounding pleased.

"That one and *Danny Boy* and *The Last Rose of Summer*. I grew up listening to music like that when my family gathered around the piano." I smiled. "There's another one I like that starts 'Just a song at twilight—'"

"'When the lights are low?'" he asked.

"Yes," I murmured. "I wish you'd sing that for me sometime."

"I'll work on it," he promised before tucking into his pork chops.

I invited Bryce to my suite, and we reached for each other several times that night. I never tired of his embrace, which made me feel cherished and safe, and when the alarm went off at 7 a.m., I wished I could stay in his arms. But I hopped into the shower, where Bryce joined me. Then we ordered room service and drank coffee in white terrycloth robes embroidered with a lion's head atop a crown, the Ritz-Carlton logo.

"It's better if we head to the Shubert separately," I told him later when we were getting dressed in our rehearsal duds. (He'd stashed a change of clothes in my closet before our date.)

"The tech will be rocky," Bryce said before giving me a sweet, lingering kiss. "Should we meet at the corner deli when we break?"

"Good idea." I leaned forward to kiss him again as someone banged on the door. Thinking the housekeeper would've been less noisy, I wasn't surprised to find Nate Wicker in the hall, wearing a Yankees cap and wool jacket. "Sorry to intrude, kids," he said, entering my parlor. "There's a problem." He twisted his imaginary pinkie ring. "Look, I know you weren't invited, but some of us had a party in Richard's room last night."

"We had a party of our own," Bryce said, standing. "What's up?"

"Julie was with us for a while, and when she was about to leave, Richard asked if he could join her. She declined, and later on, he called her room and told her he loved her. I gather she didn't reply in kind because Richard threw the receiver down. Then the phone rang, and he said, 'I love you, Julie, but you obviously don't love me.' And he suddenly stormed out. Since I was blotto, I conked out on his couch, but when I woke up, I recalled his parting words. And here I quote: 'I'm done with this whole fucking mess.'"

"Whoa," I said.

"Yeah, and as the Brits say, he's gone walkabout," Nate drawled. "Jane, you better call Brock Remsen. Then we should fan out and try to find the king. I'll check with the doormen here and visit some hotels where they put the chorus. Bryce, you knock on doors at Parker House."

"Maybe he's with Nell," Bryce said.

"I called Nell, but they're not a couple anymore. I also checked with Roddy." Nate paused. "Jane, you go to the theater and see if he's in his dressing room."

"Let's hurry," I said. "With all our other problems, Alan doesn't need an AWOL star."

"I wouldn't have drunk so much if I knew I'd be playing Arthur today," Nate said before leaving us.

I dialed Brock while Bryce grabbed his jacket and let himself out. "Richard Burton didn't come home last night," I told my boss. "Worse, he told Nate he's done with *Camelot*. And you can't say Philip Burton didn't warn us. Richard's been strong for the cast, telling them everything will be fine. But deep down, he's had big doubts."

"What a fiasco, but thanks for letting us know," Brock said. "Alan and I are about to leave for the theater."

"Bryce and Nate are going out to search for Burton," I added. "See you at rehearsal."

Ten minutes later, a taxi dropped me in the alley that ran alongside the Shubert. I passed a series of unmarked doors until I reached the last one, which was unlocked. A young bald security guard at the desk told me to sign in.

"Is Richard Burton here?" I inquired, but the guard hadn't seen the leading man. I then asked him to describe the backstage layout, which he did in some detail.

"It's a maze," he said, "and it's haunted. I'd never want to be alone here at night."

Duly warned, I walked through an adjacent door, entering a long hallway, too narrow for two people to walk side by side. I passed an exposed brick wall, a lavatory, and dressing room 2 marked "Miss Andrews" before I finally reached dressing room 1 marked "Mr. Burton." I slipped inside the latter, which had a single makeup mirror illumined by many bulbs—the lights were on—and a mirrored counter with blue drapes hiding the base. There were two chairs with padded seats, a sink at the far left, and a bathroom with a shower and toilet. But since the place didn't reek of smoke, Richard clearly hadn't been there.

I made my exit and continued walking toward the stage-left wings straight ahead. But at the end of the hall on my right was a winding concrete staircase which, according to the signage, led up to the principal dressing rooms or down to the basement. Since Richard would have no reason to visit his colleagues upstairs, I ran down two flights.

Switching on the lights, I saw a huge chorus dressing room on my left containing six sinks and many chairs in front of mirrors. Swiveling right, I wandered through a sprawling all-purpose space with costume racks and bins; a washer and dryer; a couch and easy chairs; two metal tables and chairs; a partitioned nook, likely for stage managers; and another principal dressing room all the way across the floor near a second set of stairs. Nobody was around, so I ran up the latter and saw the stage manager's console at stage right.

Taking care not to trip over rubber cables and assorted wires, I emerged in front of the act one-set with its enormous birch tree. At center stage, I nearly smacked into the theater's ghost lamp, but since the house lights were on, I had a perfect view of the Shubert, a jewel box with a red and crème decor.

"Is Richard Burton here?" I called to nobody in particular, though the production tables were occupied out front.

"No sign of him," Bernie Hart yelled from behind. "Brock called Sybil in New York, and she has no idea where he's gone. But we're moving ahead with the tech."

Crew members were talking at stage right, and I asked one to show me the pass door to the house. As I joined the team, Oliver Smith and his assistants were conferring at one table while Brock and Alan sat at the other. Yet all of them stared at the stage as though they could make Richard appear by dint of their concentration; no one acknowledged my arrival.

Brock and Alan were still staring ahead when the tech began at 10 a.m. with no sign of their leading man. But I thought Nate was remarkably polished as Arthur. He'd studied Burton closely, memorizing each inflection, and if you closed your eyes while Nate was speaking, you would've thought Burton was playing the king.

We had to endure a constant round of starting and stopping, allowing lights, sound, and scenery to be adjusted. When the lunch break was called, I hightailed it to the corner deli and bought sandwiches and Cokes for Bryce and me. I carried my tray to a small table and was sliding into a rickety chair as Bryce came in, followed by Dan, who went directly to the counter.

"Hope you don't mind, Cookie," Bryce said, sitting across from me, "but I told Elsdon he could join us. He says he needs to speak with you."

"Any sign of Richard?" I asked, and Bryce shook his head.

"Jane, I have a bone to pick with you," Dan said a bit later, slapping his tray on our table.

"Hold on, Elsdon," Bryce said. "I didn't know you planned to fight."

"Kitty Hart called my fiancée," Dan snarled, plopping into a chair. "Kitty told her about Sarah, and I've never heard Dominique so irate. She might call off our engagement."

"Can you blame her?" I asked.

"Who told you to get involved in my business?" Dan asked.

"Everyone in the cast knew why Sarah left," I said, "even Mrs. Lerner and Mrs. Hart. So why are you blaming me? Those women aren't *my* friends."

"But how did Mrs. Hart know I slept with Sarah in *New York*?"

"Simple math," I said. "Sarah knew she was pregnant two weeks into our Toronto run. That would've been too early to do a test if you'd knocked her up there."

"Dominique is coming for opening night," Dan said. "I'm going to explain things to her and suggest we take the baby and raise it. Sarah's talking about putting our child up for adoption, but it's my kid, and I should have a say. Will you call her, Jane, and intercede?"

Outraged by his insensitivity, I hastily wrapped my sandwich in a napkin. "Bryce, I'm going to finish my lunch at the Shubert. Otherwise, I might lose it." I glared at Dan. "As for you, Elsdon, you can go to hell."

"Jane, please," Dan said. "Call Sarah. She'll listen to you."

But I grabbed my coat and bag, then my sandwich and Coke, and took off. I thought Elson had a nerve imagining that Sarah would allow him to raise their child with another woman. (Yet, as far as the poor baby was concerned, having one biological parent might be preferable. I half-wondered if I should pass on Dan's request, distasteful as it was.)

When I reached the production table at the theater, Brock came over and gleefully whispered, "The prodigal son has returned. He's backstage, apologizing to everyone."

"That's good," I said. "Where has he been?"

"He didn't say, but he's meeting with Alan and Fritz after the tech. I just hope he isn't planning to quit."

————◆————

Bryce and I stayed apart that night so he could blow off steam with some guys in the ensemble. I slept well and felt rested when I showed up for Thursday's dress rehearsal before our one Boston preview.

From the back of the house, I saw Alan and Brock blocking the aisle near the production table, and when I approached them, a tall, bespectacled man rose from his chair and offered a moist palm. "Miss Conroy, isn't it?"

"Yes," I replied, shaking Philip Burton's hand. "Hello."

"It's all arranged, Jane," Alan told me. "Philip will fill in for Moss, and Brock will also take some rehearsals."

As the Other Burton returned to his place, Brock and I also sat. "Richard has offered to rehearse the understudies," he whispered. "And you'll continue working with the Toms."

"Philip and Brock will have a lot on their hands," Alan observed. "But I'm giving an interview to *The Boston Globe* in which I'm announcing *I'll* take over directing duties."

At center stage, a crew member was toting the ghost lamp into the wings, and I wondered if Philip Burton could actually whip the show into shape. Would his presence placate Fritz?

"Philip," Alan said, "your first task is to decide whether Goulet can cut the mustard, acting-wise. If not, we'll need to hire someone or promote one of his understudies."

(My heart did a cartwheel. Bryce might be playing Lancelot on Broadway.)

"What does Mr. Loewe think of Goulet?" Burton asked.

Alan sighed. "He's solidly in his corner, and so is Franz Allers."

"Curtain tonight is at eight-twenty-five," Philip Burton said, "which means rehearsal should end by midafternoon. Suppose I decide about Goulet in a day or so?" He paused. "I'm thankful you brought me on for Richard's sake."

"And we appreciate your coming to Boston on a day's notice," Alan said. "With you at the helm, I can tackle the writing I couldn't do in Toronto."

Feeling restless, I used the pass door to enter the wings at stage right; then I snuck around the back of the set, entering the long hall off stage left. Richard was ranting behind his closed dressing room door, so I snuck closer as he yelled, "Alan just told me." He coughed and resumed speaking in a huskier tone. "It's ridiculous. If they fire Bobby, I'll leave, too."

"It's unfair," Julie said calmly. "But wouldn't it be best to persuade Philip that Bobby's worth keeping? Alan's at his wit's end. If we add fuel to *his* fire, he'll explode."

"Julie's right," Roddy McDowall said in a muffled voice.

"It won't be a cakewalk tomorrow night," Richard said. "But since I still believe in this bloody show, I'll go to bat for Bobby with my father later tonight."

"I'm relieved," Roddy said. "Bobby shouldn't be the company scapegoat."

Believing the stars' meeting was about to end, I ran up the stairs. The principal dressing rooms were in a hallway off the landing, and I found the one marked "Messrs. Christmas and Elsdon." I knocked, and when Bryce invited me inside, I was surprised. The dressing room was a rectangular shoebox with one vanity, two mirrors, two folding chairs, and one sink. No bathroom, no daybed, and scant space for a costume rack. "Where's everyone?" I asked.

"In the basement where they can breathe. Hey, we've heard there's a new director."

"There is," I said, leaning against his vanity. "Richard's father, Philip."

"Great," Bryce said. "Another Burton who'll hate me." He paused. "Hey, I'm sorry about the scene at the deli. Elsdon ambushed me, too."

"I wasn't upset," I said, realizing I hadn't told Bryce about seeking Kitty's help with Dan's fiancée. "Maybe I should phone Sarah. I mean, Dan *is* the baby's dad."

Over the intercom, Bernie Hart called, "Ten minutes till rehearsal, ladies and gents."

"Come with me," Bryce said, taking my arm. "I want to show you something nifty." He pulled me into the hall and down the winding stairs, offering a hand when we slipped into the dark stage-left wings. We walked across the spongy black floor to a door at the edge of stage right, where we entered the crew's utility room containing sinks, a coffee pot, a fridge, equipment trunks, and assorted tools.

"Wonderful, isn't it?" Bryce asked, pointing to the rear wall where a scenic artist had recreated posters of the legendary shows that tried out at the Shubert. Beneath each poster, the stars had signed their names: Mary Martin and Ezio Pinza in *South Pacific*; Gertrude Lawrence and Yul Brynner in *The King and I*; James Britton in *Paint Your Wagon*; Judy Holliday in *Bells Are Ringing*; and Mary Martin and Theodore Bikel in *The Sound of Music*.

"It's special," I whispered.

"Look down at the end," Bryce said. "They're painting the *Camelot* poster."

"Let's hope it brings us luck," I said, squeezing Bryce's hand.

The sound of thunder echoed from the wings: the chorus climbing upstairs.

By the time I returned to the house through the pass door, the company had lined up across center stage. I glanced backward and saw Fritz pacing the carpet behind the last row. I took my usual seat next to Brock while Alan and Philip Burton walked down the aisle and stood before the pit. The cast grew pin-drop quiet, then Alan introduced Philip, who read some remarks he'd jotted on cards. I cringed, recalling our first enchanting read-through in New York. How could this prim Other Burton replace the witty, urbane Moss Hart?

Brock handed me a clipping from the morning *Globe*. The headline said, "Creators in Arduous Task of Condensing *Camelot*." I skimmed the story, which predicted that Boston's version of the show would run three hours and a half at tomorrow's opening. It also reported that Alan was directing, filling in for Moss, who remained hospitalized in Toronto.

"There's no mention of Philip," I whispered.

"Consider his participation an open secret," Brock whispered back. "The cast will know, but Moss might not hear for a while. Philip will be well paid and get program credit on opening night, and Richard will be happier."

I didn't answer my boss, but it seemed the behind-the-scenes plot of *Camelot* was thickening by the hour.

10.
REWRITES
AD NAUSEAM

Bryce

Bryce waited in the wings after Philip Burton had restaged the knights' rowdy "Fie on Goodness!" number. He needed to stay loose since he had solos in the next scene, but he felt tension creeping from his shoulders down his back. If you'd told him Lerner and Loewe would move *Camelot* to Boston and hire a director who'd undo the cleverness—and brio—Moss Hart had given the show, he would've called you insane. Even if Lerner's book was too long, Moss's direction had been inspired.

But after running through "Fie on Goodness!" and hearing Philip Burton's ideas, just hours before the Boston preview, Bryce and his castmates muttered curses when the new director released them. He'd asked for "less testosterone," though the song was about the knights' pining to commit violent acts now banned by Arthur's civil court.

What was the man thinking? Or, more to the point, what was Alan thinking? After introducing Burton, Lerner had decamped, allegedly to continue revising. Loewe had left, too, making Bryce wonder if the composer had already washed his hands of *Camelot*. Right now, he was likely at the Ritz with that chick Tamara, who whitened her face and looked like a Beatnik out of central casting. All she needed was a beret.

Bryce shifted from foot to foot, thinking the only person who seemed unhappier than the rest of them was Elsdon. His fiancée was flying in that night, but she'd already told him their engagement was off unless Dan could think of one reason why she should forgive him for "screwing that little nobody from the chorus during rehearsals."

"The weirdest part," Dan told Bryce earlier in their airless dressing room, "is that I find myself missing Sarah and wondering how our baby's doing."

"Why is that weird?" Bryce asked.

"Because as often as I've gone on the road, I've never missed my fiancée. So now I'm wondering if I was blinded by Dominique's money and social cachet. But that's not love, is it, Christmas? And you'd know since your face lights up like New Year's Eve whenever you see Jane." He grimaced. "Face it, I've loused up the lives of three people, and there's a tender fourth life to consider."

"I hope you work it out," Bryce said, meaning it. But now, as he stood stage right, he forgot about Dan's misery while watching tall, balding Philip Burton on the proscenium.

"Miss Andrews and Messrs. Wicker, Christmas, and Elsdon to the stage," Bernie Hart called from the production table. "We'll be doing 'Then You May Take Me to the Fair.'"

Bryce saw Julie enter from stage left and stop near Philip. Nate ran in with Dan. Then Bryce joined the others while Franz Allers mounted his podium.

Julie smiled at the new director. "I thought the 'Fair' number might be cut," she said, looking nice in a beige blouse and slacks (which Bryce had come to think of as her "uniform").

"Mr. Lerner's on the fence," Philip Burton replied in a light tenor that was the opposite of Richard's amber-hued voice. "We'll keep it for Boston, but he wants to pick up the pace." The director called to Franz Allers. "Can we speed this number up?"

"It's fast enough, I assure you," Allers replied.

Burton looked pained. "Then let's see how it goes," he muttered before heading for the pass door to the house. The actors took the places they'd assumed for Moss: Lionel and Sagramore on Julie's left and Dinadan on her right. The scene was set in the palace garden after Guenevere met Lancelot during the May Day picnic.

When Allers nodded, Guenevere launched the number a cappella, calling Sir Lionel, who stepped forward. The music came in, and Jenny mentioned the night she'd asked Lionel to take her to the town fair. Yet since the arrival of the younger, stronger Lancelot, she archly wondered if *he* would be a better protector.

With his honor on the line, Lionel vowed to challenge the Frenchman to a joust, promising he'd make mincemeat out of the guy. The queen sang that Lionel could take her to the fair if he followed through on his boasts. Then he gallantly stepped back as the queen called to Sagramore.

"Stop," Philip Burton yelled from a seat in the orchestra. "Mr. Christmas, is it?" he asked. "Guenevere's baiting you, but each of your rebuttals sounds more brutal than the one before."

Bryce stared at the director, flummoxed. Moss had told him to act increasingly more aggressive with each salvo Julie tossed at him.

"Tone it down," Burton said. "Act amused. You don't actually believe the queen wants you to do horrible things to Lancelot."

"That's exactly what I think," Bryce sputtered. "She's put off by Lancelot's hubris and wants to make him pay. As for Lionel, he feels insulted and gets worked up."

"That may have been Mr. Hart's approach, but I'd like you to try it my way."

Bryce decided he detested this man. "More tongue-in-cheek?"

"Quite right," Burton said, and Bryce turned upstage where Nate and Dan looked incredulous since Moss had given them the same macho suggestions. "And Miss Andrews," Burton added, "I'd like you to be more flirtatious."

"Flirtatious?" Julie asked.

"Why, yes," Burton said. "She's asking each of them to compete for time with her."

"As her bodyguards," Julie observed. "They wouldn't dare imagine she had other ideas."

"Why not?" he asked. "She has other ideas with Lancelot." He shrugged. "Guenevere uses her feminine wiles to get whatever she wants. That's her intention here anyway."

"Very well," Julie said, but turning upstage, she rolled her eyes, causing Nate, Dan, and Bryce to smirk.

"Let's start again," Burton called.

Bryce took his place, wishing Julie would baldly reject the new director's cynical view of Jenny's motives. To his chagrin, though, the leading lady now flirted with the knights.

Bryce signed in at the stage door around 6:15 p.m. that Friday, hoping Jane would also come early. Unlike their opening night in Toronto, the "simple folk" were not invited to a soiree in Lerner's suite, so he and his mates put together an after-show bash for the ensemble. Jane had decided to celebrate with the cast instead of the producers, and Bryce looked forward to relaxing with her since all they did lately was fret about *Camelot*.

Before heading inside, Bryce glanced at the call board and read a telegram:

Dear Company: Love and luck tonight from the loneliest man in Toronto. Moss Hart

He shook his head, knowing Moss would be lonelier if he could see the hash Philip Burton was making of his work. And things might get worse if the Boston reviews were bad.

Bryce walked down the hall past the star rooms on his left and climbed the stairs. Inside his own dressing room, he threw his canvas bag on the vanity and noticed a bottle of cognac that Jane had left for him and Dan. Then he read telegrams from his folks, his agent, Mr. Sardi, and a few actor friends. And he was surprised to find another wire: *Break a leg in Boston. Cyril Ritchard.*

He smiled, having heard on the grapevine that Ritchard was starring in *Happiest Girl* as well as directing. He thought he must be under serious consideration for a lead, though Andy hadn't called. Even so, this was a hopeful way to start *Camelot's* Boston run.

He sat at his mirror, thinking he better tell Jane about his new prospect, though he was superstitious about sharing such news before he auditioned. Yet he was determined to forge ahead with *Happiest Girl*, which had music by Jacques Offenbach and lyrics by Yip Harburg—his agent had sent him the details. But he honestly had no idea how Jane would react.

"Knock, knock," she called, waltzing in, and when Bryce turned, he was stunned anew by her beauty. She wore a blue gossamer gown that floated when she walked, and showed tasteful cleavage. "Do you like it?" she asked, and when he stood, she lifted her face to be kissed. "Julie lent it to me," she told him.

"That was nice of her," Bryce said, inhaling Jane's natural fragrance of Breck shampoo and Dove soap.

"She and I explored Newbury Street this afternoon and then had tea in her suite with her gray poodle, Shy. She was feeling happy about her story in the *Globe* today. We also talked about clothes, and when she found out I only have two party dresses, she offered me this one. She's lost weight from stress, but it's perfect for me."

"You're perfect, period," he said, leaning down to nuzzle

the space between her breasts.

"We'd better not start," Jane said. "I just saw Dan outside and accidentally met Dominique. She looks like a beauty queen, and she's wearing enough emeralds to choke a horse.

"How are she and Dan doing?" Bryce asked.

"Their problems are written all over his face." As Bryce sat, she added, "Julie told me some dish. Bobby tries to kiss her in the bedroom scene."

"A crush works for the show."

"But she doesn't want to encourage him since kissing's not in the script."

Someone beckoned from outside, and Jane opened the door to Alan and a tall man with shaggy white hair and a white beard. "Hello," Alan said. "Is Christmas around?"

"I'm right here," Bryce said, rising again as Alan and the stranger came in.

"Bryce Christmas and Jane Conroy," Alan said, "I'd like to introduce T.H. White, the esteemed author of *The Once and Future King*." He addressed White adding, "Bryce used to bring a copy of your marvelous novel to our rehearsals in New York."

"I did, and I loved it," Bryce said. "It's an honor to meet you, sir."

"Tim," the author said. "As I told Lerner here, I was flying from London to New York with Tony Walton when our plane made a detour to Boston. Fog or some such piffle, which means my visit is fortuitous. And since you're still working on the show, I'll reserve judgment."

"We're grateful for your patience," Alan said. "And now I'm placing you in the capable hands of Miss Conroy, who'll take you to the star dressing rooms. I'll see you and the Waltons at the Ritz after the show. We'll have drinks, food, and a candid discussion."

"Thank you, Lerner," Tim White said before Alan disappeared. Then he thanked Bryce for reading his book.

"Have a good show, Bryce," Jane said before escorting the author into the hall.

A surprise visit from T.H. White was the last thing Alan needed, Bryce thought, noticing the tiny costume rack someone had delivered. He exchanged his street clothes for a robe and began patting on his foundation. As Dan burst in, he said he'd met the author downstairs.

"What the hell happened?" Bryce asked when he noticed Dan's left eye and cheek. They were red and starting to swell, and he recalled Jane's cryptic remark about Elsdon's face.

"Dominique punched me, which I definitely deserved." He sighed. "Apparently, she doesn't want to raise anyone else's 'brat,' as she put it, especially since she's unable to have her own children, a tidbit she withheld. Can you believe her brass, deceiving me like that? Well, it's a moot point since our engagement is over."

"What are you going to do?" Bryce asked.

"What would you do, Christmas? Sarah won't even take my calls."

"Excuse me a second," Bryce said before jogging to the payphone near the stairs. His mission took three minutes, and when he reclaimed his place at the mirror, Dan was seated on the adjacent chair, head in hands. "Listen, roomie, I called Bernie Hart and asked him to send up some ice for your face. It should reduce the swelling."

"Thanks, man," Dan said, looking up. "That will help."

"And I've thought about your problem. Albany's three hours away, so don't bother calling Sarah. Rent a car for Sunday and drive to her house. You can apologize and propose."

"Just like that? Out of left field?" Dan asked.

"You'll have the element of surprise. She'll be so relieved I bet she'll accept."

"You may be right," Dan said. "I'll try it. And you want to hear the irony? Even if Dominique hadn't cut me loose, I would've ended it, and for the right reasons. I'm in love with Sarah and want to raise our baby with her." He grinned. "I owe you, Christmas."

"Forget it," Bryce said. "I just hope they bring the ice. You're getting a real shiner."

"I look like holy hell," Dan said, glancing in the mirror. "But real knights probably looked worse."

"Yeah, they were missing eyes and teeth," Bryce said, and they both roared.

———— ◆ ————

From Bryce's perspective, *Camelot's* opening at the Shubert seemed as magical as any spell Merlyn could cast. Alan had slashed lines, so act one was shorter—and every cut helped. Another bright spot was that, unlike the Canadian audience, the Bostonian crowd caught the wit in Alan's dialogue and lyrics. Peals of laughter often echoed through the house, lifting everyone's mood backstage.

Perhaps to avoid being accosted in the lobby at intermission, Alan and his wife slipped on stage through the pass door and chatted with Oliver Smith, Abe Feder, and Hanya Holm. Standing stage right was Joyce Haber, who was still doing background interviews. Bryce noticed that Fritz and Tamara were absent, but he made his way upstairs—not easy on that crowded staircase—and took a slug of tea from the cup he'd brought from the deli. Then he sat at his vanity, thinking the "Fair" number had seemed out of sync with Julie acting sexy while the knights repressed their virility. Musically, though, it had gleamed.

Dan arrived—his eye was getting black and blue under his makeup. While changing costumes, they shot the breeze until Bernie Hart called "Five minutes 'til curtain," followed by "Places for act two." Since Bryce and Dan's next number, "Fie on Goodness!" was just ahead, they ran downstairs with Roddy close behind. Bryce, Dan, and Roddy waited until others cleared the stairs, then walked ahead, single-file, into the stage-left wings.

Hemmed in by his colleagues, barely able to breathe in the musty space beyond the set, Bryce listened to Bobby's "If Ever I Would Leave You" and was awed. Goulet's bass-baritone was like molten silver pouring from his cords. His timbre was beautiful, and his singing made Bryce believe he truly loved Jenny. (So far, smoking hadn't hurt the guy's instrument.)

Act two moved quickly. Halfway through, Bryce infused his verses of "Fie on Goodness!" with extra testosterone, ignoring Burton's instructions. Then he sang his heart out in "Guenevere" and the "Camelot" reprise. During the latter, Bryce could hear loud sobs and sniffles coming from the first few rows of the house, and he almost cried himself.

Was it too much to hope this star-crossed musical was finding its feet?

The applause at the curtain call was deafening, and downstairs in the basement, bottles of champagne sat in buckets on a table, compliments of the Black Angus, a neighborhood bistro. When Bryce got down there after removing his makeup and changing into his navy suit, he found Jane sipping bubbly with Mr. White, who looked dazed. Bryce took Jane's arm, his way of telling her they should go, and she turned to the author, saying, "Tim, Julie and Tony will fetch you here. Alan's ordered a car that will take all of you to the Ritz."

"Much obliged, Jane dear," the author said, pouring himself more champagne.

Bobby Goulet and the other knights had booked a party room at Steuben's Café Midnight on Boylston, a nightclub that stayed open until 3 a.m. Bryce and Jane arrived at twelve-thirty, and an hour later, when the gypsies were blitzed on beer, Bobby climbed onto a long table and waved the first review. "This is from *The Boston Globe*," he called. "The headline says *Camelot Needs Work—Gorgeous But Dull*."

The cast members groaned in unison, and a few yelled, "Boo."

"Who wrote that?" Leena Lear called. She was Julie's petite main understudy.

"A critic named Cyrus Durgin," Bobby answered. "Suppose I pass it around?"

Since Bryce was sitting at Goulet's feet, Bobby threw the paper to him, and Bryce read the review, growing more confused with each paragraph. Though Julie earned kudos for being "a dream performer," Richard was called merely "interesting" and "virile." Durgin saved his highest praise for Robert Goulet's "dark good looks and strong voice," dubbing him "the real romantic lead of Camelot."

"It's ironic," Bryce told Jane who'd been chatting with Nate. "Bobby got good reviews because he's doing better without Moss's harping. This should end all talk of his being fired."

"Let me see," she said, grabbing the *Globe*. "Wow! Durgin slays Alan's book. He called the two big speeches for Arthur 'a crushing letdown for the audience.'"

"He doesn't like the 'peace and justice' theme, either," Nate remarked after his turn reading the review. "Which is bizarre since that's the main point of Arthur's 'might for right.'"

"It's late," Bryce said, yawning, turning to Jane. "Your place or mine?"

"Yours," she said. "I don't want to see the producers tonight."

They made the rounds, saying goodnight to their colleagues. When they were strolling up Tremont in the morning chill, Bryce asked, "Don't you want another glimpse of the famous Dominique? You could stop by Alan's suite while I wait in yours."

Jane yawned. "I'm not interested. Dominique resembles Mrs. Lerner with her blonde hair, designer duds, and jewels. But she did thank me for saving her from Dan."

"I don't understand," Bryce said, steering Jane past a sleeping man on the sidewalk.

"Remember in the deli the other day when Dan accused me of speaking to Kitty Hart? He was right. I did a favor for Kitty in Toronto, and she agreed to tell Dominique about Sarah."

"Cookie, you astonish me." Bryce stopped under a street lamp and kissed her with a rush of desire. She went limp in his embrace, and for the first time in his life, he fervently believed in God. How else could he explain the wondrous gift of Jane Conroy? "I forgot to tell you," he said as they resumed walking. "You did a fine job with the kid playing Tom."

"You think so?" Jane asked.

"You have talent," he said. "Directing is a field worth exploring."

Bryce felt discouraged by the poor *Globe* review. When they reached his room, he switched out the light but didn't make love to Jane. She seemed happy to snuggle in his arms, and they fell asleep, but he awakened too early on Saturday. He brushed his teeth, then donned some slacks and a knit pullover and went downstairs to fetch two cups of java, which he brought back to his room. After serving Jane coffee in bed, he climbed in with his own cup, using pillows to support his back.

Jane eagerly took a few sips before asking if the *Globe* review had been a bad dream.

"We wish," he said. "The desk clerk downstairs told me the main Boston critic is Elliot Norton. His review should be out this afternoon, and maybe it'll be better. He's also known as a play doctor, and I wish they'd hired him to fix *Camelot*."

"I don't think Alan would let anyone touch his script."

After they made small talk for a while, Jane ran to the bathroom. When she returned, she jumped onto Bryce's lap, straddling it, and kissed him with minty breath.

"I don't know how I'd get through this without you," she whispered. "I had no idea things would be this chaotic on the road."

"I've heard about try-out travails from many actors, but *Camelot* takes the cake."

"When the show opens on Broadway, Brock will leave and I'll lose my job. Then what?" Jane slid to the edge of the mattress and walked to a damask armchair, sitting with her legs crossed under her. "I'm sure that literary agent won't take me back, and even if I apply to Yale, I wouldn't start until next fall. It's dawned that I'd need to ask my parents for help with tuition, and they might turn me down."

Bryce put his feet on the floor. "Live with me," he said.

"You mean as your lover?" she asked.

"I hope you'll always be my lover," he said while crossing to her chair and getting down on one knee. "But I want you to be my wife. I know we're moving fast, but will you marry me, Jane?" (He'd lately concluded that having a traditional family wasn't his main priority.)

"When?" Jane asked, stroking his wavy hair.

"Depends on what kind of wedding you want. My folks will be blasé. Yours?"

"I'm their second daughter. They might be relieved not to throw another pricy country club wedding especially—uh—"

He chuckled as he stood up. "Especially if the groom's a part-time waiter."

She stood, saying, "Maybe we could have a small wedding after *Camelot* opens. Maybe they'd give me the reception money for grad school."

"I'd prefer a small wedding. So, what's your answer? Will

you have me, Miss Conroy?"

"Hell, yes!" she said, laughing, throwing her arms around his neck. "Can we tell people?"

"I think we can share the news with friends. But I'd like to give you a two-carat rock before you tell your folks."

"Two carats? That would cost a fortune."

"My *nagymama* left me money, and my *Camelot* pay is a lot more than at Sardi's."

"Let's order food and celebrate before the matinee."

He kissed his new fiancée and began to whistle while jumping in the shower. He felt grateful that while the fortunes of *Camelot* were worsening, his own were improving. He'd met the love of his life and sensed that his first Broadway lead was in his sights. And he also decided *Camelot* might limp along on the strength of its marquee stars, even if the other Boston reviews were tepid. Regardless of the show's fate, however, it was enough that Jane would become his wife.

Jane

After Bryce and I shared a room-service brunch, we decided to walk through the Public Garden, a place we were eager to explore. We walked down to Boylston and chose a paved path that was nearly empty. We passed acres of brownish grass, assorted statues, and the Swan Boat Pond (minus the boats, which didn't operate in winter). The morning was cold and overcast, but I thought the day was glorious, at least until Bryce took off for the Shubert.

Now I had time to process the gravity of having gotten engaged, and I felt flustered passing a statue of George Washington on horseback before I crossed Arlington Street. I loved Bryce, and when I was in his ebullient company, enthralled by his looks and talent, I was sure we were supposed to marry. But as I cleared the Ritz's revolving door and ran up the steps to the foyer, I wanted to wail like a lost child. Was Bryce the right partner for life? Was I truly in love or merely in the grip of lust and infatuation?

He'd voted for Nixon, for God's sake.

My mind was a swamp. I was so distracted I passed the elevator and the grand staircase and wound up in the lobby with its couches, coffee tables, and vases brimming with flowers.

"Jane," said a familiar male voice, and when I looked up, Richard, clad in a white shirt, red tie, and dark slacks, was leaving the Ritz Café, which served light meals. "You look down in the mouth, love. Have you read Elliot Norton's review in the *American*? Alan got some early copies, and it's worse than the *Globe*."

"I'm heading up to Alan's now," I said.

"Why don't you come upstairs and read my copy. That way, you'll know how to speak to Alan and Fritz. I don't imagine they're pleased."

When I hesitated, Richard guffawed. "You can trust me."

"All right," I said, since Richard had a point about my need to be informed before seeing Alan. (I didn't worry about Fritz since he ignored me.)

Richard steered me to the elevator, and on the tenth floor, he showed me to his grand suite overlooking the Garden. I sat on a white couch as he sauntered to his bedroom and retrieved the *Boston American*. He opened it to the right page as he returned, then tossed it in my lap.

"*Camelot Disappoints*," I read aloud. "What's wrong with these blockheads?"

"They're out for blood," he said, sitting next to me, lighting a cigarette. "But they're misleading the public. The book needs tightening, but it's a damn fine show."

I skimmed the column by the critic I'd heard lecture at Catholic University, a man respected by Father Hartke. And I got upset reading his main impression, which echoed the headline in the *Globe*: the show was dull. He loved Bobby's voice and Julie's comic timing and thought Richard was strong, even delightful, except when he was forced to be too serious. He loved Fritz's music but found *Camelot* less than entertaining.

"Holy shit," I cried, feeling self-conscious as the words escaped from my mouth. I'd been taught it was uncouth to swear, but Norton's review made my blood boil.

"My thoughts precisely," Richard said as I placed the paper on his coffee table. He moved sideways and faced me. "You're new to this madness, Jane, but it all blends together after a while. Whether reviews are good or bad, I give my utmost to my role and hope the audience approves." He stared at me pensively. "But you weren't thinking of our show in the lobby just now, were you? Your melancholy was caused by something personal."

"You're right," I said. "I told someone I'd marry him, and now I'm having doubts."

"How old are you, love?" Richard asked.

"I'm twenty-five."

"I was twenty-four when I married Sybil, and God knows I'm a poor husband, but she was a brilliant mate for me. Maybe you'll come round to that."

"You're a man of the world, Richard. How do you know it's a good time to take a step like marriage? And how do you know you've chosen the right person?"

He furrowed his brow. "You consult your intuition and take a leap of faith. Knowing is something that happens in hindsight, but you strike me as a person who makes smart decisions." He smiled. "Who's the lucky bloke?"

"Someone you're not fond of," I mumbled. "Bryce Christmas."

"Ah, Yuletide. He and I fell out in New York. But he's gifted, and Moss thinks he'll be a Broadway heartthrob." He paused. "Roddy says he's heard that Christmas will soon quit *Camelot* for a leading role elsewhere."

I was caught off guard because Bryce hadn't shared this news. But I calmly stood, saying, "I should let you get ready for the matinee."

"I shouldn't have promised you could trust me," he said, walking my way. "A romp with you would get my motor running. How about it?"

"I'm flattered, Richard," I said. "I wish I could throw caution to the wind. But cheating on Bryce would make me feel guilty, and I feel cheap enough having sex outside marriage."

"Before you go, I'd like to put a thought in your mind about engagement. It's a wise anonymous poem from the seventeenth century." And in his sonorous voice, he intoned:

> *Love not me for comely grace*
> *For my pleasing eye or face,*
> *Nor for any outward part,*
> *No, nor for a constant heart.*
> *For these may fail or turn to ill,*
> *So thou and I shall sever.*
> *Keep therefore a true woman's eye*
> *And love me still but know not why,*
> *So hast thou the same reason still*
> *To dote upon me ever.*

"Lordy," I said. "That was sublime."

"Was it?" Richard asked.

"I might just faint."

"This way," he said, offering his hand. "Getting you horizontal is the idea."

"I can't," I said. "Oh, Richard, please. I have to—say no."

But then I reached out and stroked his unshaven cheek, staring into his gray-blue eyes. It was like peering into a bottomless mysterious sea.

With a grave smile, he briskly pushed my hand away. "Off you go, love."

I returned his smile but didn't delay.

When I was walking toward the elevator, my heart pounding, I felt furious at myself for going to Burton's suite. Because I'd been sorely tempted. He was unbelievably sensual but also vulnerable, and when he'd recited the poem, I pictured myself in his arms, then in his bed. But I loathed smoking, especially the reek of tobacco breath, and since Richard had just finished a cigarette before propositioning me, the smell of his clothes and hair brought me to my senses.

Still, it had been a close call, and I was glad I didn't have to confess a sexual misstep to Bryce. And now I'd learned my lesson and wouldn't be alone with Richard again. We'd all heard he'd cut a swath through the female chorus after ending his fling with Nell. But didn't his philandering wear his "brilliant mate" down? How did Sybil Burton stand it?

My mouth went dry, guessing that if Bryce even looked at another girl, my heart would snap like a twig, and as this thought washed over me, I thought, *Forgive me, Bryce.* I suddenly recalled a remark Julie had made over tea: that Richard was catnip to men, women, children, and animals, the most charismatic person she'd ever met. (But Julie, ever loyal to Tony, stopped short of confiding she was attracted to her leading man.)

Well, Bryce had proposed to me, and while it was sooner than I'd expected to find a husband, I was learning that life as an adult was neither predictable nor controllable. I remembered nights in my college flat in seedy northwest D.C. when Sarah and I had shared our fantasies about conquering the New York theater. We'd longed to be modern women who supported ourselves on Broadway, she as an actress and I working backstage. But nothing we'd imagined matched the pitfalls of being out of town with *Camelot,* and we'd both grown up fast. (I felt helpless knowing my friend was alone in her misery, but Bryce advised me to be patient.)

———◆———

While the Saturday matinee was happening at the Shubert, I took notes at another meeting with Alan, Madame, Fritz, Tamara, and Brock. Alan began the session by reporting that he'd had breakfast with T.H. White before Tim and Tony Walton flew to New York, and the author was more generous in his appraisal of *Camelot* than the critics. "He told me not to worry about being faithful to his novel. In fact, he exhorted me to do whatever's best for my book."

"Terrific," said Brock, though his tone was dubious.

"I don't think there's anything dull about *Camelot*," Madame said. "Neither does Joyce Haber. I had breakfast with her before she went to New York on that flight with Tim and Tony."

"Thanks, darling," Alan said. "But the show's still too long. On the positive side, the scenes are playing better, thanks to Philip Burton and Brock here. And Tom of Warwick is livelier, thanks to Jane."

"Fine, fine, but I don't agree with most of Philip Burton's ideas," Fritz said. "He's made the 'Fair' song look like Guenevere plans to bed all three knights."

"I don't see that," Alan snapped.

"I do," Tamara said.

"*Moi aussi*," Madame said.

Alan stared at his wife, whose overpowering Shalimar scent made my nose twitch. "Let's give Philip free rein while I hack away at my book. I'm rewriting from the middle of act one."

"When should we let Roddy sing his new song?" Fritz asked.

"Before we close in Boston," Alan said. "And we need to write a new French song for Lancelot that proclaims his love for Guenevere at the top of act two."

"In French?" Madame asked. "Should I translate those lyrics for you?"

Brock sighed in response to Mrs. Lerner's offer, whereas Fritz slowly crumpled an unlit cigarette, rolling it between his fingers until it flaked all over his clothes. (Why didn't Alan and Fritz meet alone instead of subjecting themselves—and us—to these frustrating chats?)

———◆———

On Sunday, Bryce and I went sightseeing. We explored the steep streets of Beacon Hill dotted with brick Federal-era and Victorian row houses and had a prime rib dinner on pewter plates at a communal table in Durgin Park, a famous restaurant where waiters slammed food in front of their patrons. "I wish Mr. Sardi could see these jokers," Bryce had said, feigning disgust but enjoying himself.

Later we returned to the Ritz, where we made fast, fierce love. Afterward, we were lounging in Ritz robes in my parlor when the phone rang. "I hope that's not another crisis," I said. But when I picked up the receiver, I heard Sarah chirp, "Jane, did you know?"

"Know what?"

"That Dan was coming here today," Sarah said. "I was so shocked I didn't know what to tell him when he proposed. My parents hated him on sight, of course. But after he left, I had a heart-to-heart talk with them, and now they're on board."

"Bryce told me Dan might visit you today," I replied.

"He and Dominique are done," Sarah said. "And I don't

care if it was her decision. The idea of giving up my baby depressed me so much I could hardly get out of bed." She laughed. "That was convenient, since I'm supposed to rest. But God help me, I still want the man."

When I asked where things stood, Sarah explained that she and Dan hoped to marry soon. "Maybe two Sundays from now if you can find a Boston priest who'll skip the banns. My folks will drive me over next week, and since Dan's a Catholic who's never been wed, we're free and clear. Isn't that something? So, would you call Father Hartke and see if he can pull strings? I'm too ashamed to tell him I got pregnant, but maybe he'll help us if you ask."

"I'll call him tomorrow," Jane promised.

"Dan says he loved me from the start of our affair," Sarah said. "He realized it after I left Toronto. And listen, Jane, he has a big apartment with room for a nanny, and I'll be able to pursue my career." She'd been talking a mile a minute and paused to exhale. "We want you and Bryce to be our witnesses, and I want you to be our baby's godmother. You've always been there for me, Jane, and I'll be there for you. No matter what."

I covered the receiver and told Bryce that Dan wanted him to be his best man. "With pleasure," he replied.

"We'll be delighted to stand up for you. I'll call you tomorrow after I speak with Hartke. He'll know a priest here. He knows everyone." After I hung up, I returned to the couch. "I guess we misjudged Dan Elsdon."

"I'm glad he's doing the right thing with a nudge from you and Mrs. Hart."

I was so thrilled by Sarah's news I had trouble sleeping. On Monday morning, however, Brock assigned me an annoying daily task that I'd resent for the rest of our Boston run. Since the book and the scene numbers were changing daily, the program in the preprinted playbills didn't match what the audience saw on stage. Alan's remedy was to have me visit his suite at 4 p.m. on regular performance days, learn what scenes had changed since the day before, type up the alterations, and bring this info to a print shop on Boylston by 6 p.m.

I'd have to wait while the printer made half-page inserts, then carry two boxes—one for the orchestra and one for the balcony—to the Shubert so the ushers could stuff them into playbills. (For Thursday and Saturday matinees, I'd have to ask the printer to double the number from the night before, which meant toting four boxes, a haul requiring a cab.)

As I dove into this chore, I found myself hating my job, hating the November weather, which had turned bleak, and hating *Camelot,* which was not improving with the Other Burton's changes. (All right, I was overreacting, but the inserts were sending me over the edge.)

When I sat in on Brock's rehearsals with the chorus, I understood why he was a general assistant to the producers: he was a skilled director, and I belatedly gleaned his worth to Alan. In baseball parlance, he was a utility player. When he coached the actors—or corrected their line readings—he buoyed their confidence and reinforced their best instincts. If Richard hadn't needed shoring up by Philip Burton, Alan might've asked Brock to take all the rehearsals. (As for my directing experiment, I'd done such a good job with the Toms they didn't need me anymore. I was back to being a full-time gofer.)

"You seem edgy lately," Nate said when we accidentally met outside the street bar at the Ritz late Friday night. I was by myself since Bryce, fearing he was catching a cold, had gone to his own hotel.

"Everyone's edgy," I said.

He shifted from foot to foot. "Jane, I've been meaning to

speak with you. I had no business kissing you in Toronto. Shari's my world, and I'd never do more than flirt with someone else. Will you accept my apology?"

"I shouldn't have kissed you, either," I said. "Shall we forget it?"

"Forgotten," he said with a wide grin.

"Hey, Nate. The other day you said Richard told Julie he loved her on the night he disappeared. Does he really think he loves her?"

"Arthur loves Guenevere," he said. "Maybe Richard has to fall for Julie as part of his creative process. He told me he's had flings with all his other leading ladies. But I think Bobby's the one with the biggest unrequited crush." He smiled. "Speaking of romance, I hear you're engaged to Bryce. He's a lucky man."

"I am, too."

"Be happy, love," he said before giving me a bow, then ambling into the bar.

"Goodnight," I called, thinking Nate had picked up the endearment 'love' from Burton.

Was everyone going bonkers from the pressure? Look at what I'd almost done with Richard. I still blushed at the memory of touching his acne-pocked cheek. Yet I believed Nate when he said he didn't cheat on Shari because I'd never heard gossip about him on the company grapevine. (Or even Bobby, who had a wife named Louise in New York. I figured his crush on Julie was innocent.)

Pushing the elevator button, I decided the one person I wished I could consult was Moss, and I wasn't alone. Alan had confided the same thing that afternoon when I'd arrived to type up the changes for the inserts. He also mentioned that Goulet's job was secure despite lingering rumors to the contrary. "We briefly considered replacing Bobby when we arrived in Boston," he admitted. "But Richard wouldn't hear of it, and the rest of us realized he was right." He shrugged. "All's well that ends well, I suppose."

But it sure didn't hurt, I concluded later on, that Bobby had scored a better review from "the dean of Boston critics" than either Richard or Julie. (In Bobby's shoes, I might've sent a huge box of Belgian chocolates to Elliot Norton.)

11.
JANE'S
LITTLE LAPSE

Jane

Knowing how much I despised my new task, Bryce offered to meet me at the printer nightly and help me tote the playbill inserts to the Shubert. Sometimes we reached the theater quite early, allowing us to grab a sandwich at the deli and have a quickie in Bryce's dressing room. Other nights, we lingered over a hot meal at one of the bistros on Stuart Street. Then we'd sign in at the security desk and part ways at the stage-left staircase. He'd go up to his dressing room while I ran down to the basement, where the stage managers were usually kibitzing with each other. (I spoke little at their gab sessions but learned a lot.)

Thursday, November 10th, was Richard's thirty-fifth birthday. Alan and Fritz surprised him with a party at the Paddock Café, the restaurant next door to the theater. The manager, Sean Hurley, closed the place to others at 11 p.m. so the *Camelot* cast could relax. Though I passed the Paddock daily, I'd never gone inside before and was now disarmed by its coziness. The brown Formica-topped bar was shaped like a horseshoe with red cushion stools, and the dining room boasted adjoining cherrywood booths resembling pews in colonial churches.

I was among the first to arrive, and I shyly greeted Sybil Burton, who'd taken the evening train from New York. I still felt ashamed that I'd nearly succumbed to Richard's advances, but I chatted with his wife as we accepted coupes of Bollinger from the bartender. Alan, Madame, Fritz, and Tamara joined us, along with Brock and Philip Burton. When a few gypsies showed up, Sybil and Philip, old friends apparently, moved to the end of the bar, and since I was sitting several stools away, I leaned toward them to eavesdrop.

"How's the show coming?" Sybil asked the Other Burton. "Can it be saved?"

"I believe so," he murmured, "but much depends on Mr. Lerner. We work together on the book far into the night, and I barely get four hours' sleep."

"I can't thank you enough for taking it on," Sybil said. "Rich is much calmer."

Sybil calls him *Rich*, I mused, whereas nobody had ever used that diminutive in my hearing. I got lost in my thoughts until someone kissed my neck from behind.

"Howdy, ma'am," Bryce said, claiming the next stool. "How's it going?"

"I'd rather be alone with you," I said.

"Likewise. I hate two-show days, but at least we didn't have to rehearse." When the barkeep was in front of us, Bryce said, "I'll have what the lady's having." Then he grimaced. "Pellinore's dog pooped three times before he left the stage tonight. We all had a hard time keeping a straight face, but it smelled pretty rank."

"Sorry," I said, watching the door where the cast and crew were trickling in.

"Have you heard the news?" Bryce whispered. "Our New York opening has been postponed from November 26th to December 3rd. We're staying in Boston an extra week."

"Brock must've been afraid to tell me," I said. "He knows I

hate doing the inserts."

The guest of honor slipped inside the Paddock, and his colleagues broke into a ragged chorus of, "For he's a jolly good fellow." Richard froze, visibly stunned, especially when Sybil ran over and kissed him.

Seeing Richard's eyes shine with tears, I felt happy for him. He was a mass of contradictions, and I longed to know him better. But he wasn't the kind of man who'd have a platonic female friend.

The next day, the citizens of Boston were still celebrating the November 8th victory of their native son, John Fitzgerald Kennedy, who'd won the presidential election. And when I stopped by Alan's room around 4 p.m., he, too, seemed pleased by the success of his former Choate and Harvard classmate. But he also mentioned he felt frustrated that his script was still in flux. "I keep cutting but also adding. And I've yet to find the best place for Lancelot to declare his love for Jenny except in the madrigal Fritz and I are writing. Maybe that will suffice."

That night, after giving Bryce a long French kiss outside the deli, I found Brock in the Shubert lobby, staring at a carton of orangeade. "Why do I drink this awful stuff?" he asked. Then he complained he was weary of directing, weary of Philip Burton's pomposity, weary of living in hotels; lonely for his wife, and worried that the more Alan tinkered with *Camelot*, the worse it got. "We lack a guiding vision," he intoned.

"It wasn't like this with *My Fair Lady*?" I asked.

"No, because we had Shaw's *Pygmalion* script," Brock said. "That man had an unerring sense of drama, so we rode a wave of success from our first New Haven preview straight to Broadway." He laughed, confessing he'd once made a journal entry about *Camelot* that ended with *Who needs George*

Bernard Shaw? "This show's a train wreck like *Paint Your Wagon*."

I remembered a recent chat with Jack Dabdoub from the chorus who'd done *Wagon* nine years ago. He'd told me Lerner and Loewe nearly broke up while reworking that show, which flopped on Broadway.

"Hey, congrats on persuading Elsdon to marry Miss Wilkins," Brock added. "I heard the ceremony's happening next Sunday at some Boston Catholic church."

"The Paulist Center," I said. "Paulist priests are liberal, and they're going to waive the banns." I smiled. "Sarah and Dan had a rough start, but I think they'll make a go of it."

"Madame told Alan that you asked Kitty Hart to call Dan's fiancée. That was ingenious, Jane. Have I told you lately how much I appreciate your calm efficiency? I bless the day Max sent you my way."

"Thanks." I was gratified since Brock gave me few compliments.

"Some night next week, let's skip the damn show. I'll take you to dinner at the Ritz, and we'll unwind. What do you say?"

For a fleeting instant, my female guard went up. But this was Brock, after all. "I'd like that," I replied.

"Good, and be advised that the Ritz dining room is ultra-formal." He crumpled his empty drink carton. "Why didn't you mention you got engaged to Christmas?"

"We're trying to keep it quiet," I murmured.

"Is that why you're not wearing a ring?" he inquired.

"I will be soon," I said, sensing Brock still didn't approve.

———◆———

Bryce and I were asleep in my suite at 10 a.m. on Sunday when I was awakened by a knock. I donned a Ritz robe and closed Bryce into the bedroom. Bracing myself for a new calamity, I answered the door and came upon Francine Tristan, waving a copy of *Time*.

"This baby hits the stands tomorrow," she explained. "I took an early train so I could give a preview copy to Alan and Fritz. But nobody's stirring on their floor. Hope I didn't wake you, Jane. Can I wait here for a while?"

"Of course," I told Francine, who brought to mind Mrs. Tiggy-Winkle in her bulky brown mink coat.

"Thanks, doll. And I'd kill for a cup of joe."

"I'll call room service," Jane said. "Anything else you'd like?"

"A prune Danish if they have one. Traveling's murder on my digestion."

By the time I ordered breakfast, Francine was settled in a wing chair. "Want to read the *Time* story?" she asked, offering me the magazine.

I accepted her copy and studied the cover photo of Alan and Fritz seated on gilt thrones before a medieval coat of arms. "The picture's impressive," I said, but then I read the blue banner slanting across the top: *The Rough Road to Broadway*.

"It's a bit of a hatchet job," Francine said. "And I blame Haber. She's one of the 'dear shits' who couldn't resist crowing at our misfortunes." She shrugged. "But there's something I don't get, which is one reason I stopped by. Everyone in the cast knows Alan and Fritz have barely spoken since the show moved to Boston. Everyone knows they fell out over Alan's refusal to hire a name director. Yet while the *Time* writer John McPhee mentions Abelard's death, Alan's ulcers, and Moss's heart attack, he gives the impression that Alan and Fritz are a united front. How did Haber miss their estrangement?"

"Alan's wife kept Haber busy day and night, according to Brock. They became fast friends, and Haber's interviews with cast members were brief because Mrs. Lerner tagged along and kept butting in. Now whether Alan asked her to do this, I don't know."

"But Julie called Alan and Fritz 'the loneliest men in town.'"

"Doesn't that imply they're in this debacle together?"

"I suppose. Toward the end, John McPhee calls *Camelot* 'Lerner's *Parsifal.*' On the heels of '*Gotterdammerung* without laughs,' that makes the show sound grim."

"It *is* grim," I said. "The more I watch act two, the more tragic it seems."

"Well, I'm moving the photo call to our last Tuesday here. Leo Friedman will come in from New York, and we'll do it after the show. It's an ordeal, but why wait until the Broadway previews? It's not as though the cast will be any less stressed."

After another knock, an elderly waiter wheeled a silver cart to the sofa. As soon as I signed the bill, the man limped away.

"I see three mugs?" Francine said. "I didn't realize you had company."

"Uh, Bryce Christmas," I said. "We just got engaged." I handed the Danish on a napkin to Francine and poured her coffee from a silver carafe.

"Two sugars, please," she said. "And good for you, doll. It's a pity your fiancé will be leaving us, but *Camelot* might not make it past New Year's Eve."

Though I'd already heard this news from Richard, Bryce still hadn't mentioned his plans, and I hadn't asked. Was it because I didn't want to know? Because it would be harder for us to deepen our relationship if we weren't sharing the same ups and downs?

"I gather from your expression he hasn't told you," Francine said. "It's likely still up in the air. Press agents hear gossip, and someone said he'll be the lead in Harburg's new musical."

The bedroom door squeaked open, and I turned too late to warn Bryce about our visitor. He stumbled into the parlor stark naked, stopping when he glimpsed Francine. "Miss Tristan," he said without missing a beat. "Nice to see you again."

"I assure you, the pleasure's mine," Francine said, eyes widening.

"Excuse me a moment," Bryce said before retracing his steps.

"Mazel tov, darling," Francine drawled. "He's a stallion." After emitting a wicked cackle, she bit into her Danish, and I wished she'd move on. I was looking forward to a day of sightseeing with Bryce and Dan, as well as Sarah, who'd moved into a single room at the Parker House. We planned to rent a car and drive twelve miles to Concord, where I hoped to tour the home of Louisa May Alcott.

Bryce returned in a white Ritz robe and poured himself some coffee. He sat near me on the sofa and asked Francine, "How's our box office in New York?"

"Healthy despite poor notices on the road." She pointed to Lerner and Loewe on the front of *Time* which I'd placed on the coffee table. "I'm not sure this article will help, but it may not hurt. People might be curious. Even sympathetic."

"Alan should get a medal," Bryce said. "He's rewriting around the clock."

"Speaking of the clock," Francine said, rising slowly, "I've detained you lovebirds long enough. I have to find the courage to rouse L and L, though it's barely eleven."

I showed Francine to the door, saying, "Hope Alan and Fritz like the story."

"They won't," Francine said before she lurched away on her high heels.

"You didn't look embarrassed when she caught you in the nude," I told Bryce when I returned to the couch.

"Actors show their bodies all the time," he said with a shrug. "I'm not ashamed of mine." After a pause, he added, "You seem annoyed."

"Francine was nearly drooling," I said. "But, no, I'm not annoyed. Are we taking our field trip?"

"I forgot to tell you. Sarah's under the weather. Dan mentioned last night that he didn't think they'd be going anywhere today."

"She should rest. But you and I could take a cab to Cambridge and walk around, couldn't we? I need to get away from King Arthur's court."

"I second that motion," Bryce said, putting down his cup.

I wanted him all to myself, which was why it bothered me that Francine saw him naked. But instead of explaining, I said, "Before we get ready, I want to know if you're quitting *Camelot*. I've heard rumors you'll be doing a new show, but you've kept me in the dark."

"My agent called me about a possible leading role, but I don't have a contract."

"Oh, Bryce, I think I'll feel abandoned if you leave me alone."

"You better get used to it. We won't always work together. If I move ahead with my career, I might be on the road more than I'm in New York, And if you pursue directing, you'll be off to regional theaters. Truthfully, it'll be hard to make a marriage thrive that way."

"Are you saying I should give up my dreams to support your ambitions?"

"No, I'm just describing what we'll face with a two-person theater career. Unless we both get jobs at a rep company like Arena Stage in D.C. or the Guthrie in Minneapolis."

"Would that be feasible?"

"Could be." He stroked my cheek. "I think you had a good idea. Let's visit Cambridge."

"You're on. We can stroll across Harvard Yard and discuss why JFK, their star alum, will be a better president than your shifty candidate."

"Kennedy didn't win by a landslide," Bryce said. "Nixon will be back."

"Like a bad penny," I told him.

By Thursday, November 16th, as I sat in on a chorus rehearsal, I realized that Boston theatergoers were seeing a far different *Camelot* from those who'd attended the last Toronto show four weeks earlier. And I also saw that Alan's daily rewrites were exhausting the cast. The actors got altered scenes at their 11 a.m. rehearsal each morning, and they practiced the changes that day and the next morning, directed by the Other Burton (principals) and Brock (chorus). They performed the new version the second night, so Monday's changes were played Tuesday night, and Tuesday's changes were played Wednesday night. Thursday was a two-show day, which meant that Wednesday night's changes stayed in until Saturday. (On Sunday, they were off, but then the tiring routine began again Monday.)

At least the production was getting shorter. Julie's original solo toward the end of act one, "Face to Face," was removed in Boston because it was a response to Lancelot's "Quests," which they'd cut after Toronto. Alan and Fritz still planned to write her a song that would serve as a bridge from "the Jousts" (when Guenevere fell for Lance) to the "proposition" speech (when Arthur confessed his fears about his wife and best friend). Poor Julie would likely be learning the new one just before we opened on Broadway, and she was such a pro she wouldn't bat an eye.

Standing in the Shubert's rear wings, I recalled that *Camelot* had fourteen act-one scenes in Toronto, but there would be twelve when we left Boston. Act two had nine scenes when we began, but would wind up with eight. Alan was unsure about cutting "Fie on Goodness!" but he'd allowed Roddy to perform his new number, "The Seven Deadly Virtues." And the partners had finished their piquant madrigal for Lancelot that would introduce "If Ever I Would Leave You." The lyrics, sung in both French and English, revealed that Lance and the queen had carried on for two years between acts one and two. This would heighten the drama, though Bobby hadn't yet performed it on stage.

———◆———

Each night while I ordered the inserts, Bryce showed up to help me. But on Friday, November 18th, I met him wearing the slinky cocktail dress my mother had sent me. "Going somewhere tonight?" he asked.

"Brock invited me to dinner," I said as we sat on a bench in the print shop. "I won't be around during the show."

"Good timing," he said. "The boys are throwing a bachelor party for Elsdon at a club in the Combat Zone. Bobby's coming and maybe Richard. We even hired a girl to jump out of a cake." He chuckled. "Dan should be thrilled. But I'll be late, so I'll stay at Parker."

I was relieved since he'd certainly reek of smoke and booze after carousing at some sleazy bar. "I have something to tell you," I began. "Since Sarah's parents are coming to the wedding on Sunday, she invited my parents, which means you'll meet my folks sooner than we planned." I touched his arm. "I couldn't talk her out of it."

"Are you going to tell them about us?"

"Well, since Sarah and Dan know we're engaged, it might be awkward not to."

"Don't look so worried, Cookie. *You're* not pregnant."

"I'm not worried. I'm just not looking forward to dinner tonight with Brock. He's been out of sorts." I sighed. "Let's invite my folks for a drink on Sunday night and tell them about us privately. It's Sarah's day, and I don't want to steal her thunder."

Bryce was on board with my plan, and when the inserts were finished, he offered to carry the boxes to the Shubert so I could return early to the Ritz.

"Have fun," he said, closing me into a cab, then paying the driver.

Brock and I had arranged to meet in the street bar at 7 p.m. When the host ushered me into the dimly lit, dark-paneled room with windows facing Arlington, I found my boss seated on a banquette along the wall. It seemed like an oversight that Bryce and I hadn't stopped at this cozy hideaway, and I made a mental note to bring my fiancé here soon.

When my boss got to his feet, I admired his tailored charcoal suit and red tie. His aftershave smelled expensive, and it was flattering that he'd dressed up for me. "I'm sure our table is ready upstairs," he said.

"You look debonair, Mr. Remsen," I said as we entered the foyer.

"You look swell yourself," he replied. "But do you mind if we take the elevator instead of the staircase?" I agreed, and we presently arrived inside the hotel's legendary second-floor restaurant. The maître d' greeted Brock by name and brought us to a table at the front window where a bottle of Veuve Clicquot was chilling.

Though I'd eaten once or twice at the Café overlooking Newbury, the main dining room was swankier than I expected. The cobalt-blue water glasses matched the dark-blue chandeliers which were its hallmarks, according to Brock. The tables had crisp linen cloths, and I loved the twinkling lights in the Public Garden across Arlington Street. A tuxedoed waiter promptly poured our champagne, and Brock lifted his crystal flute, saying, "Here's looking at you, kiddo. You're indispensable."

Hadn't Moss told me this should be my goal? I touched my glass to his, then tasted the Brut champagne. "You're in a good mood, Brock. Did Alan and Fritz like *Time*?"

"Alan thought it was fair," he said. "Fritz hasn't said much." He sighed. "We've heard Elliot Norton is coming again next week. We're hoping he'll like the changes and give us a boost as we head into New York. Last we heard, theater parties have begun to cancel, so our record-breaking box-office advance is waning."

Since we'd heard Moss Hart had gone home to New York, I said, "Maybe Moss will return before we open. Maybe he can undo some of Philip's—er, changes."

"That won't happen," Brock said. "Moss was told to rest until February, and God only knows if *Camelot* can limp along till then." He finished his champagne, and a waiter poured more for both of us. "Shall we look at our menus? It's some of the best haute cuisine I've tasted anywhere."

I shyly copied Brock's choices, and after the waiter took our orders, my boss asked to see the sommelier, telling him we'd selected *consommé, les médaillons de veau saute à la moutarde, pommes Lyonnaise*, and *salade de saison*. Brock insisted on white wine, so the sommelier picked a Louis Jadot Pouilly-Fuisse for the entrees, though he "preferred" Cote du Rhone with veal.

"You're gutsy," I said after the sommelier huffed away. "Standing up to a wine snob."

"If you can stand up to Alan and Fritz at their temperamental worst, a sommelier's a teddy bear." He paused. "So, Jane dear, are you enjoying your job? The truth."

"I like everything except doing inserts," I assured him. "Being your assistant has given me a bird's-eye view of production. I can't thank you enough."

"Do you plan to keep working after you marry?" he asked, buttering a roll.

"Yes, I'll work after I go to grad school," I said, eager to solicit Brock's support.

"Grad school?" he asked sharply. "You're getting rigorous on-the-job training. You could move directly into stage management as an assistant."

"I'm hoping—well, I was inspired watching Moss. I'd like to try directing."

Brock's mouth curved into a moue of surprise. He refilled his flute and topped mine with white foam. "That's still a man's field," he said. "There are one or two women who've gotten their feet in the door, but you couldn't pick a harder goal. Did someone advise you otherwise?"

"Moss," I replied. "I spoke with him in the hospital."

"Moss's mind was fuzzy from his heart drugs," Brock said. "Which grad school?"

"Maybe Yale. I could also return to Catholic. Father Hartke respects me."

"Dear Jane," Brock said. "You have a flair for directing. You did a great job with Tom of Warwick. But why do you want to climb this particular mountain? I'd sincerely like to know."

I put down my flute. Though my head was buzzing from the champagne, I was aware that neither Moss nor Bryce had probed my motives. "Brock, from the time I was a teenager, I loved to read plays. And when my high school drama club took me to the theater for the first time—a matinee of *The Crucible*—I was hypnotized. The play dispensed vital truths about life."

"Miller's a genius," Brock said.

"Yes, and when I watched what Moss did in the early rehearsals of *Camelot*, I realized the director is the one who pulls everything together and brings out the text and sub-text."

"Moss Hart is brilliant at what he does. But remember, Jane, he brings years of experience as a playwright that deepens his directing ability. He's unique."

The waiter interrupted our discussion when he brought our salads, and since Brock had turned the Veuve bottle upside down in the bucket, the sommelier presented the Pouilly-Fuisse.

"Very nice," Brock said, so the man poured our wine.

"I like this wine," I murmured after tasting the crisp Pouilly.

"You won't be drinking the good stuff on what you earn as a lady director."

Biting my tongue, I took a dainty bite of romaine lettuce dressed with oil and vinegar. (Brock had asked for the salad course after the *consommé*, distressing our waiter since the salad normally came after the entrees.) "Brock, may I ask you something? My uncle Max is aloof with our family, but he stays in contact with you. Is there a reason you're so close?"

Brock looked away, but I got the feeling he was gazing inward. "The war," he said sadly. "I rarely talk about it, but I'm surprised your father didn't tell you."

"Max's hands are badly scarred," I said. "I've always wondered what happened."

"I'll give you the short version without much gore."

He explained that in 1942 Lt. Maxwell Conroy and Lt. Edmund Remsen were among 697 sailors aboard the USS *Juneau*, a Navy light cruiser, when it was torpedoed by the Japanese during the Battle of Guadalcanal. The boat exploded and broke in half, killing all but ten men. The survivors spent the next three days treading water in the Pacific, fighting the pain from their wounds and fending off sharks. Max and Brock eventually climbed aboard an inflatable raft dropped from a U.S. warplane and slowly paddled to San Cristobal Island.

"Your uncle saved my life," Brock said. "His hands were badly burned in the fire, but he knifed a shark that devoured two of my toes and was about to eat the rest of me." He flinched. "I'm sure you've noticed my limp. Anyway, the shark attack happened before the raft came down to us like manna from Heaven, and Max got the Bronze Star for bravery."

"I had no idea," I murmured. "You've taken such an interest in me, I—"

"Jane," he said, patting my hand. "Max is closer than a brother. You're family."

"I'm—touched," I replied. "I feel the same about you."

Blinking back tears, I was relieved to know Max and Brock's history since it explained why Brock had been my company guardian angel. But when our entrees came, he changed the subject, sharing his fond and funny memories of *My Fair Lady* and *Brigadoon*. He ordered a second bottle of wine, and afterward, we devoured luscious citron tarts with our coffee. Then we drank Remy Martin from snifters the size of soup bowls.

"I may need help leaving," I said when my head began to spin after my first sip of cognac. "I'm not a drinker." Punctuating this claim, I broke out in a cold sweat, and when the waiter brought the check, I felt a wave of nausea. I figured an antacid might help, and though I didn't have those tablets in my room, Brock kept a supply. While he walked me to the elevator—I was weaving—he looked wary when I asked to visit his suite. "I need Alka-Seltzer."

"All right, but let's make it fast," he said, pushing the button for the tenth floor.

When I was seated on the couch in his parlor, he fetched two tablets and a glass of water from the bathroom. After the fizzing ended, I downed the cloudy drink in two long gulps and hoped I wouldn't burp. "Thanks so much," I said, aware that Brock was watching me with alarm.

"Jane, you're much too pale," he said. "I need to get you upstairs right away." He took my arm and guided me toward his door, but I stumbled and collapsed in a heap on his carpet.

"Judas Priest!" he cried, crouching down. "Are you all right?"

I giggled and slowly got up. "I'm too blitzed to walk. I'll have to camp out here."

"That's a bad idea," Brock bristled. "There'll be talk if anyone finds out."

Nonetheless, I staggered into his bedroom and fell, facefirst, onto his mattress. My limbs felt like boulders weighing me down, and I couldn't move. I closed my eyes, head throbbing, and waited for the Alka Seltzer to take effect. Then—dreamless sleep.

When I awoke, I had a low-grade pain in my stomach and head. Sitting up, I realized I was alone and completely dressed except for my shoes. I assumed it was 11 p.m., perhaps midnight, but when I crept into Brock's parlor, sun was streaming in through open drapes, casting a glare that hurt my eyes. Brock was snoring on the sofa in his suit from the night before, and when I checked the clock, I was aghast to learn it was 7 a.m.

I fell into a wing chair and struggled to conjure details from the night before. Brock surely hadn't meant to ply me with booze or lure me here. It had been my fault for drinking too much, and maybe he wouldn't recall the shameful way I'd passed out. But staying the night in my boss's suite hadn't been proper, and if anyone saw me leave, they'd think the worst of us as he'd feared.

I scooped up my shoes and tiptoed to the door. In the hall, I found the fire stairs, climbed them, and dizzily walked to my suite. When I unlocked my door, my drapes were closed (as I'd left them), but a lamp cast shadows in the parlor, which seemed odd since I hadn't left any lights on. Yawning, I made my way to the next room, nearly fainting when I saw Bryce sitting up in bed, his eyes red from Dan's bachelor bash.

"Where in Hades have you been?" he asked hoarsely. "I've been worried sick."

"I—fell asleep in Brock's suite," I said, unable to concoct a good lie.

"Brock's suite?" he asked. "Where was he?"

"He was there," I said, plopping into the wing chair. "We had too much champagne and wine at dinner, and I accidentally passed out."

Bryce stroked his mustache, and I guessed he wasn't buying my story.

"It was completely innocent," I said. "So, how was the party? I thought you were staying at the Parker House."

"Did you 'accidentally' sleep with Remsen?"

"Don't be silly, Bryce. Brock would never touch me—" But when a knock interrupted my explanation, I feared my boss had come to check on me, which my fiancé might misinterpret. *God help us,* I thought as Bryce disappeared into the bathroom. While I was answering the door, he stomped into the parlor in a Ritz robe.

"I can't speak to you from the hall, Jane," Brock said, and when I stepped aside to let him pass, he nearly collided with Bryce. "Hello," he added, pulling back. "I brought Jane more Alka-Seltzer. Your darling girl was sick last night, and I've been playing nurse."

"Nurse?" Bryce asked, glowering. "Or doctor?"

"I'll forget you said that, Christmas," Brock grunted before dashing out the door.

"I swear to you, Bryce, nothing happened," I said.

"Something happened, all right," Bryce said, crossing his arms.

"I had a small lapse of judgment," I insisted.

"Two lapses," Bryce said. "You drank too much with a male companion and went to his room. You showed incredibly poor judgment, Jane." He paused. "Look, I'm going back to my hotel to get some sleep before the two-show marathon."

"Fine," I said. "Maybe you'll be in a better mood later."

"I'm not in a bad mood," he said. "You betrayed my trust."

"That's a strong statement. I'm not allowed two missteps?"

He sighed. "Let's take a break until I can assimilate all this."

I wanted to hide from his scowl. Instead, anger overtook me, and I said, "If that's how you feel, we better cancel our engagement. Then you won't have to 'assimilate' my betrayal."

Bryce gaped at me, apparently too shocked to reply.

"I'll be seeing the show with my parents and Sarah's folks tonight," I continued. "You might have to meet them since you're the best man. Then I'll see you at church tomorrow."

"Jane," he said, "you're being hasty. Let's talk about this when we cool off."

"You're the one who wanted a break, Bryce. Now you've got one."

"Fine," he mumbled. "I'll get my clothes and clear out."

"One last thing," I said. "Brock never showed a smidgen of interest in me, even when he was drunk."

"He's a frigging saint," Bryce snapped. "But if you're going to have a theater career, you better damn well recognize how appealing you are. Somehow you grew up thinking you're average in every way, and I'm here to say you're a knockout." He frowned. "I'll miss you."

I wanted to hurl myself into his arms and beg his forgiveness, but pride held me back. He'd questioned my morals and my honor, and I was hurt—also too hungover to think straight

Right now, I wanted to be alone. So, I let Bryce dress and leave without another word.

But I was too upset to return to bed, and by noon I was telling myself to call Bryce at his room and apologize. I didn't, and the idea resurfaced at the matinee's half-hour: I should call Bryce backstage and make amends. But I was paralyzed by fatigue and guilt. Instead, I cried and cried. I'd been reckless to go to Brock's suite, especially after my close call with Richard, and I'd acted bratty when Bryce called me on it. But I sure as hell hadn't meant to break up with him.

My parents phoned from the Parker House after they checked in at 4 p.m. They'd run into Sarah's folks, Ron and Ellen Wilkins, at the front desk. I told Tish that I'd made a 6 p.m. reservation at Dini's, a seafood joint Bryce recommended.

As the afternoon wore on, I spent time reflecting on what Brock had revealed about himself and Uncle Max. They were both scarred for life from their war wounds, and Max was even viewed as a hero. (Why hadn't my father told me? He knew how much I cared for his brother.) Amazingly, both men had bravely moved on, and I shed tears for their fortitude, or maybe I was weeping over my broken engagement. Having no other antidotes for misery, I took more Alka-Seltzer, and by the time I greeted my attractive, gray-haired dad and stylish mom in the Parker House lobby, I resembled my usual self. My heart, however, was in shreds.

My mother gave me a probing look. She asked if something was wrong.

"It's been a crazy few weeks," I confessed, longing to cry on Tish's shoulder.

Sarah emerged from the hotel elevator, clad in pink chiffon, accompanied by her tall, sandy-haired father, a food marketing exec, and her brunette homemaker mother. The older four greeted each other warmly, having met at college events through the years.

"I can't believe it's tomorrow," Sarah said, threading her arm through mine as we strolled past King's Chapel, heading to Dini's. "Thanks for moving heaven and earth to do this for me."

"You're welcome," I said. "And it's true what they say

about pregnant women, Sare. You're glowing."

"I can't wait to move into Dan's place when we get back to New York. You and Bryce will be our first dinner guests."

I forced myself to smile, envying my friend's happiness. I'd never been to Bryce's walkup, which he'd described as a railroad flat, and now I might never see it, thanks to my rash declaration of independence.

The four parents raved about the seafood at Dini's, and as the curtain fell on act one of *Camelot*, all of them seemed moved. Nobody spoke until Sarah leaned toward me, saying, "Alan's changes have made a big difference, so I'm surprised Bryce is quitting. But Dan called me at the matinee intermission and said Bryce got a lead in a new musical."

"He told me it was in the works," I mumbled before rising and helping Sarah to her feet. We followed our parents out to the lobby for refreshments.

When act two began, I marveled at the latest improvements. The pace of the show was faster, and I adored the new French madrigal for Lancelot. I also thought Mordred's "Seven Deadly Virtues" was more devilish than his former reprise of "Fie on Goodness!"

Alan had beefed up the drama in the "Guenevere" number, sung by Bryce, Dan, and the chorus, and I was impressed by Garry Whitson's acting in the finale. *Camelot* seemed romantic, poignant, and exactly what the Boston critics had claimed it wasn't: a delightful polished successor to *My Fair Lady*.

After the curtain calls, while the orchestra played the exit music, my parents stayed in their seats, Tish wiping her eyes. Mr. and Mrs. Wilkins stood in our row talking with Sarah, and I was glad all of them had seen the show during our third week in Boson instead of earlier. But my spirits were lower than dirt since I'd probably have to endure the misery of seeing Bryce before I swept Sarah back to the Ritz. We were planning a pajama party before the wedding, a throwback to our college years.

We stayed put until the crowd dispersed. Then the six of us made our way outside, where we waited under the Shubert marquee. Chorus members dashed past, avoiding the crush of fans at the stage door. Bryce and Dan soon emerged through the front doors along with Roddy and Robert Coote, who waved to Sarah and me before walking away.

"You were sensational," Ron Wilkins told his future son-in-law, extending his hand. Ellen Wilkins rose on her toes and kissed Dan's cheek, echoing her husband's praise.

"His technique is flawless," Sarah declared, and the Wilkins family formed a circle around Dan, who seemed startled by everyone's approval.

I shyly greeted Bryce, saying, "I'd like you to meet my parents," and as I uttered those words, my folks moved toward him. "Mom, Dad, this is Bryce Christmas, who'll be the best man tomorrow. You heard him sing the first two verses of 'Guenevere.'"

"Indeed we did," my father said, extending his hand. "You have a sterling baritone."

"Nice to meet you, sir," Bryce said, shaking hands. "And you, Mrs. Conroy."

"It's Owen and Tish," my mother said. "You were impressive in the 'Fair' number, too."

"You're both too kind," Bryce said, sounding pleased.

"Where are you from, Bryce?" my father asked.

"Princeton," Bryce said, "but I went to Rutgers." He laughed. "My day job was being a waiter at Sardi's while auditioning for Broadway."

"Nothing wrong with that," my father said. "I waited tables in college myself."

"I have to admit," Bryce said, "I enjoyed the rush each

night around seven-forty when all the patrons had to pay at once so they could get to the theater."

"You have a positive attitude," my father said.

"Bryce," called a lady from over his shoulder, "shouldn't we be going?"

I swiveled around and saw Leena Lear, the loveliest soprano from the chorus. She was dressed in a wool coat and mink hat, and I recalled that Leena and Bryce had been rehearsing together as the understudies for Julie and Bobby.

"You'll have to excuse me, Owen and Tish," Bryce said. "My friend and I are joining some castmates for supper."

"It was nice meeting you," my father said.

"I'll see you at the wedding," Bryce said before nodding curtly at me. Then he made a point of warmly bidding goodnight to Sarah, Dan, and Sarah's folks before guiding Leena next door to the Paddock Café.

"Could you excuse me?" I asked my parents. Then I hurried down to the ladies' lounge, reaching the toilet seconds before I lost my dinner. When the siege ended, I rinsed my mouth, reapplied my lip gloss, and returned to the sidewalk where my parents were chatting with the Wilkins family and Dan.

"Should we go?" I asked Sarah.

As soon as Dan hailed a taxi, I said goodnight to the four parents and slid inside. From there, I watched Sarah kiss her groom before he helped her into the cab and shut the door. The driver sped away, and while peering out the side window, I knew that as soon as I was safely ensconced at the Ritz, I'd howl like a banshee. I'd never imagined that Bryce might start dating someone else on the same day we broke up.

"Jane," Sarah said. "You haven't been yourself tonight, and I saw Bryce leave with Leena. Did you two fall out?"

"I made a terrible mistake," I cried. "I broke up with Bryce. Can you believe I was worried my folks wouldn't like him? Instead—"

"They adored him," Sarah murmured.

The taxi sped over Charles Street between the Common and the Garden, and I wondered if Bryce and Leena liked each other. Or were they congenial colleagues? Well, I would see him at the ceremony tomorrow and the wedding dinner and then around the Shubert, so there was reason to hope. As soon as I could muster the nerve, I'd apologize profusely and try to repair the damage I'd done. But I'd never felt more helpless, or miserable, in my life.

———————◆———————

The next Tuesday night during our last week in Boston, Leo Friedman and Francine Tristan arrived to conduct the photo call. Bernie Hart had been asked to corral the actors, but over dinner at the Paddock before the show, Francine warned the photographer to expect a topsy-turvy night. Leo, a man with elfin ears who was my idea of an aging leprechaun, wondered why Francine was concerned. "Haven't we seen it all before?" he asked.

"Some of these actors drink *during* the show," Francine said. "And they've been through hell with Lerner's changes. Remember, Leo, they've been rehearsing daily—though not to-day—and doing the show at night, and now we're asking them to work again after midnight when they'll be ready to drop. Add booze, and we might get bupkis." The press agent turned to me. "All set with the food?"

"The deli up the street will deliver at midnight," I said.

"Look, Francey," Leo said, "I'll sit in the front mezzanine during the show and see if I can get good stuff then. It would be nice to dismiss them early."

"I suppose we're as organized as we can be," Francine said. "I think I'll have a second drink myself. The buzz will wear off long before we have to rally the troops."

Leo chuckled, and I glanced furtively at Francine, who was dressed, as usual, for a cocktail party. Should I tell the press agent I'd ended my engagement in case I had any issues? No, I decided, digging into my bowl of Irish stew. Bernie would call the cast to the stage; at most, Francine might ask me to fetch a few props.

I'd worn a navy sweater over a white blouse and dark slacks, hoping to blend into the woodwork. I didn't want to speak with Bryce, whom I'd last seen at Sarah's wedding, where he'd been polite but hadn't given me the slightest hint he wanted to reconcile. And if he spent the photo call flirting with other women, I'd try to ignore him.

Just before joining the press agent and photographer, I'd dropped off enough program inserts for the entire week since Alan had frozen the show (even though it still ran three hours and thirty minutes). At least that soul-numbing task was behind me.

I stood under the marquee at 11:50 p.m., eager to greet the caterers. I waited for twenty minutes in the cold, but when they didn't come, I cursed aloud and raced up the block. The deli was closed, and I felt stupid because I hadn't written down an emergency number. Yet I'd confirmed my order with the deli manager that afternoon, so what had happened?

Since the Shubert's front door was locked, I had no choice but to use the stage door, where I pushed through the boisterous crowd waiting to meet the stars of *Camelot*.

"You can't cut in line, little girl," a plump matron screamed, but I told everyone I worked for the show and had to get inside. It took another two minutes to reach the security desk, and by the time I'd returned to the stage, Francine was wringing her hands. About two dozen actors were skulking around the set, no doubt impatient to eat.

"The deli guy didn't show," I told the press agent.

"That's unfortunate," she said. "The actors won't cooperate without food."

"Let me call Sean Hurley, who runs the Paddock," I said. "They're still open."

"In the meantime," Leo Friedman said, "someone should ask Burton and the boy to pose for the last scene." He turned to me. "We shoot the show in reverse, as you know."

"I'll find Burton," Francine said, "while Jane speaks with Mr. Hurley."

"Richard may be stuck at the stage door," I said before stalking through the wings. It was my bad luck to bump into Bryce in the hall, where we both jumped as though we'd been struck by cattle prods. "Excuse me," I said, before racing outside.

"It's an emergency," I told the security guard, who wore a super-large uniform that hung off his thin frame. "I need to use your phone." When I got the Paddock manager on the line, Sean Hurley agreed to help us and took my order. Then he cheerfully inquired why the producers hadn't asked him to cater the photo call in the first place.

Caught off guard, I couldn't think of a reason.

"Cost, I imagine," Hurley said. "Well, I get plenty of business from Shubert patrons, and I'm glad to bail you out."

"Your delivery guys should use the stage door and ask for me," I said before racing back to Francine and reporting my progress.

"Brava," the press agent said. "Otherwise, we'd have a mutiny on our hands."

"I'll go find Richard and Garry," I offered, retracing my steps until I saw Master Whitson lounging against some scenery next to his toothy mother. "Miss Conroy," his mom said, "Bernie Hart promised me the photographer would shoot Garry first. It's getting late."

"Yes, please head to the stage now," I said, then I returned to the deserted main hall and knocked on Richard's door. Bobby opened up, drink in hand, and I saw Richard seated at his vanity, pouring a vodka. "The food's been delayed," I said, "but Richard, could you pose with Garry now so the kid can go home?"

"He's *young*," Richard said. "He's the only one who won't be knackered tomorrow."

"We heard you screwed up," Bobby said. "The cast has a dartboard with your face on it."

"The deli was at fault," I said wanly. "So, Richard, will you come now?"

"All right, but it'll cost you," Richard said, gulping his shot. He stood stiffly, then followed me through the wings, now crowded with cast members shouting questions about their supper. I assured them the food would arrive soon as Richard, wearing his costume from the finale, loped in my wake. As we reached center stage, he said, "Give us a kiss, love," before pulling me close and smooching me tenderly. "Marvelous," he said after breaking away. Then he strolled over to Garry and tousled the kid's hair.

"I saw what he did," Francine said when I joined her at stage right. "Is Burton a good kisser? On a scale of one to ten?"

"He's an eleven," I said, and Francine guffawed.

Leo Friedman crouched before Richard and Garry. Then Bernie Hart emerged from the rear, asking the pair to run their scene from Tom's entrance.

Leo made a series of loud clicks with his camera as Burton fed a line to Garry, turning slightly toward the front, a stage bit known as "cheating." I began to relax, thinking all might be well, until Francine asked me to find Bryce and Dan so Leo could shoot the "Guenevere" number. "The rest of the chorus is here," Francine said, pointing to some singers, "except for those two. I know Bernie paged them."

I watched the crew start to change the set before I ran again toward the main hallway, where I found Bryce, trailed by Dan, both wearing their "Guenevere" cloaks. "Mr. Christmas and Mr. Elsdon," I called, "could you get your sweet asses to the stage?"

"Care to rephrase that?" Bryce asked.

"Sure," I told him. "Could you *please* get your sweet asses to the stage?"

"Christmas, are you going to let her talk to you like that?" Bobby called from Richard's doorframe. "How 'bout you, Elsdon?"

"They're late," I yelled. "And that's enough from you, Goulet. Put a sock in it."

"I'll tell you what's late," Bobby snarled. "Our chow. You're incompetent, Conroy."

I turned and stomped toward the wings with Bryce and Dan in tow. Other singers took their places in the chorus, and Bernie asked them to warble a cappella phrases of "Guenevere" while Leo caught the moment on film. As the photographer finished, four men entered the wings with trays of sandwiches, carafes of coffee, and six-packs of soda, plus bags of utensils and napkins. I asked them to follow me to stage right, then down the stairs and across the basement, where they placed everything on one of the two tables. Afterward, while escorting the delivery guys back to the stage door hallway, I heard Bernie on the loudspeaker, calling, "Dinner is served downstairs. Dinner is served!"

Exhaling, I returned to stage right, where Bryce accosted me, saying. "You were rude."

"You're supposed to come when you're called," I said, folding my arms.

"We were on our way," Bryce said. "To be frank, Jane, you're pushing your luck. Bobby's riding high. How do you know he won't tattle on you to Alan? He could get you fired."

"I must've lost my head," I said, stung by his criticism.

"Is that a trend?" he asked, but when I glanced up, he was grinning.

"I'll apologize to Goulet. And I'm sorry for being rude to you and Dan."

"I'll tell Dan," he said, gazing at me with a glimmer of sympathy.

"I've been making bad decisions, Bryce. It may be stress, which is no excuse. Look—

"Bryce, dear, we better eat while we can," Leena Lear called.

"She's right," he said. "I'm hungry, and it might be a long evening." He studied me for a moment before saying, "Later, gator." Then he strode toward Leena.

Was he needling me by alluding to happier times or just being flip? Either way, I wanted to run after him and smack his face. Instead, I crossed to stage left.

"What's up, doll?" Francine asked. "You look distraught." When I didn't answer, she said, "Now that the food's here, we'll be fine."

"Francine, I managed to insult Bobby, Bryce, and Dan."

"Bobby's hanging out with Richard," she said. "Bring him a sandwich as a peace offering." She paused. "But you and Christmas?"

"We broke up," I said, trying not to cry. "He seems to be dating Leena Lear."

"I'm so sorry," Francine said, patting my arm. "I've had theater flings that went awry. But you hold your head up, Jane, and I'll deal with 'Mr. Well-Endowed.'"

"Thanks, Francine," I said, grinning at her wit. "I'll make nice with Goulet."

"Tell him we're doing the bedroom scene next. I'll have Bernie call Julie and Roddy."

As if on cue, the crew began dragging the queen's canopy

bed to center stage. When I reached the basement again, I decided I'd bull through the next few hours by dint of Francine's kindness. I'd formerly viewed the press agent as a tough broad, but I'd been wrong.

I had much to learn, I thought, heading for the food table. But one thing I knew for certain was that I wouldn't feel whole again until I'd cleared the air with Bryce, who was now chatting with Leena, Dan, and Nate at the second table. (If Bryce knew I was nearby, he didn't glance my way.)

I grabbed a turkey sandwich for Goulet while warning myself I might need to grovel at Bryce's feet. I couldn't predict when I'd find the courage, but my darkest fear was that I'd already lost him. And if this was the case, I thought, trudging back up to stage left, I might never recover. Worst of all, I'd have no one to blame but myself.

PART
FOUR

BROADWAY-PHILLY FOLLIES
DECEMBER 1960 - MARCH 1961

"'Once there was a fleeting wisp of glory,' cries Richard Burton as he awaits the last curtain alone. And there was. But, for *Camelot* as well as for Arthur's court, it is the glory of a steadily setting sun."

- Walter Kerr, *New York Herald Tribune*, December 1960

12.
BRIEF SHINING
RUN-THROUGH

Bryce

As many times as he reread Elliot Norton's second review of *Camelot*, Bryce couldn't see where the critic was coming from. Norton said the show was "a shadow" of what it should've been, and though Bryce was back at his flat, it still rankled him that he'd found a copy of the November 27th *Boston American* at his door before checking out of the Parker House. Couldn't Norton wait until the cast left town before dumping his second dose of vitriol?

Happy to be home, Bryce skimmed the review one last time. Norton loved the title song; he liked the new French ballad for Bobby and "The Seven Deadly Virtues" for Roddy but seemed irked that Lerner and Loewe's new song for Julie hadn't debuted in Boston. And he didn't like Roddy's nastier take on Mordred. Strangest of all, he was more critical of Richard than he'd been after opening night, concluding the star had lost his way. For this failing, Norton blamed the lack of dramatic action and humor in Alan's book.

Mainly, though, Norton bemoaned the absence of Moss Hart's guiding hand and minimized the contributions of "an assistant named Philip Burton." Julie Andrews, he wrote, was giving an "exquisite performance," and Robert Goulet sang "richly and magnificently." Yet Norton declared that four weeks in Boston had left *Camelot* "unperfected."

Jeez, Louise.

Bryce tossed the paper on his coffee table-trunk. He fetched a Heineken and returned to the couch. He was dying to discuss this bizarre review with Jane, but wasn't sure how to contact her. Had she returned to the Barbizon? Surely the new Mrs. Elsdon knew her whereabouts.

He took a slug of beer and wondered how things had gone so horribly wrong with the girl he loved and hoped to marry. He'd felt justified getting upset that she drank too much and passed out in Remsen's room. But he'd also felt consumed by overpowering jealousy, and now he realized he'd been unreasonable and unwilling to hear Jane's side. When he said they needed "a break," however, he'd meant the rest of the day, not that excruciating last week in Boston.

When Jane hadn't called to apologize that first Saturday, he'd decided to rattle her cage by taking Leena Lear to dinner. But he and Leena were friends—she was engaged to a dancer in *Bye Bye Birdie* and not inclined to stray. Anyway, the last thing he wanted was a fling with anyone. Though he'd had affairs with castmates in previous shows, he didn't view sex as a casual method of stress relief or ego-building as some actors did. He craved intimacy with Jane.

He drank his beer, musing that he'd gotten on well with Dr. and Mrs. Conroy after *Camelot*. The next day at Dan and Sarah's wedding, Jane's dad had been downright convivial, and at one point, they repaired to the Parker House bar, where they had a meaningful talk about their stints in the Army. (Owen had proudly mentioned he'd been deployed overseas during World War II, though he still felt sad that his brother Max had suffered grievous wounds. Bryce admitted he'd felt ashamed of his stateside posting during Korea.) They also discovered they were avid golfers with the same handicap: ten.

Owen seemed so impressed he said, "It would be fun to play sometime." And, irony of ironies, Bryce later heard Owen tell Jane, "You should find a real man like Christmas, but you must prefer the artsy types."

"I don't, Dad," Jane had meekly replied.

Bryce thought Jane seemed melancholy while they witnessed their friends' vows in the sanctuary of the Paulist Center, and she'd mostly ignored him during dinner in a private room at the hotel. Bryce had thought their rift was a tempest in a teapot, but a stubborn streak prevented him from reaching out to her. Why had he gone upstairs to his room that night and let Jane's father wait with her while the hotel doorman hailed a cab? Why hadn't he dashed out to the street and insisted on escorting her back to the Ritz so they could have steamy make-up sex?

After the photo call in Boston, Jane avoided the backstage hallway, and maybe it was his imagination that Julie stopped speaking to him, too. He'd seen Jane and Julie hop into a cab one night after the show and guessed that Jane had complained about Bryce to the leading lady. Yet, coincidentally, Richard and Bobby were friendlier lately, though he couldn't fathom why.

Well, they were back in New York, but he had no idea where he stood with his ex-fiancée. The only sane thing to do at this moment was to watch *Maverick* on his small black-and-white TV and hit the sack. Tech rehearsals this week would be challenging, and nerves might get raw before they opened on Saturday.

He kicked off his loafers and loped to the kitchen for another Heineken and a carton of Hunan Chicken, rooting around a drawer for a fork. He brought his meal to the couch and dove in, eating his chicken cold because he was too lazy to turn on the stove. And as he swallowed, he realized his chosen career was daunting. Since he'd been offered a lead role in

Harburg's spring musical—without an audition—he needed to weigh the pros and cons of staying in *Camelot* or moving on. Which posed the bigger risk?

———◆———

On Monday, while Brock Remsen was supervising the installation of the set at the Majestic Theatre on 44th Street, another Shubert house, the company met on the New Amsterdam roof. When Bryce arrived at 10:45 a.m., Alan and Fritz were huddling at the production table with Hanya Holm and Franz Allers. Philip Burton stood in a corner chatting with Richard.

Bryce took a seat five rows behind Julie and Roddy and was joined by Dan, whose smile was brighter than usual. "Howdy, Elsdon," Bryce said. "How's married life?"

"Better than I could've imagined," he said. "And since we don't have to perform at night until Thursday, my bride and I would like to invite you to dinner tomorrow."

"I'll be there," Bryce said. "Just us three?"

"Four—you, me, Sarah, and Jane, who's bunking with us for now. You should know that Sarah hopes to play peacemaker for the two of you."

"Sarah's an angel," Bryce said. "I'll bring some champagne I've been saving."

"How about seven?" Dan asked, handing Bryce a scrap of paper with his address.

"I have an idea," Bryce said. "You and Sarah can help me woo Jane if you'll play along. I assume you have a piano, yes?"

His castmate nodded, and after Bryce explained his plan, Dan chuckled. "You're planning to bring out the heavy artillery, huh? Good for you." Then, after saying he and Sarah would do their parts, he asked, "Have you heard the wags in town are calling us *Cost-a-lot?*"

"Better than 'a medical,'" Bryce replied. "That's what the

writer called us in *Time*."

Their chat ended when Philip Burton walked up to them. "I just spoke with Alan," the director said as Bryce and Dan stood to greet him. "He's cutting some verses in the 'Guenevere' number to make the finale come faster. But we both feel the success of the song depends on the urgency of your singing. You're telling the story oratorio style, and it's got to be intense. Even more intense than it is now."

"Should we ask Mr. Allers?" Dan asked. "If we're going to change our vocal approach?"

"Don't change anything," Burton said. "Just add more emotion. Sing as if it's 'life or death' because that's what it is for Guenevere."

"We'll do our best," Bryce said. "Anything else?"

"Go ahead and act completely crass in 'Fie on Goodness!' These knights aren't joking. They want to molest virgins and murder their foes." Burton shrugged. "I know I said 'less testosterone' in rehearsal, but I believe I was wrong."

After the director strolled away, Bryce said, "You had the right idea about Allers."

"He's not busy now," Dan said. "Let's ask him. Burton doesn't realize that 'adding emotion' could disrupt our vocal line." When his colleague set off, Bryce followed, impressed by Dan's knowledge of technique.

Bryce didn't see Jane on Monday and caught a mere glimpse of her on Tuesday as he rehearsed his choral numbers. Maestro Allers had given permission for Bryce and Dan to use Burton's suggestions, and after working on "Guenevere" and "Fie on Goodness!" again, they decided the director was on point this time.

The unexpected pleasure of Tuesday afternoon was watching (and hearing) Julie learn her plaintive new ballad, "Before

I Gaze at You Again." She was a quick study and sang the number flawlessly after three repetitions.

"It's more powerful than her old song, 'Face to Face,'" Nate told Bryce as they sat at the rear of the New Amsterdam.

"It shows her attraction to Lance," Bryce said, "but also her wish to stay loyal to Arthur."

He discreetly checked his watch, eager to leave so he could dress for his dinner at Dan's.

At 7 p.m. sharp, Bryce emerged from a taxi and surveyed the façade of 585 West End Avenue, one of those stately brown-brick buildings dating to the twenties. The doorman in a green uniform ushered him inside a marble lobby with fresh bouquets on pedestals and crystal sconces. He took the elevator to the seventh floor and found apartment G. Having pressed the buzzer, he expected Sarah to greet him, but Jane answered, wearing a crisp white blouse, a black pencil skirt, and higher heels than usual, her wavy auburn hair falling to her shoulders. He felt glad he'd dressed nicely in a tan corduroy jacket, white dress shirt, blue silk tie, and brown slacks. He smiled while handing her the champagne. "I haven't seen you at rehearsals," he said, trying to sound offhand.

She shrugged. "Brock and Alan have me running all over town again."

Glancing around, Bryce said, "This is quite a place."

"Wait until you see the living room. It's big as a ballroom. And I feel so lucky they asked me to stay." She laughed. "I took the maid's room off the kitchen. I even have a bathroom."

Bryce followed her down a long narrow hall to an immense parlor with parquet floors, a fireplace, floor-to-ceiling windows facing West End, and a black Steinway grand jutting out from the northwest corner. Dan had chosen a nubby caramel-hued couch, teal easy chairs, and a brown low-slung coffee table. There was a small TV on a stand, an immense cherry stereo console, and a couple of lamps on black-lacquered side tables. The room had an unfussy masculine feel that would likely change after the baby arrived.

"Evening, Bryce," Dan said, wearing a navy blazer over a blue dress shirt and tan slacks.

"I like your home," Bryce said.

"My aunt lived here for years," Dan said. "I was lucky to inherit her rent-control deal."

Sarah joined them, clad in a gauzy hostess dress that reached the floor. "So glad you're here," she told Bryce, kissing his cheek before placing a platter of cheese and crackers on the coffee table. Jane handed her Bryce's Bollinger, which Sarah passed to Dan. "We don't have flutes," she said apologetically.

"It'll taste the same in goblets, honey," Dan said before popping the cork. He poured the bubbly, and as each took a glass, he asked, "Shall we toast to new beginnings?"

"To the newlyweds," Jane replied. "And screw Tiny Tim."

"Cheers," Bryce said, and they all clinked glasses.

"Delicious," Sarah said. "What's that about Tiny Tim?"

"Moss said that before our first read-through," Jane said. "And God bless us, everyone."

Jane took a gulp of champagne before asking if Sarah needed help in the kitchen.

"I do," Sarah said, "but Dan will do the honors. You two can relax."

As their hosts vanished, Bryce gestured to the couch and waited until Jane sat before joining her. "What's new, Cookie?"

"New? Well, I had time to think about my future, so before we left Boston, I called Father Hartke. He heads the Catholic University drama school, and he said he'd let me start the directing master's this spring. If I wait for Yale, I couldn't start until '62."

"You might move to D.C.?" he asked, allowing this distressing news to sink in. "I'm sure glad I found out what's what before we got any further."

"What does that mean?" Jane asked, sounding defensive.

"You're a great girl, but we might not mesh in the long run." He sighed. "You're rigid."

"I'm rigid?" she asked. "You made me feel like a slut for a small lapse in judgment." She stood, frowning. "Well, two lapses." She left the room, and Bryce nervously wondered if he'd chased her away for the evening. But Jane soon returned wearing the pink cashmere shawl he'd bought her on the carefree day they toured Cambridge.

Was this an olive branch? He didn't know, but before she could escape, he took her in his arms and kissed her until she trembled. "You're unperfect," he said. "That's what Elliot Norton called *Camelot* in his second review."

Jane threw her arms around his neck and hugged him tightly. "I'm unperfect, all right."

"So am I," he said. "But kissing you again is heaven."

She pulled away. "You have no idea how I longed to visit your dressing room that last week in Boston and smack your gorgeous face."

"Really? You have no idea how I longed to visit your hotel room that last week and tan your sweet ass."

She smiled at his reference to the photo call. "What stopped you?"

"I did," Dan said, joining them. "This guy was furious. I was afraid he'd act like Dominique and go too far."

"Hell, I did *Kiss Me, Kate*," Bryce protested. "I know how to spank someone without leaving bruises. My Kate actually got off on my technique."

"Yeah, mine, too," Dan said. "She even quit wearing the pads."

"Will you two stop?" Jane asked. "I liked it better when you hated each other."

"What did I miss?" Sarah asked, her dress rustling as she returned.

"Nothing worth repeating," Jane said.

Dan grabbed the champagne and topped off their glasses. He glanced pointedly at Bryce before saying, "Hey, Sarah, do you know Christmas can play while he sings?"

"That's something I'd like to hear," Sarah told Bryce. "Will you perform for us?"

"Please," Jane murmured.

"How could I say no?" Bryce asked, tickled by his friends' participation in his surprise. He strolled to the Steinway, opened the cover, and stretched his fingers. Then he played a lyrical introduction, all the while staring at Jane. In a tone filled with longing, he sang:

Once in the dear dead days beyond recall,
When on the world the mists began to fall,
Out of the dreams that rose in happy throng
Low to our hearts Love sang an old sweet song;
And in the dusk where fell the firelight gleam,
Softy it wove itself into our dream.

Just a song at twilight when the lights are low,
And the flick'ring shadows softly come and go,
Tho' the heart be weary, sad the day and long,
Still to us at twilight comes Love's old song,
Comes Love's old sweet song.

He continued with an instrumental riff on the first verse, then reprised the second with barely controlled emotion. As he finished, the three of them clapped and Dan called, "Bravo."

"Thanks," he said, rising from the piano.

"Thank *you*," Jane said, brushing away tears.

"You should do a recital," Sarah said. Turning to her

husband, she added, "One last trip to the kitchen, Danny, and we'll be ready." Then she grinned hopefully at Bryce and Jane before she and Dan noiselessly slipped out.

As Bryce returned to the couch, Jane said, "I told you I loved that song in Boston."

"Yeah, so I bought the sheet music at a shop near the printer where we got the inserts. I guess something good came out of that irksome job."

"The song suits your voice," Jane said.

"I communicate best through music. It's how I share my real self."

Jane smiled. "Like that famous quote, 'When words fail, music speaks.'"

"Exactly. A lot of singers feel that way. It's why we put up with all the crap."

From the corridor, Dan called them to dinner.

"Jane, listen," Bryce said as they stood. "I was steamed at you that last week in Boston, and Dan kept me from confronting you in anger. He was right."

"I was steamed, too, Bryce. But my anger was mostly at myself."

Bryce placed her hand through his arm, and they strolled up the hall to Dan and Sarah's dining room, lit with tapers casting yellow light. As he pulled out her chair, Bryce decided he might not ultimately "mesh" with Jane, but he couldn't help noticing Dan and Sarah's newfound ease after all their misery. And while taking the seat across from Jane, he wondered if the two of them could find a way forward.

Jane

We enjoyed a meal of roast leg of lamb, mashed potatoes, glazed carrots, and salad—Sarah was an accomplished cook—

followed by a homemade apple pie with coffee. Bryce left at 10 p.m. since the company had a full schedule the next day, and I began to clean up. Sarah and Dan vanished for half an hour, and when Sarah reappeared in her velveteen robe, I asked her to sit in the breakfast nook, knowing she'd feel tired from entertaining. "But I came to help you," she protested.

"You went to a lot of trouble for me," I said. "Let me at least do the dishes."

"Well?" Sarah asked. "Did you and Bryce make up?"

"We made a little progress," I said, washing the last plate.

"Dan says he's been depressed. He asked us if he could serenade you tonight."

"That was unexpected. Even so, he thinks I'm rigid, and I think *he's* rigid. Oh, Sare, I'm so lost. I may need to stay here for a while. Or should I start looking for a place?"

"The large room across from ours will be the nursery," Sarah said. "But the maid's room is yours for as long as you want. Danny and I will always be grateful to you, Jane."

"I'm glad you're happy, Sarah." I began to dry the plates in the drainer, stacking them on the counter. "Look, I was a fool. I shouldn't have gone to Brock's hotel suite, drunk or sober. Even worse, though Bryce doesn't know it, I went to Burton's suite, and when he began reciting poetry in that voice of his, I barely got out intact."

"But from what you've told me, you'd just gotten engaged to Bryce, and you must've been scared, or you wouldn't have been so reckless." She sighed. "I *had* to get married, and I've made my peace with it. But in all our talks at college, Jane, you always said you wanted to focus on stagecraft. You never mentioned marriage or kids."

"And then I fell in love," I moaned. "And even though it's inconvenient and I got cold feet in Boston, I don't want to live without him."

"You looked like you might devour Bryce tonight during his song."

"I wanted him to sing forever, just for me. And I found myself vowing never to cross a man's threshold again unless it's his."

"You and I have come a long way." Sarah stood and kissed my cheek. "I should toddle off, but maybe you need to swallow your pride and apologize to Bryce. Soon."

After Sarah left me, I dried the wine glasses and concluded I'd reached another crossroads. After *Camelot* opened, Brock would start helping Alan with his next project, whatever it turned out to be, and he wouldn't need me. The idea of being at loose ends made my back seize up, but for now, I had a nice place to stay and a chance to save my relationship with a man I loved and my parents liked. (Before leaving Boston, I'd called my mother and confessed my brief engagement to the actor they'd met. "Your dad and I would approve," Tish said. "He's a lovely man.") Yet from Bryce's comments, I thought he was firmly on the fence about me.

Sarah was right: I shouldn't let another day end without baring my soul to him.

———◆———

I saw the backstage of the Majestic for the first time on Wednesday night at 5 p.m. while the cast moved in with their mementos and lucky charms. Unlike most Broadway stage doors which were a few feet from their theater's marquee in either direction, I had to enter an interior alley through a pair of gray industrial doors on West 45th, one street away from the Majestic's front entrance on West 44th.

I walked along a dark concrete passage, which doubled as the service entrance to the Manhattan Hotel, until I came to a second set of gray doors on my left. Moving inside, I found a mostly covered alley hosting the stage doors of the Golden, Royale, and Majestic Theatres. Continuing east, I detected a bit of sky and a few distant fire escapes in an open area above some exposed pipes. I passed garbage cans and six red doors to the Majestic—an emergency exit?—until the stage door loomed ahead on the right. After entering, I climbed a few stairs and cleared another door where a gray-haired guard sat in a cubicle. I introduced myself and scanned the sign-in sheet, learning that Bryce was early as usual.

Feeling apprehensive, I crept along the narrow corridor, passing Julie's dressing room. Up ahead was Richard's room, but I turned left at a narrow cement staircase that led upstairs to several floors of principal dressing rooms—Brock had told me the layout. (The ensemble rooms were upstairs on the other side of the building overlooking 44th Street.)

I passed Bobby and David Hurst's room and Mr. Coote and Roddy's room on the second floor—their names were on the doors—hoping to find Bryce and Dan's room on the third floor across from Nate and Garry Whitson. It was a relief when I reached the next landing and Bryce promptly answered my summons. He invited me inside, where I gave him a peace offering, a box of black and white cookies, freshly made, from the William Greenberg bakery.

"My favorite," he said. But then we stared mutely at one another as though we'd never been alone before. The cramped room had two vanities and mirrors, a sink, and a rack for costumes, but no chairs for visitors and no daybed. (Brock had told me each floor had a communal toilet. It was spartan, all right.)

"I heard tonight's run-through won't have costumes or scenery," I mumbled.

"Alan wants to see it on a bare stage," Bryce said. "With lights, of course."

"Ten minutes till act one, ladies and gents," Bernie Hart called through the intercom.

"I should let you, uh—get ready," I stammered.

"Thanks for the cookies, Cookie," he said, meeting my eyes but not moving.

"My pleasure." I opened his door, then closed it again. Turning, I said, "Bryce, I want you to know how sorry I am about Boston. I should've apologized the day we broke up. I did betray your trust, but I've learned from my mistake. Please don't give up on us."

"I wasn't at my best, either, Cookie," he said, touching my arm.

"You won't have to worry about me directing. It's the wrong path." He looked nonplused, so I said, "I know I sounded certain last night, but that was bravado. Truth is, after I called Father Hartke, I knew I couldn't move to D.C. or anywhere else. I need to be with you."

"Oh, Jane," he said, stroking my cheek. "We don't have time right now for a serious talk. Can you come out with me later?"

"I have to take notes at a dinner meeting," I groused.

"Figures," Bryce said. "If anything changes, meet me outside the gray doors on 45th."

On a whim, I moved forward and kissed him hard on the mouth. Then Dan burst in, and I fled into the hall, relieved I'd told Bryce my feelings. He hadn't echoed my declaration, so maybe last night's serenade was his parting gesture; maybe the date he'd just suggested would've been our last hurrah. *At least I tried.*

A short while later, I was standing outside the Majestic's entrance on 44th Street, aware of the many marquees dominating the block, including *Becket,* which was playing at the St. James across the lane. For a moment, I studied the light-brown brick Majestic with its loggias and an ornate overhang above a series of bronze doors. It definitely had a "royal" façade.

I slipped into the foyer, then the immense lobby with its

frescoes and chandeliers, then the elegant house with its salmon-hued seats, muted red carpet, and more chandeliers. After inching down the aisle to the production table in Row M, I slid into a seat at Brock's left. Up ahead of us, the velvet curtain was closed, but the orchestra was tuning up in the pit.

Next to Brock was Alan, Robert Downing, his stage managers Ed Preston and Jonathan Anderson—Bernie was backstage—and Francine, whom I now viewed as a friend. At the next table were Oliver Smith, Hanya Holm, Tony Duquette, Abe Feder, Trude Rittman, and the orchestrators, Robert Russell Bennett and Philip Lang.

Behind the main production team (and spread out through the orchestra section) were the general manager and his assistant; the hair designer; the sound designer; and the assistants to Smith, Holm, Duquette, and Feder; the assistant conductor; and the rehearsal pianists. I had to grin because everyone who'd helped to mold *Camelot* had flocked to this final run-through before the public previews on Thursday and Friday.

But where was Fritz? I guessed he'd sneak in when the lights went down and pace the carpet past the last row. Glancing at the mezzanine, I spotted familiar faces: Mrs. Lerner, Fritz's "Tamiboy," Sybil Burton, Nate's wife Shari, and dear Sarah, all in Row A, one of the best locations in any theater. I also noticed a stunning blonde woman, but had no idea who she was.

The house lights dimmed, and Franz Allers entered the pit and bowed to applause from his colleagues. I sat back as the lyrical overture—yet another new one—echoed throughout the auditorium. The curtain rose on a stage devoid of scenery. Sir Dinadan and Sir Lionel, wearing collared shirts, ties, and slacks, stood center stage. Upstage were lords and ladies of the court, also in street clothes. Merlyn presently entered, dressed like the knights. He chatted with Dinadan and Lionel, then summoned Arthur from his hiding place.

The king, having no tree to jump out of, entered from the wings, and the scene began.

As act one progressed, I decided it was the most moving performance I'd witnessed to date. Stripped of its lavish settings and costumes, this barebones *Camelot* threw Alan's witty dialogue into relief. The acting seemed fresh, as though the stars were improvising. Philip Burton's work receded, and Moss Hart's brilliance shone through like a master's colors on a canvas that some minor artist had tried, but failed, to paint over.

With fewer scenes in act one and the addition of "Before I Gaze at You Again," the pacing was faster, and the characters' motivations were clearer. By the "proposition" speech, I heard a few people sniffling, and everyone clapped as the curtain closed.

"Finally!" Alan said to Brock as a ten-minute break commenced. "It's the show we knew it could be. Let's go to Patsy's tonight after I speak to the cast."

"The new solo for Julie is a winner," Brock told Alan. "But where's Fritz?"

"Fritz is the phantom of the opera these days," Alan said. "He slips in and out unnoticed."

"He'll come 'round when the show's running," Brock said. "The advance is over two million even before we've released the cast album."

"We still have to face the critical gauntlet," Alan said, lighting a cigarette.

"Maybe the team should ditch the sets and costumes," I whispered to Brock. "The drama is richer without the trappings."

"I think the cast feels it also," Brock said. "Christmas is damn good, Jane. But I thought he might deck me when I came to your room in Boston."

"I told him nothing happened," I assured my boss.

"Did you notice my Lisa in the front mezz? She's the blonde lady sitting next to the new Mrs. Elsdon. I'll introduce you on Saturday."

Ten minutes flew by. Then Franz Allers returned to his podium and launched the spritely Entr'acte. The house lights dimmed, and the curtain opened as two couples strolled along the terrace of the castle. When Lancelot was alone with Guenevere, who sat embroidering on a bench, he sang his French madrigal. At the end, he declared his love before easing into his big solo, "If Ever I Would Leave You," moving seamlessly from spoken word to song.

I could've squealed with happiness. "If Ever I Would Leave You," which stopped the show in Toronto and Boston, originally began with an orchestral intro that had dwarfed Lancelot's feelings. Without the intro, Lance's voice conveyed his passion for Guenevere, and his conundrum evoked my sympathy: how could he leave her? (He couldn't.)

Act two continued as Mordred spread dissension among the knights and trapped Lance and Jenny in the queen's bedroom as they pledged to end their affair. After Bryce sang his trenchant solos in the "Guenevere" number, Arthur dithered about whether to accept the sentence of his civil court and burn the queen, and I was on tenterhooks. But it was Bryce's golden baritone—and Dan's—that allowed me to picture what was happening off-stage as Lancelot rode in to save Jenny. And near the finale, after Arthur knighted Tom of Warwick, I got teary as the embattled king realized his legacy would live on.

Amidst boisterous applause, the curtain came down after three hours and fifteen minutes, which was still long. But the performance had been superb, which Alan told the cast as they gathered on stage for notes. Then he smiled and said, "Go home and rest. If you can recapture half of what you did here at the preview tomorrow night, *Camelot* will triumph. Thank you, friends, from the bottom of my heart."

I assumed I'd accompany Alan and Brock to Patsy's, but Alan abruptly canceled dinner. As soon as I was dismissed, I raced to the lobby, exited under the marquee, and dashed around to 45th Street, where Sarah was waiting outside the huge gray doors. "Hey, Sare," I called. "If I don't come home tonight, don't worry. It'll mean I'm with Bryce."

"Hallelujah," Sarah said, giving me a quick hug.

"I'm not celebrating yet," I murmured. "He might still break up with me."

"You're a silly goose," Sarah said before Dan and Bryce appeared. The four of us exchanged greetings, then Dan and Sarah walked off to hail a cab. Bryce and I stood under a street lamp, gawking at each other as cast members passed by.

"I'm free," I squeaked. "How did you know Alan would cancel our meeting?"

"Just a hunch he might feel bushed after the run-through," Bryce said. "Cookie, I know a place for a quiet drink, but we're blocks away and it's cold. Should we take a cab?"

"No, let's walk," I said before Bryce grabbed my hand and pulled me west. We crossed Eighth and strolled past bistros and townhouses to Ninth, where we turned uptown, expelling breaths in the damp air. Ladies of the night stood on corners in jackets, short skirts, and fishnet hose, flapping their arms to stay warm. A toothless man asked Bryce for spare change—he gave him a buck—and a pair of hoodlums with greasy duck-tails offered us "prime Mexican weed," which Bryce politely declined.

"That was the best performance of *Camelot* I've seen," I told him as we walked faster. "Alan was nearly speechless af-terward, and I heard Oliver, Abe, and Tony congratulate him.

But Fritz was nowhere to be seen."

"Oh, we saw him," Bryce said. "He came backstage."

When we reached West 56th, Bryce gestured east. "If you hadn't guessed, I'm taking you to my place. I'm afraid it's not as nice as Dan and Sarah's."

"I can't wait to see it." I'd secretly hoped we'd wind up at his flat, so I'd packed my toothbrush and diaphragm in my shoulder bag. "I love brownstones," I said as we reached his building. "They give New York real character." I followed him up the steep front steps, then up three double flights. He entered his flat ahead of me, switching on some lamps.

"It's cozy," I said when he showed me the living room with his mahogany Steinway console, built-in shelves crammed with books, and simple furniture. The place smelled fresh since he'd cracked a window, but a hissing radiator made it toasty warm.

"Let me take that," he said, helping me out of my coat before stashing it with his leather jacket in the closet. "I'm drinking brandy. What can I get you? I also have beer and soda water."

I asked for brandy and perched on the edge of his couch, thrilled that Bryce had brought me here. (If he'd planned to dump me, he would've picked an impersonal bar, wouldn't he?) I glanced around his front room until he handed me a snifter with amber liquid and sat near me.

"Cheers," he said, touching his glass to mine, but I was too keyed up to respond. I took a sip of the brandy, and it warmed me going down. Then I put my snifter on the antique trunk that served as a coffee table.

"Bryce, even if I went out with Alan and Brock, I was going to swing by here later and ring your bell. Tonight's the night, and I'll do anything to win you back."

"Anything?" he asked, his eyes alight with mischief.

"Just about." I laughed nervously. "You said you wanted to

tan my hide—"

"You started it, lady. You said you wanted to smack my face."

"An idle threat. I'd never slap you or anyone, but I was livid that you were with Leena."

"Leena's a pal," he said before downing his cognac. "And Dan and I were teasing you last night, though he did help me keep my cool after we broke up." Bryce took my hand and kissed it. "Look, Jane, we've said and done some unfortunate things. You apologized before, so let me do the same. I acted like a jealous ass when I should've trusted you, and I'm truly sorry. But can we forget all this and start over?"

"I'd like that," I said. "But I should probably confess I nearly slept with Richard in Boston."

"*That* I understand," Bryce said. "The man is charm incarnate." He paused. "While we're confessing, I should admit I slept with Rina in Toronto."

"Fine. And now I think we're square." I leaned over and kissed him until our tongues danced a tango. Breathless, breaking away, I asked, "Will you give me a tour of your flat?"

Catching my meaning, he laughed while pulling me to my feet. He tugged me down the dark hall to his bedroom, switching on a banker's lamp with a green shade. His lair appeared neater than any bedroom I'd called my own, and I examined the only items on his dresser, two plastic cubes that held baseballs signed by Joe DiMaggio and Lou Gehrig.

"These balls are collector's items," I said.

"I'd never part with them," he said. "My dad and I are diehard Yankee fans."

"You told my father you love golf," I said.

"I play golf," he said. "But I *love* baseball. You?"

"I like baseball. My dad roots for the Senators. Don't let on, but I like your team."

"Good thing," he said. "I couldn't be with anyone who

didn't like the Yankees."

In the corner was a card table with a portable stereo and a crate of records on the floor. But before I could survey his album collection, Bryce twirled me around and kissed me until I saw stars. "I can't wait another minute, Cookie," he said, pulling me toward his bed.

We made dreamy love on top of Bryce's soft sheets smelling of Canoe. I kept sighing, feeling happier than I'd been since that awful morning when I'd called off our engagement.

Later, he riffled through his closet for the cotton robe he'd worn backstage in Toronto. Then he handed me a long white tee shirt that I donned without leaving his cozy bed.

"I learned something from the run-through," I told him. "Lavish costumes and sets can weigh a show down. I began to wonder if they're hurting *Camelot.*"

"I wondered, too," Bryce said, perching on his mattress. "It seemed effortless tonight."

"If I ever direct," I said, "I'll remember tonight's version and restrict the clutter."

"You don't have to move to D.C. or New Haven to explore directing."

"You're right," I said. "But ironically, I went to the wrong Hart brother for advice. I should've talked to Bernie because I think I'd make a better stage manager."

"Stage management would use your experience with *Camelot,*" Bryce said, "and we'd be able to work together sooner. You'd start as an assistant, so you could apprentice and join the union." He paused. "But don't lower your sights for me, Cookie."

"I'm not," I assured him. "I like the hands-on nature of stage management and the fact that you stick with one show for a long time. With directing, you're finished when the production opens. Also, directors need to be endlessly inventive, but I'm more of a nuts-and-bolts person."

"Stage managers are directors in their own way," Bryce observed. "When the name director leaves, it's the stage manager who gives notes and rehearses the replacement cast. It might be the best of both worlds."

"Oh, Bryce, it feels so good to talk like this again," I said. "I may be rigid, but during the time we spent apart, I felt I'd lost half of myself. I promise to do better."

"Me too," he said. "How about a second cognac?"

"I'll take soda water." I'd lately decided to limit my alcohol to one drink a night. But as I watched him pad away, I thought it seemed unlikely that Bryce would ask to renew our engagement. Our reconciliation was new, and he had a lot on his mind with two previews and Saturday's opening ahead. Maybe all I could expect this soon was an invitation to stay the night.

"Hope you're staying over," Bryce said, reading my mind as he returned.

"I brought my toothbrush," I said, accepting the soda water.

"Be my date for the party at Luchow's on Saturday," he said before walking to the card table and switching on the phonograph. The cut he played was "The Best Is Yet to Come," sung by Tony Bennett. "Did you know the Broadway composer Cy Coleman wrote this?" he asked.

I was sitting against his bedboard, propped up by pillows, and he joined me.

"I've heard it before," I said, "but I had no idea who composed it."

"The lyrics are by Carolyn Leigh," Bryce said. "It's one of my favorite tunes."

I listened to the sensual words and music as Bryce and I

gazed shyly at one another. And as he leaned over to kiss me again, I prayed Cy Coleman's hopeful song described our future.

13.
MAJESTIC
DEBUT

Bryce

It was cold and growing dark as Bryce walked downtown on Saturday, December 3rd, at 4:30 p.m., heading to the Majestic for *Camelot's* 6:45 p.m. premiere. He and his colleagues had felt encouraged the past two nights when the preview audiences laughed in the right places and clapped loudly at the finale, but tonight might be different. The New York critics had heard all the carping and read the latest Boston reviews; they might come looking for flaws.

As Bryce passed familiar markets and coffee shops on Eighth, he thought about his luck. He and Jane were blissfully back together, and he'd just signed a one-year contract with producer Lee Guber to appear in his new musical, *The Happiest Girl in the World*. His name would appear on the playbill's title page along with the two female leads, Janice Rule and Lark Weiss, although the only name over the title would be Cyril Ritchard, who was also directing.

He fumbled in his pocket for a fifty-cent piece to give a beggar, musing that rehearsals for *Happiest Girl* would begin next month. Next Monday, his agent would tell the *Camelot* producers that his last outing as Sir Lionel would be Saturday, January 14th. And knowing the end was six weeks away made his Broadway debut even more precious. He liked playing one of the knights who sang the best lyrics in several songs, and he'd savor his immediate future as a featured actor, aware that he'd soon become a leading man. He would tell Jane later tonight, and next week when his parents saw *Camelot*—he'd bought them orchestra seats for Friday—he'd take them to Sardi's afterward, introduce Jane, and announce his news. (He'd already stopped at Sardi's and told his former boss, who exclaimed, "Kudos, Bryce! I told you in Toronto we'd soon have to commission your portrait, and Hirschfeld will be drawing you for the *Times*.")

After his stroll through two alleys, which might have been the entrance to a factory instead of the Golden, Royale, and Majestic Theatres, he passed through a side door, walked up a few steps, and entered another door to sign in. But instead of going to his dressing room, he found his way to stage right, illumined by the ghost lamp, and gazed at the shadowy house. It was still early, and he figured his colleagues wouldn't come in for a while. He put his canvas bag and wool topcoat on the floor, pulling a pitch pipe from his tuxedo pants. Returning to center stage, he stood up straight and took imperceptible breaths before singing "ay-ee-ah-oh-oo" on a single note.

He continued the exercises he'd sung in voice lessons since 1944 (except for his time in the service). His teacher had wanted Bryce to pursue a classical career, but he felt more at home with American musicals than with European opera and Lieder. At fifteen, he'd persuaded his parents to take him to *Carousel* on Broadway, and watching twenty-eight-year-old John Raitt, the show's leading man, had changed his life. Tonight, Bryce would tread the same boards his baritone idol had owned as Billy Bigelow, Raitt's signature role, and when this coincidence dawned on him, he stopped vocalizing and thanked Divine Providence for *Camelot*.

After his warm-up, Bryce retrieved his bag and coat and

walked from the wings to the stairs, climbing three flights to the cell he shared with Dan. Nell Dean was also on this floor, and when they met on the landing, he kissed her hand for luck. As everyone knew, Nell was sad that Richard was often seen at Downey's with his newest paramour, a leggy showgirl from one of the supper clubs.

Inside his dressing room, Bryce smelled the roses on Dan's vanity, probably sent by Sarah; his table held a stack of telegrams but no flowers. He put his jacket on the clothes rack and hung his bag on his chair, and as he moved to his vanity, he saw an eggshell-blue Tiffany box with a white bow and card. He opened the envelope and read Jane's message wishing him "luck and love." Then he looked inside the box and found a silver frame holding a photo of himself in his orange velvet costume for the joust scene. The top of the picture was engraved *Bryce as Sir Lionel in CAMELOT*; the bottom read *Broadway Debut, 12-3-60.*

He grinned, thinking it was the perfect talisman, more meaningful than anything else Jane might've given him. He'd also sent her gifts: a dozen roses and a wooden Noah's Ark with hand-carved animals from F.A.O. Schwarz. On the card he'd written, *Cookie, I'm glad we "paired up" in Toronto and didn't stay lone wolves. Thanks for all the ways you helped us get to Broadway! xoxo Bryce*

He wished he could've seen her face when the messenger delivered the ark, but he and Jane had decided not to meet until after the premiere. Now that he'd be doing eight shows a week, with two on Wednesdays and Saturdays, he planned to conserve his voice on performance days. He'd learned that even normal talking before he sang took a toll on his cords.

Bryce rose and stripped to his jock strap. He wriggled into cream-colored tights and slid into flat shoes. He donned a tee shirt for doing his makeup. Just before curtain, he'd add the long velvet salmon-and-cream tunic, his costume for the single line he spoke at the top of act one.

When Dan arrived, their dressing room seemed full to bursting. Though both of them used deodorant and cologne, Bryce could smell his castmate's sweat. It was a mercy that Dan didn't smoke like Burton and Goulet. As it was, the air was too dry, and Dan had brought in a vaporizer whose warm steam was helping their sinuses.

"I saw Jane before I left," Dan said. "She bought a dress to dazzle you."

"She could wear a gunny sack and dazzle me," Bryce declared. He'd arranged his makeup on the table and now patted foundation on his cheeks with a sponge. He used a brush that set the base, then added a brown powder for contouring around his nose, along his cheekbones, and across his forehead. He chose another sponge to pat the contour powder into his skin, lightly moving it outward. His proficiency now gave him planes that would be visible from the second balcony, and he employed a soft powder brush to set the makeup he'd put on so far. Next came the brown eyeliner along his top and bottom lash line, then he penciled his eyebrows.

Bryce jumped when Bernie called through the intercom, "Good evening, ladies and gentlemen. Mr. Lerner will address the cast on stage in fifteen minutes. That's fifteen minutes."

He reached into his bag and removed a thermos. After taking a swig of warm tea, he put the thermos on his table for later. He added light rose lip color with a pencil, then stood, did a few stretches, and found his tunic on the rack. He and his roommate had a little more breathing room in Boston, but nothing could beat the thrill of waiting to perform in New York.

As Bryce dressed, he noticed Dan was just starting his makeup since he didn't enter until halfway through act one. Feeling jumpy, Bryce offered his hand, saying, "Good show, roomie!" As he reached the landing, he willed himself not to vomit. He'd never had a sick stomach before a show until now.

After taking a few deep breaths to steady himself, Bryce ran downstairs and heard the makeup lady chattering to Julie, whose door was open. Richard's dear friend and dresser, a handsome Black man named Bob Wilson, nodded to Bryce as he left the star's room with the king's satin cape. Bryce followed Bob into the wings at stage right and realized he was the first of the cast to arrive. He wished Jane would show up, but she'd be out in the lobby with Brock, schmoozing with VIPs.

Now Philip Burton emerged from the shadows. Earlier, Bryce had thumbed through the first-night playbill and realized the de facto director was listed as "Assistant to Mr. Hart" under Staff for Messrs. Lerner, Loewe & Hart. He'd thought it was paltry recognition for the man who'd come to Lerner's rescue in Boston, but that was show biz.

"Good evening, Mr. Christmas," Philip Burton said, crossing the stage. "Good show!"

"Same to you, sir," Bryce said, glad to be distracted from his jitters.

"I believe Alan Lerner's happier with the length," Burton said with a shrug.

"Here he is now," Bryce said as Alan ducked into the wings through a pass door from the house. At the same moment, members of the ensemble marched on stage, trailed by Richard, Julie, Bobby, Roddy, and Robert Coote. Bryce couldn't spot Dan or Nate in the crowd, but he nodded to Leena Lear, bless her heart, and Jack Dabdoub.

Alan stepped forward. He looked so tired Bryce wondered if he'd make it through his pep talk, much less tonight's show and party. He wore black tie, and his pompadour glistened with hair cream. The *Time* author had claimed he looked like a graduate student during those early days in Boston. Now he resembled a haggard author in his forties who survived on caffeine, nicotine, and if you believed the gossip, amphetamines.

"Ladies and gentlemen," Alan said, "we've come a long way since the early rehearsals. After watching that moving run-through the other night, Fritz and I couldn't be prouder. You've brought *Camelot* to life in ways we never could've imagined, and if ever a cast deserved success, it's you. But I should remind you that a first-night audience might not laugh or applaud in the usual places. My best advice is, forget them and play the play."

"And God have mercy on us all," Richard called, the last line of his "proposition" speech.

"Amen," Alan said, and the company erupted in applause.

Bernie called, "Places in five minutes," over the loudspeaker, and the cast scattered.

Bryce, inspired by Alan's words, suddenly felt eager to be on stage. As he slipped into the wings at stage left, he saw Richard peering through a small opening in the curtain, cursing the opening night crowd, and felt reassured. As utterly brilliant as Burton was as King Arthur, he was a wreck before facing an audience, just like everyone else.

Bryce got in position for his entrance, knowing one of his favorite moments would happen soon: the scraping sound as the stagehands opened the curtain.

———◆———

A Broadway premiere was not exactly what Bryce had anticipated when he'd watched John Raitt and dreamed of supplanting him. He was so well rehearsed he lived the show moment by moment and nearly forgot the audience. When they applauded, he barely noticed, and at times his mind wandered out front to Jane. Did she like his performance? Was she as eager to sleep with him later as he was to have her?

Cripes, was he losing it? He was *on* Broadway, but as the evening trudged along, he felt deflated, as though this was any average night in *Camelot*. In some ways, it was less thrilling than others since the audience was cool, as Alan had predicted. The only number that got an ovation was "If Ever I Would Leave You."

Waiting in the wings, he decided a visitor from Mars would've thought Goulet, not Burton, was the name-over-the-title star. Then, in the blink of an eye, the show was over and the full company was on stage, hidden behind the closed curtain as the audience noisily left the house. Alan and Fritz arrived with their ladies, Mrs. Lerner in a gold sleeveless gown with long black gloves and Loewe's Tamara in a navy-blue cocktail dress. The production folks swarmed around the cast, offering congratulations. When Bryce felt a smack on his back, he turned to face Richard Burton, who grinned and said, "Nice job, Yuletide. There's hope for you yet."

"I was moved by you tonight, Mr. Burton," Bryce said. "You didn't fall short."

When Bryce's pun sank in, Burton roared. "It's Richard or Rich," the star said. "Stop by my dressing room some night for a drink. Bring that lovely girl of yours."

Bryce nodded, amazed by the actor's warmth, and then he spotted Jane. He wove his way through the crowd and swooped her into his arms, twirling her around.

"I never heard you sing so well," she whispered. "And thanks for my toy ark."

"Thanks for my photo," he said. "You look stunning." And she did, modeling a royal-blue dress with a scoop neck to which she'd added long white gloves and a tiny blue bag.

"Hey Christmas," Brock said, "you were on fire in 'Guenevere,' pun intended."

"That's nice of you to say," Bryce said. "I hope the producers were proud tonight."

"Alan's sanguine," he said. "Fritz hasn't said much." He patted Jane's shoulder. "See you at Luchow's. We'll have a jolly time since we won't know the reviews for hours."

"Luchow's is way down on 14th, isn't it?" Jane asked Bryce. "Will we go by subway?"

"Not tonight," Bryce told her. "The producers hired limos to take us. Let me change, and I'll meet you back here." He took off, gliding past Kitty Hart in satin and pearls (but no sign of Moss), Gloria Swanson, Burgess Meredith, Noel Coward, and Marlene Dietrich. His Broadway debut was over, and the best part was he'd felt vocally secure and had aced his solos. Of course, he might feel less relaxed when his agent and his parents came next week.

As he climbed the stairs to his dressing room, he ignored the bedlam in the hall and decided the one person he hoped to impress was his father. During Bryce's career in summer stock, his dad had never praised him, but Professor Christmas was a Julie Andrews fan, and Julie had promised to meet his parents. Bryce felt he'd rack up points for influence, whatever his dad thought of his acting and singing. (It seemed serendipitous that he'd performed for Jane's parents, and they'd admired his work without knowing he might one day join their clan.)

Jane

It was an evening of firsts. My first time watching the opening performance of a Broadway show I'd worked on; my first ride in a limousine with a group of theater folks I viewed as comrades; my first visit to Luchow's, a New York landmark with free-flowing champagne and a string quartet playing waltzes; my first time feeling proud of a boyfriend who'd made a big contribution to the show's success.

But I felt worried despite the warmth of Luchow's with its dark wood panels, wooden bar, and turn-of-century light fixtures. The owners had arranged for their regular patrons to leave early so the *Camelot* cast could have a private party—or wake—depending on the reviews. I told myself, "Don't borrow trouble," one of my father's maxims, but I had a sinking feeling the critics would carp despite the valiant efforts of those who came here dressed to the nines, hoping to toast their show's success. Craning my neck, I saw Richard, Sybil, and the Other Burton sitting at one table and Julie and Tony with several friends at another. The lights were low, and the dance floor was full as cast members jitterbugged to let off steam.

I retreated to a private corner while Bryce got our drinks. But I felt let down, thinking the production had seemed less vibrant than during its luminous run-through and two previews. Of course, the audience had been quiet, and maybe their lack of enthusiasm had rattled the actors.

I waved to the photographer Leo Friedman. I'd loved seeing his pictures displayed in glass cases outside the Majestic; he'd captured both the pomp of *Camelot* and the rapport between the actors. And I knew glossy color prints would adorn the original cast album, which the company would record a week from tomorrow. Soon, theater lovers across the U.S. would get a preview of *Camelot* from playing its glorious score on their stereos and seeing Leo's photos. Would ticket sales pick up?

"I have a proposal for you, doll," Francine Tristan said, walking toward me in a mauve gown straight from the pages of *Vogue*. "As you know, I work for a theater publicity firm. There are three senior press agents, and we're looking for a junior agent to write releases and do office chores. You'd still work on *Camelot* plus your boyfriend's new show. Any interest?"

"May I think about it?" I asked, feeling tempted.

"Natch," Francine said. "But I need to know soon." She smiled. "By the way, I'm glad you and Mr. Christmas are back together."

I thanked my friend for her support as Bryce returned with champagne, gallantly handing his flute to Francine. Then Alan and his wife joined us, and after Alan asked for a word with the press agent, Mrs. Lerner raised her glass to Bryce, saying, "To the best singing babysitter in *Camelot*."

Bryce chuckled, and when the orchestra struck up another waltz, he asked me to dance. We moved past the tables to the floor up front and swayed to "The Embassy Waltz," composed for *My Fair Lady*. I felt giddy, clinging to my boyfriend and watching Julie and Tony dance cheek to cheek. Brock and Lisa joined us, and after the music stopped, Brock finally introduced me to Mrs. Remsen, a math professor with movie-star looks.

"You're what I call his work wife, Jane," Lisa said.

"That's a fair description, my sweet," Brock said, "but Jane's getting a big promotion."

"I am?" I asked. "I just got an offer to join Miss Tristan's firm."

"You'd be wasting your talents," Brock said. "Listen, kiddo, Bob Downing will call you tomorrow. You should accept his offer and become the assistant stage manager for *Camelot*."

"Oh, Brock," I said. "How did I rate that?"

"You're a team player," Brock said. "Nobody wants to lose you, Jane."

Before I could ask more questions, the Remsens floated away. "Uh-oh," Bryce said, "Reviews must be out. Lerner's walking up to the mic."

The room grew still as all of us gazed intently at Alan. "Ladies and gentlemen," he said, "our first review was just read to me. It's by Howard Taubman of the *Times*, and the headline is '*Camelot* Partly Enchanted.' He loved the stars—indeed the whole cast; he liked the sets, costumes, music and lyrics, and some of act one. Alas, he didn't like act two or most of my book." He shrugged. "We also got a preview of John Chapman's notice in the *Daily News*. He called the show magnificent. He said the songs are lovely and unfailingly right, and the cast is superb." Alan looked up. "Our first unqualified rave."

Bryce and I clapped along with everyone else.

"We'll have to wait until morning for Walter Kerr in *The Tribune* and some others, but since it's late, I want to thank you again for your dedication. Allow me to wish you a fond goodnight, and remember, limos are waiting to take you home."

Applause erupted again, and when I saw Alan walking toward Fritz, I wondered if the partners would move past their rift and collaborate again.

The string quartet played tunes from *Camelot* as the party broke up. Bryce and I headed for the door, followed by Sarah and Dan, Nate and Shari, and Nell Dean and her date, a ringer for actor Tab Hunter. We piled into a limo and yakked about the party. When Bryce and I got out at the corner of Eighth and 56th, we watched the car race north, and I put my gloved hand in Bryce's palm. "I'm dancing on air," I said. "Two job offers! And one would get me involved in your new show, so I'd sure like to hear the details."

We reached Bryce's building, and while climbing up to his flat, he cheerfully told me about *The Happiest Girl in the World*. Inside, he switched on a lamp in the living room, adding, "I planned to share this with you tonight. I signed the contract just today."

"You're going to leave *Camelot*?" I asked, removing my wrap.

"You bet," he said, hanging his coat in the closet. "This is a huge break for me. Billing in the program, leading man status, and twice the salary I'm making as a knight."

"Well, it might be tempting to publicize you," I said as we sat together on his couch.

"I'll be happy if you take either of those jobs, Cookie. Our talks about your moving away for grad school nearly broke my heart."

"Mine too," I said, meeting his winsome gaze.

———————◆————————

When I awakened the next morning, sun was streaming in through gossamer curtains and I heard a jazz riff from a saxophone on the radio in the living room. Feeling groggy from the champagne, I squinted at the clock on the night table and learned it was 11 a.m. I jumped out of bed and found a long flannel shirt in Bryce's closet. After visiting the bathroom, I padded to the living room, where Bryce was at the table reading the Sunday *Tribune*. He'd set out bagels, lox, cream cheese, capers, and sliced tomatoes, and as soon as I appeared, he said he'd made coffee.

I grabbed the pot from the kitchen and carried it to the table, filling a mug for myself and refilling Bryce's cup. Then I sat down and cut a sesame bagel, smearing it with cream cheese. "What does Kerr say in the *Tribune*?" I asked.

"The headline is '*Camelot* Is Better When You Take It In Reverse.'"

I sipped Bryce's fragrant brew. "What on earth does that mean?"

"He loved the early scenes, but felt the meat of Lancelot and Jenny's affair is missing."

"We've heard that before," I said. "I feel sorry for Alan."

Bryce shrugged. "Alan's a survivor who'll live to fight another day. What I learned a long time ago is that theater brings much more rejection than success. It takes you to the highest of the highs and the lowest of the lows, with little in between." When the phone rang, he rambled to the table beyond the sofa to answer. "It's Sarah," he said before turning off the radio.

I ran to the phone, then asked my boyfriend for a pencil and paper. After scribbling a number, I thanked Sarah for acting as my answering service. "Robert Downing just called," I told Bryce. "He wants me to call him back."

Remaining on the couch, my hand shaking, I began to dial. Three minutes later, recalling Brock's advice, I accepted the job of *Camelot's* assistant stage manager. It paid far more than my Gal Friday post, and Mr. Downing asked me to start a week from Monday.

"Congratulations, Cookie!" Bryce said after I shared my news. "I think you made the right decision." He returned to the table, and I soon followed.

"But will *Camelot* close soon?" I asked. "Brock told me the advance might dry up if the ladies who book theater parties hate the reviews and cancel."

"It'll probably limp along," Bryce said.

Though I felt astounded by Mr. Downing's offer, I added lox and capers to my bagel as though it was any other morning. But my mind began to reel with new possibilities.

"We have a free day today," Bryce said, "and it might be nice to put *Camelot* out of our minds. How would you like to see *The Fantasticks*? It's playing in the Village at three."

"I've always wanted to see that show. And a 3 p.m. curtain gives me time to get back to Sarah's so I can change. Why don't I meet you at the theater?"

"You should pack a few things and come back here. I'll spring for a cab downtown."

"So, Bryce," I began shyly, "if you're asking me to bring clothes, does that mean you want us to live together?"

"Not quite yet," he said. "We moved too fast before, Cookie. You weren't ready."

"I'm fine with whatever you want," I told him. "After I start my new job and you begin rehearsals for your new show, we'll be on different schedules, and that'll be an adjustment. In the meantime, you need to make room in your closet. I'll hang a few things in there tonight."

When I stood, Bryce tugged me onto his lap. I put my head against his shoulder, and we sat without moving for a while. When I shimmied out of his arms and walked down the hall, I heard his footsteps behind me and guessed we'd land in bed.

And though I had a room at Dan and Sarah's for as long as necessary, I knew I'd spend little time at my friends' home in the future. Bryce could place artificial limits on our living arrangements if he liked, but from this day forward, I belonged to him, body and soul.

I was ready at last.

14.
CHANGES
ALL AROUND

Bryce

He was surprised he and Jane were so simpatico, despite their opposite schedules. They seldom had time for long discussions since she was sleeping when he left each morning and had gone to work by the time he returned. But now, as he kissed his snoozing lover's cheek before heading to rehearse *The Happiest Girl in the World*, he looked forward to April. His show would be running at the Martin Beck on West 45th, and he and Jane would be free on weekdays (except Wednesdays and Saturdays) and Sundays; they'd both work Monday through Saturday nights.

And though he planned not to speak much before he had to sing, he was sure they'd share some exploits—in and out of bed. Truth be told, Jane was so enthralled by his singing she was more protective of his voice than he was. "Those small bits of gristle in your throat are your meal ticket," she'd joke, and she wasn't far off. In the new show, he had one lyrical solo, three romantic duets, reprises of duets, and two choral numbers.

Bryce took an apple from the fridge and grabbed his jacket, scarf, and the sleek leather messenger bag Jane had given him for their first Christmas together. He locked his door since she had the luxury of sleeping till noon. After racing downstairs, he cleared his building's front steps, whistling. Heading east, he strode past the old brownstones on his street, moving fast because the wind was damp. It was Wednesday, February 1, 1961, and he'd bid farewell to *Camelot* two Saturdays ago. Dan and Nate had taken him to Downey's after his final show, and as they drank a few beers, Bobby and Jack Dabdoub joined them. Bryce had felt sad to be leaving his *Camelot* comrades, especially Dan, to whom he'd grown close. But when rehearsals for *Happiest Girl* began, his exhilaration outpaced any traces of regret. In the new cast, he was the romantic lead, though Cyril Ritchard and Janice Rule were the stars.

Bryce loved his role as the macho, sex-obsessed General Kinesias. He enjoyed singing with the sensual Lark Weiss, who played his wife, Lysistrata or "Liz." The only slog ahead would be leaving for the Shubert in New Haven on February 16th, a two-week run, and then moving to the Shubert in Philadelphia for a month. The company would return to New York on March 26th, a week before their opening, but he'd promised Jane he would rent a car and drive home on Saturday nights in March so they could spend their Sundays together.

At the corner of Eighth and 56th, Bryce touched his bushier chin. For *Happiest Girl*, set in Athens in 400 B.C., all the featured actors had facial hair, so he'd allowed his goatee and mustache to expand into a neatly trimmed beard. Crossing the street, he thought about Cyril, a thin Australian in his sixties who stood six-two and was famous for playing TV's Captain Hook. The director had warmed to Bryce and Michael Kermoyan, another actor he'd poached from *Camelot*. But Cyril was a whirling dervish, and Bryce found it hard to pin down his ideas. Otherwise, he had few complaints. The script was a well-crafted farce, and he doubted it would change daily (like *Camelot*) on the road.

He passed familiar storefronts and kept walking until he

reached a nondescript stone building. After the attendant took him to the tenth floor, he entered a foyer that led to an immense rehearsal hall with windows fronting 46th Street. The production team was at their table, and the rehearsal pianist was at his Yamaha. Bryce waved to Yip Harburg, a friendly, pleasant-looking man in his sixties who'd written the book and lyrics for *Finian's Rainbow* and the words for film ballads like "Somewhere Over the Rainbow."

For *Happiest Girl*, Yip told Bryce he'd adapted the story from *Lysistrata* by Aristophanes and had penned the lyrics for songs borrowed from Offenbach operettas. The plot focused on a campaign to stop the soldiers of Athens from fighting endless wars, so the women, led by Liz, vowed to withhold sex from their husbands until they sought peace. In the hands of Harburg, the show was a merry free-for-all and a showcase for Cyril, who played eight parts.

Bryce sat on a bench and removed his script from his bag. All the actors were off book by now, but when he wasn't needed for scenes, he continued to study his lines. So far, he'd made three pals in the cast: tall Michael Kermoyan, his understudy, whom he hadn't known well in *Camelot*; beautiful Joy Claussen, a young actress making her Broadway debut; and Joy's wise-cracking friend, Lainie Kazan, also new to Broadway. (His leading lady, Lark Weiss, was cordial when they were rolling around a large prop bed, but they hadn't socialized. He knew little about her except that she'd just left Broadway's *Becket*, in which she portrayed the mistress of the title character played by Laurence Olivier.)

This morning Bryce watched Cyril (as the naughty Pluto) and Janice Rule (as the chaste goddess Diana) learn a dance number, "Vive le Virtue!" while the choreographer Dania Krupska called the beats over the piano. From the song's rhythm and lyrics, Bryce knew it would be a crowd-pleaser, but since he'd watched it before, his mind wandered.

Though his domestic life and career were going well, he was bothered by a complication that cropped up when he'd taken his parents to dinner after *Camelot* and introduced them to Jane. His father, Edward, had seemed enthralled, but his mother, Magda, a.k.a. *Anya,* hadn't approved of his beloved.

Anya was an entrepreneur who'd opened a clothing boutique in Princeton, catering to the girlfriends of the Ivy League boys and wealthy local ladies. Striking at age fifty-two, with flawless skin and platinum hair, she'd always worn the latest fashions, unlike the other housewives in Bryce's old neighborhood. And while *Anya* hadn't actively encouraged Bryce to perform, she'd driven him to voice lessons because she liked his initiative.

After seeing *Camelot,* his mother offered fulsome praise of Bryce's performance over drinks at Sardi's. But when she began to grill Jane about her ambitions, *Anya's* mouth grew pinched. "You're going to be a stage manager?" she asked. "Is that a job for a *lady?*"

"Why wouldn't it be?" Jane murmured, which evoked an icy stare from his mother.

"The production team recruited Jane," Bryce explained. "They're going to train her."

"All men, I suppose," *Anya* replied with a sniff. "Now I could understand if you wanted to work with costumes. That's a feminine pursuit. But this other field sounds crass."

"Crass?" Jane asked, glancing at Bryce, who'd been rendered speechless by *Anya's* narrow attitude. "I've never heard anyone say that, not even my own parents."

"And speaking of your parents," Professor Christmas said, "I gather they live in Chevy Chase, Maryland, and your father's a dermatologist?"

"They live in Bethesda," Jane said. "My dad's a cardiologist."

"And your mother?" *Anya* asked. "Does she work outside the home?"

"My mom raised my brother, sister, and me," Jane said, smiling. "Now she does volunteer work. She recently campaigned for Kennedy."

"Bryce," *Anya* said, patting her son's hand, "remind me what's good here, will you, *kedves*?" ("Kedvesh," he later told Jane, meant "dear" in Hungarian.)

Bryce drew his mom's attention to the cannelloni, realizing that Jane's face was turning pink. She was probably angry, and so was he. But having dealt with his prickly mother all his life, he knew it was better to humor her and wait for her mood to improve. She starved herself to stay thin, and drinking two martinis on an empty stomach had given her a harder edge than usual.

Later, after they'd returned to Bryce's flat, Jane had sounded worried when she said, "And to think I was afraid my dad wouldn't accept my being involved with an actor. But he liked you in Boston, both my parents did. It's your martinet mother who hates me."

"She'll come around," he said. "She's found fault with every woman I've ever dated."

"I wish you'd told me that before tonight," Jane moaned.

———◆———

"Hey, Bryce," called Roberto Quilico, a fortyish actor who played a couple of roles and served as *Happiest Girl's* assistant stage manager. "You're on. We're doing 'Adrift on a Star.'"

"Right away," Bryce said before moving to the center of the wooden floor. He slipped into character as the lusty General Kinesias, capturing the hand of his wife, clad in a silky blouse and tight leggings. The pianist played an intro, then Kinesias and Liz recalled their blissful honeymoon while singing a sensual duet based on "The Barcarolle" from *Tales of Hoffman*. At the end, the general swooped his wife into his arms and kissed her, then carried her to a high mattress while proclaiming his love. But as he lunged toward her, she eluded his embrace, pretending she wanted to get him a drink, then a blanket. Savoring her game, Liz gulped a second drink before she and Kinesias partly disrobed.

The general pleaded with Liz to stop delaying their bliss, but she put him off until he overpowered her. As Kinesias pulled his wriggling wife on top of him, the goddess Diana entered the boudoir, pulled an imaginary arrow from her quill, and shot Liz in the rump. She screamed and rolled off the bed, yelling that she wouldn't sleep with Kinesias again until he renounced war. Then she chased him around the room with his sword as the act-one curtain fell.

Cyril called, "Wonderful, darlings! Now you can piss off for a while." The stage manager called places for act two, so Bryce ducked out to the foyer and grabbed a drink at the water fountain. Afterward, he sat on a bench along the wall and closed his eyes, thinking his acting in the bed scene had lacked pizzazz.

Conjuring memories of Julie Andrews last September, he decided Julie always behaved like a leading lady, infusing her role with charm and charisma. Which meant that if Bryce was to be a leading man, he'd have to act like one. *Starting now.* Because the smooch he'd given Lark was tepid; at the time, he was thinking that Jane wouldn't like him kissing his costar. And while Cyril hadn't noticed, Bryce knew he must display palpable sexual longing; otherwise, his General Kinesias would be as one-dimensional as Goulet's Lancelot in early *Camelot* rehearsals.

"You look discouraged," Lark said, joining him on the bench.

"I didn't feel I was convincing before," he blurted out.

"You sang well," she said. "But you always seem afraid to get close."

"I'm intimidated," Bryce admitted. "Your last scene partner was Laurence Olivier."

"I feel the same. Your last singing partner was Julie Andrews."

"Actors," he said with mock disgust. "Why don't we run through it now. And I hope you won't mind if I ramp up the kissing."

"Please do," she said with a come-hither smile, assuming Liz's persona.

He offered his hand to help her stand. "Let me know if I do anything that puts you off."

"Oh, husband," she replied. "Show me the man who plans to take what's his."

"The bench will be the bed," he said, moving a few paces away before he sang his opening line. *Jane will have to understand*, he thought.

After they finished singing, he kissed her with a lover's urgency. When they parted, they were both breathless, and Lark said, "That's how I pictured Kinesias."

"Progress," Bryce said, thinking his leading lady was a trouper. Yet he nonetheless missed Jane, whose female essence was intoxicating.

———— ◆ ————

By the end of that week, Bryce arranged an early dismissal to meet Jane for supper at Dinty Moore's, the Irish bar where he'd gone last August to celebrate landing his role in *Camelot*. But so much had happened in the interim that triumphant morning seemed another lifetime ago.

Dinty's host told him his "lady friend" was already seated in the quiet back section, and Bryce hurried through the dining room. When he found Jane, she told him she'd ordered two Guinness Stouts, and he kissed her before sitting across from her. He never tired of studying her expressive face.

"I read the whole script of *Happiest Girl* last night while you were sleeping," Jane said. "The plot rises and falls on whether your character, the general, will get laid again after his wife rejects him for going to war. The other women of Athens withhold sex from their husbands, and the general gets so frustrated he considers a divorce." Jane shrugged. "How many times can you beg your wife for sex in one show? Other than Diana's wish to learn about human love, there's not much meat."

"You haven't heard the songs." He knitted his brows. "They're beautiful and funny."

"I'm not judging, Bryce, just observing. You must be having fun." She took a slug of Guinness. "Is there a lot of action on beds with your leading lady?"

"Some," he replied. "We're in our clothes mostly, but while the doublets in *Camelot* are short, they're paired with hose. In this show, I wear short tunics, but my legs are bare."

"Sounds risqué," Jane said.

When a waiter came to take their order, Jane ordered Irish stew and Bryce asked for a rare steak and baked potato. "I get ravenous during rehearsal," he said. "I'm on stage a lot."

"Do you like working with Cyril Ritchard?"

"He's suave and couldn't be more encouraging. But I have a feeling I'll never know the man, sort of like Moss Hart." He laughed. "Still, as you've guessed, I'm having a grand time."

"No problems?"

"I see one possible problem," he admitted. "Our show has gods and goddesses who'll be flown in on a cloud that will be a moving platform. Just the thought of it makes me queasy." He took her hand. "Let's talk about you, Cookie. Do you still enjoy your new job?"

"It's terrific," she said. "I love working with Bernie Hart

and Robert Downing and the other guys. I also visit Richard in his dressing room, where he spent several hundred dollars of his own money building a bar. And before you wonder why I go there, one of my tasks is escorting his guests to see him after the performance. You wouldn't believe the people I'm meeting."

"Like who?"

"The stars of every show on Broadway," she said as the waiter brought their food. "Mike Nichols comes a lot since he's working at the Golden next door. Elaine May, too. And this stunning showgirl who's Richard's mistress."

Bryce speared a piece of steak but didn't reply. Since accepting the role of Kinesias, he'd learned that half the backstage chasing was done by actresses who longed to bask in the fame of leading men. He was getting a lot of female attention at *Happiest Girl* rehearsals, which was one reason he liked Joy Claussen, who treated him like a brother. Other girls in the chorus, however, had let him know they were interested in "seeing" him outside rehearsals.

"You seem far away, Bryce," Jane remarked. "I said I'm sorry I have to eat and run."

"You barely ate three bites, Cookie, but go ahead. I'll see you when you get home."

Jane got up and stroked his hairy chin. "Your fuller beard makes you look more handsome, if that's possible." She took off toward the front room, and Bryce ordered a second Guinness. He tasted the foam, wishing his show had already returned from the road. He'd probably field a few more propositions out of town, which he'd resist, and he'd keenly miss sleeping with Jane. He was more in love with her than ever.

Jane

I felt lonely after Bryce decamped to New Haven, so I moved back to Sarah and Dan's flat. When Bryce called late one night—we needed to decompress after our shows, so 1 a.m. was a good time to chat—he sounded whipped. The New Haven reviews had been mixed, but on February 28th, the night his show opened in Philadelphia, he promised he'd come home the following Sunday.

"They held a party for us at the Players Club," Bryce said, "because our producer Lee Guber is a Philly boy. It was something like the opening night shindig in Toronto. I wish you'd been there."

"Ditto," I said. "How was the first show?"

"Uneven," he said, then began to cough. "Can you tell I'm getting a cold? Anyway, a wheel fell off Cyril's chariot during an entrance, and the cloud platform began to rock back and forth when it descended. The actors were bobbing up and down, too." He coughed again. "I've heard Lark and I are losing a song. Frankly, we don't mind."

When he hacked a third time and seemed unable to catch his breath, I told him he should take some cough syrup and go to bed.

Eager to see him that next Sunday, I packed a bag and returned to his flat on Thursday, March 2nd. His phone began to ring as I let myself in, and without thinking, I picked up.

"Who is this, please?" Bryce's mother snarled.

"It's Jane, Mrs. Christmas. How are you?"

"I just remembered Bryce is away. But what are you doing at his apartment?"

"I baked him some banana bread," I lied. "He's due back Sunday, so I'm leaving a treat to welcome him. The super let me in." I asked if I could help her, and she said she was calling to arrange house seats for clients who wanted to see *Camelot* on Friday, March 10th. "We're not full that night," I lied again, "so I can arrange comps. Would you and Mr. Christmas like to come again with your clients?"

"They'd love it if we came with them," she said. "Why— thank you, Jane."

"I'll leave four orchestra tickets in your name. And if you wait for me afterward under the marquee, I'll take you backstage to meet either Julie or Richard."

Magda chuckled. "You're canny, aren't you, dear? Meeting one of the stars will certainly impress my clients. Thank you *very* much. I'd love to meet Julie again."

"Of course. I'll see you next Friday."

"Goodbye, *kedves*," Magda said. "Give my love to Bryce when you speak to him."

After hanging up, I giggled. I *was* canny, though Bryce would have to pay almost forty bucks for his mother's house seats. (Why would the box office manager comp them after Bryce had left the cast?) Yet my boyfriend might consider it a fair swap if I gained his mom's goodwill, and I'd definitely speak to Julie about meeting Magda and her guests.

I hauled my bag to Bryce's bedroom, relocked his front door, and set off for the Majestic. Each time I went there, I was amused that the actors had to pass through that hotel service entrance, then trudge through that open alley full of garbage cans to reach the stage door. It was the opposite of glamorous, just like the theater's cramped, draughty backstage. But I adored every inch of it and wished my parents would visit so I could introduce them to Mr. Downing, Ed Preston, Jon Anderson, and Bernie Hart, my four bosses.

I was in the basement office with Mr. Downing and the stage managers when Alan slipped in, followed by Moss. We'd been told to expect the director, and I felt elated to see him again, though he was thinner than last time. Moss shook hands with each of us, and when he got to me, he said, "Bernie mentioned you'd joined his team. I think you made a wise career choice." He smiled. "Kitty and your dad have become pen pals. We're both grateful for his insights."

"He enjoys helping you," I said, unaware that my dad and Kitty Hart were still in touch.

"I called this meeting," Alan said abruptly, "to announce that Moss and I have watched the show for the past three nights and clearly see its problems."

"We've consulted Fritz," Moss said, "and we think we can fix what's not working. Thus, we've persuaded the unions to allow us to rehearse here on stage next Monday, Tuesday, Thursday, and Friday from ten to two."

"Bob," Alan said to Mr. Downing, "please have the stage managers visit the dressing rooms tonight and alert the cast."

"I shall," the production stage manager replied. He was a balding man in his forties with an impish grin, but I couldn't call him by his first name. "What if some actors aren't available?"

"Unless they're on their deathbeds, they have to rehearse or risk being replaced," Moss said. "This is our last chance to get the show right."

"Understood," Mr. Downing said.

"Jane," Moss said, "I want you to sit out front with Alan and me tonight. I'll whisper my notes, and you'll jot them down. I mean, if it's all right with your team."

"Anything you want, Moss," Bob Downing added.

"Good," Alan said. "Let's meet back here after the bows to discuss plans for next week. But for now, Jane, get your things. We're going for a bite at Patsy's."

Thrilled that Alan and Moss were taking me to dinner, I grabbed my coat and bag and followed them into the hall.

Moss swiveled around, saying, "Jane, in case you're wondering, this plan is irregular. I can't think of another show that went back into rehearsal once it was running."

We climbed up the cement stairs, and while walking up the hall, Alan said, "We'll also soon announce another big surprise, a way to help ticket sales." He waved to the security guard, then asked me, "How's Christmas doing with Harburg's new show?"

"Great," I said as we exited the stage door.

"Well, the ensemble's not as strong without him. Please assure him he can always return to *Camelot*. I'll make sure he replaces Goulet, if and when Bobby leaves. And we'll have tours."

"I'll tell him," I said, feeling my pulse quicken as we rambled through the alley. But after Bryce had attained leading man status, wouldn't he balk at rejoining the chorus? Even so, he might be flattered when I relayed Alan's offer.

———◆———

I awakened on Sunday feeling grumpy because Bryce's cold had kept him in Philly. "I hope I didn't give it to my leading lady," he'd said late Saturday night when he called to cancel. "We kiss a few times." I calmly told him to drink tea, but I'd seen photos of his gamin costar, Miss Weiss, and hated picturing her in Bryce's arms. But then I laughed at myself since Bryce was true blue.

Feeling lonely, however, I spent the morning reading the *Times* and learning that John F. Kennedy "enjoyed" being president. (Was the paper joking? This seemed like a trivial topic for a front-section article. Why wouldn't JFK like the job he'd worked so hard to get?)

I was delighted by the enormous advertisement for *The Happiest Girl in the World* in the Arts section, announcing

Bryce's name in big black letters. While scanning the show listings, I learned *The Miracle Worker* was having a 3 p.m. matinee, and because I needed a distraction, I walked to the Playhouse Theatre on West 48th Street near Fifth. I bought a ticket in the center orchestra and lost myself in William Gibson's scalding drama. The physical struggle of Annie Sullivan (played by Suzanne Pleshette) to reach blind-deaf Helen Keller (Patty Duke) was riveting, and as I strolled home afterward, I felt renewed. The temperature was balmy, and the afternoon rain had stopped. I mused again how blessed I was to be a member of the Broadway community.

After buying a pizza for supper, I returned to Bryce's flat and spent the night reading *The Once and Future King,* which barely resembled Lerner's version of the Arthurian legend. When Bryce called around 10 p.m. to say he felt better, I passed on Alan's invitation to rejoin *Camelot.*

"Oh, Cookie," he said, "I feel liberated being a principal. I've realized how much of my personality I had to hide in the chorus."

I sighed after he hung up. I missed Bryce terribly and still felt disappointed that he'd taken me to lunch at the Piccadilly on Valentine's Day and given me a gold heart pendant from Tiffany's. It was nice, but I'd expected an engagement ring. And now that he was "liberated," would he want to stay single? Was that the real reason he hadn't come home?

Did he have doubts about commitment? The same doubts I'd resolved since Boston? Though it was late, I phoned Sarah and poured out my fears. "You two just got back together," Sarah said. "Dan tells me Bryce has never been happier, and men don't lie to one another about such things." I thanked my friend for her counsel, but then I sobbed for the next two hours in Bryce's bed. I told myself I'd need to get a tougher hide if Bryce and I were going to pursue separate careers. As he'd told me before, we'd likely work apart more than together.

I met Bernie Hart at the stage manager's office at 8:30 a.m. on Monday, glad to have my usual duties that week, plus the tasks I'd take on for the "irregular" rehearsal period. The actors were due at ten, so Bernie and I went upstairs, entering the wings at stage right. He asked the crew to move the act-one set to the rear, leaving the stage as empty as possible. One techie removed the ghost lamp as another guy switched on the work lights.

"Your first task, Jane," Bernie said, "is to pass out the scripts that Alan rewrote last week. We'll start from the top of the show and get through as much as we can. No sets today."

"Why are we rehearsing three months after we opened?" I asked.

"You're busy during the show and probably haven't noticed, but some nights as many as two hundred people walk out. And advance ticket sales have dried up because word of mouth is poor. I assume the producers are making a last-ditch effort to prevent us from closing."

"I didn't realize it was so bad," Jane said.

Bernie shrugged. "Christmas made the right move to leave."

An hour later, I checked the sign-in sheet and assured Mr. Downing that everyone was present. I'd stacked the revised scripts on a table in the wings and gradually placed them in the actors' eager hands. Then I waited while the cast gathered on the proscenium.

Moss was seated at the production table out front with Alan, Fritz, and Brock, and the stage managers waited at an adjacent table. But nobody else was around. I saw Franz Allers mount his podium in the pit where a pianist sat at her keyboard.

Moss rose stiffly and walked down the aisle. The cast applauded, whistled, and cheered, and a smile lit up his sallow features. "Thank you, dear friends," he said in a clear voice. "Allow me to return the favor. I watched you several nights last week, and you're doing fine work. And though the box office is slow, your efforts are far from futile. Alan, Fritz, and I believe that with a few changes, the audience will see a much-improved *Camelot* and word will spread."

"Hear, hear," Richard called.

"Now for the details," Moss said. "We're cutting 'Then You May Take Me to the Fair' and a full scene in act one, as well as 'Fie on Goodness!' in act two. We're tinkering with the 'Guenevere' number, and Alan has rewritten or shifted dialogue in other places. The show will be sleeker and shorter. Please use your scripts until you memorize the changes."

Cast members darted into the wings. Edward Preston was calling the show from the console, and I soon heard "Places, everyone" over the backstage speaker. Jonathan Anderson and Mr. Downing remained at the production table while Bernie approached me with a script. "You'll be the prompter today. I put a chair at the edge of the wings for you, stage left. Watch carefully. Shout, if necessary."

"But they're on book," I pointed out.

"Oh, they'll still get lost," he said.

"I'm on it, boss." I ran to my chair as Bernie disappeared through the pass door into the house. After Ed Preston bellowed, "House to Half," then "House Out," the lights dimmed out front. Then Ed called "Music," and Franz Allers lifted his baton. The rehearsal pianist played the end of the overture, and since the curtain was open, the stage lights came up to reveal Nate as Sir Dinadan and Jack Dabdoub as Sir Lionel, waiting on the hillside with members of the court.

I sighed, wishing Bryce was on stage with his colleagues.

That evening when I showed up early for the Monday night performance, I felt hopeful. The new version had played well in rehearsal, even with the actors holding scripts, and by Friday, when Bryce's folks and their guests saw the show, they'd probably experience the visceral magic of *Camelot* that was hiding in plain sight all along. It astonished me that tightening the book, making Lance and Guenevere's love more vivid, and cutting two songs could help so much. But Moss had a clear vision after being gone, and Alan and Fritz were seasoned enough to see the value of more rehearsals.

But what was the other surprise Alan had mentioned?

Tonight, my main task was to check the props, an easy job I finished quickly. Since I had time, I ran to the stage right hallway. Richard's room was dark, but Julie was doing scales in her dressing room with a pitch pipe. I waited until she stopped vocalizing. When I knocked, Julie opened the door and gave me a warm hug. "What a lovely surprise," she said, wearing a striped cotton robe. "Am I getting a note from stage management?"

"Oh, Jules, you're exemplary. If anyone had a note for you, Mr. Downing would come."

"Perhaps," Julie said humbly, pointing to her loveseat. "How's Bryce doing? We all miss him." She laughed. "But he wouldn't be thrilled to lose two of his three songs."

"No, he wouldn't," I said. "I think he's content with his new show. They're in Philly, and his own reviews have been excellent." I glanced around the modest room with its mirror and fluorescent lights, a sink in the corner, and a rack that held her silk and satin gowns.

"If Bryce is fine, what's wrong?" Julie asked, sitting at her vanity. "You're not yourself."

"I'm worried because Bryce isn't coming back to see me on weekends as he promised. He says he has a cold, which doesn't seem bad enough to keep him in Philly."

Julie turned to make eye contact. "A cold could threaten his job, Jane. He's making his debut as a principal, and when a show's out of town, anyone can be replaced. Remember what almost happened with Bobby? If Bryce thinks his singing is off, he's smart to rest on weekends."

"I appreciate your insight," I said.

"Bryce probably feels a lot is riding on his success, and he may be running scared. And another thing. Relationships are a juggling act when you're apart. I know because Tony and I are often on different continents. Maybe if you tell Bryce your worries, he'll be honest."

"Well, speaking of Bryce, his parents are coming again Friday with two guests. Would you mind if I brought them back?"

"Not at all," she said. "It'll be just us. No one else is coming that I know of."

"Thanks for everything," I said, standing. "I'll let you get dressed. Good show!"

"Darling," Julie called when I was almost out the door. "Speak to Bryce."

I ran down to the basement, thinking I'd take Julie's advice, but not until I saw Bryce in person. While heading toward my office, I heard steps from behind and turned to see Brock.

"Hello, kiddo," he said. "It's hard to believe you're not working for me anymore. To paraphrase Lerner, I'd grown accustomed to your face."

"I know what you mean. I miss you, too, Brock."

"Thanks for that parting bottle of Dom Perignon. I'm saving it for a special occasion."

"Your next Lerner and Loewe opening night?" I ventured.

"Doubtful. Alan and Fritz aren't getting along any better. Things changed forever in Boston when Alan told Madame she could sit in on work sessions. I suspect Fritz has decided, 'Never again.' But Alan has a slew of new ideas. He'll find a collaborator."

"He has you, Brock, and you're the one he needs most."

"That's kind of you to say, and completely accurate." Brock snorted. "Well, I better fly. I'm having a drink with Alan at Sardi's. But if you need anything, Jane, give me a buzz."

"I will," I said. "Thanks, Brock."

He headed toward the stairs, then retraced his steps. "Hey, did I hear Max lost his job?"

"Kennedy cleaned house. But Max got a nice consulting post with a Navy contractor."

"I'll call and congratulate him," Brock said.

As my old boss ran upstairs, I realized my work life wasn't the same without him. But while slipping into my office, a stuffy gray room with five small desks and chairs, a scuffed linoleum floor, overhead fluorescent lights, and a single phone, I felt at home. I was shadowing the stage managers nightly and learning new skills, and they were generous with their knowledge and patient with my mistakes. I'd relished all my assignments so far.

It would likely be years before I could call a show on my own, but I glimpsed a discernible career path. And when Bernie Hart greeted me upon entering our dingy cell, I knew I'd found a niche that was essential. Broadway shows could run without message-toting Gal Fridays, but curtains didn't rise until a stage manager gave the signal. Which meant that one day, if I worked hard, the union pro manning the backstage console would be Jane Conroy.

"I finished the prop check," I told Bernie.

"Good," he said from the desk adjoining mine. "We'd also like you to monitor the call board at half hour to make sure everyone has signed in, and then you'll call the pre-show cues."

"Will do, boss," I said, beaming at the man I viewed as my new mentor.

15.
MARCH
MIRACLE

Bryce

His throat felt sore and swollen during his second week in Philly, but he pushed through each performance, drinking tea with honey in his dressing room and gargling with saltwater in his hotel room. It was fortunate the John Bartram was a few steps from the theater.

He liked the Philadelphia Shubert with its 1,870 seats, though it was much larger than the Boston Shubert. Given his head congestion and stuffed nose, he had to work hard to project his sound, and by his evening show on Saturday, March 11th, he felt too ill to drive home, though he'd rented a car. It was the second time he'd canceled on Jane, and while she'd been busy with his parents on Friday night, he heard the disappointment in her voice when they spoke at 1 a.m. on Sunday morning.

Now it was 4 a.m., and Bryce was pacing his narrow room. He'd fallen asleep on one of his twin beds, then awakened in a panic. He was drenched in sweat, and his head ached. He gulped aspirin but felt an itch near his navel, and when he pulled down his pajama pants, he discovered an angry rash on his belly. It felt rough and raised, and he wondered if he was the victim of bed bugs. Using the little energy he had, he pulled up his mattress but saw no vermin.

Feeling chilled, he climbed under his threadbare covers—the Bartram was old and rundown—and remembered the call he'd received from his mother on Saturday before his matinee. *Anya* had extolled Jane's thoughtfulness and charm, but she was underwhelmed by the Majestic's cramped backstage, where she, his dad, and their guests had met Julie Andrews. "Her dressing room is small," she'd told Bryce. "Is the backstage in Philadelphia any nicer?"

"I'm afraid not," he'd replied with a yawn.

"As you know, I was far from sold on Jane," *Anya* said, "but I saw a different side of her last night. She's a respected member of the staff. I think Miss Andrews adores her."

"Everyone does," Bryce said. "So be honest. How's *Camelot* without me?"

Anya surprised him by raving about the show, saying it moved faster and ended by 10:45 p.m. But she also told him some of Sir Lionel's solos were gone. "I'm sure no one else could sing them as well, so they cut them."

"Yeah, that must be the reason." He chuckled, having heard from Jane that Moss had returned and done judicious pruning.

"This call's costing me," his mother said. "Let's set up a dinner with you and Jane after your new show opens. I'll make her an authentic Hungarian meal. She'll need to learn your *nagymama's* recipes if she's going to cook for you."

"We'd like that," he said, thinking Jane could barely boil water, much less make Hungarian dishes, which was fine with him. He'd learned a lot from watching the chefs at Sardi's and loved to cook.

After Bryce hung up, he knew he would've been restless continuing in *Camelot* without the "Fair" number and "Fie on Goodness!" And since Dan was also affected by these cuts, he wondered how his former roomie was faring. He looked forward to catching up with friends after *Happiest Girl* opened, but mainly he couldn't wait to resume his life with Jane. Being out of town in New Haven and Philly seemed empty without her except when he was on stage.

He fell asleep, and when he awoke around ten, he felt better. He ordered coffee, toast, and eggs from room service and asked the front desk to send up copies of *The Philadelphia Inquirer* and *The New York Times*. He planned to rest all day and watch the Boston Celtics play the Syracuse Nationals on TV.

After breakfast, Bryce thumbed through the papers, but soon felt chilled again. He took a hot shower and afterward returned to a slip-covered armchair and mused about *Happiest Girl*. He liked playing a macho general in flamboyant costumes, especially the flowing cape over his short tunics. At one point, his chest was partly exposed while he coaxed Liz into bed, and he was glad he'd returned to the gym after *Camelot* opened.

But the notes Cyril gave him last night were pickier than usual. The director had no idea he was under the weather, and Cyril ordered him to behave like a sex-starved warrior who needs a woman. "Remember," he said, "this man thinks with his willy."

"Yessir," Bryce replied with a military salute that made Cyril grin. But he knew he'd lacked stamina and focus at both Saturday shows, and he'd warned Lark beforehand that he planned to kiss her neck instead of her lips since his cold might be contagious. She'd thanked him, but Cyril told him to "kiss Lark properly" going forward.

Since the start of his theater career, Bryce hadn't informed stage managers of his ailments, and as a chorus member or featured actor, his shortcomings had gone unnoticed. But illness was harder to hide as a lead. So far, he'd sung over his sore throat and received no notes from the musical director, Robert De Cormier. He assumed that if he rested on Sunday,

he'd feel fine on Monday when the company had a brief afternoon rehearsal and an evening performance. The book authors Fred Saidy and Henry Myers and the lyricist Yip Harburg
were cutting the show, which some critics thought was long.
(Shades of *Camelot* on the road.)

Bryce dozed off during the basketball game and awakened
to noise in the hall. When he peeked outside, he found Joy
Claussen and Michael Kermoyan on his threshold.

"Hi, Bryce," Joy said. "We were hoping you'd join us for
dinner." She was a willowy blonde with a dazzling smile, and
he loved watching her play Aphrodite.

"Dinner?" Bryce asked. "Is it that late?"

"It's six," Michael said in his booming voice. "We're going
to Latimer's Deli."

"You know, I haven't eaten much today," he said. "Come
in." He headed for the bathroom to comb his hair and brush
his teeth, and when he returned, Joy was on his phone.

"It's for you," she told him. "Someone named Jane."

Bryce quickly grabbed the receiver and said, "Cookie,
hello."

"Who was that?" Jane asked. "I thought you had to rest
today."

"I did," he said. "I just woke up when friends from the cast
came by. We're going to dinner, so can I call you later?"

"Sure, but are you better?" she asked. "I'm worried about
you."

"I'm back to the world of the living," he assured her before
hanging up.

Jane

I thought the new rehearsals had done wonders for the cast's
morale, but ticket sales for *Camelot* hadn't picked up. All of us

were on tenterhooks on Tuesday night, March 14th, after Alan, Fritz, and Moss called a meeting. Were they going to announce we were closing? The entire cast returned to the stage after the bows, and I waited with the stage managers near our console until the orchestra stopped playing in the house.

"We have sensational news," Alan said, "and we wanted to tell you in person. It mainly concerns Richard, Julie, Bobby, Nate, and Jack Dabdoub, but all of us should benefit."

"This Sunday at eight," Moss said, "Ed Sullivan will broadcast a tribute to Lerner and Loewe. Originally, Sullivan planned to honor the fifth anniversary of *My Fair Lady*. Instead, we've asked him to spotlight *Camelot*."

"And he graciously agreed," Fritz added.

"So," Alan said, "if our stars will give up their day off to rehearse and appear live on Mr. Sullivan's TV show, we'll get priceless publicity."

"I'll be there," Richard yelled

"*Absobloominlutely!*" Julie called, and Jane guessed that the producers had already secured the stars' consent.

After the meeting, Bob Downing asked the stage managers to gather downstairs. "I spoke with Sullivan's staff," he announced, flopping into his chair on wheels. "They need me and one other stage manager. Jon, Ed, Bernie—you decide who'll go. Jane, you'll have Sunday off as usual." He smiled. "Thanks so much, everyone. I think Mr. Sullivan might well be our savior."

——◆——

It was a long week for me. Bryce and I spoke little, but he'd promised to come home without fail on Sunday, March 19th. And by luck of the draw, I wouldn't need to spend my day and evening at the CBS-TV Studio 50, where Ed Sullivan beamed his show to America. The day before, however, I carried

messages from Mr. Downing to Sullivan's production manager, handing envelopes to the guard at the stage door on West
53rd—yes, I was back to gofer duties. But since the weather
was warming up, I didn't mind the sixteen-block, round-trip
walk before *Camelot's* Saturday matinee.

When I returned to my office around noon, Bernie gave
me a message: Bryce was ill again and wouldn't be home the
next day. I felt my facial muscles tighten, and Bernie said, "You
look crestfallen, Jane. Was this news you didn't expect?"

"Yes," I whispered, sliding into my chair.

"I hardly have to remind you that flu travels through com-
panies."

"Can a man have the flu three weekends in a row, Bernie?"

"Moss did in Toronto."

When Bernie clammed up, I felt that unmistakable prickle
along my neck that hadn't happened since the day I first saw
Bryce at the Piccadilly. But this time, the sensation was a foreboding. Something was wrong; *very* wrong. I couldn't guess
why my boyfriend wasn't being frank with me, but a strong
intuition warned me to fly to his side.

"Bernie, I'm new to your staff," I began. "I'm not eligible
for time off. But I feel an urgent need to check on Bryce in
Philly. I hate to ask since we have a big day tomorrow, but
could you cover for me at the matinee and the performance
tonight?"

"In a heartbeat," Bernie said. "I'll call the Shubert stage
manager and ask him to leave a courtesy ticket at the box office. I'll also tell him to alert Bryce you'll be there. You go
straight home and pack. Trains run hourly from Penn to
Philly, and it's only ninety minutes away." He pursed his lips.
"I think you're smart to find out what's up. But I've known
Christmas for years, and he's a damn good egg. He must have
trouble on the road and doesn't want to alarm you."

"How can I ever thank you?" I asked.

"No need. Richard asked for you, and we gave you the thankless job of taking visitors to his dressing room after the show. You wind up staying late every damn night without a peep of complaint. You're aces." He paused. "Now get out of here, Conroy. I'll see you Monday."

I saluted, then grabbed my things and ran upstairs. Nobody else was around this early, and as I dashed through the alley, I felt a wave of gratitude for Bernie's kindness.

I reached the 30th Street Station in Philadelphia around 5:30 p.m. and took a cab to the Shubert. The ride along Market Street, then Broad, was pleasant as the taxi passed stately buildings and department stores and big hotels looming in the dusk. But the wide boulevard of South Broad was declining. The crumbling blocks near the theater reminded me of Boston's Combat Zone, and since the white-and-pink Shubert was elegant, it seemed out of place.

As Bernie promised, my ticket was waiting at the box office. The envelope held a note:

Cookie,
I got Bernie's message. I'll meet you under the marquee after the show to avoid the stage door—Cyril and Janice have many fans. And thanks for coming. I've sure missed you. Sorry you won't hear me at my best tonight.
xo Bryce

I'd traveled light with a canvas tote bag which I placed on the seat of my booth at a nearby coffee shop. When my sandwich came, however, I had no appetite. I hadn't seen Bryce since he left for New Haven a month ago, and lately, when we spoke, he seemed preoccupied and not too interested in what

I was sharing. Since this was unusual, I wondered if the pressure of his role was getting to him. (Amazingly, until Julie had raised the issue, it hadn't occurred to me that Bryce might be worried about his vocal performance. But then I recalled the night in Boston when he went back to the Parker House alone, fearing he'd caught a cold.)

At 8 p.m. sharp, I headed to the Shubert, whose marquee was immense, with small light bulbs illuminating the sidewalk below. Heading through the tall front doors, I admired the lobby's crystal chandeliers and wide marble staircase. When I entered the gold auditorium with crimson seats, an usher escorted me to Row H and gave me a black-and-white program whose cover said *The Playgoer, Shubert Theatre.* I thumbed to the title page, where Bryce's name sat on the second line below the show's title. Mr. Christmas had arrived!

The rows in the Philly Shubert were already crammed with people. And as the house lights dimmed at 8:20 and maestro Robert De Cormier bowed from his podium, I felt the same excitement that goosed my heart whenever an overture began.

Suddenly, I couldn't wait for the songs and scenes in this fledgling show to unfold. The audience clapped at the entrance of Cyril Ritchard, who moved center stage as the Chief of State, and when General Kinesias entered in his cape, brass helmet, and white tunic, I launched another round of applause. Bryce grinned faintly but didn't break character by glancing my way.

An hour later, though, as the lights came up, I felt like a balloon losing air. *The Happiest Girl in the World* featured sensual waltzes and ballads by Offenbach; witty, often naughty lyrics by Harburg; lively dances; and superb singing and acting by all, though Bryce stood out. Like *Camelot,* the plot extolled the benefits of peace, a message delivered with comic timing by Mr. Ritchard, but it lacked what Brock would call "a big idea."

Indeed, it posed one banal question: how long could the

women of 400 B.C. Athens withhold sex from their soldier-husbands? Bryce's character was the horniest man since the other featured actors played gods like Pluto (Mr. Ritchard), Jupiter (Michael Kermoyan), Bacchus, and Apollo. And when their heavenly "cloud" drifted down, then up, then down again, the effect was impressive, but the platform looked as wobbly as Bryce had described. I felt sorry for the actors.

As I hurried to the lobby to buy an orangeade, I realized I'd never read *Lysistrata*, the Greek comedy on which the show was based. Yet I could've skipped act two and known all the wars would cease, allowing Kinesias and his wife to reunite. I felt butterflies in my stomach while waiting in the refreshment line because I was dying to see Bryce and hoped the rest of *Happiest Girl* flew by.

Act two went smoothly until Bryce's solo, "Five Minutes of Spring," in which he tried again to seduce his beautiful wife. The song required a smooth vocal line, known as legato, but at the end of each phrase, his voice faded into laryngitis. And by the end, he sounded raspy and went flat on the high note. The audience clapped, but I sensed his mortification. Fortunately, he had no more solos, and by the finale, when he sang a reprise of the title song, he'd recovered enough to fudge his notes.

I clapped hard for Bryce at the curtain call—his applause was decent—and concluded that the audience had enjoyed the show's bawdy humor. As I walked up the aisle, the orchestra replayed the overture, and I enjoyed hearing Offenbach's lush melodies again. But how would this racy bit of fluff survive among the truly memorable musicals on Broadway this season?

Well, that was their producers' problem. I had bigger fish to fry.

Outside the Shubert, I moved to the curb so theatergoers could pass me. They quickly cleared the sidewalk under the marquee, and I pulled my coat tighter against the cold. I was gazing across the street when chapped lips kissed my neck. Turning around, I saw Bryce and almost gasped. His face was flushed, and he was sweating. "Hi, Cookie," he said hoarsely before wrapping his arms around me.

"You were terrific," I mumbled.

"You're a bad liar," he croaked. "I'm losing my voice, and my throat hurts like it's been slashed with a razor. And I have a rash near my navel that feels like sandpaper."

I put my hand on his forehead. "Dear God, Bryce, you're burning up."

Ignoring my concern, he pointed left. "My hotel's half a block away. We'll order room service since I can't manage going out."

"Oh, you're going out, mister," I said, hoping to hide my fear with humor. I stepped into the street and put my hand in the air, knowing my earlier foreboding had been about his health. He'd told me the truth when he'd claimed he couldn't travel.

"What are you doing?" Bryce protested when a cab pulled up. "We don't need a taxi."

"We do," I said, opening the passenger door. "Get in."

Bryce glowered at me before sliding across the cracked leather seat. I joined him and shut the door. Moving close to the plastic partition to address the middle-aged driver, I asked, "Where's the nearest hospital with a good emergency room?"

"For God's sake, I don't need an ER," Bryce snapped.

"The Jefferson," the driver replied, pulling on the brim of a Phillies cap. "Five minutes away."

"Please take us there," I said. "We need the emergency entrance."

The driver glanced at Bryce in his rear-view mirror. "Sir," he said, "my money's on the lady. You look terrible." Then he pulled onto Broad Street and sped away.

"Jane, when this is over," Bryce said, "we're going to have a talk about boundaries."

"Sure, Bryce. Right after we discuss the dangers of ignoring medical symptoms. Why didn't you call the house doctor? Every theater has one."

He exhaled. "I'm too ill to fight with you."

"I rest my case," I said. "But you did look awfully sexy in your costumes."

Bryce sulked, peering out the window. I knew he was angry, but I didn't care.

The driver turned on several streets whose names I couldn't read in the dark, stopping before a well-lit Emergency sign. I pulled money from my wallet, giving the man a fat tip before jumping out. I held the door for Bryce as sweat dripped down his cheeks. He seemed unsteady, so I grabbed his hand and led him through a set of doors. We walked down the hall to a reception desk, and while Bryce stumbled into a chair in the waiting area, I spoke to a matronly nurse in a starched white cap and white uniform.

"I'm Mrs. Christmas," I said, and the nurse smirked. "Yes, like the holiday. My husband's burning up and has a raw throat."

"I see," the nurse said, handing me a clipboard. "Fortunately, we're quiet tonight. I'll call for an orderly. You may fill out the health forms inside while you wait for the doctor."

"Thanks so much," I said, and before I could join Bryce, a statuesque Black woman arrived with a wheelchair. I followed the two of them down another hall through a set of automatic doors. The orderly steered Bryce into a treatment room and helped him move to a narrow bed before leaving. A silver-haired nurse bustled in and placed a thermometer under Bryce's tongue.

"What's the bad news?" I presently asked.

"It's 102.5," the nurse replied. "Do you know how long it's

been this high?"

"Not sure," I said. "I've been in New York while my husband's been performing at the Shubert."

"With Cyril Ritchard?" the nurse asked, turning to Bryce. "They sent us free tickets for the first preview, so we've all seen it. From your dark hair and beard, you must play the general. You sing like a god, young man."

"He does," I said. "But he has another troubling symptom, a sandpaper rash."

"Ah," the nurse said before walking to a cabinet and removing a cotton hospital gown. "Sir, please remove your clothes down to your briefs and put this on." She turned to me. "Don't worry, hon. The resident on call tonight is tops. We'll fix your hubby right up. But that's a high fever for an adult."

Jane winced, thinking, *Don't I know it.*

Bryce placed his feet on the floor, kicking off his shoes. "You have some nerve, Jane."

"Let me help you," I offered, but he stubbornly insisted he could manage. I sat on a folding chair while he changed and returned to the bed, propping his back against the slanted mattress. "I'll need your Equity insurance card," I mumbled. "For the health forms."

Bryce told me to look for his wallet in his messenger bag.

After I completed the paperwork, a nice-looking man in scrubs hurried in and extended his hand to Bryce. "I'm Dr. Maxon," he said. "I had the pleasure of seeing you at the Shubert last night. But I understand you have a rash? Could you show me?"

Bryce raised his gown and let the physician look.

"Now stick out your tongue and say 'ahhh,'" Dr. Maxon said. Then he felt the glands at the base of Bryce's neck and listened to his heart with a stethoscope. "Sir, you have a severe strep infection. We'll treat it with a hefty shot of penicillin, and that should knock it out. But you're dehydrated, so I'm going to admit you for fluids."

"I'm staying?" Bryce asked in a barky tone.

"You'll be discharged in a day or so, but you shouldn't return to work until next Saturday night. Rest at your hotel, gargle, and talk as little as possible."

"Am I contagious?" Bryce asked.

"I assume so," the doctor replied. "It'll take twenty-four hours for the drug to kick in." He turned to me. "Mrs. Christmas, how did you know the significance of the rash?"

"I had a raw throat and sandpaper rash in college," I said. "It was scarlet fever."

"Bingo," said the doctor. "I'll send in the nurse to start an IV." He grinned at Bryce. "You have a smart wife. If you hadn't come in tonight, you would've gotten much sicker."

After the doctor raced away, I stood and took Bryce's hand.

"I'm sorry for getting mad about your concern," he whispered. "I feel like a jackass." He grinned sheepishly. "I do have a habit of ignoring symptoms and hoping they'll disappear. But I was afraid I'd lose my voice altogether. In which case, I might've been fired."

Bless Julie, I thought, for diagnosing the reason he'd been so evasive on the phone. "I'm just glad I made it here before you got worse," I said.

The nurse entered the room with the IV fluid bag hanging from a pole. Another nurse followed with a tray that held a large hypodermic.

"I have to powder my nose," I told Bryce, preparing to flee. Needles scared me.

"Go ahead," he said, wincing as the nurse wielded the needle.

The next morning, I awakened at 7 a.m. when a nurse crept in to check Bryce's vitals. Because the ER staff viewed him as a VIP, they assigned him a large private room on a quiet floor. They brought in a cot, blanket, and pillow for me, and since I'd packed a nightgown, I'd slept in relative comfort. By the time Bryce awakened, I'd gotten dressed and gone to the cafeteria for coffee. I was reading *The Philadelphia Inquirer* when he called me.

"How do you feel?" I asked, moving to his bedside.

"Like a new man," he said. "Nothing hurts."

"Thank God. I was beside myself when I saw you last night."

"Typical guy; I hate admitting I'm ill, so I didn't tell anyone. But I won't do that again." He took my hand. "Jane, I've been lost without you. Can you sit on the bed?"

Facing him, I edged onto his mattress with my right knee crossed and my left leg on the floor. "I've missed you, too. Life in *Camelot* has been drab since you left. I'm glad we can spend today together."

"How 'bout the rest of our lives?" he asked, sitting up straighter. "I loved hearing you call yourself Mrs. Christmas."

"I had to, or the hospital staff wouldn't have dealt with me."

"I figured that, but I've been doing some thinking while I've been away, and my career goals have shifted. I'm not sure I want to play leading roles anymore. You see, everything's drab for me, too. I think we should try to work on the same shows in the future. And I want to make things formal, so here goes. Will you marry me, Jane?"

"Oh, Bryce. When you canceled on me three weekends in a row, I was afraid you were having second thoughts about us."

"I'm a piss-poor communicator. I should've told you I was sick, but I have a lot invested in being strong for you."

"Maybe we'll have to take turns."

"Maybe so. You're a strong woman, Jane." He took my hand. "Will you have me?"

"You bet I will," I said. "In sickness and in health."

"I wish we could seal the deal with a kiss," he replied with a sly smile.

"I love you, Bryce. But you better tell me everything from now on, cowboy."

"Yes, ma'am," he drawled.

"I need to excuse myself for a few minutes," I said, then I slipped into the hall. Thinking I'd have to buy Bernie Hart a steak at Downey's when I got back, I planned to find a pay phone and share my wondrous news with my mother and Sarah.

Bryce's temperature was normal when the nurse checked on Sunday at 7:45 p.m. By then, he'd received flowers from Janice Rule and Lark Weiss, a visit from Joy Claussen, and a call from Cyril Ritchard. "Don't rush back, my boy," Cyril had said. "Protect your pipes. We have our Broadway opening to think about."

At 7:55 p.m., I said, "Are you ready for a surprise?" I turned on the room's black-and-white television on the movable stand near his bed, switching the channel to CBS.

"What's going on?" Bryce asked while I pulled my chair close to his bed.

"Ed Sullivan's doing a tribute to Lerner and Loewe. They persuaded him to focus on *Camelot*, so if you'd stayed, you would've been on the show with Nate."

"Maybe I should've stayed," Bryce said. "I didn't know how hard it would be to have part of a show's success depending on me. I'm starting to view it as a burden."

"You said that before," I said. "But it's premature, isn't it,

Bryce? Because whatever you think now, you're going to be sensational. You're the best singer in the company, even at a quarter of your vocal strength. But you have to promise me you'll follow the doctor's orders."

"I will," he said. "My voice is my best asset."

"Your legs are a close second in those skimpy tunics."

He chuckled, and *The Ed Sullivan Show* began. Neither of us spoke as Julie, Rex Harrison, and Stanley Holloway performed pre-recorded numbers from *My Fair Lady*. Then Ed gave a brief introduction, and Richard sang *Camelot* to Julie and gave his speech about how he became king. They wore their act-one costumes, but Julie hadn't bothered with wigs or false eyelashes, so she looked younger than she appeared on stage. Alan and Fritz came on next, with Fritz playing "How to Handle a Woman" on the piano as Alan crooned his own lyrics. Then Bobby in doublet and hose performed "If Ever I Would Leave You," followed by Julie and Richard singing "What Do the Simple Folk Do?"

As the stars finished their dance, the crowd in the CBS-TV Studio 50 clapped and cheered, and I wished the audience at the Majestic could react with the same enthusiasm. And maybe they would, now that Moss had worked his alchemy, but who'd be there to see it?

"It would've been fun to appear on 'Sullivan,'" Bryce said as I turned off the TV. "But I'm glad I had the courage to try something new." He sighed. "I wish you didn't have to leave tomorrow."

"You'll be home in a few days," I reminded him.

"It'll be great when I'm at the Martin Beck and you're at the Majestic. We can meet for late suppers after our shows and go home and make love until dawn." He smiled. "Unless—?"

"You're not suggesting we—?"

"The doc said I'd be less contagious by now. And after the

nurse comes in at eleven and removes my IV, nobody will bother us."

"That's a fun idea," I said. "But let's see if you feel up to it."

While the train chugged along the tracks from Philadelphia to New York the next morning, I looked out the window and felt at peace after weeks of turmoil. I'd felt anxious since that night in Boston when I'd seen Bryce leave with Leena Lear, and I'd known I wanted to renew our commitment two days after moving into his flat. I had no inkling he felt the same until he proposed for the second time.

And though he'd had a good reason for staying in Philly on weekends, I wished he'd confided in me instead of hiding his illness. Then again, he was the guy who didn't tell me he had a new job possibility for weeks and who failed to warn me about his hard-to-please mother. But perhaps honest communication would come more easily as our relationship deepened.

As for my career, I knew in retrospect that watching Moss Hart had dazzled me during the New York rehearsals and the early weeks in Toronto. In my soul, however, I was a detail person like Brock who thrived on organizing what already existed. Stage management called on my natural strengths, and I was growing more adept at each performance. The best part was, I couldn't wait to get to the theater each day, and I doubted most people felt as content in their jobs. Again, I mentally thanked Uncle Max for helping me since, without his influence, I might still be at the Barbizon sending letters to producers.

I yawned, having spent another night on that hard hospital cot. Bryce had second thoughts about making love after the nurse removed his IV, claiming he'd been selfish to suggest it since he might infect me. Then he closed his eyes and was out for the night. Today, we both awakened early, and he told me to go home and rest up for work that evening. When I kissed his forehead, it was cool. Then I took his hand, and when his eyes grew moist, mine did, too.

"I'll see you soon," I said. "Take it easy. And by the way, I liked your friend Joy."

"I'll call you this afternoon, Cookie," he said.

I napped until the conductor called, "Penn Station, five minutes. Next stop, Penn Station." Then I opened my eyes and grabbed my bag. The train moved into the dark tunnel under the Hudson and, with a series of hard jerks, pulled into Penn. I crossed the crowded platform to a steep staircase. In the terminal, I found the exit, and after climbing two more sets of stairs reached the street. I breathed the damp March air and saw the usual stream of yellow cabs zigzagging in and out of lanes on Eighth Avenue.

Feeling restless from the train, I decided to walk to Bryce's flat, a distance of twenty-five blocks. The sun was peeking through the clouds, and I was glad to be back. I picked up my pace, passing drugstores, delis, and coffee shops. It was after 11 a.m., which explained why my stomach growled at the aroma of hot dogs warming on carts.

I bolted across 42nd Street with all its girly shows, but the city's seamier side didn't bother me. If you were going to live here, you had to accept the shady stuff along with the glamorous parts, and as long as you walked fast and looked confident, you'd stay relatively safe.

When I reached 44th Street, I glanced toward the Majestic and was shocked to see a thick line of people snaking around the corner toward the Manhattan Hotel. There were policemen on horseback and a TV news crew under the marquee.

What in heaven's name was afoot?

Feeling protective of my show and its theater, I crossed the avenue but couldn't get near the Majestic. I ran back to the corner and returned to the opposite sidewalk, heading east until I saw Brock under the marquee of the St. James. Glad to come upon someone who could explain the commotion, I rushed up to my old boss.

"Hello there, kiddo," Brock said. "Can you believe this?"

"What happened?" I asked.

"Ed Sullivan's nod to *Camelot* happened," he said. "And now we're watching a miracle, a goddamned miracle. All these folks are here to buy tickets."

"Really?" I asked, eyeing the crowd.

"The box office manager called Lerner. Then Alan called me and said to get down here. Frankly, I never saw so many ticket buyers in the same line, even for *My Fair Lady*."

"Oh, Brock," I cried. "How splendid."

"Listen, I'm going to call Lerner from the pay phone at Sardi's and give him a full report. How about I take you to lunch so we can celebrate?"

"How about if I take you for a change?" I asked.

"I accept," Brock said. "And by the way, Jane, this is why I love the theater. You do your level best, and the critics weigh in, then the fans decide. It's a roller-coaster ride, but I wouldn't want to work in any other field."

"Me either," I said as Brock offered his arm.

"Richard canceled for tonight," Brock said as we set off. "Rehearsing all day yesterday and doing Sullivan at night wore him out. The fans won't be happy, but the house will be full for Nate's debut as Arthur."

"Never a dull moment," I murmured, aware that Brock had become a dear friend.

We continued strolling up the block, beaming at each other as we talked. And as we got close to Sardi's with its cherry-red canopy, I wasn't surprised when Brock vowed to tell everyone—from the restaurant's owner to the VIP patrons seated up front—that Lerner and Loewe's *Camelot*, once deemed a money-sucking debacle, would be a musical for the ages: a big, gleaming, boffo Broadway hit.

EPILOGUE

Letter from Jane to Sarah

Camelot Company
War Memorial Opera House
301 Van Ness Avenue
San Francisco, California

July 3, 1963

Dear Sarah,

Bryce and I were thrilled to get your letter and learn that you and Dan will be joining New York City Opera this fall. Your voices will shine there. Many congratulations!

We were also happy to see that our precious godchild, Anne Kirsten, is growing fast. Thanks for the snapshot.

I also have good news. Ed Preston, production stage manager of *Camelot's* national tour, has promoted me to stage manager. You can imagine how proud I feel when the curtain comes down, knowing I've called the show. I've found my dream job, and it's as rewarding as I hoped.

All in all, this tour's a blast. Kathryn Grayson is warm and friendly, and she and Bryce have good chemistry as Jenny and Lance. Louis Hayward has joined us as Arthur, and he shares fun stories about Hollywood. As you can see from the address, we're playing the Opera House in San Francisco, a grand old theater with great acoustics. Bryce stops the show every night with "If Ever I Would Leave You."

As you pointed out, it was a blessing in disguise that *Happiest Girl* only ran ninety-six performances, allowing Bryce to rejoin *Camelot* at the Majestic. He got other Broadway offers after earning stellar reviews as a leading man but biding his time in the *Camelot* chorus gave him Lancelot when Bobby moved on. Then came this glorious chance for us to travel together.

Of course, 1961 brought as much sorrow as happiness. It's still hard to accept Moss's death. I like to remember his gleeful remarks at Sardi's during Bernie's fiftieth birthday party that April, a month after *Camelot's* triumph on *Ed Sullivan*. Mostly I find myself remembering the shock and grief we all felt at Moss's memorial service, two weeks after his fatal heart attack in December, a little more than a year after *Camelot* moved to Broadway. As 1962 wore on, Bryce and I spent a lot of time with Bernie, taking him out for drinks, trying to comfort him. Though he had his work on the show, it was also a painful reminder of what he'd lost. (Bernie's better now, though he's not a faithful pen pal.)

Anyway, our time in San Francisco has been a working vacation. On days off, we rent a car and sneak off to Napa Valley or drive down the coast to Monterrey and Carmel. I think our life would be perfect except for the constant nagging by mail and phone. Bryce's mother and my father are disgruntled that we've chosen "to live in sin" instead of getting married. (He gave me a two-carat diamond from Tiffany's. I'm not sure what they're worried about.)

Truth is, Bryce would like to elope, though the minute we say, "I do," our folks will expect us to start a family. And while I've never longed to be a mother, Bryce wants kids, so I'm considering the idea. We both realize that mixing parenthood with our careers will be tough, but I'm sure it's no harder than mixing parenthood and opera. So maybe you and Dan will blaze the trail for us.

Make no mistake, Sare. Bryce is my soulmate and true love. Our bond keeps growing.

Have a great summer! We miss you all.

Love,

Jane

P.S. - Our *Camelot* tour ends at the National Theatre in D.C. next summer, a year from now. We're hoping President and Mrs. Kennedy will come to see us since Alan's heard JFK likes the cast recording. And because we'll be near Catholic University, maybe I'll call Father Hartke and ask him to marry us at Little Flower Church in Bethesda, my folks' parish. Remember, the National is where I saw *Oklahoma!* and pinned my hopes on theater, so I'm sensing synchronicity in this plan. I hope you'll be our matron of honor, Dan our best man, and little Kirsten our flower girl, but for now, stay tuned. In the words of Bryce's favorite song, "The best is yet to come ..."

APPENDIX

SYNOPSIS OF LERNER AND LOEWE'S *CAMELOT*

(As performed after March 19, 1961)

<u>Act I</u>: The court magician Merlyn lectures his royal pupil, King Arthur, who's hiding in a tree, spying on his bride Guenevere, a princess he's never met. Arthur sings "I Wonder What the King is Doing Tonight." When she runs away from her entourage, Guenevere sings "The Simple Joys of Maidenhood." Arthur jumps down and pretends to be a commoner named Wart. He extols the charms of "Camelot" in song, but Guenevere longs to go home. When his top knight Sir Dinadan approaches, bows, and leaves, Arthur sheepishly tells Guenevere how he pulled a sword from a stone and became king. Smitten, Guenevere agrees to marry him. Merlyn is soon bewitched by the nymph Nimue (who sings "Follow Me") and leaves Arthur without a counselor.

Five years pass, and Arthur creates a new moral order based on "might for right," requiring knights to make decisions at a Round Table and strive for peace instead of war. A young idealistic knight, Lancelot du Lac, arrives from France to swear his fealty, singing "C'est Moi." Guenevere, also called "Jenny," dislikes Lance, who is pompous and pious. An aging king named Pellinore also comes to Camelot, crashing a picnic during which Jenny and the chorus sing "The Lusty Month of

May." Pellinore quietly resumes his old relationship with Arthur, becoming the king's confidante. Jenny asks three strong knights—Sir Lionel, Sir Sagramore, and Sir Dinadan—to challenge Lance to a joust on the same day. Arthur wonders what his wife could be thinking in "How to Handle a Woman" before "The Jousts." After Lancelot kills Lionel, Lance invokes his purity to bring the knight back to life. Jenny and Lance exchange glances, and their former animosity turns to instant, if unspoken, attraction. Alone on a terrace, Guenevere sings, "Before I Gaze at You Again," wishing Lancelot would leave court. Moments later, Arthur is heartbroken when he notices that his wife and best friend have fallen in love. He knights Lancelot and, in the stirring "proposition" speech, vows to ignore the passion Jenny feels for Lance and focus on strengthening the Round Table.

Act II: Two years later, though Lancelot and Jenny have not slept together, their infatuation remains strong. Lancelot conveys his passion by singing a sensual madrigal and "If Ever I Would Leave You" to her. Arthur's illegitimate son Mordred shows up and sings "The Seven Deadly Virtues." He convinces the knights to resume their old violent ways. The royal marriage grows strained as Arthur and Jenny wonder "What Do the Simple Folk Do?" And after Mordred persuades the sorceress Morgan Le Fey to trap Arthur in a forest one night during "The Persuasion," Lance sneaks into Jenny's bedchamber. They embrace, then guiltily renounce one another as Jenny sings, "I Loved You Once in Silence." Mordred bursts in, accusing them of treason. Lancelot escapes, but the civil court sentences Jenny to death. As she goes to the stake, the chorus sings "Guenevere," and Lance rides in with an army off stage, rescuing the queen and killing many knights. Arthur must declare war, but before the battle, he meets with Lance and Guenevere and pardons them, learning his wife has entered a convent. After Lance and Jenny leave, the despondent king encounters a fourteen-year-old stowaway who yearns to become a knight. The king dubs the boy Sir Tom of Warwick, then tells him to run behind the lines and return home so he can tell everyone he meets about the Round Table. Arthur heads into battle, knowing his legacy will be remembered through people's stories about "Camelot (Reprise)."

AUTHOR'S NOTES & ACKNOWLEDGMENTS

It takes a village to research, write, and revise a novel. I want to extend my warmest gratitude to Barry Eisenberg, who believed in me before I believed in myself. Also: Nancy Peck and Joyce Dormady, my first trusted readers; Stephanie Cowell, my historical fiction godmother; Lisa Baron and Joan Ebzery, who made insightful manuscript suggestions; and Kirsten Erdosh, who gave me the title. I'm also grateful to the following for ongoing support: Carolyn Bayer, David Dormady, Susanne Dunlap, Hannah Eisenberg, Marc Eisenberg, the late Lindsay Edmunds, Marion Edmunds, Georgiana Francisco, Kendra LaDuca, Elizabeth Lee, Monica Maxon, Louise Nayer, Sydney Price, Tony Scully, Madeline Svendson, the late Francine L. Trevens, and Henry A. Young, Jr. Also, Donya Hubby.

I also want to thank the versatile staff at Atmosphere Press, including my editor Colleen Alles, managing editor Alex Kale, acquisitions editor Kyle McCord, art director Ronaldo Alves, cover designer Matthew Fielder, copyeditors Chris Beale and BE Allatt, production manager Erin Larson-Burnett, interior book designer Cassandra Felten, digital director Evan Courtright, ebook designer Travis Schilling, book publicity director Cameron Finch, and book publicity manager Hayla Alawi. They are members of a talented and energetic team, and I am deeply grateful for their individual and collective efforts to move my novel from page to print.

Why was I inspired to write about Lerner and Loewe's seventh musical *Camelot*? I fell in love with the music and lyrics—

and its charismatic stars—after my parents bought the original cast album in 1961. And though I missed its 1960-1963 Broadway run, I saw the Lincoln Center revival with Richard Burton, Christine Ebersole, and Richard Muenz in 1980. It moved me deeply, especially Richard Burton's tour de force as Arthur.

For years I worked as an arts publicist and, later, arts journalist, but I didn't consider writing a novel about *Camelot's* travails until I read *The Street Where I Live*, Alan Jay Lerner's witty 1978 memoir. My interest grew when I had the pleasure of interviewing Stone Widney, the longtime right arm of Alan Lerner and a fine director in his own right, for a *Huff Post* article celebrating *Camelot's* 50th anniversary in 2010. (My first novel, *The Voice I Just Heard,* released in 2012 and still available at Amazon, is also a backstage yarn.)

Though I have written a work of fiction, I did extensive research to give the novel a sense of authenticity. *Camelot's* troubles have been well documented, namely the early death of its costume designer (in reality, Adrian; in my book, Abelard); the hospitalization of Alan Lerner for ulcers in Toronto; the volatility of Lerner's fourth marriage (1957-65); the coronary of Moss Hart in Toronto, resulting in Hart's withdrawal as director and premature death in 1961; the musical's extreme length; and the negativity of the critics even when the show reached New York. In truth, Ed Sullivan's role in saving *Camelot* from closing can't be underestimated!

All the dates are as accurate as possible (except the costume designer's death, which happened in 1959). I have intermingled famous public figures with fictional characters. But when it comes to the historic theaters where *Camelot* played, I hope to give my readers a "you are there" experience. I interviewed actors and production people who worked at the former O'Keefe Centre (now Meridian Hall), the Boston Shubert, and New York's Majestic. I visited the Majestic's unique stage door alley and toured every inch of the Boston Shubert backstage, and I stayed at Boston's Newbury Hotel, the former site of the historic Ritz-Carlton. Much has been written about Richard Burton, who ranks among the greatest actors of his (or any) generation. By all accounts, he was an incomparable leader of the cast of *Camelot* during those chaotic out-of-town weeks in Toronto and Boston.

Dame Julie Andrews's grace, elegance, vocal and acting talent, and devotion to the late Tony Walton, her husband during *Camelot,* have been well publicized. As Guenevere, Dame Julie was a north star to the cast, never complaining about the endless changes and never losing faith in the show. My portrayal is meant to be a valentine to this iconic singing actress.

For all manner of help, I want to thank (in alphabetical order): Michael Abourizk, Senior Manager of Research, the Broadway League, who offered information about the backstage of the 54th Street Theatre where *Camelot* rehearsed. The late Joy Claussen, the stage-and-TV actress who made her Broadway debut in *The Happiest Girl in the World* and shared memories of Cyril Ritchard, the out-of-town tryouts in Philadelphia, and the shaky "gods/goddesses" platform on which she performed. Eric Colleary, Ph.D., Cline Curator of Theatre and Performing Arts, Harry Ransom Center, the University of Texas at Austin, who gave me information about the papers of Robert Downing, production stage manager of *Camelot.* He directed me to a 1961 master script that helped me see how Alan Lerner changed the musical's book from rehearsals to Broadway. Ryan Fox at Ryan Fox Law, PLLC, for invaluable legal advice. Andrew Garland, opera baritone, who shared his memories of the Boston Shubert. Alicia Ho, production manager of TO LIVE, who sent me info about the dressing rooms and the Green Room at Toronto's O'Keefe Centre prior to its renovation. Dominic McHugh, Ph.D., Lecturer in Musicology at the University of Sheffield in the U.K., who emailed me about Alan

Jay Lerner. Cristina Meisner, Research Associate III at the Harry Ransom Center, who tracked down the *Camelot* scripts in Robert Downing's papers, scanned them, and sent me PDFs. I also want to thank Cait Miller, Librarian, Music Division, the Library of Congress, who helped me view Alan Jay Lerner's papers. Julia Noulin-Merat, stage designer for the Boston Lyric Opera, who spoke with me at length about the Boston Shubert's backstage. Richard Poole, a veteran actor who recently appeared in *The Phantom of the Opera,* who clarified details about the stage door and backstage of the Majestic. Darcy Pulliam, an actress who shared memories of the Boston Shubert. Ann Rexe and her researcher Pat at the Toronto Branch, Ontario Genealogical Society, who tracked down reviews of *Camelot* by Nathan Cohen and Herbert Whittaker. Josiah A. Spaulding, Jr., President and CEO of the Boch Center-Shubert Theatre in Boston, who described the Shubert's backstage. Also, his Boch Center staff: Rebecca Margolis, Associate Director of Development, who arranged a tour of the Shubert; and Scott Towers, Director of Special Projects and Historian, who cheerfully showed me around the Shubert in June of 2022 and let me explore its nooks and crannies. Mark E. Swartz, Archive Director of the Shubert Archive, who clarified the location of the star dressing rooms in the Majestic Theatre during *Camelot.* Emily Sweeney, *The Boston Globe* journalist, who gave me information about the Paddock Café, the restaurant located next door to Boston's Shubert Theatre in 1960. Lisa Vroman, the actress-soprano who starred on Broadway and elsewhere in *The Phantom of the Opera* and shared key details about the stage door, backstage layout, and star dressing rooms of the Majestic Theatre. The late Roger Watson, who sent me emails about Toronto in the 1960s. Susan Watson, the star of Broadway's *Bye Bye Birdie,* who answered questions about the dressing rooms at the 54th Street Theatre. Finally, three theater-savvy contributors to the Broadway World Message

Board: "Tourboi," who offered a description of the Boston Shubert's stage door and backstage; "Bowtie 7" who sent me online to Stage Specs (1999), produced by the Broadway League; and "Morosco" who sent me to the same publication.

I drew upon the following resources for inspiration and information:

The Novel Alan Jay Lerner Adapted:

The Once and Future King by T.H. White. New York: G.P. Putnam's Sons, 1958.

Books:

A Wonderful Guy by Eddie Shapiro. New York: Oxford University Press, 2021.

Act One, An Autobiography by Moss Hart. New York: The Modern Library, 1959.

Alan Jay Lerner by Edward Jablonski. New York: Henry Holt and Company, 1996.

Alan Jay Lerner, A Lyricist's Letters, Edited with Comments by Dominic McHugh. New York: Oxford University Press, 2014.

B'Way, Broadway: The American Musical, by Michael Kantor and Laurence Maslon. New York: Applause, 2020.

Dazzler, The Life and Times of Moss Hart by Steven Bach. New York: Da Capo Press, 2002.

Home, A Memoir of My Early Years by Julie Andrews. New York: Hyperion, 2008.

Mike Nichols, A Life by Mark Harris. New York: Penguin Press, 2021.

Moss Hart, A Prince of Players by Jared Brown. New York: Back Stage Books, 2006.

Richard Burton by Melvyn Bragg. Boston: Little, Brown and Company, 1988.

Richard Burton, Prince of Players, by Michael Munn. New York: Skyhorse, 2008.

Richard & Philip: The Burtons, by Philip Burton. London: Peter Owen, 1992.

The Complete Lyrics of Alan Jay Lerner, Edited with Annotations by Dominic McHugh and Amy Asch. New York: Oxford University Press, 2018.

The O'Keefe Centre, Thirty Years of Theatre History by Hugh Walker. Toronto: Key Porter Books, 1991.

Off the Wall at Sardi's by Vincent Sardi, Jr., and Thomas Edward West. New York: Applause Books, 1991.

The Musical Worlds of Lerner and Loewe by Gene Lees. Lincoln: University of Nebraska Press, 2005.

The Secret Life of the American Musical: How Broadway Shows Are Built by Jack Viertel. New York: Sarah Crichton Books, 2017.

The Untold Stories of Broadway, Volume 3, by Jennifer Tepper. California: Create Space Independent Publishing, 2016.

The Street Where I Live by Alan Jay Lerner. New York: W.W. Norton and Company, 1978.

The Wordsmiths, Oscar Hammerstein 2nd and Alan Jay Lerner by Stephen Citron. Milwaukee: Applause Theatre & Cinema Books, 2014.

We Danced All Night, My Life Behind the Scenes with Alan Jay Lerner by Doris Shapiro. New York: William Morrow and Company, 1990.

Articles:

"The Rough Road to Broadway," *Time*, John McPhee with research by Joyce Haber and Kenneth Froslid, November 14, 1960.

"Sorority on East 63rd Street," *Vanity Fair*, Michael Callahan, April 2010.

"Stone Widney Recalls the Magic of *Camelot*," http://www.huffpost.com, Susan Dormady Eisenberg, December 2, 2010.

"He'd Rather Be Right" (Hart), http://www.vanityfair.com, Meryl Gordon, May 30, 2012.

"Eleven Broadway Landmarks That Are Gone," http:///www.playbill.com, Jennifer Ashley Tepper, Ruthie Fierberg, October 21, 2016.

"When the Barbizon Gave Women Rooms of Their Own," *New Yorker,* Casey Cep, March 1, 2021.

Musical Scripts:

Camelot, Book and Lyrics by Alan Jay Lerner, Music by Frederick Loewe. New York: Random House, 1961.

The Happiest Girl in the World (1961) Book by Fred Saidy & Henry Myers, Lyrics by E.Y. Harburg, Story by E.Y. Harburg, Music by Jacques Offenbach. Performing script: Concord Theatricals.

Programs-Playbills:

Program, The O'Keefe Centre, Toronto, *Camelot,* October 1960.

On Stage, Shubert Theatre, Boston, *Camelot,* October-November 1960.

Playbill, Vol 4, December 1960, Majestic Theatre, New York, *Camelot.*

Playgoer, Shubert Theatre, Philadelphia, March 1961, *The Happiest Girl in the World.*

Playbill, Vol. 5, April 10, 1961, Martin Beck Theatre, New York, *The Happiest Girl in the World.*

Playbill, San Francisco Light Opera Assoc., Vol 1, July 22, 1963, *Camelot* National Tour.

Newspaper Reviews:

Nathan Cohen, the *Toronto Daily Star,* October 3, 1960 (*Camelot*).

Herbert Whittaker, *The Toronto Globe and Mail,* October 3, 1960 (*Camelot*).

Cyrus Durgin, *The Boston Globe,* October 29, 1960 (*Camelot*).

Elliot Norton, the *Boston American,* October 30, 1960, November 27, 1960 (*Camelot*).

Alan Frazer, My Boston, the *Boston American,* October 31, 1960, about *Camelot's* opening night.

Elinor Hughes, *Boston Herald,* November 6, 1960, November 25, 1960 (*Camelot*).

John Chapman, *New York Daily News,* December 4, 1960 (*Camelot* on Broadway).

Howard Taubman, *The New York Times,* December 4, 1960 (*Camelot* on Broadway).

Walter Kerr, *New York Herald Tribune,* December 6, 1960 (*Camelot* on Broadway).

Henry T. Murdock, *The Philadelphia Inquirer*, March 5, 1961 (*The Happiest Girl in the World*).

Kevin Kelly, *The Boston Globe*, June 4, 1961 (*The Happiest Girl in the World*).

Online Clips:

Lerner & Loewe: Broadway's Last Romantics, a documentary created for Public Television, may be found on Youtube.

Also, *The Broadway of Lerner and Loewe.* They both contain rare live clips from *The Ed Sullivan Show* on March 19, 1961.

ABOUT ATMOSPHERE PRESS

Atmosphere Press is an independent, full-service publisher for excellent books in all genres and for all audiences. Learn more about what we do at atmospherepress.com.

We encourage you to check out some of Atmosphere's latest releases, which are available at Amazon.com and via order from your local bookstore:

Icarus Never Flew 'Round Here, by Matt Edwards

COMFREY, WYOMING: Maiden Voyage, by Daphne Birkmeyer

The Chimera Wolf, by P.A. Power

Umbilical, by Jane Kay

The Two-Blood Lion, by Nick Westfield

Shogun of the Heavens: The Fall of Immortals, by I.D.G. Curry

Hot Air Rising, by Matthew Taylor

30 Summers, by A.S. Randall

Delilah Recovered, by Amelia Estelle Dellos

A Prophecy in Ash, by Julie Zantopoulos

The Killer Half, by JB Blake

Ocean Lessons, by Karen Lethlean

Unrealized Fantasies, by Marilyn Whitehorse

The Mayari Chronicles: Initium, by Karen McClain

Squeeze Plays, by Jeffrey Marshall

JADA: Just Another Dead Animal, by James Morris

Hart Street and Main: Metamorphosis, by Tabitha Sprunger

Karma One, by Colleen Hollis

Ndalla's World, by Beth Franz

The Courtesan's Daughter, by Susanne Dunlap

ABOUT THE AUTHOR

Susan Dormady Eisenberg began her writing career as a teenager when she contributed a regular column to the *Cohoes Newsweekly* in her hometown of Cohoes, New York. After earning a bachelor's in Humanities from Michigan State, she promoted the performing arts as a publicist and/or marketeer for the Goodspeed Opera House, Syracuse Stage, and the Joffrey Ballet. After moving to Washington, D.C., she became a freelance promotional writer, creating publications for banks, hospitals, schools, and other organizations. She also studied fiction writing with the late novelist and critic Doris Grumbach at American University.

As an arts journalist, Susan has written articles for the *Hartford Courant*, the *Albany Times Union, Classical Singer* Magazine, *Opera News,* and the *Huffington Post* (where her work often appeared on the front page). A proud member of the Authors Guild, she released her first novel about an aspiring soprano, *The Voice I Just Heard,* in 2012. Her next novel will explore the life and times of American icon Annie Oakley.

Susan lives in Baltimore with her husband, a senior living executive. They have a beautiful daughter who works in theater.

Please visit her website at www.susandeisenberg.com.

Printed in the USA
CPSIA information can be obtained
at www.ICGtesting.com
LVHW092318221123
764747LV00008B/157